Half-Light Harbor

Scottish Isles Series

Book One

Samantha Young

Half-Light Harbor

Scottish Isles Book One

By Samantha Young
Copyright © 2025 Samantha Young

Without limiting the rights under copyright reserved above, no part of this publication may be reproduced, stored in or introduced into a retrieval system, or transmitted, in any form, or by any means (electronic, mechanical, photocopying, recording or otherwise) without prior written permission of the above author of this book.
This is a work of fiction. Names, characters, places, and incidents are either the product of the author's imagination or are used fictitiously. Any resemblance to actual events, locales, or persons, living or dead, is coincidental.
This work is registered with and protected by Copyright House.

Cover Design by Hang Le
Edited by Jennifer Sommersby Young
Proofread by Julie Deaton

About the Author

Samantha is a *New York Times*, *USA Today*, and *Wall Street Journal* bestselling author and a Goodreads Choice Awards Nominee. Samantha has written over 60 books and is published in 31 countries. She writes emotional and angsty romance, often set where she resides—in her beloved home country Scotland. Samantha splits her time between her family, writing and chasing after two very mischievous cavapoos.

Also by Samantha Young

Other Adult Contemporary Novels by Samantha Young

Play On

As Dust Dances

Black Tangled Heart

Hold On: A Play On Novella

Into the Deep

Out of the Shallows

Hero

Villain: A Hero Novella

One Day: A Valentine Novella

Fight or Flight

Much Ado About You

A Cosmic Kind of love

The Love Plot

On Dublin Street Series:

On Dublin Street

Down London Road

Before Jamaica Lane

Fall From India Place

Echoes of Scotland Street

Moonlight on Nightingale Way

Until Fountain Bridge (a novella)

Castle Hill (a novella)

Valentine (a novella)
One King's Way (a novella)
On Hart's Boardwalk (a novella)

Return to Dublin Street Series:

On Loverose Lane
A Royal Mile

Hart's Boardwalk Series:

The One Real Thing
Every Little Thing
Things We Never Said
The Truest Thing

The Adair Family Series:

Here With Me
There With You
Always You
Be With Me
Only You

The Highlands Series:

Beyond the Thistles
Among the Heather
Through the Glen
A Highland Christmas: A Novella
Skies Over Caledonia
Northern Twilight
Forever the Highlands

Young Adult contemporary titles by Samantha Young
The Impossible Vastness of Us
The Fragile Ordinary

Other Titles by Samantha Young

Drip Drop Teardrop, a Novella

Titles Co-written with Kristen Callihan

Outmatched

Titles Written Under S. Young

Fear of Fire and Shadow

True Immortality Series:

War of Hearts
Kiss of Vengeance
Kiss of Eternity: A True Immortality Short Story
Bound by Forever
Bitten by Destiny

War of the Covens Trilogy:

Hunted
Destined
Ascended

The Seven Kings of Jinn Series:

Seven Kings of Jinn
Of Wish and Fury
Queen of Shadow and Ash
The Law of Stars and Sultans

But to see her was to love her;
Love but her, and love for ever.
—Robert Burns, *Ae Fond Kiss*

Prologue
Tierney

The restaurant was crowded. People were squeezed together like strands of multicolored dry spaghetti shoved into a jar as they waited for a table to become free.

A guy at the next table was on his phone loudly berating a colleague for a screw-up at work while his lunch date studied her menu, mortified. On my other side, two women spoke over each other as they discussed their latest failures in the dating scene.

"I mean, if your penis is pierced, you're basically advertising that you're good at sex!" the brunette yelled over the noise of the other diners to her friend. "Well, I have a severe case of buyer's remorse. I was scammed!"

Once upon a time I might have laughed at that with London, but I felt crowded by all the people. And outside the restaurant windows, Manhattan was abuzz with foot and road traffic. There was noise and lights and smells and *feelings* everywhere.

So many feelings I could barely feel my own.

My chest grew uncomfortably tight, and I breathed a little sharper, a little faster to alleviate it.

"You're not happy," my best friend, London Wetherspoon, said.

I tried to focus on her pretty face and drown out the surrounding chaos. "Am I supposed to be?" I asked.

She flinched. "That's not what I mean. No one is saying you need to be over your grief. I only mean ... you're not happy here."

She was right.

The itch to leave New York had started long before the death of my parents. But family was what mattered most to me. My parents were here. London was here. And, I reminded myself because I constantly needed to remind myself, Hugh was here. Hugh, my boyfriend of eighteen months.

He'd seen me through losing my parents. A lot of new partners might have bailed at having to support someone through something so big so soon.

I wasn't very present with him these days.

But he didn't seem to mind.

Maybe I should mind that he didn't seem to mind.

"You're the only family I have left," I told London truthfully.

She reached across the table to cover my hand with hers. "And I will always be your family. Even if you need to be somewhere else to be happy."

"Somewhere else?"

"Scotland." She gave me a melancholy smile. "I know you've missed it since your grandmother died. You should go. Even if it's just to visit for a while. Get out of the city. Figure out what you want."

The thought of Scotland scored a new ache across my chest, and it was the first positive spark I'd had in a while. I'd been numb for months, going through the motions, not doing anything. Sure, I could afford not to do anything, but that didn't mean I should mindlessly laze about.

For four years, I'd worked as the general manager of a five-star hotel on the Upper West Side. It was a boutique hotel, not part of the Silver Group. However, my parents' reputation and standing in the hospitality industry snagged me the job. At the time, I was the youngest general manager in New York. But I'd kept the job because I was damn good at it.

Until the two people who mattered most to me died in a helicopter crash.

I returned to work two months after my parents' funeral, and I made a lot of mistakes. Losing my shit at an entitled guest was the final straw for my boss and he "let me go."

Now I was aimless.

Lost.

Yet the thought of Scotland cut through the noise.

"What about you? What about Hugh?"

London rolled her eyes. "Who gives a fuck about Hugh? As for me, I'm here, babe, whether I'm sitting across a table from you or an entire salty ocean."

Gratitude was the second positive emotion to pierce my numbness that day. "Scotland." I nodded. "I'll think about it."

My best friend smiled. "That's all I ask."

———

After lunch with London, I was supposed to go to a job interview with the Silver Group. The CFO, Ashlyn Waters, had reached out to invite me to interview for general manager at their hotel in Midtown. It was a favor to my parents, I knew that.

Despite the kindness behind the offer, I couldn't make myself go.

Now that London had planted the idea of Scotland, the thought of burying myself in another job here in Manhattan made me more numb than usual, which was saying something. Instead, I returned to the apartment that belonged to Hugh. The truth was Hugh was different from any guy I'd dated. Confident, more forthright. Arrogant. He was a nepo baby too. Son and heir of one of the biggest automotive brands in the world. Now Hugh was CFO of the electric vehicles division, and once his father stepped down, he hoped to become CEO.

His job meant he traveled a lot. He wasn't around much.

And maybe that was why we'd lasted as long as we had.

After I lost my parents, I'd seen a caring side to him I hadn't expected. He'd moved me into his apartment to keep an eye on me and I'd dazedly gone with it despite London's reservations. My friend had grown quiet over her dislike of Hugh since he'd reintroduced her to Nick whom we knew of in high school. Nick and Hugh were two peas in a pod as far as I was concerned, but London had been dating him for a month and seemed to like him. Despite not liking Hugh. Strange, but true. But I'd seen her sneer today at the mention of my cohabitee.

I'd noted it.

I'd *noticed*.

Huh.

As I walked into the apartment building, the doorman/security guard, Harvey Collins, a large gentleman in his early thirties, raised his eyebrows. "Ms. Silver. I ... Good afternoon."

I frowned at his strange expression. "Good afternoon, Mr. Collins."

"It's Harvey, Ms. Silver," he reminded me like he always reminded me, but his eyes darted to the elevator with nervousness.

My parents, Maura Gordon and Carter Silver, had instilled in me that if someone showed me the respect of calling me by my surname, I showed that respect back. Harvey Collins didn't work for me. He protected Hugh's building from unwanted visitors.

His nervousness, however, was strange.

Even stranger that I was noticing.

It was as if my conversation with London today had woken me out of a thick fog.

I swiped the key card and then hit the button for the penultimate floor, noting Harvey scowling at the wall. The doors closed before I could ask him if he was all right.

A minute later, I let myself into the apartment. As I stepped into the open-plan living space, an unfamiliar woman came hurrying out of the main bedroom, barefooted and buttoning up her silk blouse. Her hair was a mess, her expression frantic.

And Hugh came rushing out after her, barefooted, wearing his suit trousers and shrugging on his shirt.

My boyfriend was a handsome, smooth type of attractive. Perfect hair, perfect teeth, perfectly straight nose, lips just full enough, and a strong, sharp, masculine jawline. He worked out obsessively, so his sculpted body was a thing of beauty.

As I took in the situation, I realized that I felt nothing.

He was cheating on me with this woman—oh, I did recognize her. She worked in his office. Carolina or Catalina. Something like that.

Her cheeks flushed ruby red as she hurried into her high heels and grabbed her jacket. "I'm so sorry," she murmured as she rushed past me and into the elevator.

I watched the doors close behind her and turned to Hugh.

He sighed in exasperation, running a hand through his hair. "You were supposed to be at an interview."

"Yes." I nodded. "You're correct. You fucking another woman is my fault because I was supposed to be at an interview."

Hugh flinched at my flat tone. "I ... I don't know what to say."

"Sorry is usually a good go-to."

"I don't think I am." He shrugged. "I have needs, Tierney. Having sex with you is like jerking off. You just lie there. You don't do anything."

Disgust soured my gut. "I'm sorry grief has gotten in the way of my libido."

"Your parents died nearly a year ago!" He threw his hands up in exasperation. "And it still feels like I'm living with a fucking ghost! Excuse me if I need a little attention from someone who enjoys having sex with me."

The last of my numbness melted away as I stared in horror at this man I was sharing a life with. But I wasn't, was I? Because he was right. He was the best lover I'd had—which wasn't saying a lot—but after my parents died, I completely lost interest in Hugh. In every way. We were just two people sharing an apartment. I'd thought him patient. That I'd gotten him wrong before their deaths. That he was kind and understanding.

Like fuck he was!

He was screwing around behind my back. "The right thing to do is break up with a person. Not fuck around with other women. Jesus! I need to get a sexual health check, you absolute selfish prick!"

Hugh's jaw dropped. Then he took a step toward me. "Do you realize that is the most impassioned thing you've said to me in a year?"

Seriously? "You're an asshole."

I shoved past him, striding into the large bedroom and into the walk-in closet. Finding my suitcases, I rolled them out into the room.

"What are you doing?" Hugh grabbed my wrist as I reached up to begin pulling clothes down to pack them.

I shrugged him off. "I'm leaving."

"No." He bent his face to mine and now it was my turn to gape at the aggression in his features. "I haven't put up with your shit for a year for you to walk away now."

I curled my lip in revulsion. "If you need people to believe you ended it, tell them that. I don't give a damn."

He grabbed my biceps, yanking me toward him, his grip bruising as I tried to squirm out of his hold. "I put up with your shit because I love you," Hugh hissed. "You don't walk away now that you're finally here *looking* at me. If I'd known screwing around with Caro would elicit this reaction, I'd have told you sooner!"

"You didn't tell me—you got caught." I shoved at him. "Let go of me!"

"I've been waiting for this." His eyes heated as he jerked me against him, and I shuddered at the feel of his arousal. "I've missed this. I've missed you."

He'd barely finished the sentence when my knee connected with his hard-on.

Agony blazed across his face as his lips parted on a silent yell.

"I'll get my stuff later." I skirted past him, shaking. "But we're over, Hugh. *Over.*" I rushed into the living area and out to the elevator. I hit the button frantically.

It seemed to take forever for the doors to open and as I got on, Hugh burst out of the apartment, still clutching himself between the legs. "Tierney, don't you dare leave."

I already had my cell out. "Come near me and I will call the police."

He straightened, rage blazing in his eyes. "This isn't over, sweetheart."

"It's over if I say it's over." I bristled with my fury. "Don't mess with me, Hugh. I'm on the edge and I might do something really crazy in self-defense. Don't push me."

He blanched at the innuendo in my threat before the doors closed and the elevator descended.

Trembling with anger and fear, I slumped against the car wall and tried to pull myself together before the doors opened again.

The concern on Harvey's face told me he knew. He'd have seen Hugh go up to the apartment with Caro. Seen Caro leave.

Yet whatever he read on my face as I stepped out, he asked quietly, "Ms. Silver, are you all right?"

"I'm fine." I waved a shaky hand. "Thank you, Mr. Collins. I won't be back, so this is goodbye."

He opened the exit, holding the door for me. "It's been a pleasure, Ms. Silver. Good luck to you."

I gave him a wan smile. "Thank you. You too."

Walking out of the building, I felt a weight lift from my chest.

Turning to glance back up at the high-rise as life buzzed by me, I realized my relationship, my existence here, was an anchor weighing me down in the wrong place.

Scotland.

The word whispered through my mind.

Yeah, maybe it was time to go back.

"Tierney Silver?"

I spun to find a strange woman peering at me. A man in a suit bumped into her and she huffed and stepped to the side. She had pixie-cut brown hair and wide, curious brown eyes. There was a small, sparkly blue stud in her nose, and she wore a blue knitted vest top over a white T-shirt paired with slouchy brown trousers. Brown loafers completed her casual office outfit. On anyone else, it would look frumpy, but she made it look effortlessly cool.

I'd definitely never met her before.

"Do I know you?" I asked wearily.

I was tired and needed to find a place to stay.

She held out her hand. "Perri Wilcox. I'm an investigative reporter."

Oh great. "Look, I don't—"

"My colleague Ben Rierson was killed two days after your parents died in a helicopter crash."

I froze.

"I've been investigating Ben's death and recently discovered the two were connected."

Shaking my head, I took a step back, like I could sense what was coming.

"I believe my colleague was murdered because he was helping your parents with an investigation. I believe your parents' death was not accidental, Ms. Silver. I think someone shut them and Ben up."

The sidewalk began to spin, and I stumbled against the side of the building.

Perri Wilcox reached out to steady me. "Whoa, you're okay," she murmured in her husky voice.

I took a few calming breaths before I met her dark gaze. "Tell me." My tone was hard. "Tell me everything."

1. Tierney

Isle of Glenvulin, Scotland

The handsome Scot at my side kept talking as we wandered through the derelict guesthouse, but his voice had become like background music. Mostly because the question *What have you done?* kept repeating over and over in my mind.

Only a week ago, buying the old guesthouse that had once been a pillar of the community on this part of the island had seemed like a good idea.

"Tierney? Tierney?"

The Scottish accent changed my name from "Teer-Nee" to "Teer-Neh" and pronounced "Teer" so quickly, it took me a second to realize the Scot was calling my name.

I whipped around to find Quinn McQuarrie, my main contractor, standing in the doorway of what had been a dining room, waiting expectantly for me to follow him. His brows drew together. "You all right?"

Pasting on a smile, I nodded and followed him out of the room.

"Starting to feel overwhelmed?" Quinn guessed as we strode down the dark hallway and out the front door. We hadn't finished our final tour before renovations were set to begin, so I didn't understand why he was leading me outside.

"Um ... maybe a little," I admitted. "Where are we going?"

"To remind you of something." He walked around to the back of the house, and I followed him, my hiking boots trampling overgrown weeds, unkempt hedgerow scratching into my jeans as we waded through it.

Quinn stopped in the garden on the cliff top. Even though I'd already seen the view, my breath caught again as I looked out at the harbor to the sound of Glenvulin. Beyond the deep blue waters was the rugged coastline of the mainland of Scotland.

The large guesthouse was built on the hill above the harbor. Below was the main street with colorfully painted buildings that lined the coastal front of Leth Sholas. Leth Sholas was a tiny harbor town on the Isle of Glenvulin. Leth sholas meant *half-light* in Gaelic and the town was colloquially nicknamed for its English translation.

Half-Light Harbor.

I'd fallen in love with the tiny village while backpacking around Scotland in search of the perfect place to start over. Half-Light Harbor, like many of the towns on the cluster of isles off the west coast of Scotland, was a dying community trying desperately to rejuvenate so they could provide opportunities that tempted their younger generation to stay. I was concerned as an American that I'd be viewed as some outsider intruding on their island. However, the community council had been more than helpful aiding me in obtaining the planning permissions needed to turn the guesthouse into a modern bed-and-breakfast.

"Once we open up the front"—Quinn gestured to the frontage with its too-small windows—"the views will be spectacular. I've always thought this place could be tremendous." His look was warm and reassuring. "We're all with you, Tierney, and grateful someone is investing their time and money into this old lady." He nodded back to the house. "She deserves it."

Gratitude suffused me. Since arriving a week ago to stay permanently on Glenvulin, I'd vacillated between excitement and panic. However, every time I slid toward the panicked end of the spectrum, someone from this tiny harbor town made me feel good about my decision. They were the most welcoming people I'd ever met. Some gruff and blunt, but always friendly. Well, almost always. There were one or two members in the community council who enjoyed making me sweat and uttered passive-aggressive comments about my not understanding how island life worked.

Scanning the stunning view, not for the first time, I was drawn to the small island off the coast of Leth Sholas. A causeway road connected the two islands, but only when the tide was out. Otherwise, the smaller island sat isolated and disconnected in the middle of the sound.

"That's Stòr." Quinn pointed to the tiny piece of land.

"Is it inhabited?"

"Only by the bloke who owns it." He flashed me an attractive grin that crinkled the corners of his blue eyes. "You'll meet him soon enough. Ramsay McRae is my business partner. We own the building company together. He was an ... engineer. But he's also a dab hand at woodwork. Some of the custom work we'll be doing around the house will be Ramsay's."

"I look forward to meeting him." I cocked my head in curiosity. "So, are people allowed on his island?"

Quinn considered me. "I'm sure he wouldn't mind if you

wanted a wee look around. Just remember to check the safe crossing times if you do decide to venture over."

Last year when I drove around Scotland looking for the perfect place to either build or renovate to start my B and B dream, I'd gotten used to the driver's seat being on the right side of the vehicle and having to drive on the left side of the road. However, while the main A road around the coast of the island was large enough for passing vehicles, most of the B roads were single track. Having learned the hard way last year driving the NC 500 around Scotland, I'd opted to buy the smallest SUV I could find.

My cute Suzuki Ignis in bright turquoise bumped along the rough causeway that connected Leth Sholas to Stòr. There was water on the road, which made me a little nervous, but I guessed the tide never fully went out. When I was a kid, my parents were forever joking about my curiosity and how it was going to get me into trouble one day.

A nagging ache gnawed at me as I passed the tide times warning sign because as it turned out, my parents' curiosity had gotten them into trouble first.

"Nope." I squeezed my hands around the steering wheel. "I'm not going there today. Today I'm going to Stòr to wander around the island and have a peaceful, lonesome picnic."

A glance in my rearview showed the coastline growing farther behind. The causeway connected to a road outside of town.

Growing closer to the island, I discovered it was larger than I expected.

As I reached it, I noted another tide time warning sign. I was surprised to learn that high tide could shut Stòr off from the mainland for as long as eight hours. But I had the rest of the afternoon and the evening to explore. According to the safe crossing times, the tide would stay out from now until almost eleven o'clock tonight.

The road was single track and climbed upward through thick forest. Taking it easy, I drank in the views back to Glenvulin through the thicket of trees. Following the road around the island, it didn't take me long to drive it. A third of the land didn't even have a usable road, it seemed. What I did drive, according to my vehicle, was only around seven miles long. The trees opened up as I crossed the island. A few miles passed and then the landscape transformed into fields and rocky terrain. Eventually, I spotted a white house on the opposite side. It was perched right on the coast, looking back toward Leth Sholas, and had its own dock. Deciding it was only polite to introduce myself since Ramsay McRae was partners with Quinn, we'd be working together, and I was on his land, I drove toward it.

However, there was no vehicle in front. Parking my SUV, I got out and strolled up to the house that was typical of island homes. One story, small windows, white render. I knocked first. I inhaled the crisp salty sea air and enjoyed the mild breeze that blew through my hair.

There was no answer, so I meandered around to take a nosy peek in one of the windows. From what I could see, it was a small snug. Around the back was the kitchen. There was a lot of clutter, almost like it was being used for storage.

Was this *not* Ramsay McRae's home?

There was a large bank of solar panels positioned next to the house, so obviously someone was using it because it had power.

Frowning, I noted the lack of a boat at the dock. Perhaps my new co-contractor was not home.

Returning to my car, I drove back the way I came but stopped around the halfway point between the white house and the causeway. Parking as far off the road as I could, I grabbed my backpack, which held my picnic along with my latest paperback romance obsession. Then I hiked down through the wooded coastline until I came to a tiny, pebbled beach.

I sucked in a breath at the turquoise waters surrounding the inlet. It was stunning. Finding a grassy knoll, I sank down and listened to the water lapping at the shore. From here, the mainland of Scotland was even closer. Quickly, to get it out of the way, I took a snapshot of the view. Part of my marketing plans for the B and B was to share the progress of the renovation on social media. I interspersed photos and videos of my old Victorian building with photos of the setting. As someone who didn't particularly enjoy documenting experiences and preferred to live in the moment rather than break out of it for a photograph, I had to constantly remind myself to take pics. Quinn had politely declined my request to upload videos of him and the men working to socials (he and some of the guys were hella hot), and I respected that. With a sigh, I put my cell away and drank in the view.

For a moment, though, I felt like the only person in the world.

All my stress and anxieties, all the responsibility I felt weighing on me, for a few beautiful minutes, it all just melted away.

This is why I came here, I reminded myself.

This was why I'd traveled across a continent to start over.

Venturing onto Stòr today might have been out of my growing curiosity, but it was also from a need to enjoy some "me time" before the chaos of renovation and running a business changed my daily life.

Opening my backpack, I took out the sandwich I'd bought from Leth Sholas Bakery & Tearoom. There were a surprising number of businesses within those rainbow-colored buildings along the harbor. The bakery, I'd discovered, was run by married couple Harry and Bryan Weaver, Australians who had moved to the island seven years ago. They were warm and friendly, and their cakes and sandwiches were so far among my favorite discoveries in my new home.

I had to force myself to slow down and savor the spicy salami, pancetta, and Monterey Jack cheese ciabatta. There was a whole lot of other stuff going on inside the loaded gourmet sandwich, and it was a whole lotta amazing.

"Oh my gawd," I moaned around a mouthful. This sandwich was better than any of the orgasms I'd had with a partner (I'd had pretty amazing orgasms on my own, so the distinction was necessary).

Orgasmic snacks—check. Peace and isolation—check.

It was perfect.

For about fifteen minutes.

I didn't even hear him approach.

"*You* are on private land," the deep, male voice growled ominously behind me.

2. Tierney

"Arggggh!" I launched off my knoll, whirling around and stumbling on pebbles as I backed up toward the water.

Towering above me on the grassy dune was a mammoth, bearded, would-be killer. My heart hammered in my chest as I gaped up at the intruder.

I could barely make out his face for the bushy salt-and-pepper beard surrounding his lips and covering his cheeks. He had massively broad shoulders and his navy plaid shirt strained against thick, muscled biceps. Long, long legs were clad in dirty jeans, his big feet in well-worn hiking boots. His brown hair was as shaggy as his beard. Piercing wolf eyes glared at me. They were the most striking pale gray I'd ever seen.

A warning growl drew my terrified gaze to the stunning dog sitting perfectly at his side. The Alaskan Malamute had startling blue eyes. Its white, black, and tan fur was better groomed than its apparent owner.

"Hush, Akiva," the stranger rumbled, and the dog quietened.

Uncertain of its nature considering the glowering man at its side, I took another step back.

"Watch it or you'll end up in the water," the man said blandly. "I won't hurt you. Neither will Akiva." He patted the dog's head. "Unless I tell her otherwise." He crossed his arms over his broad chest. "Unfortunately, you're not the first tourist to bumble their way onto my island and get stuck. You all seem to deliberately miss the private land signs."

Realization dawned and a little relief with it. "You're Ramsay McRae?"

The man gave me a brief nod. "Who are you?"

"I'm Tierney Silver."

He raised an eyebrow. "The American who bought the guesthouse?"

"That's right. We're ... Quinn told me we'll be working together. Right?" The reminder was more for me. Surely, the stranger was harmless if he and Quinn were business partners.

Right?

Instead of answering, he scowled and asked in his anglicized Scottish brogue, "Do you not know how to read then, Ms. Silver?"

"The private land signs? I didn't see them and Quinn said you wouldn't mind me taking a look around the island. I'm afraid my curiosity sometimes gets the better of me." I offered an apologetic smile that usually charmed people.

Not the yeti, apparently.

"I'm talking about the safe crossing times."

I frowned. "I did check them. I'm good until nearly eleven o'clock this evening."

His wolf stare was magnetizing. I felt caught in it. Sudden awareness heated through me and my cheeks turned hot under his attention. "You read the wrong side of the timetable. Tide came in as you came over. You're *stuck* here until eleven o'clock this evening."

Oh shit.

My shoulders slumped. "You're kidding."

He stared stonily in reaction.

Even though it might cost me my life, I couldn't help my lip twitch. "I'll take that as a *no, you're not kidding*."

With a sigh, he turned on his heel. "Follow me." Ramsay did this whistle thing I could never hope to emulate, and Akiva tore her beautiful eyes from me and followed her owner. I gaped after him.

"I meant you," he called over his shoulder.

Grabbing my backpack, I lunged up onto the grass after him, almost tripping over a tree root. "Where are we going?"

"There are only two places you can go on Stòr. Unsurprisingly, both belong to me."

I rolled my eyes at his gruff, vague response. "I can wait it out in my car. I don't want to impose."

"Is that why you ignored my private land signs?"

"I told you—Quinn said you wouldn't mind."

At that, Ramsay grumbled something under his breath I couldn't quite hear.

As I clambered uphill out of the woodland after him and his gorgeous dog, I noted the Defender parked behind my car. That thing had to be twenty years old.

"Follow me," he ordered again.

Before I could respond, Ramsay and the dog were in his vehicle and backing out. At my just standing there watching him, he waved impatiently for me to get into my car.

Ugh, this was going to be fun.

Hurrying into my Suzuki, I watched as Ramsay executed an impressive three-point turn on the narrow road and then I tried to do the same. It took me a little longer and I think I scratched my alloys.

He waited for me, and I could practically feel his impatience vibrating from his very cool Defender into my turquoise baby SUV.

Wondering if I was following him to my death, I was only half joking to myself about that when he didn't drive to the house at the dock. He drove us toward the causeway but then pulled off onto a track hidden in the woodland.

Starting to get nervous, I considered reversing out but realized there was literally nowhere for me to go.

I was trapped on this guy's island with him.

"Well, you wanted an adventure in Scotland," I muttered to myself. "Dying gruesomely here is pretty adventurous."

Ahead of the Defender, the woods suddenly opened.

Pulling the SUV to a stop beside the Defender, I gaped at the house and barn sitting in the middle of a clearing, surrounded by mostly birch trees and a few oaks. Two large oaks had been planted, one on either side of the buildings, almost like guardians of the smaller birch and Ramsay's home.

The yeti had two houses on the island.

Ramsay got out of the Defender, Akiva at his heels. He waited while I got out of my car, bringing my backpack with me because it had my phone. Not that I'd noted if we had a signal on Stòr. That would have been the action of a smart, cautious person.

Damn it.

Belated butterflies fluttered to life in my belly as the tall, imposing Scot stared at me in that way that seemed to not only see right into me but electrify every nerve in my body. My throat was very dry all of a sudden.

"I'd return you by boat, but I let Quinn's sister borrow it today to deliver furniture to a house on one of the smaller islands."

Quinn's sister Cammie (Cameron) was working with me on the interior design of the guesthouse. "I know Cammie."

"Aye. Anyway." He gestured to the house. "You're stuck with me here for a while."

It was quite diplomatic of him, considering his real thought was probably *I'm stuck with you here for a while.*

"I'm sorry. Quinn said ... I'm sorry for trespassing."

He nodded. "*Quinn*. Anyway, it happens. Until the council gives me the go-ahead to put barriers up at the causeway, it'll keep happening."

"Why won't they let you?"

"I own the island, not the causeway."

"Right."

Akiva barked from her spot on the porch.

Ramsay jerked his chin. "Tea? Coffee?"

"Sure. Thanks." I started after him. Now that I'd spent a couple of minutes in his presence, he didn't give off the would-be killer vibes after all. However, I was still a woman alone with a strange man twice my size on an island. Trapped.

I reminded myself he was Quinn's partner and the likelihood of Ramsay doing anything nefarious was slight.

"Nice Defender," I said to his back.

Ramsay glanced over his shoulder, his attention swinging from me to my Suzuki. "Aye." He turned to open the front door and I was pretty sure I heard him mutter, "You could see yours from space."

Frowning, I looked back at my little SUV.

Okay, so she was vivid. But I liked her. I'd even painted my nails to match.

Ramsay held the door open for me and when I met his stunning gaze again, he seemed to read my mind because his lips twitched ever so slightly. As if I amused him.

I murmured my thanks, but when he closed the door, a sudden panic tightened my chest and my grip on my backpack.

Perhaps he heard my intake of breath because he said as he reached for something on the wall, "Signal on the island is patchy at best and nonexistent inside the house." I realized he had what appeared to be a walkie-talkie in his hand. "This is a VHF radio handset, and it patches into the same frequency as the voluntary lifeboat service back on Leth Sholas," he explained as he held my stare and pressed a button on the handset. "Half-Light, this is McRae. Over."

The handset crackled and a woman's voice sounded in the house. "McRae, this is Half-Light. Annie here. Problem on Stòr? Over."

Still holding me in that startling gaze of his, Ramsay replied, "The new guesthouse owner got caught out by the tide times. She's here with me in case anyone is looking for her. I'll get her back safely tonight. Over."

Warmth suffused my cheeks when I realized what he was doing.

He sensed my unease at being alone with a strange man in his cabin in the woods.

He was letting someone else know where I was for my sake.

If Annie at the voluntary lifeboat service thought this interaction odd, she didn't let on. "Understood. Enjoy your guest. Over." Laughter rumbled in her voice like she knew he'd find me a complete inconvenience.

Ramsay smirked and I huffed, even though relief loosened my shoulders and my grip on my pack. "Sure. Over." He held up the handset to me and pointed to a button. "This is the button you press if you need to contact Leth Sholas."

"Thanks."

He hooked the handset back on the wall and strode past me. Akiva bounded excitedly around his legs, and I understood why when he pulled a can of dog food out of the cupboard. As he fed the Malamute, I finally took in my surroundings.

It was a large open-plan space with vaulted ceilings—a

kitchen, dining, office, and a living area. There was plenty of lighting, but it had the dull glow of energy-saving bulbs. I wondered if he had another bank of solar panels somewhere powering the home.

There were no paintings on the walls, no artwork, no photographs. No cushions or throws on the large leather sectional. No rugs on the floor. No television in sight.

If it weren't for the tall bookshelves lining the entire length of one wall, there were no signs of anyone living here. It was utilitarian.

Except for the books.

There must have been thousands shelved along the length of the house.

And there were small piles of them on side tables and on his desk in the office area.

"You like to read, huh?"

He grunted.

I glanced over at him.

"Tea or coffee or water?" he asked.

"Uh, coffee. No cream, no sugar. Thanks."

He nodded and set about making said drink.

"So, books?"

"Aye."

I dropped my backpack on the floor by the sofa with a sigh. This was going to be a *long* afternoon. "You have a barn?" I tried again.

"Workshop."

"Workshop?"

"Aye."

I gritted my teeth in irritation and then wrangled my patience. A few minutes passed. Finally, I attempted conversation again. "What is the workshop for?"

Ramsay crossed the room, holding out the coffee to me. He didn't have one for himself. I took it as he continued, "I do custom woodwork for clients across the islands and mainland."

"Right. Quinn mentioned you might be able to do some stuff like that for the B and B."

He jerked his chin in what I assumed was confirmation that he could in fact do custom work for me and then strolled into his kitchen to remove Akiva's newly cleaned plate.

The dog, now fed, ambled toward me.

I tensed as she stared at me with eyes as penetrating as her owner's.

"She's friendly. Do you not like dogs?" Ramsay asked from his place at the sink. "I can call her back."

"I like dogs." I smiled at Akiva as I tentatively held out my free hand. "And you are a beauty."

As if she understood my words, the large dog sniffed at my fingers and then swiped them with her tongue. She bussed her face into my hand, and I scratched behind her ear. Her beautiful tail whomped rapidly on the ground as I said, "Oh, aren't you the most gorgeous girl I've ever seen. Yes you are. Yes you are. Look at those beautiful eyes." I placed the coffee mug on the side table so I could lower to my knees and give Akiva all my attention.

She bussed and wriggled into my pets, trying to swipe her tongue over my face. I laughed, lifting my chin to avoid her attempts. When I looked over her head, I locked eyes with Ramsay's and my breath caught again.

I couldn't see much of his face because of the beard, but I could make out the soft curve of his mouth and those eyes ... I'd never seen eyes like them. There was also the fact that he was as beautifully formed as some onscreen comic hero.

Attraction flushed through me. "She's really stunning," I murmured.

"Aye, and she knows it." His tone was warm with affection. "She doesn't usually take to new people like that."

"Really? She seems so friendly. How old is she?"

"Four. I got her as a pup not long after I moved here."

"We had a Husky growing up. His name was Odin. He was my protector. But when he passed, my mom couldn't handle the grief, so we never got another dog."

There was a moment of silence and then he said, "I heard about your parents. I'm sorry. Tragic accident."

"Right," I murmured, pushing down the rising rage that always accompanied thoughts of my parents' death.

A tingling on my neck had me looking up from Akiva to Ramsay. Tension tightened my grip on the dog because Ramsay McRae's furrowed brow told me he'd noted my strange response.

"Thank you," I replied quickly. "It's been hard without them."

"They left quite a legacy."

They had indeed. Not one they were particularly proud of.

"Why give it up and come here to run a small B and B?"

So, he had done his research.

My reasons for giving up my rights to the hotel empire my paternal grandparents built, my parents had inherited, and then I inherited when my parents died in a helicopter crash, were too complicated to explain to a stranger. Especially one who barely answered normal questions. Kind of unfair of him to hit me with the hard ones.

"It suits me." I shrugged. "I was thinking ..." I stood, giving Akiva one last scratch behind the ear. "Since we're stuck here, maybe I could show you the mood boards Cammie and I put together for the B and B? Since you'll be doing some of the custom stuff."

The Scot gave me a short nod. "Sure."

I sat down on the sofa and rummaged in my backpack, looking for my phone, pulling things out to get to it. "Ah-hah." My fingers curled around my cell, dragging it out. Ramsay had crossed the room to sit on the couch beside me and as I reached to return items to my backpack, I noted his raised eyebrow and focused attention.

On my paperback.

Heat hit my cheeks. But I had nothing to be embarrassed about, I reminded myself. I slid the book into my backpack unhurriedly.

"Was that ... *three* men and a woman?"

Now I flushed for a whole different reason. "Yup."

"And ... she's a nanny? And they're her neighbors?"

Hearing the strangled laughter in his voice, I settled down on the couch with all the primness I could muster. "Uh-huh. It's called *Why Choose Romance*." I stared directly into his eyes. "Any other questions?"

Those pale eyes twinkled, but he shook his head.

Tapping on my phone screen, ignoring my damp palms, I brought up the mood boards Cammie and I were working from. I didn't care what he thought about my reading preferences, Mr. I Own Every Literary Classic Under the Sun and Probably Read the *Eclogues of Virgil* for Fun.

And yet my brain wanted to zoom off on a tangent, wondering what he thought about me. If he thought I was merely some dumb, nepo baby who came here on a whim with my trespassing tendencies and kinky romance novels.

Why did I care? I didn't know this guy from Adam. He was clearly older than me and totally not my type with his gruff, short sentences and unkempt appearance.

I'd always liked my men classically handsome and charming.

Then why did it feel like every inch of my skin was abuzz with awareness?

I had to force myself not to suck in a breath when Ramsay leaned closer to see my phone. Oh, of course, he smelled amazing too. A spicy, woodsy scent either from shower wash or shampoo (it couldn't be cologne—he didn't cross me as the cologne type), mingled with sea air. I fought the strange and sudden urge to nuzzle my face in his corded throat.

What the hell kind of instant attraction crap was this?

3. Ramsay

She smelled like she looked.
　　Expensive.
　Sexy.
　I shifted in my seat, focusing on the phone in her manicured hand and frowned at her perfect nails that matched the color of her silly wee SUV. Nails that would no doubt feel fucking amazing raking down my back. I threw out the image and opined gruffly, "If you're going to get your hands dirty, you should clip those off."

Tierney Silver glanced up from the device in her hand, her hazel eyes wide. "What?"

"Your nails."

"Cut my nails?" she asked, as if I'd suggested she shave her head. "No way. I can help without cutting my nails." Her frown was disapproving as she turned back to her phone, muttering under her breath about yetis or some such nonsense.

I studied her profile as she swiped on her screen looking, I supposed, for the mood board she and Cammie had come up with.

The photos online of Tierney didn't do her justice.

She photographed as a pretty, well-turned-out young woman but nothing extraordinary. Not some raging beauty. But if anything my world travels had taught me was that beauty was subjective. Some people just had a magnetism in real life that didn't come through in a photograph. Something untenable and indescribable that made you unable to look away. That made them the most gorgeous person you'd ever met in your damn life.

Tierney Silver was that. And I hadn't expected it from the spoiled heiress. Even in jeans, a Henley, hiking boots, with her blond hair tied back in a ponytail, she was stunning. One of those women who would look good in a black plastic rubbish bag.

Up close I could see a smattering of freckles across her nose and cheeks. There was a larger freckle right on the corner of her lush top lip. I stared at it as she muttered to herself about the mood board.

What the fuck was happening here?

I wrenched my gaze away, annoyed at myself for acting as doe-eyed as the young lads on the island. They were all twittering like fools over the American hotel heiress.

Even if I didn't have a rule against sleeping with women from the island, I wouldn't touch Tierney Silver. Spoiled, rich, pampered twenty-seven-year-olds didn't really do it for me. At least not usually.

Though it was clear she was something more. My previous career had taught me to see beyond what people presented to the world.

There was a dark grief in Tierney's hazel eyes.

And secrets.

I was a bloodhound when it came to secrets. Could smell them from miles away. Once it had been my business to ferret out secrets. But this ... her ...

Not my business, I reminded myself.

"Aha!" Tierney held the phone up to my face. "This is what we're thinking for the dining room." She scrolled through the mood board. I was pleasantly surprised to see a contemporary twist on traditional Victorian coastal design. I'd half expected her to turn the B and B into a too cold, too modern guesthouse along the lines of some of the hotels in the empire she'd given up.

And who gives up their rights to a multibillion-dollar hotel chain?

I tried to focus on the B and B since it was where I would be working for at least the next six months. "That looks out of place." I tapped on the image of the antique Welsh dresser.

"Right." She looked up at me and gave me a smile. Her smile was too sweet. I felt it in places I really shouldn't.

Okay, aye, this was a problem.

"I included it because my grandmother had one like it and I'd love to incorporate the idea into the dining room but with a modern twist. So far, I'm having no such luck finding a piece of furniture that will work with the design." She shrugged. "I'll keep looking." Turning back to her phone, she tapped the screen a few times. "Now this is one of the bunk-bed rooms, and I saw this design where they custom built three bunk beds, two beneath and then one on top going the opposite way, like this. Do you think you could build something like that? It would be a great way to increase capacity in what is a smaller room."

I studied the photo she showed me, moving in closer to her. It was a clever design. "Aye, I can do that."

She turned to stare up at me, her eyes widening ever so slightly upon realizing how close we were. A little splash of red on her cheeks and an almost imperceptible intake of breath told me she was affected by my nearness. Her pupils dilated.

So the pampered princess was attracted to me too.

Aye, this was a problem.

Too young. Too sweet. Too much my client.

Deciding the best path forward was to ignore the unspoken awareness of each other, I asked more gruffly than I intended, "What?"

Tierney swallowed and looked away. "Uh, can I see your workshop?"

"Want to know if I'm any good?" Now, why did that sound dirtier than intended?

"Something like that."

A minute later we were walking across the clearing to my barn.

"Do you have solar panels somewhere?" my companion asked.

"Aye. Beyond the trees where they get constant light."

"Do you have plumbing?"

Her curiosity was endearing and also annoying because I wondered what else she'd become curious about. "Aye. It was a bitch to put in and more expense than any normal person would spend to connect to Glenvulin's sewage line."

"Oh, I'd spend it in a heartbeat." She gave me a smile filled with camaraderie. It really was the sweetest smile I'd ever seen. "I once stayed with some friends on an island in the Philippines. Beautiful. Stunning. But no plumbing. The owners of the rental were using composting toilets. Sounds fine, right? It's not fine. They weren't maintained properly and three of us got food poisoning. The smelly kind. These composting toilets were not equipped to deal with that shit. Literally."

I grunted with amusement as I let her into my workshop. The earthy aroma of wood hit my nostrils in a comforting, familiar way as we entered.

"And I'm talking to you about fecal matter," she murmured, her cheeks flushing ever so slightly. "I'm doing great. Got stuck on your island. Inconveniencing you. And now I'm talking about disgusting bodily functions."

"Everyone shits." I shrugged, brushing past her to switch on the lights. "Even the king."

Tierney laughed, and the sound, for some reason, made me think of these wee silver bells my mum used to hang from an arched doorway that divided the living room from the entrance. She hung them there every Christmas. The sound of her laughter was fitting, considering Tierney's surname. "I think that's blasphemy."

"Only if he heard me." I turned to watch the bulbs taking a second to warm up and illuminate the space.

"Maybe he did. He is the king." Her gaze darted around the workshop and landed on my current piece. A client on the Isle of Skye had commissioned me to make a rocking chair based on a photo of her grandmother's old chair.

"This is gorgeous." Tierney strode over to it, her hand hovering above the carvings along the side panels. "You're not merely a carpenter. You're an artist."

Uncomfortable with her effusive compliment, I stared down at the chair I'd spent the past few weeks working on between other projects. "I'm just copying the photo my client gave me."

"Well, it's amazing. Also this place *smells* amazing."

It did. At least it did to me. I worked with a lot of hardwoods, which had a smoky scent. There was something calming about it. I always felt myself unwind while I crafted items out of wood.

The large barn might have been filled with half-finished work—a dining table Erin Mull from the island had commissioned; bookshelves that would slot perfectly into place in a home on Skye; a live-edge wood coffee table for Cammie's client on the mainland. But my tools were meticulously organized—squares, table saw, saws, chisels, fastening tools, clamps, sanders, brushes. Other than Akiva, this workshop was my baby.

"What got you into carpentry?"

Living on a very small island had prepared me for people's natural curiosity about their neighbors. Once the questions had made me uncomfortable, like I'd squeezed on too small boots. Now, I skirted the details of my history with ease. "Military put me through my engineering and construction degrees. Picked up some skills along the way. Woodwork became a bit of a hobby."

"A hobby." She strolled casually around my space, eyeing my equipment and the pieces of furniture lying around in different levels of repair and finish. She stopped at the coffee table with its live edge and tentatively ran her hands along it. "Beautiful. Pretty awesome hobby. I can barely put together something from Ikea." Her tone went beyond self-deprecating to disparaging. She flicked me a look. "But I can shoot a target from two hundred yards. Maybe I should have gone into the military. Did something useful."

Not many people surprised me. But this did. "How did you learn to shoot?"

"My dad." Tierney turned, crossing her arms over her chest in a move I knew she didn't realize was protective, defensive. "He used to take me to the outdoor rifle range at his club every second Saturday."

"Do you like guns, then?"

"Nope. But I liked spending time with my dad. And I happened to be good at it. Do you like guns?"

I tried not to smile at the attitude in her question, like my enquiry had been judgmental. It was not. "They have their uses."

Our eyes held for a second too long, that awareness raking over my skin. Her arms dropped from her chest as her attention dropped to my mouth. I wasn't sure she even realized how much she gave away.

Damn it.

"How long were you in the military? Which division? Navy, army?"

"Royal Marines." *Subject change*. "I actually really need to finish up some work. Are you all right to head back to the house? Keep yourself occupied for a bit?" It was rude, but I needed some space from the blond and her many questions.

Embarrassment tinged her cheeks and she nodded rapidly. "Of course."

"I'll be over in a wee while," I said, trying to ignore the prickle of guilt.

"Take your time." She waved those manicure-tipped fingers at me without looking back and disappeared out the barn door.

A few seconds later, I heard the front door of my home shut and Akiva give a welcoming bark inside. My dog, who barely liked anyone but me, liked Tierney Silver, of all people.

I blew out a breath, running a hand through a beard I kept meaning to cut. "Well ... fuck."

4. Tierney

Being a little sneaky, I'd had a quick, curious look around the rest of the house. I'd discovered two rooms down a hallway off the kitchen. One was a bedroom and had a book on the bedside table and a TV on a cabinet opposite it, so I guessed it was Ramsay's. The other room was full of expensive gym equipment, which, gathering from his impressive physique, the man used daily.

I also noted a set of bagpipes propped up against the farthest wall and wondered if Ramsay played.

I'd always liked the bagpipes, but I had friends who couldn't stand the sound. When I was a kid, my parents had taken me to Scotland every other summer to visit my grandmother. My mom was born in Edinburgh and raised in Scotland and had left to attend college in the US. She'd ended up getting a job after graduation and staying in the States.

One summer, Dad had gotten tickets to the Royal Edinburgh Military Tattoo, which was this event on Edinburgh Castle's esplanade. Military bands played along with other performers from across the world. I remembered hearing the drums from the military pipe band and then the wail of the bagpipes before I even saw the musicians. The sound thrummed through my chest and caused goose bumps to spring to life along my arms and down my spine.

I'd been enthralled by it.

Mom had sat through it with a pained expression. She hated the bagpipes. I didn't understand it. I didn't understand why she couldn't hear what I heard. There was something so mournful and haunting about them, and yet, triumphant and resilient. A strange dichotomy for a musical instrument.

If Ramsay played the pipes ... one, it made him hotter than I already thought he was; and two, I wanted to hear him play.

He was such a mystery. A tall, muscular, talented, woodworking, book-reading, hot Scottish hermit of a mystery.

There was no ring on his finger. No sign of a woman or a man or any companion except for Akiva.

That, of course, didn't mean he was single.

He could have a girlfriend or boyfriend on the island.

Not that I should care.

The man was clearly a bachelor, even if he had a partner out there somewhere.

And I was pretty sure by the way he dismissed me earlier, he found me annoying.

Around six o'clock, I was three quarters of the way through my romance book, which was way too steamy for me to be consuming in my current situation. The last thing I needed was being turned on while trapped on an island with my sexy yeti.

I heard his footsteps on the porch first so I'd lowered my book to watch him stride into his house.

A house I'd made myself at home in.

I had my legs stretched out on his sectional and Akiva was asleep across my lap. My eyes met Ramsay's as he stepped inside. He took in his dog. I felt the tension in Akiva's body, like she was trying to decide if saying hello to her owner was worth giving up my comfy lap.

"Thrown over so easily," Ramsay murmured, amusement in his pale beautiful eyes. "I'll remember that."

As if she understood, Akiva suddenly jumped off me and the couch, hurrying over to greet her dad.

He lowered to his haunches, scratching behind her ears while murmuring affectionate words.

Attraction rippled in my belly as I watched this tender side of him.

In fact, the level of attraction really was ridiculous considering how little I knew about Ramsay.

"Do you play the bagpipes?" I blurted out.

Ramsay turned to me, his piercing gaze still surprising, knocking the breath right out of me. Slowly, he stood from petting Akiva. "Been snooping, Silver?"

My cheeks flushed because I had been. I also might have grown hot at the familiar use of my surname as a nickname. "They're right there." I gestured to the other side of the room where I knew the bagpipes laid.

"Aye, I play."

"Where? When?" I got up off the couch to follow him into the kitchen. I kept the island between us as he opened the refrigerator.

"Pipe band. Quinn's in it too."

Which meant I might get to watch and hear Ramsay play. "Do you play locally?"

"Sometimes. Sometimes at events on the mainland. Why?" He glanced over his shoulder.

"I like the pipes. My mom was Scottish, and we'd visit my grandmother in Edinburgh every other summer. After my first Tattoo, I made my dad take me every time we visited my gran."

"Sounds like you have Scotland in your blood. In more ways than one."

"Yeah."

"Dinner?" he asked abruptly.

In answer, my stomach gave a rumble of approval. "Sure. Thanks. I really appreciate your hospitality."

He grunted in response.

Thirty minutes later, I sat across from Ramsay at his dining table eating the basic pasta dish he'd thrown together. It was far from a culinary masterpiece. Now that I was pretty sure he found me annoying, I felt self-conscious and remembered to keep my questions to myself.

It was interesting because growing up the way I had, I'd become a pretty confident person. The last time I remembered feeling self-conscious was when I was thirteen. It was the first time a boy kissed me and I'd agonized over if I was any good at it.

I'd barely taken a bite of the bland pasta when I felt Ramsay's attention on me.

Looking up, sure enough, Ramsay searched my face.

"What?"

"You're quiet."

"Am I? Do you know me well enough to ascertain that quiet isn't my usual mode?"

"Our earlier interaction suggests otherwise."

I frowned.

"I'm not suggesting you're overly talkative, Silver. You just ... are less so than before."

Silver. Why was him calling me by my surname so hot?

"I'm already imposing. Just trying to stay out of your way as much as possible before it's safe to cross back to Leth Sholas."

We ate in silence for a bit after that and I tried not to be hurt by Ramsay's lack of response or denial that I was imposing or needed to stay out of his way.

"So ... you really plan to stay here permanently?" Ramsay

asked out of nowhere. "You're not planning to move on once the B and B is up and running? Leave someone else to manage it?"

"No." I frowned. "Why? Is that what people think?"

He shrugged. "I think we think you don't know what island life is like. It'll be hard for someone who has had every convenience at her fingertips."

Irritation heated my skin. "*You* got used to it. You're not an islander by birth."

"No. But I was in the military. I know life without convenience."

Anger overtook my irritation. So that was his problem, huh? He thought he had me pegged. Just like everyone else.

Spoiled little rich girl playing dress-up with a building on Glenvulin. That I'd get bored and go running back to my life as it was before.

Well, news flash.

That life no longer fucking existed.

"If I can get up every day and move through a world in which my parents are dead, I can go without having designer stores and fancy restaurants at my fingertips." I shoved a forkful of pasta in my mouth before I told him to go fuck himself.

Tense silence thrummed between us.

"I didn't mean to insult you," Ramsay finally offered.

"No?" I cocked my head, smirking unhappily at him. "Or was it more that you didn't think I would recognize the insult?"

Something gleamed in his eyes. "Fair enough." He studied me for a second too long, making it difficult for me to catch my breath. What was it about this man? Even annoyed at him, I was hot and bothered. "Did you finish your book?"

Taken aback by the question, it took me a second to respond. "Almost."

"Did ... she enjoy all of her neighbors?"

At the seriousness with which he asked, I couldn't help but laugh.

Ramsay flashed me a quick grin and there went my breath catching again.

I wanted to see him smile like that without the bushy beard.

It crinkled the corners of his eyes in the sexiest way.

"Yes," I answered primly, lips straining against amusement. "She thoroughly enjoyed all three neighbors, and they thoroughly enjoyed her in return. They are currently being typical dickheads at this point in the book, but I expect copious amounts of groveling in the next few chapters."

"Groveling?" He frowned incredulously.

"Oh yeah, it's hot. I love a good grovel." At his bemusement, I grinned and gestured to his books behind me. "You have quite the library. Though I'm guessing there are no *Why Choose Romance* novels on those shelves."

"No, there aren't." He shook his head, staring past me to the books. "I inherited them."

"Have you read them all?"

"Not all. But I've made a dent."

"How old are you?" The question was out before I could stop it. I flushed.

Ramsay quirked an eyebrow. "How old do you think I am?"

Hearing the teasing in his tone, I relaxed ever so slightly. "Midthirties?"

"Forty."

That surprised me. I knew he was older than me, but I didn't know he was thirteen *years* older.

I wasn't usually attracted to older men.

But now I didn't know why because this man was more man than I'd ever encountered in my life.

"I'm twenty-seven," I replied to have something to say so I didn't blurt out how sexy I found him.

"I know." He chewed on another bite of pasta and looked down at Akiva who sat by his chair, eyes round with begging. "No, sweetheart. You'll get something later."

He called his dog *sweetheart*.

This man was trying to kill me.

"What's your favorite book?" I asked, changing the subject.

Ramsay took one last massive bite, chewed while not quite meeting my eyes, and stood. Finally he said, "Dunno." He dumped his plate in the sink. "Just put your plate here when you're finished. I'll be in my workshop if you need me. I'll be back at eleven to take you over."

The man was gone before I was finished gaping in astonishment at his abrupt departure.

I looked at Akiva, and she stared back at me expectantly. "Has he always been the human version of whiplash?"

I could have sworn Akiva gave me a commiserating jerk of her snout.

―――

Sure enough, Ramsay stayed away for the rest of the evening.

Bored, I'd washed and dried the dishes. I'd also gone out to ask about Akiva's dinner and Ramsay hadn't even looked up from the rocking chair when he provided me with her feeding instructions.

The rest of the night, Akiva and I lazed on the couch. I finished my book (there *was* a good grovel) and then I ran the battery down on my phone playing solitaire until my eyes blurred. I tried to connect to the internet because according to my phone, there was a network. But it was private so I couldn't connect without a password. A thorough search of the house revealed no router so I could only assume my phone was picking up networks from Leth Sholas.

How Ramsay survived over here without the internet, I did not know. Connection on the island wasn't the strongest, but it did the job. Here on Stòr, there was nothing. How did people contact Ramsay? How did he work with clients when he was so unreachable? Other than the VHF radio, the man had no way of communicating with people from his island.

I, of course, wanted to ask him about it, but I was still stung by the way he'd walked out after dinner. There was being a man of mystery and then there was just being a dick.

By ten fifty I had my backpack together and I'd already hugged Akiva goodbye. I stepped out onto the porch, car keys at the ready, and stopped, contemplating letting Ramsay know I was leaving. Despite his rudeness, he had let me stay in his house and he'd fed me. He wasn't all bad.

Sighing, I moved along the lighted porch toward the barn and startled to a stop when the tall Scot stepped out of his workshop. He took long strides toward me. "Ready?"

"Yeah, I was going to let you know I was leaving."

"I'll follow you."

"Really, there's no need. You've done enough."

"I'll follow you," he said, his tone brokering no argument as he brushed by me on the porch. His earthy, musky scent caused this weird fluttering in my chest. "Just let me grab my keys."

Stubborn yeti.

I made my way down to my car, eyes wide in the dark. I was barely in it when Ramsay reappeared again, Akiva at his heels. They jumped into his Defender with ease, and I did a three-point turn, driving out of the woodlands first. It took me a second in the dark to remember where I was supposed to turn, but thankfully, I made the correct choice. I had a feeling Ramsay already thought I was a useless nepo baby (and was now concerned the town did too), I didn't want him thinking I was also directionally challenged.

Ramsay kept close behind me, his headlights kind of glaring, actually. But I made it to the causeway. There was still a little water but not enough to stop me from driving right onto it.

I frowned at the sight of Ramsay following me across.

Where the hell was he going?

Leth Sholas was quiet at this time of night. The only commercial building lit up was the volunteer lifeboat service building at the end of the main harbor road. There was no parking on the harbor front, other than in the designated tourist parking lots, so I drove down a side street that led me to the back of the apartment block that overlooked Half-Light Harbor. I was renting a guest apartment from Aodhan MacDuff, one of the local councilmen and property owners. He had quite a few rental properties across Glenvulin.

Parking was tight behind the apartment, but my spot was empty. Even with the beam of Ramsay's headlights trying to fluster me, I swung the Suzuki around and reversed back into the space. Ramsay's Defender sat in the entrance of the parking lot.

Hmm.

Getting out of the vehicle, I grabbed my backpack and gave him a wave as I hurried across the small lot to the back entrance. I fumbled with my key, but as soon as I opened the door, the headlights dimmed, and I watched as Ramsay reversed out. He paused suddenly, but I couldn't see him beyond the glare of his lights.

Realization dawned.

He wasn't leaving until I was safely inside.

Huh.

I darted into the building and locked the door behind me.

A mystery.

The man was a mystery wrapped up in well over six feet of delicious manliness.

Yes, he had been a dick.

But he was also kind of not.

That night, Ramsay McRae consumed my thoughts as I lay in bed trying to sleep. I hadn't mooned over a guy like this since I was seventeen years old.

Oh my god.

I clapped a hand to my forehead in embarrassment.

I had a *crush*.

A girly, stupid crush.

"Kill me now," I groaned, rolling over onto my side and pulling the covers tightly around me.

5. Tierney

A week later, my first coffee of the morning in hand, I opened my phone to a new text from Perri. My heart leapt and I clicked on it.

> I've finally tracked Adila. Flying to Sydney today. Will let you know if I make contact.

I quickly typed a response.

> Okay. Please be careful.

I stood and walked over to the living room window of the apartment. It had a view over the harbor but nothing like the elevated vista my guests would have from the B and B. My stomach churned as it always did when I let my mind wander to the crusade I'd decided to fight.

My phone binged, drawing me out of my melancholy. Cameron:

> Are we still meeting at 10 a.m.?

I quickly typed one-handed.

> Absolutely. See you then.

Beneath that text thread was an unopened message from Hugh.

I ignored it as I had been ignoring it for the past few days.

At the sight of a new text from London, however, I tapped on it:

> Tell me Scotland is worth missing London.

I grinned at her pun. London Wetherspoon had been my best friend since the ninth grade. We'd both attended a private New York high school that wasn't quite as vicious as *Gossip Girl* depicted, but we knew kids who lived in actual hotel rooms, who partied hard and dirty, and lived in a world of privilege beyond most people's imagination. London's parents were both top surgeons and she barely ever saw them. They were neglectful at best, emotionally abusive at worst. My parents were loving and hands-on and my mom was adamant I didn't get sucked into a life of crazy ostentatiousness because of our wealth.

Despite her own privileged upbringing, London never acted like a pretentious asshole or superior to anyone who had less. She'd envied those whose parents were around and cared. Her parents only cared when London's grades weren't high enough. They'd stopped caring altogether when she refused to go to medical school and she'd used her trust fund to put herself through culinary school. London was now a sous chef at a restaurant in Manhattan and worked long hours.

To my surprise, she was still dating Nick. Nick had attended our school but was a few years ahead of us. I remembered him being gorgeous, popular, and a bully. London promised he'd matured since then, but I had my reservations. Nick was a successful stockbroker, and I thought he was wrong for my best friend. He wanted London to quit her job, and it had become a point of contention between them. I thought Nick didn't really know London if he thought she'd give up her career for him. However, London seemed infatuated with him, despite their differences.

> It'll never be worth that. But London could come to Scotland 😊

It was too early to get a response. I'd need distraction elsewhere. Keeping busy. That's what I required. The past week, I'd spent my time sightseeing, in between traveling to antique stores on the mainland and across the isles with Cameron to find pieces that might work for the B and B. I attempted valiantly not to think about Ramsay.

I saw him yesterday, bringing his small boat into harbor, the rocking chair he'd been working on in the back of it. He'd obviously finished it and was bringing it to Cammie. Ramsay hadn't seen me and I'd hurried away before he could.

Cammie had asked me about getting stuck on Stòr. Apparently, Annie at the volunteer lifeboat service had told everyone. I shrugged it off like it was no big deal and changed the subject.

There was no point letting everyone know I had a big ol' silly crush on a man who had left his beloved dog alone with a stranger rather than converse with said stranger.

Throwing back the last of my coffee, I grabbed my keys and purse, glancing around the apartment to make sure I had everything I needed. It was a small one bedroom with an open-plan living and kitchen. It had a nice view over the harbor, though the windows weren't big enough to really take advantage of it. Aodhan usually rented the apartment out as a vacation let and it wasn't purpose built for someone to stay in long term. But it would do until the B and B was ready. We were designing an owner's suite where I'd live permanently.

I hurried down the stairwell, out the front entrance of the building, and almost walked into a group of tourists. Murmuring apologies, I strode down the harbor road that bustled with life. As long as the weather allowed, there were regular ferries to the mainland not only for tourists but for locals. Many people on Glenvulin worked on the mainland, so they had to catch a ferry in the mornings and afternoons. There were also tourists, of course, and fishermen and excursion boats already filling the harbor. The smell of seawater, fish, and the sound of gulls crying overhead had become a familiar and welcome assault on my senses. Cammie had joked that there were only two seasons on Glenvulin—June and winter.

It was June and I was going to enjoy the heck out of the mild, calm weather while we had it.

For the past few weeks, I'd ventured all over Glenvulin, snapping photos for my social media, starting with the colorful row of buildings that curved along the coastline. For a tiny village, the rainbow Main Street overflowed with businesses. There was everything from the volunteer lifeboat service and ferry crossing to vacation apartments, two hotels, a hostel, a beauty salon, a convenience store, a coffee/bookshop, a bakery, two gift shops, a museum, a hardware store, a chocolate shop, a whisky distillery, pharmacy, Italian restaurant, and a fish-and-chips shop. And that was just on Main Street. In the village beyond were more stores, a fishmonger, a butcher, a doctor's surgery, a fire and police station, and a small supermarket. Farther out on Glenvulin were a couple more cafés and restaurants, a cheese farm, Quinn and Cammie's parents' farm and their farm shop with fresh produce, as well as a few more hotels and B and Bs.

I'd been warned I'd miss my conveniences living on the

island, but so far, so good. Certain services managed to do overnight to the isles, which amazed me, but getting some of the supplies we required for the renovation was a little more involved. I had to pay extra on delivery for the more unwieldy and larger materials. But I could survive with only a handful of takeout choices and stores.

Maybe not having everything at their fingertips, having to wait to receive things they wanted and/or needed, or having to travel for them was why the people of Glenvulin seemed a lot more laid-back and patient than the people from the world I'd left behind.

Work started today and Cameron had offered to meet me there. I enjoyed hanging out with Cammie and was pretty sure we'd remain friends after the B and B renovation was complete.

My first stop was my favorite place second to the bakery—the coffee shop/bookstore. It was housed in a pink and white building next to the blue and yellow building of the bakery next door.

It was called Macbeth's Pages & Perks.

It was already busy inside the cozy store. Along the back wall was the coffee counter and all the machinery. The adjacent side of the room was lined with bookshelves and the front of the store with bistro tables. There was a comfortable couch and coffee table near the bookshelves, but it was always occupied whenever I ventured in. There were two armchairs next to an actual fireplace, but those were always the first spots to get taken.

Framed literary posters hung on the wall, interspersed between metal signs with sayings about coffee and books like "That's what I do: I drink coffee. I read books. And I know things." "Death to Decaf." "Drink Coffee: Do stupid things faster with more energy." "Heaven is a never-ending supply of coffee and books. Welcome to Heaven."

The signs made me smile and wonder about the owner, whom I'd yet to meet. The store was run by Ewan and Martha, who had told me during a quieter moment in the shop that the owner, Isla Macbeth, was currently off sick.

Today, I was greeted by a new face behind the coffee counter. A beautiful brunette with large dark eyes gave me a smile that didn't quite reach said eyes. "What can I get you?" she asked in a Scots accent similar to the locals. Yet I hadn't seen her around the village before because I definitely would have remembered her.

"Americano for Tierney!" Ewan called from the opposite end of the counter, flashing me a grin of welcome.

I smiled back and nodded at the brunette. "He's right."

"Oh, you must be the American who bought the guesthouse," the brunette said before turning toward the machine to start making my drink. She glanced over her shoulder. "I'm Taran Macbeth."

"Oh, are you Isla's daughter?"

Undeniable pain tightened Taran's features. "You met Mum, then?"

"No." I hesitated, not sure what was happening but feeling not-great vibes. I glanced down the counter toward Ewan who gave me a shake of his head, his eyes suddenly bright with emotion.

Oh god, what was happening?

Taran finished making the Americano in silence and then set it down in front of me. "I hope you like it here."

"I do. Thanks."

I paid for my coffee, aware there was a line behind me but weirdly feeling the need to say something else.

"If you ever need anything ..."

Taran's expression softened. "That's my line. But thanks. Same. If you're a regular in here, I'll see you a lot now. I've come home to take over the store."

I heard what she wasn't saying and battled the urge to tell this stranger how sorry I was. Now I recognized that look on her face. I'd seen it on my own whenever I looked in the mirror after my parents' death.

Gesturing with my cup, I gave her a little wave and walked out of the coffee store feeling unbelievably sad for her.

"Tierney!"

I glanced up to find Cammie strolling toward me. The McQuarries were a tall bunch. Cameron was five ten, built like a glamor model, and had a thick mass of long blond hair. Every other week there was a new streak of color in the two bands framing her face; today it was fuchsia pink. Her nose was a little too long and her mouth a little too wide—but she had that thing, that quality, that made her attractiveness transcend the nonsensical lie referred to as "traditional beauty."

She wore a tight-fitting rain jacket with a belted waist with her jeans and hiking boots, barely any makeup, and yet still managed to look put together. Slim gold rings with varying stones decorated almost every one of her blunt-nailed fingers, and when her right sleeve was pushed up, it revealed her tattoo, a beautiful, delicate branch of heather to symbolize her niece Heather. When her nephew was born, she had his name, Angus, wound into the tattoo in script.

Usually of a sunny disposition, I tensed at Cammie's somber facade as she approached. She gestured to the store behind me. "Did you hear?"

"Hear what?"

Her blue eyes glistened. "Isla Macbeth has metastatic breast cancer. It's not ... They didn't catch it in time. She's decided not to seek treatment."

I'd known it was something like that. I'd seen it written all over a devastated Taran Macbeth. I squeezed Cammie's arm. "I'm so sorry. That's why Taran is home."

Her head whipped toward the coffee shop. "She's in there?"

I nodded.

Cammie stared at the store for a few seconds, hesitating. Then she gestured for me to walk with her. "Taran is ... *was* Quinn's girlfriend in high school."

I thought about my handsome contractor and the pretty brunette and could absolutely see it. "How sweet."

She made a huffing noise. "It was until it wasn't. We all thought they'd end up together. Finding love here isn't easy. But Taran left Leth Sholas for Glasgow Uni and things fell apart between them. They broke up and my brother in a drunken, miserable state, made the stonkingly bad decision to sleep with Kiera."

"That's his ex?" So far, I hadn't been given many details about the personal lives of the villagers I now found myself among, but it felt good that Cameron trusted me enough to share.

"Heather and Angus's mum." She referred to Quinn's children. I'd learned over the past few weeks that Quinn was a single dad to a seventeen-year-old girl and twelve-year-old boy of whom he shared joint custody with his ex.

"He became a dad at eighteen and because our own father bolted when we were kids, leaving Mum to raise us alone, Quinn didn't want that for Heather."

"Wait. I thought your parents owned a farm."

"Greg is our stepfather," Cammie explained. "He came back to Leth Sholas to take over his parents' farm and he and Mum reconnected from their childhood. Don't get me wrong, we think of him as Dad now, but he didn't come into our lives until Quinn was eleven and I was eight. Quinn remembered how hard it was for Mum. He didn't really get a chance to be a wee boy because he had to help her out so much, even taking care of me so she could work nights. Anyway, he married Kiera because he didn't want Heather to grow up without a dad in the house. They tried for years to make it work, even going so far as to deliberately have Angus. I love my brother, but he should never have ... Anyway, Kiera did what was best for her in the end and left. She's moved on and is happy with her new partner."

I'd noted the lack of ring on my contractor's wedding finger. "And Quinn? Did he move on?"

Cammie huffed. "One thing you should know about island life is that it makes for a very shallow dating pool."

That I didn't mind at all. I wasn't here to date. I shoved thoughts of Ramsay McRae from my mind. "Now Taran's back ..."

"Aye, that's not going to happen. Taran ... When she found out Kiera was pregnant, she was beyond devastated. She never came back to Leth Sholas. Taran and I were close, but she cut me off too." Cammie gave me a sad shrug. "I understood. Quinn broke her heart so badly she hasn't returned to Leth Sholas in eighteen years. Isla and Taran's brother, Laird, would always leave the island to go visit Taran in Glasgow. Last I heard, she was engaged ... I wonder if her fiancé is here too."

Not only was her mom dying, but Taran had to return to a town where everyone knew her painful history ... where she had to face the man who broke her heart. I hoped her fiancé *was* with her to support her. "That is too much for anyone to deal with all at once."

"Aye." Cammie took a shuddering breath. "Her dad died when she was eight. So all she'll have left is her brother Laird and Laird's wife and their kids too. But maybe if she has a fiancé ... I don't know. I wish she'd let me be there for her."

"Have you tried?"

"I don't think she'd want me to."

"Cammie, I just looked into the grief-stricken eyes of a

woman who probably needs all the support she can get right now."

My new friend halted in her steps, biting her lower lip as she considered this. "You're right. I'll ... I'll make an approach. Let her know I'm here if she needs me."

"Good. And I know I'm new here and all, but I would like to be helpful. And I ... unfortunately know what it's like to lose a parent."

"You more than anyone will be able to offer her comfort. You don't have the baggage we all do. And you get it. I'm sorry that you get it. But you do."

"I'll check in with her," I promised.

Cammie smiled. "I'm so glad you chose our wee island to start over on."

Grateful she'd offered her friendship so easily, I returned her smile. "Me too."

The B and B was bustling, organized chaos as the demolition crew tore down walls and pulled out the old kitchen and bathrooms under Quinn's direction.

He greeted us at the door. "We're making this quick," he said stone-faced. "Too easy for accidents to happen in this midden."

"We need to talk after this," Cammie replied, her tone pointed.

Sorrow flickered over Quinn's expression. "If it's about Isla, no need. I heard."

"Did you know Taran is back and working at Pages & Perks?"

His chin jerked back, nostrils flaring. "What? No."

"Wanted to give you a heads-up."

Quinn's gaze darted to me and apparently that was the end

of the discussion. He handed us hard hats, insisting we put them on. As we moved through the dust-clouded building, I tried not to get anxious at the wreckage as Quinn shouted over the noise, explaining everything that was going on.

That's when I saw him again.

Ramsay McRae was in the old kitchen, ripping out the cabinets, muscles straining against his tight, sweat-soaked T-shirt.

He might as well have been in a porn movie for the impact the sight of him had on my body. I felt a deep pull low in my belly and an answering wet tingle between my thighs.

What the ever-loving fuck?

"McRae!" Quinn shouted.

Feeling heat on my face, I turned to find Cammie staring at me, lips straining with laughter, eyes wide with knowing.

That's when I realized my mouth was hanging open like a panting dog.

I snapped it shut.

Cammie leaned in and spoke in my ear, "Apparently, *we* also need to talk."

My cheeks heated. "What? I don't ..." I laughed lamely and then whirled around, giving the men my back. "Am I that obvious?"

"Eh, only a wee bit."

"Oh God." I grimaced. "Okay." I wiped my expression clean. "Better?"

"Aye. But you and I are going to talk when we're alone," she murmured before she stepped toward her brother and Ramsay.

The men were frowning at us and Quinn practically barked, "Problem?"

"No!" I answered a little too loudly. "Cammie and I were talking about the design for in here. But the demo is going great. Obviously." I couldn't make eye contact with Ramsay.

"Oh, hey, I need to show you two something." Cammie pulled her phone out of her back pocket, shooting me an amused look. I could kiss her for saving me from my own awkwardness. "I posted a video last night from your gig on Skye last week and it went viral." She held up her phone screen, and I heard the pipe band music ever so slightly beneath the sounds of the demo going on around us.

My curiosity had me straining to peer at her phone, but Ramsay snatched it out of Cammie's hand, his fingers flying over it.

"What are you doing?" Cammie yelled over the noise.

Without a word, Ramsay handed the phone back to her.

"Uh! You deleted it. And you deleted it from my video folder. The brazen cheek of it!"

Ramsay glowered at Quinn who turned to his sister with an exasperated sigh. "Cam, I told you not to post any videos of the band online."

She crossed her arms over her chest. "You know it's interesting, because I see a ton of people videoing your performances but somehow there's nothing online ... though curiouser and curiouser, there are hashtags for the band name."

"What's the band's name?" I hadn't thought to ask Ramsay last week.

"Leth Sholas Pipe Band," Cammie supplied. "So there's no mistaking that at some point there were videos of the band uploaded to the internet that mysteriously disappeared." She raised her eyebrow. "Don't you find that curious?"

I did. My eyes were round with a million questions. "I do."

"See? Tierney thinks it's weird too."

Quinn gave another long-suffering sigh. "Cam, stop reading into things, eh. Right. I think that's enough of a tour for now." He eyed me. "How about you come back at four and we can talk about the progress?"

Awareness prickled over me and my attention pulled to Ramsay. Just like last time, I found myself caught in his wolf-gray eyes. What was that?

I tried not to suck in a visible breath as my heart rate accelerated. "Sure," I said to Quinn and then, weirdly desperate to have some kind of interaction with Ramsay, asked, "Where's Akiva?"

"Annie at Leth Sholas lifeboat service watches her when I can't have her around for safety reasons."

"I could watch her," I blurted without thought. "She and I kind of bonded."

"You did?" Cammie pouted. "I always thought Akiva was aloof with everyone but Ramsay."

Not me, I thought, feeling a little smug.

However, Ramsay gave me a small shake of his head. "She's fine with Annie." And then walked out of the room to continue the demo. I felt dismissed. And rejected.

My cheeks heated as I shrugged, flashing a forced smile at Quinn. "Four o'clock."

A few minutes later, Cammie and I walked downhill back toward Main Street. I braced myself, waiting for the interrogation.

Cammie didn't make me wait. "So, hot for McRae, huh?"

I rolled my eyes. "Say it louder, why don't you? I don't think they heard you on the other side of the island."

She chuckled. "Sorry. It's not like you're alone in your attraction. There are many women here who cursed being married when he first appeared. You have to tell me what happened between you two on Stòr."

"Nothing. He abandoned me for most of it to hide in his workshop while I snuggled up with Akiva."

"Akiva snuggled with you?"

"Yes. We snuggled."

"Wow." Cammie shook her head. "But you and Ramsay didn't ..."

"Didn't what?"

She wiggled her eyebrows.

I huffed indignantly. "I'm not the *sleep with a guy I just met* kinda person. And anyway, if you didn't notice, Ramsay McRae isn't interested. I think he finds me mildly irritating."

"Uh, no." Cam shook her head, her hair bouncing with the movement. "I picked up on definite vibes between you two. The way he was looking at you ..." She fanned her face with a laugh. "That's why I thought something had happened."

So ... it wasn't only me? There really was something electric between us.

"Nothing happened."

"Well, despite the crackle in the air, I wouldn't anticipate anything happening." Cammie gave me a smile to soften the blow of her words. "Quinn has done a good job of pulling Ramsay out of his hermit ways, but as long as he's lived here, he has never slept with a woman from Glenvulin. Quinn says Ramsay doesn't do serious relationships and he won't ever sleep with a woman from the island because he wants to avoid complications. Last I heard, he was casually seeing a woman over on the mainland."

Disappointment deflated my crush-induced butterflies. I didn't know why. It wasn't like I was looking for a relationship right now. Only eight months ago, I was living with someone.

"Look, it's nothing," I assured Cammie. "I'm not interested in anything right now. I have enough on my plate. Just ... don't tell anyone."

She chuckled, wrapping her arm around my shoulders to give me a quick squeeze. "Aw, Tierney, you don't need to ask me that. A little over two thousand people live on Glenvulin ...

which means you get very good at keeping secrets unless you want every bloody person in Leth Sholas to know every minute detail of your life. I'll keep you right and let you know who you can trust to keep their mouth shut and who fancies themselves the town crier."

I laughed, leaning into her. "Thank you. I honestly don't think I'd be able to make this transition without you."

And I meant it. Despite all the darkness I had gone through and still had to go through, in that moment, I felt very lucky to be in Leth Sholas with a friend like Cameron McQuarrie at my side.

6. Ramsay

As soon as I knew the women had left, I found Quinn and pulled him out into the garden that was now covered in rubble from the ongoing demo.

"Problem?" Quinn asked, wiping sweat and dust off his forehead with the back of his arm.

"Aye, there's a problem. Cammie's videoing our performances and uploading them online."

Quinn nodded. "You have someone dealing with that stuff, though, right?"

"That's not the point. Tell her to stop."

"I have. You saw for yourself. It only makes Cam more bloody inquisitive."

I knew that. I knew it wasn't Quinn's fault. That my request had the rest of the band wondering what the fuck I'd gotten up to in a past life that I didn't want my face on the internet. "Fuck."

"Why don't you tell the guys and Cam that you were involved in some operations that left you with a few enemies?"

"And bring that baggage to the pipe band? Something these guys do to literally blow off steam?"

"Well, I don't know what else to suggest."

"Aye, me neither."

Quinn turned to stare out at the water. I sensed tension radiating off him. Tension I suspected had nothing to do with *my* past. "Did you hear about Taran, then?"

My friend's jaw clenched. "Cammie told me."

"I met her."

"When?"

"This morning. In the coffee shop." I studied his face for a reaction as I murmured, "Bonny." It was true. Quinn's ex was a stunner.

"Aye, I don't need the reminder."

At his flat tone, I pushed. "You going to reach out?"

I thought he might not answer, but he turned from the water and nodded. "Aye, we'll eventually run into each other, anyway. Sooner rather than later. And it's only right that I do." His features tightened with pain. "Isla and I ... well, she forgave me, even if Taran couldn't. I owe her. For her, I'll talk to Taran and offer my support. Though I know she'll throw it back in my face."

"Heard she was engaged."

Quinn cut me a betrayed look. "Are you trying to wind me up?"

Fuck.

"No." I clamped a hand on his shoulder. "Just trying to see where you're at so I can have your back. My shitty way of trying to say I'm here if you ever need to talk."

One night, maybe a year after I'd moved to the island, Quinn and I got shit-faced and traded war stories. His was about Taran Macbeth. The one who got away. I knew what it was like to have a woman haunt you, even if my circumstances were different.

"I know. Thanks." He eyed me. "Did I pick up on a vibe between you and Tierney?"

I smirked to hide the truth. "Vibe?"

"Heather's teen speak rubs off on me sometimes." He referred to his seventeen-year-old daughter.

"Well, there's no *vibe*," I lied outright.

"You sure?" The fucker eyed me knowingly.

I'd lied for a bloody living and yet Quinn McQuarrie could see right through me, and I knew it. "She's our client. She lives here. She's thirteen years my junior. Three reasons why if there is a 'vibe,' I'm ignoring it."

"There's definitely a vibe."

"If you say *vibe* one more time …"

Quinn snorted and walked toward the house. "She's back here at four so you might want to be done for the day by then if you're avoiding the *vibes*."

Aye, I'd make sure I was gone by four.

Despite wanting to avoid her, I couldn't say I hadn't indulged my curiosity a little. I'd known she was Tierney Silver of the Silver Hotel and Resort empire. I'd known she'd given up her fancy life in New York to buy a rundown guesthouse in the middle of fucking nowhere, bringing a spotlight to Leth Sholas that made me uncomfortable since I'd picked the middle of fucking nowhere to live for a reason.

What I hadn't known until I'd dug a little deeper was that Tierney Silver hadn't merely given up her rights to the hotel empire … she'd sold the twenty percent share in Silver Hotels that she'd inherited upon her parents' deaths. She then donated all that money (more than $100,000,000) to multiple charities. It had been all over the news.

Why did a hotel empire princess donate her inheritance?

Why did she pick the middle of fucking nowhere to start over?

I didn't like unknowns.

My very nature tempted me to get close to her if only to learn the answers to these questions.

However, the pull between us, that strange, heightened awareness that crackled in the air every time I looked at her, was enough to bury my curiosity.

I didn't need nor want to be pulled into Tierney Silver's orbit.

It was just asking for trouble, and I'd had enough of that for a lifetime.

Pulling my phone from my back pocket, I sent a quick text to Jay, a hacker friend and computer genius, asking her to do a quick check to make sure there was no trace of Cameron's video online.

7. Tierney

Two days later, I'd just finished dinner when my phone rang.

I reluctantly turned it over to look at the screen, hoping it wasn't another call from Hugh, hoping it might be London who'd texted back to promise she'd visit as soon as she'd saved enough for the flights. I'd offered to fly her over, knowing my prideful friend would say no and wishing for once she would say yes, but the restaurant kept her so busy. Still, London was the only family I had left, and I missed her more every day.

The call wasn't from London. My pulse leapt at the sight of Perri's name. Fumbling in my hurry, I dropped it and scrambled to pick it up.

"Hey!" I said, sounding out of breath.

"Hey, you okay?" Perri asked in husky, calm tones. From the moment Perri Wilcox contacted me, I'd found her voice soothing and her capable, take-charge demeanor reassuring.

"Fine. Just dropped my phone."

"How goes it in Scotland?"

"It's what I needed," I answered honestly.

"I'm glad to hear that."

I frowned, realizing the time difference. "Isn't it like three or four in the morning there?"

"It's after five. I have an early flight out."

"So, do you have news?"

"I do." Perri sighed. "It's not exactly the news I was hoping to impart."

"You met with Adila?"

"I did. She was very anxious and jittery and kept looking around, but I managed to get her to tell me that she has now accepted a settlement figure from the Silver Group. Signed off by Halston Cole."

Disappointment crashed over me. "So she can't talk to you."

"Legally, she can't go on record or that fucker could sue. I told her I could still quote her as an anonymous source, but Adila got very frightened. She thought someone in the restaurant was watching us, someone she recognized and thought was following her that morning. She left."

"Shit, shit, shit." I stood and kicked the bottom of the sofa, the dull pain not enough to satisfy the frustration raging through me.

"I got back to my hotel room and after I showered, I found a note shoved under the main door. It was typed—and it was a threat. It said I needed to get the hell out of Australia and to mind my own business or I would end up dead like my friend."

She said it so matter-of-factly that it took a second for the threat to register.

"Perri ..." My phone shook against my ear as my body trembled at the reminder of what happened to my parents and Perri's colleague, Ben. "This isn't worth your life. Maybe you need to stop."

"Isn't it? They killed Ben and they killed your parents and they know that one more 'incident' is going to fuck them. I don't work for some small-time newspaper, Tierney. I work for one of the biggest fucking papers in the country and every single one of us at the *Chronicle* is gunning for this guy. Don't think for one second he doesn't realize that. If one more reporter dies investigating this, it is a nail in his own fucking coffin. So don't you worry about me. Okay?"

Heart racing, my whole body vibrating with adrenaline, I let out a shaky breath. "Okay."

"Good. I'll reach out when I return to New York. Adila is a setback, but it's not the end of the world. We can still do this."

"Okay. Thank you, Perri."

"Talk soon."

After we hung up, I stared around the tiny apartment suddenly feeling so restless it was claustrophobic.

I needed to get out.

I needed to expend the rage and fear and frustration building inside me.

In my mess of emotions, I didn't even remember walking to the guesthouse. One minute I was in my rented apartment, the next I was letting myself into the dark building on the hill. There were solar lanterns at the front door. I picked one up and walked into the dining room. There was currently a wall between it and what was a sitting/leisure area. It was the room with access to the gardens and views of the harbor. I wanted people to see it from the dining room. However, the wall obstructing it was a supporting wall.

Quinn had told me they were putting temporary support braces in place today so they could take the wall down tomorrow.

I noted the braces at either end of the wall. And I noted the sledgehammers.

He'd invited me to be there since it was one of the changes I'd most been looking forward to.

Now it felt like if I didn't take the wall down right this second, everything whirling inside would suck me into a black hole.

Roughly putting on a hard hat I'd found discarded in the shell of my B and B, I picked up the sledgehammer, surprised by the weight. Back in New York, I'd gone to the gym every other day. There was no gym on Leth Sholas, but I was a mere ferry ride to some of the best hiking trails in the country.

Still, I felt the weight of that sledgehammer in a way I wouldn't have felt eight months ago. It was a good kind of heavy, though. The kind of ache I needed as I bashed the flat end of the tool into the wall with a forward motion rather than a swing. The impact juddered up my arms, satisfying my writhing rage. Mindless, I thrust the hammer again, watching the plaster work crumble and the brick beneath loosen, the dust irritating my eyes and throat.

But I didn't care.

Sweat dampened my neck and underarms and my muscles ached as I expelled my burning wrath with each destructive blow. Suddenly, there was a gaping hole in the middle of the wall. But I wanted it all gone. Gone, gone, go—

A large hand wrapped around the sledgehammer, and it was suddenly yanked from my grip with such force, I stumbled backward.

Wiping the sweat and dust out of my eyes, I stared directly into a wide, muscular chest. My gaze moved upward and locked with Ramsay McRae's. His pale eyes burned with anger and his knuckles were white around the sledgehammer I'd just wielded like a therapy tool.

My heart raced and I was a little out of breath. I could feel the ache in my shoulders and upper arms and knew I'd pay for it in the morning.

But it was worth it.

"What the fuck?" Ramsay bit out, his fury palpable.

Suddenly uneasy, I took a step back. "What are you doing here?"

"I left a tool I need, and it's a bloody good thing I came to get it. Are you trying to bring this building down on top of you, woman?"

Confused, I looked at the wall that now had a hole in the middle of it. "Quinn braced it. He was going to let me do this in the morning, anyway, so I don't see what the problem is."

My attitude seemed to enrage Ramsay even more. "The problem is you are unqualified to take down a supporting wall. Propped braces can move, which they have done." He pointed the sledgehammer at one of the steel braces. "You need a professional on hand throughout the whole process to make sure everyone is safe." He stepped into my personal space, looming over me. "You don't fucking whack at it like a demented banshee with no one else in the fucking building!"

"Stop yelling at me!" I shouted, my nerves snapping. The wall wasn't enough. I wanted to claw and scream and tear something apart.

"You need a good yelling at if it'll save your bloody life!"

"Fuck you!"

"Fuck *you*!"

Somehow we'd moved closer to one another, a mere inch of air separating us. Heat and frustration emanated between us, drawing us together inexplicably. Something flared in Ramsay's eyes and my breath caught as his head bent toward mine. My body bowed like a magnet, ready and willing to take on the invitation, to take out my anger on his body.

But just as suddenly, he jerked away, blinking rapidly like he was taken aback by his own actions. He glared like it was my fault. "You're leaving and I'm not leaving until you're out of here. I'll fix the supports."

Now mad at him for two reasons, I ripped off my hard hat and dropped it at my feet. Seething, I stormed past him, throwing over my shoulder, "Remember who the boss is, McRae."

"Aye?"

Something in his mocking tone had me whipping around. "I'm the one paying the wages here."

His dark, brooding look caused a deep, low flip in my belly I absolutely resented. "You might pay the wages ... but that doesn't mean you're my boss."

"That's kind of how it works."

"Don't tempt me to teach you that *nobody* is my boss, Silver."

I shivered at the heated threat. "Whatever. Make sure you lock up when you leave."

"Will do. And there are healthier, more productive ways to channel the rage you have inside you."

I scoffed. "Mr. Monosyllabic is suddenly Mr. Perceptive, full of advice?"

Ramsay gave me an annoyed look that made me feel like a five-year-old. "I have thirteen years on you, woman. More if you count the multiple lives I've led. I know rage when I see it. I know when it's gotten to a point where you either let it eat you alive ... or you find a way to master it."

Just like that, the fury turned to tears that thickened my throat. "And what do you suggest as a way to master it?"

His expression was solemn. "Find something that calms your mind."

"Like you with your woodwork?"

"Aye."

"I don't think taking up knitting is going to help," I replied softly, my resentment toward him deflating as reason returned.

"No. But once this place is up and running, you'll have a purpose."

"Is it enough?"

"Most days. On the days it's not ... you ..." He looked away, and I disliked the loss of his expression. "You remind yourself that only the people who shouldn't *win* if you lose yourself to the anger."

Frustrated tears, tears he missed because he'd turned away, slipped down my cheeks. I watched as Ramsay kept his back to me, tightening screws on the braces holding up the ceiling. Wiping my cheeks, I walked away and quietly let myself out.

8. Ramsay

The mood in the Fisherman's Lantern (locally known as the Lantern) should have lifted Quinn's, but I could see as we settled on the stage, he was stiff. He wanted to be anywhere but here and I didn't blame him.

The Lantern was the most famous hotel, bar, and restaurant in Leth Sholas. Housed in a red-painted building on Main Street, its twelve bedrooms were continually occupied through the summer months. It was not only a tourist destination, it was a local favorite for a drink.

The month of June saw the pub area packed with tourists and locals alike.

The full band wasn't onstage. At smaller venues, we reduced our sound from five to three. Murray Shaw, who ran a successful fishing company, was our bass drum player, a large drum that strapped to the front of his chest and stomach. He beat the drum in a sideward motion, releasing a loud boom of beat, and so the bass was better suited for larger venues and outdoor performances.

As it was, Quinn was our snare drummer, and Forde Dallas, his best mate, was on the tenor drum tonight. That was raucous enough for the pub. I was our bagpiper as was Laird Macbeth, but the two sets of bagpipes were also too much here. At smaller venues, we alternated performances. Tonight, he'd sat this one out along with Murray, and they were at a table in the middle of the pub.

The three of us stood onstage, me in the middle of a bristling Quinn and a resigned Forde.

Quinn had been in a ferocious mood for several days.

"Ready?" I asked him.

He tried to clear his scowl but cleared his throat instead. His voice boomed out over the cacophony of the pubgoers' conversations. "*Fàilte gu* the Lantern!" He welcomed the audience in Scottish Gaelic.

Immediately the room began to quiet.

Quinn waited, expression still stony. "We're three parts of the Leth Sholas Pipe Band. If you hate the pipes, now is the time to leave."

I met Murray's gaze across the room. He shook his head with a heavy sigh. Laird stared at the fire as if he hadn't even heard Quinn. As if he wasn't here. He probably wasn't. We'd told him he didn't need to come tonight, considering his mother was on her deathbed, but he'd insisted he needed the break.

Thankfully, the tourists thought Quinn's comment was a joke and tittered.

I was certain the locals knew better—that Quinn McQuarrie was in a foul fucking mood.

Quinn and Forde began the rapid beating of the snare and tenor drums and I quickly followed suit.

Covering the mouthpiece of the blowpipe, I blew into it and the three drones let out the first wailing cry of the bagpipes. My fingers were already in place on the chanter pipe as the familiar, upbeat melody of "Scotland the Brave" filled the pub. People tapped their feet, swayed in their chairs, and began to clap along. I, personally, thought the tune sounded better with all five of us, or even better with a larger pipe band with multiple drums and pipes. But it did the trick of creating a lively atmosphere in the Lantern, which was what the owner Aodhan was paying us to do.

However, my favorite songs to perform weren't the well-known upbeat tunes.

After the loud cheers had died down at the end of "Scotland the Brave," I stepped forward to do a solo. "Sad the Parting" was one of my favorites, a haunting melody that had brought me to a standstill the first time I heard a piper play it.

The mournful deep groan of the drones played a bass note to the haunting chanter melody as I brought the pub to a hush.

I was midway through the song when Cammie and Tierney slunk in through the door, quickly finding their seats with Murray and Laird. Though I should, I couldn't tear my eyes off Tierney as the melody visibly ensnared her. Even in the dim glow of the pub, I could see the bright sheen to her eyes and her hard swallow as she tried to hold back the emotion. As if sensing her, my bloody dog suddenly leapt up from her place in front of the large fireplace and wound her way through the tables to Tierney.

It took the American a second to even notice Akiva, she seemed so enthralled by my performance. Then she gave a little jerk and blinked her eyes rapidly as she leaned down to say hello. She scratched behind Akiva's ears and placed a tender kiss on her furry head. Her blond hair wasn't in its usual ponytail, and it slid over her shoulders, shielding her face and my dog in a curtain of silken wheat-gold. I imagined how soft that hair would feel wrapped in my tight fist as I ...

Fuck.

Thankfully, Cammie jerked in her chair, pulling my mind

from fantasies it had no right exploring. Quinn's sister gaped at the interlude between dog and woman.

Akiva wasn't unfriendly, but she'd never been the kind of dog who looked for affection from anyone but me and perhaps Annie. Sometimes Quinn, if she could be bothered with him. I'd blamed it on my remoteness. That, in some way, I'd raised a dog who should be naturally affectionate to be aloof and wary of strangers.

But Akiva had taken to Tierney Silver and it shouldn't bother me as much as it did.

Then again, everything about the woman bothered me.

Lately, that night in her B and B bothered me.

The whole room had thrummed with the emotion raging in her as I'd found her hammering down the wall. I was angry at her recklessness as I saw the support braces shift out of place with each swing, realizing Quinn hadn't finished securing them yet.

Then I'd felt the fury swelling out of her and I'd known what was within Tierney Silver wasn't only grief.

I had to remind myself for the hundredth time it was none of my fucking business.

And if I didn't stop thinking about her now, I would lose my pace with the music.

However, distraction came in the form of something I wasn't grateful for, for Quinn's sake.

Taran Macbeth chose that moment to walk into the Lantern. The stunning brunette flicked a look at the stage, locked eyes with Quinn for a mere second, before ignoring him in favor of searching the room. She made her way intentionally through the crowds until she reached Tierney's table and lowered her head to whisper in Laird's ear. Whatever she said, his expression tightened. He murmured something to Murray. Murray frowned, said something back, but Laird waved him off and stood up. He placed a hand on his sister's back and the siblings pushed through the audience, ignoring the concerned attention of the locals.

Then they were gone.

It did not bode well for Isla Macbeth.

I didn't look at Quinn, but I could feel his need to jump off that stage and go after Taran and Laird. So I finished up the song before it should end and nodded at him to start the next one so he could beat out his mess of emotions on the damn drum strapped to his waist.

TIERNEY

Never in my life would I have thought the bagpipes could be this hot. I'd witnessed the Tattoo multiple times and loved it, but I'd never had this visceral reaction to it.

However, watching Ramsay play that melancholy melody up onstage hit me like an emotion-packed semitruck. And the more I watched the band, the more I shifted uncomfortably in my seat. I was distracted momentarily from what was happening on the small stage when Taran suddenly appeared to pull Laird away. Cammie and I had shared a concerned look. Word was that their mom, Isla, was deteriorating quickly. Cammie had told me on the way over so I was surprised to see Laird in the pub at all. Taran arriving and taking him away was not a good sign.

But no one could take this journey for them, and interference at this point would be unwelcome.

So, we'd attempted to turn our focus back to the band.

I succeeded only because of Ramsay.

He'd shaved off his yeti beard. There was already a salt-

and-pepper stubble growing on his cheeks but unlike the beard, it did nothing to hide his angled jawline. He was all rugged edges and soft, kissable lips. To top it off, he'd had his hair cut. With one shave and a haircut, he'd gone from sexy yeti to unbearably, ruggedly, *should have his own social media platform* HOT.

Ramsay McRae was all kinds of levels of sexy.

Damn it.

"You're drooling again," Cammie teased.

"I am not. Though ... seriously, why aren't these guys all over the internet?" I gestured to Murray Shaw and then the stage. All the men who made up the band were attractive in their own right. "I mean, was there a 'must be over six feet tall and hot' application process?"

Cammie laughed, her eyes darting beyond me.

I turned to find Murray listening in, his eyes dancing with laughter. "What was that now? Say it louder for my ego."

"Oh please, I'm not embarrassed, you know you're all good-looking."

"We're the Leth Sholas Pipe Band." Quinn's voice echoed around the room. "Thanks for listening. *Oidhche Mhath*."

As the audience clapped their thanks, I asked Cammie, "What does *Oidhche Mhath* mean?" I knew I probably butchered the pronunciation.

"Good night."

"Do you all speak Gaelic?"

Cammie shook her head. "I know bits and pieces, as does Quinn. Our parents are fluent, but I'm sad to say it is a dying language."

I nodded and surveyed the audience, noting many a person still ogling the gorgeous Scots on stage. Quinn murmured something to Ramsay and then strode out of the pub without looking at anyone.

Cammie sucked in a breath at his abrupt departure.

Ramsay stepped down from the stage, whistled low, and Akiva shot from my side to him. The big Scot had already put his bagpipes down and lowered to his haunches to greet his dog with an abundance of affection. Now that he didn't have a beard hiding his face, his smile ... it did *things* to me.

Great.

I was only distracted from his deliciousness by Cammie's tension. She contemplated the Lantern's main door. Quinn had been in a horrible mood the last few days and to my surprise, Ramsay covered for me about the wall. I'd gone to the B and B the next day to apologize for my impulsive and irresponsible behavior, but Ramsay interrupted before I could take the blame. He said he hadn't known I'd wanted to be there for the demo and had started work without everyone. I'd been grateful to him because I didn't need my main contractor thinking he couldn't trust me. When Quinn was out of earshot, I'd thanked Ramsay and promised him nothing like that would ever happen again.

The yeti (now *not* yeti) had grunted at me and walked away, which pissed me off again.

I didn't know what it was about him that got under my skin so much, but my feelings toward him were very confusing.

"Is Quinn okay?" I asked Cammie.

She shook her head, lips pressed together tightly. Finally, she sighed. "It did not go well with Taran."

I'd guessed as much. "I'm sorry for Quinn."

"I'm sorry for them all." Cammie gave me a melancholy smile. "Come on, let's grab a drink."

"I'm heading out." Murray stood too.

"You don't want a drink?"

"No, we're a man down for the chartered fishing guide, so I'm out on the boat tomorrow with a bunch of tourists."

"Enjoy." Cammie teased like she knew it was the last thing Murray wanted to do.

I knew Murray owned a large fishing company on Glenvulin. He had several fishermen, like Laird, who ran small crews, but he also ran chartered fishing guides for tourists. Salmon fishing in this part of the country was huge.

The man jerked his chin toward the bar where Ramsay and his other band member, Forde, now stood, before wandering out with a few goodbyes to locals.

"Come on. I'll introduce you to Forde." Cammie took my arm and guided me to the bar.

Akiva came over for a few pets before she returned to her dad's feet. I tried to avoid Ramsay's gaze, focusing in on Cammie's friend. I'd seen Forde out and about because he was hard not to notice, but we'd yet to be formally introduced. Forde Dallas owned the only mechanic's garage on Glenvulin, and he volunteered with the Leth Sholas Lifeboat Service. He not only volunteered to help maintain the lifeboats, but he went out on rescue operations too. Cammie had told me all of this with real fondness in her voice because she'd grown up with him. He was Quinn's best friend.

Forde, like Quinn, was thirty-six years old and seemed more suited to a stadium concert stage than the Lantern. He looked like a tattooed rock star turned cologne model.

What the ever-loving fuck was in the water here?

I clamped my lips shut so I didn't gape at the man. It wasn't that I wasn't used to attractive people. Growing up in the life I did, I'd met celebrities and some of the most attractive men in the world. However, finding a pipe band of them on a tiny Scottish island seemed farcical in a way. If more people knew about these men, a flood of people would move to Leth Sholas.

"Forde, this is Tierney Silver, our newest resident. Tierney, this is Forde Dallas, our resident Lothario." She shot him a mocking smirk.

He grimaced but his dark eyes glittered warmly. "You have the references of a ninety-year-old."

I chuckled as Cammie shoved him playfully and he laughed. Muscles, boyishly hot smile, dark hair. Perhaps an inch taller than Cammie, a bunch of tattoos that looked sort of Celtic all over his arms and even his fingers. Forde had a rough bad-boy thing going on that wasn't really my type, even if I could admit he had a sexy-ass smile.

Speaking of sexy-ass smiles ... feeling the heat of his stare, I finally looked up at Ramsay. Now here was a man I never would've guessed was my type.

But my body definitely thought he was my type.

Ramsay had a pint in his hand and he gestured with it. "Want anything?"

Guessing that was his charming offer to buy me a drink, I shook my head. I needed to stay sharp around him.

"Juice instead?" Cammie asked. "Diet Coke?"

It was weird to me that they called fizzy drinks *juice* in this part of the world, but I'd caught on a few weeks ago when Cammie first said it. "Yeah. I'll buy, though. What are you having?"

"No, it's fine, I'll—"

"What are you drinking?" Ramsay interrupted her.

"Diet Coke too."

"I'll get it." Forde stepped toward the bar but Ramsay cut him off with a wave of his free hand and leaned over to get the bartender's attention.

A few minutes later, I was situated at the counter with Ramsay while Cammie and Forde stood beside us talking about people and events I didn't know and wasn't there for. I knew Cammie didn't intend to leave me with Ramsay McRae. She seemed to forget everything else in Forde's presence, lighting up around him in a way that was hard to explain but that I knew I hadn't seen from her before. They laughed together like two kids on the playground.

Ramsay stared around the room as he sipped his pint. Akiva lay at his feet now, an actual physical barrier between us and Cammie and Forde.

Irritated that Ramsay was trying to avoid me while I stood right next to him, I asked with the deliberate intention to needle, "So, are you over your snit yet?"

His eyes connected with mine and I ignored the way my heart accelerated. Seriously, I really wanted to know how the hell he did that to me.

"Snit?" He emphasized the *t*.

"Yeah. I mean, I apologized, and you still grunted at me like a caveman." I was only half teasing.

Ramsay raised an eyebrow. "Silver, you almost brought a seven-thousand-square-foot house down on yourself."

"I apologized." I shrugged. "And promised to never do anything so reckless again."

"Are you in the right state of mind to be making those promises?"

"Yes. Trust me to know that." I sipped the soda and wrenched my gaze from his since looking at him made me feel like I'd injected espresso into my veins.

"You ever planning to tell me what sent you to drive a sledgehammer through the wall?"

"Are you ever planning to tell me why you live on an island by yourself?"

He gestured to his beautiful dog. "Not by myself."

"Mature response."

"You know all about those."

"It's not my fault you're very annoying."

Ramsay's eyes searched my face, glittering with ... intensity that felt sexual. "Is that what I am?"

"Yes." The word wheezed out, and I cleared my throat, my cheeks hot. "Somewhat."

His lips twitched. "You're somewhat annoying too."

Even though I knew he was joking, part of me still wondered if he wasn't. I didn't want to think about that too much or why it bothered me. "I'm a goddamn *treat*," I replied instead, shrugging off hurt feelings.

He grinned, and it knocked the breath right out of me.

Ramsay's eyes sharpened ever so slightly before dropping to my mouth. My lips actually tingled beneath his attention.

"You shaved. And cut your hair."

His attention jumped back to my eyes. "I do that occasionally."

"It looks good. Hygiene-wise, I mean." I shrugged.

His lips twitched. "Right. Hygiene-wise."

I tried not to, but my lips strained against a laugh and too late it huffed out, my cheeks hot. Ramsay's eyes warmed with amusement. I was breathless again. I wanted to reach up on my tiptoes and press my lips to his to settle this overwhelming awareness between us.

"Ramsay!" A woman suddenly shoved past Cammie, knocking her slightly into Forde and me out of my Ramsay stupor. "Oh, sorry!" she apologized cheerfully, almost stepping on Akiva who jumped to her feet and growled in warning. "Goodness!" The woman halted in fright, staring down at the dog.

"Akiva, heel," Ramsay ordered, patting her head in reassurance. He eyed the newcomer, a pretty, very tall, very voluptuous brunette who had attractive laughter lines around her eyes that told me she was perhaps a decade or so older than me. "Ava, what are you doing here?"

She eyed Akiva warily again as she shimmied past me, forcing me backward so she could press a hand to Ramsay's chest and lean up to kiss his lips.

Oh.

Okay, then.

When she pulled back, it forced me to retreat farther, and I had to apologize to a tourist I'd knocked into. Cammie scowled in annoyance at the rude newcomer.

"You might say *excuse me* to people," Cammie told her bluntly.

The woman's eyes widened, and she glanced over her shoulder, flushing when she saw she'd shoved me out of the way. "I'm so sorry! I've just come barreling in. I'm Ava." She turned back to Cammie. "I'm Ramsay's—"

"What are you doing here?" the man in question repeated gruffly, seeming pissed.

The brunette slumped. "I'm late. I know. I caught the ferry over ages ago so I didn't miss your gig, but then I fell asleep in my hotel room."

"You came over for the gig?"

"Aye, I wanted to surprise you." She beamed sweetly at him.

That's when I remembered Cammie telling me Ramsay was seeing someone from the mainland.

Apparently, it was more than a casual fling.

Crushing disappointment made my feet feel like they were sinking into the floor.

"And you're staying in Leth Sholas?" Ramsay's expression hadn't cleared beyond stony confusion.

"I missed you." Ava shrugged. "I know you were planning on staying with Quinn tonight, but I thought you could stay with me at my hotel. I'm better company." She flicked me a look, as if suddenly remembering I was there. And she paused. She studied me as if she was seeing me for the first time. "Sorry ... who are you?"

There was a change in her tone. A wariness. "I'm Tierney. Nice to meet you."

"Are you here on holiday?"

"No, I live here."

Ava's jaw clenched ever so slightly as she turned back to Ramsay and cocked her head in accusatory question.

And that was my cue to leave!

"I think I'm done for the night," I told Cammie as I put my half-empty glass on the bar top. "I'll see you tomorrow?"

Cammie jolted from whatever softly spoken conversation she was having with Forde. "Oh. Shall I walk you out?"

"No. I'm a few doors down. Nice to meet you, Forde. You too, Ava." I didn't look at her or Ramsay as I thanked him for the drink and then lowered to my haunches to say goodbye to Akiva.

The Malamute bussed into my pets, her beautiful pale eyes staring into my soul in the same way her damn owner's did. I kissed the bridge of her nose. "Good night, beautiful girl." She tried to swipe me with her tongue in response and I laughed, evading it before I rubbed behind her ears and turned away.

The Lantern was now elbow-to-elbow, and I had to squeeze through to make my way out. Some locals nodded good night, which warmed the disappointment chilling my limbs.

Unable to stop myself, I glanced back at the bar.

Ramsay was so tall I saw him over the crowd.

Our eyes locked as he watched me leave.

With a frown of confusion, I turned away and walked out.

9. Tierney

While Quinn assured me things were going along at a good pace, the B and B still looked like a shell of its former self. He promised me this was the point where it didn't feel like much was happening because it was all "first fit" site services—updating the electrical, the heating, the plumbing. And since I'd chosen the best eco version of everything, Quinn was constantly conferring with the experts on how to install it.

It was costing a nice little chunk of the inheritance my maternal grandmother left me, but I wanted the B and B to run as efficiently and sustainably as possible. Weeks had passed and Cammie's joke about the island only experiencing two seasons—June and winter—was proving true. It was the first week of August, there were more tourists than ever, and it had already rained the entire week. While July, apparently, had been surprisingly mild with clear skies, the temperatures only peaked at 14°C, which was around 57°F. In July.

Despite that temperateness, Scotland was more humid than outsiders realized. I only knew from my summer visits to my grandparents' house. July's clear skies did not fit the mood of the village. No, in fact, a downpour of constant rain would have been more appropriate for a village in mourning that month.

Isla passed away at the end of June, the night of the pipe band performance in the Lantern.

While I hadn't known Isla, I hurt for my new friends who did. And, of course, it reminded me of my own loss. Two years. It had been two years since I'd lost my parents, but that seemed impossible. Needing distraction, I found myself growing impatient with the progress on the building, even though we were on schedule. The B and B's social media pages were starting to attract attention, and I was fielding regular DMs asking when guests could book to stay. That was exciting! I had a friend from college whom I was paying to build my website and thus I was waiting for the booking section to be added to the homepage. I'd thought people wouldn't want to book until the finished article, but there were some eager folks out there.

After another message came in inquiring for specific dates, I decided it was time to take bookings. We could at least open the calendar for next spring because I knew the renovations would be finished by then.

I'd shot Gen, my techy friend, a text to get the booking system up and running. When stepping out of my apartment building on Main Street, an incoming call flashed on my screen. Things had been quiet on the Perri front too, so it was a surprise to see her name.

I turned my back on the bustle of the harbor. "Perri?" I answered expectantly.

Her reply was a soft laugh. "It's been two weeks. You'd think it was years. How are you?"

"I'm fine. I'm sorry for the antsy reply. How are you?"

"I understand. And I haven't called or been in touch because I wanted to make absolutely sure before getting your hopes up … but there's been a breakthrough."

Everything but Perri's voice faded into the background. "Tell me."

"Henry Copeland. He's agreed to talk again. He was scared for a while after your parents, but ... I guess his conscience won out."

Tears of relief stung my eyes. "Really?"

Triumph hardened Perri's tone. "We've got the bastard, Tierney. Henry handed over all the documentation he has. The last piece of the puzzle is the helicopter and we're pushing the crash investigators to release their report so we can see who cleared it as nonsuspicious. If we can connect the dots back to the CEO and find a paper trail to a bribe, the police will have no choice but to step in. But even without that piece, *we* have enough to publish in the next few weeks. We need to dot our *i*'s and cross our *t*'s first. Make sure everything is in order legally. Of course, we also legally need to give the Silver Group a heads-up and let that play out before we print. And I'll need you to go on record that you donated your shares because you'd discovered the CEO of Silver Hotel and Resorts covered up manslaughter and had your parents and a reporter killed when they began to investigate it."

"I'll give you whatever you need." The sob broke out of me before I could stop it. It was coming to an end. This nightmare was finally coming to an end. "W-we've r-really got him?"

"Yes. We've really got him."

A hand suddenly clamped down on my shoulder and I whirled in fright. Through the blur of my tears, I found Ramsay towering over me, scowling. "Silver, you all right?" he demanded gruffly.

Akiva nudged her face against my leg, her intelligent eyes almost questioning.

Reminded I was in the middle of Main Street, sobbing, I swiped frantically at my tears, sucking back the shaky cries that still needed an outlet. "Perri, I have to go. But thank you. We'll talk soon."

"Talk soon, Tierney."

"Thanks." I hung up and wiped my face before I lowered to Akiva to hide in her fur. I hugged her and the sweet dog leaned into me like she could sense my emotions. "Hey, beautiful girl." Pulling back, I sniffled and then laughed when she tried to take her usual swipe at my face with her pink tongue.

"Silver."

Sighing, I reluctantly stood to face Ramsay. Akiva settled at my side, pressing her warm, furry body into my legs. Resting my palm on her head in gratitude, I faced her owner whose gaze darted between me and his dog.

"Well? Why are you crying in the middle of the street?" he demanded, as if *my* tears had put *him* in an awkward position.

"None of your damn business."

Ramsay scowled. "Akiva."

The dog seemed reluctant to return to him.

"Don't make her pick sides."

"She's my dog. There are no sides but one. Mine."

"Territorial, aren't we?"

"When something is mine ... aye." He answered in a tone that almost bordered on teenage girl *duh*.

"I have to get to the B and B." I moved past him, stopping to stroke Akiva's head in goodbye, before hurrying down Main Street.

Problem was, Ramsay had a good eight or nine inches of length on me and easily caught up. Akiva happily followed along. "I'm heading that way too or did you forget I'm one of your contractors?"

"I haven't seen you around so yeah, actually, I did forget."

It was true. Not the forgetting part but the not seeing him around part. Ramsay had successfully avoided me for most of the past six weeks. We'd seen each other across the church at

Isla's funeral, which I'd attended out of respect and to be a comfort to Cammie and Quinn. Ramsay stood at the back, unmoving, face blank. I'd caught glances of him here and there, but I'd also taken myself off to the mainland a lot these past few weeks. Cammie and I had gone on interior decorating trips that sometimes had us staying overnight. We spent an entire weekend in Edinburgh, which was nostalgic and a much-needed escape for the two of us.

Ramsay didn't respond to my cheeky reply. Instead, as we turned the corner past Macbeth's Pages & Perks, taking the back road that led up the winding hill toward the B and B, he asked again, "Why were you crying?" This time his tone was softer, curiouser. Less demanding.

For some reason, that was even worse. "It's been an emotional few weeks. I'm kind of on edge, I guess."

"Because of your parents?"

I shrugged.

"So ... everything's all right?"

"I'm fine," I lied.

And he knew it too.

A muscle clenched in his jaw but he didn't push me any further on it. We stood to the side to let a couple of cars pass and then turned up onto the private road that led to my B and B in her elevated spot. My phone suddenly rang again and I yanked it out of my back pocket, thinking it might be Perri.

It wasn't.

It was Hugh. I'd blocked his last number and then he started calling me on another.

Asshole.

With a frustrated growl, I blocked him again.

"Who is Hugh?"

I glowered up at Ramsay. "No one that matters."

"Is he harassing you?"

"Not everything is ominous, you know," I teased. And

immediately changed the subject. "You didn't drive over today?"

Akiva sped upward ahead of us.

"Left my vehicle here last night and stayed with Quinn. We worked so late, I missed my safe crossing."

"Oh. You know, I can always compensate you if you need to book a room somewhere."

"It's the height of the season and, anyway, there's no need. I have Quinn's place. You're already paying toward accommodation for much of the crew."

It was true. Quinn and Ramsay's crew were men from all over the islands. Some ferried in and part of the fee I paid them covered the cost of accommodation for those guys during the week. "Okay." I knew I shouldn't, but I could feel the question vomiting up out of me before I could stop it. "How's Ava?"

There. I sounded casual. Normal.

Even though the older brunette's appearance had bothered me for days. Weeks, even. If Ramsay was avoiding me, I was avoiding him right back after Ava showed up.

I did not lust after other people's partners.

At first, I didn't think Ramsay was going to answer. Then he replied, "I don't know. She was all right last time I saw her."

"Oh." Wow. Was that what he was like in a relationship? Ugh. Poor Ava.

"We're not together," he explained as if the words were torn from him. "I don't do relationships."

"I hate to break it to you, but I think Ava thinks you're in a relationship."

"Aye, noticed that, did you?" Ramsay scrubbed a hand over the back of his neck as we leveled out onto the driveway of my guesthouse. "That's why I ended our casual ... thing."

Ah.

"I don't do serious relationships or any kind of relationships." He suddenly stopped, looking me directly in the eye as if he was warning me off. "I'm not that man. That's not who I am."

The little warmth that crept into my chest at the news he was single iced over. I looked away, staring out at the water, at the spectacular view of the Scottish coastline. "I used to think I knew exactly who and what I was."

"And now?"

I shrugged. "You know, my maternal grandmother was Scottish."

"Aye, you told me."

"I'd visit her every year with my family. She died about a year after my grandfather passed. I didn't get a chance to say goodbye to him, but I had time with my grandmother. I flew to Edinburgh for our last moment together." Emotion thickened my throat, and I had to take a minute as I recalled the image of her lying in bed, so small and frail in contrast to the larger-than-life person I'd always known her to be. "I took her hand and confessed that I didn't know who I was without her." I wiped away my falling tears, looking back out at the water in an attempt to hide them.

"And ... uh, she told me that lying in that bed was the first time in her life when she truly knew who she was. That moments and people had carved away at her every second of every day, like she was a lump of clay turning into a sculpture. And it was only now that her time was ending that she was complete. She promised me that one day it would be the same for me and that thinking you knew yourself could be a prison. That I should treat every day as a day I get to know a little more about who I am. It was just a day where the world sculpted another little piece of me."

I turned back to him and found Ramsay staring at me with a pained expression I didn't quite understand.

"How can you know everything you are when life hasn't finished sculpting you yet?"

Ramsay seemed to truly consider my words. Then he cleared his throat, that penetrating wolf gaze piercing me to the soul. "I think while your grandmother was wise ... it's also true that who we are at the core never changes."

"I think that's true too. My mom grew up with money, but she was bullied as a kid, and it made her empathetic and kind. She didn't judge people for what they had or didn't have. She raised me that way. And no matter what life threw at her, that part of her never changed." I smiled sadly, thinking about my mom who was the kindest human I'd ever known. "She made my dad a better person. He was the first to admit it."

I chuckled remembering my mom's smug, happy laugh when my dad told me the story of how they met. "My dad was on a first date with this famous supermodel the night he met my mom. I've seen pictures, and this woman was like otherworldly gorgeous. It was this international business awards thing in London, and Mom was there as an assistant to the events organizer. My dad watched as this guest accidentally poured red wine all over the host's white dress before the event started. He said that the host was practically hysterical and suddenly, this pretty blond appeared out of nowhere, efficiently whisked the host away, and the next time he saw them both, the host was in the blond's dress and the blond was in the stained white dress."

"Your mother."

I grinned. "Yeah. She swapped dresses. Dad said he watched her for the rest of the night, just doing her job and laughing off any comments about her appearance. He watched her perform little acts of kindness all night—like helping an elderly guest to the restroom. Covering up mistakes waitstaff made. He didn't speak one word to her, but he knew he needed to know her.

"At the end of the night, he put his date in a cab and returned to the event to find my mom. He asked her out. Mom said she thought he was joking at first. She knew Dad was the heir to the Silver Group empire, and she was a sweaty mess in a stained white dress." Realizing I might be boring Ramsay with my musings, I clamped my mouth shut and shrugged, feeling weirdly vulnerable.

"Your father sounds like he was a man who recognized what was important."

Relief cooled the heat in my cheeks. "Yeah. Yeah, he saw past all the bullshit. He thought my mom ... he thought there was no one else in the world like her. He would have done anything for her." Like uncover a dark secret, even if it meant ruining his family's legacy. "Anyway. Sorry ... I, uh, I'm feeling a little nostalgic today. We should get moving." I marched toward the house.

This time Ramsay didn't respond. He followed me into the B and B ... and then went his own way.

10. TIERNEY

A few days after Perri's update, I was in the B and B and finally able to see my future business coming together. Before everyone arrived, I'd taken some progress videos for socials. Now Cammie stood at my side with Quinn and a representative from the independent kitchen designer we'd selected. Arthur worked for the small, family-run business based in Fort William and had come all the way from the mainland with samples.

This was the exciting part. Choosing all the design elements.

Arthur had his laptop open and was leaning on a makeshift table Quinn had put together. He had a design app open and was adjusting the layout as we all discussed what would work most practically for a B and B kitchen.

"The range looks great and would be perfect for this Victorian building," Cammie mused as we looked at a brochure of range ovens.

"I think four fitted ovens on this wall"—I pointed to the back of the room—"would be more practical."

"Agreed." Quinn nodded.

Cammie glared at her brother and then turned to me. "What about a compromise? Two ovens on the wall and then a range oven center here." She gestured to the middle of the back wall. "It will give you your hob top, two more ovens, and a proving drawer if you want to make your own bread."

"Do you make your own bread?" Quinn asked.

I grinned cockily. "I do, actually."

"You know, I never even thought to ask if you can cook and you're opening a B and B." He chuckled.

I arched an eyebrow. "I like to bake and I'm all right in the kitchen. My best friend is a chef and she's given me some pointers over the years." Speaking of London reminded me that my best friend hadn't replied to the text I sent a week ago. I'd been so caught up in island life. I made a mental note to call her later. "But I will be hiring a chef to do all the breakfasts."

"So shouldn't the chef be here?" Arthur asked from behind us.

I glanced over my shoulder. "Oh, I haven't hired one yet."

"You do realize it might be hard to get a chef," Quinn told me. "Not everyone wants to live on an island."

I shrugged. "People are always looking for work, even if it's just seasonal. And like I said, I can cook, if I need to."

"So ... range or fitted?" Quinn pushed, sounding a bit impatient. Most likely because we'd been in what would become the kitchen for an hour already. "Gas or electric? I need to know if we need to run a new gas line in here."

"I think a chef would say gas," Cammie opined.

I could hear London disagreeing vehemently in my head. "Actually, my friend prefers induction. They have induction stovetops in the kitchen she works in, and she says they cook faster, you can better control the heat, and they're easier to clean. Not to mention better for your health."

"I stand corrected." Cammie chuckled. "I'm going to lose this one, aren't I?"

"Actually. No. I like the idea of having the proving drawer. I think two fitted ovens on the wall and an induction top range cooker in the middle is a good compromise." I glanced back at Arthur with a grin. "Did you get that?"

He chuckled. "I've got it." He picked up the laptop and brought it over. "What do you think?"

I studied the digital image of the kitchen we'd designed together in the last hour and grinned. "This is perfect." There was an island but no seats since the kitchen wouldn't be used for guests. The island had the sink and was all extra countertop and storage. There was a microwave drawer on it, a wine cooler, and cupboards on the back for whatever we needed.

"That color is going to look amazing."

We'd gone for a pale blue shaker-style cabinet. Cammie and I already selected the perfect tile for the kitchen wall and a Victorian wallpaper to really give the kitchen impact. Even if the guests wouldn't be in this room, I wanted it to match the feel of the rest of the renovation.

One of Quinn's men, a younger boy on his team, walked into the room, eyes to me. "Sorry to interrupt, but we found this package at the front door. It's not addressed to anyone."

"Oh. I'll take it, thanks." I took the package and wrinkled my nose because there was a rank smell emanating from it. It was a brown envelope that bulged in the middle with something that felt roundish and hard. There was nothing on it.

No stamp or address. No name.

Weird.

"What is it?" Cammie asked.

"I have no idea," I murmured as I tore the top open and peered inside. "There's no name—oh my God!" I dropped it instinctually, my pulse pounding in my ears.

My companions exploded with questions and Quinn marched over to pick up the parcel, his expression tight with concern.

"It's a bird," I told him quickly so he wouldn't put his hand in it. "I think it's a dead bird."

His eyes rounded a little and he moved to upend it from the envelope but suddenly Ramsay was there, as if appearing out of nowhere. "Don't touch it," he commanded.

Lowering to his haunches beside Quinn, I noted Ramsay's T-shirt was damp from sweat from whatever he'd been working on. He had pliers in his hand, and he clamped them on the opposite end of the envelope and shook out the contents.

Dismay, confusion, and dread filled me at the sight of the dead bird.

A dove.

"Is that real?" Cammie asked, keeping her distance.

"It smells real," Quinn replied softly.

"It's real." Ramsay nudged the bird over with his pliers. "Someone broke the wee thing's neck."

Tears filled my eyes. "Why?"

He looked up at me. "This was addressed to you?"

Sudden realization dawned, but I shook my head, unable to speak around the fear clamoring through me.

"No. There was no name, no stamp or address," Quinn offered.

"A dove?" Ramsay scrutinized the bird. "Whoever did this had to have bought this dove from a pet store. They bought an animal only to kill it and leave it here as a threat to someone?"

"Threat? What's going on?" Cammie stepped forward, anxious.

"A dove." Ramsay's voice was rough as he seemed to stare dazedly at the dead bird. "It's a symbol of peace and freedom."

"So … what? Someone is saying … they're going to kill someone's peace." Cammie huffed. "What does that mean?"

It meant Halston Cole knew I was onto him.

It meant … if I didn't leave the company alone in peace … I was next.

"Tierney, does this mean something to you?" Quinn asked.

I shook my head, unable to speak the lie out loud.

"Is there anyone unhappy that Tierney bought this place?" Cammie asked her brother. "I haven't heard anything. Have you?"

"No. There was some pushback from members of the community council, but none of them would do this," her brother replied. "It had to be an outsider. They must have ferried over today."

Cammie hovered near Ramsay and Quinn. "Do you have CCTV up on the house?"

"No. We didn't think we needed it. We can, though, if you want that, Tierney?"

"Should we call the police?" Cammie asked before I could respond to Quinn.

"And say what?" Ramsay rasped out, taking the bird by the pliers and placing it gently back in the envelope.

"There could be fingerprints on that envelope," Cammie insisted.

"I'll take care of it." Ramsay stood, giving Quinn a sharp look that made his brows draw together. Then he turned to me. "Authorize the CCTV, Silver." Then he walked out with the envelope that was *my* evidence.

Yet, I couldn't stop him without admitting that I knew the threat was definitely for me and it had nothing to do with me renovating the B and B.

———

RAMSAY

There were no fingerprints on the envelope.

Or the poor wee birdie.

I tested both.

Dread knotted in my gut.

Jay texted back an hour ago to assure me there were no traces of me on the internet.

Yet, it seemed someone with a grudge had found me.

Frustration and fury mingled as I petted Akiva's head and stared out at the surrounding woodland. Summer nights on Stòr lasted long into the evening, but this was the first night in August where the gloomy clouds above hadn't chased the night into an early start. Sunlight filtered through the lush leaves and I already missed the peace the sight usually brought me.

I took a pull of my beer and scratched behind Akiva's ears. She'd clung to me all day since I'd left the B and B, not only smelling the dead bird but sensing my dark mood.

There were multiple enemies who might have sent this.

If they came, I'd deal with them.

What worried me was the collateral damage.

Already, it had impacted Silver.

She'd looked like a ghost after opening that package.

I knew she had a soft heart, but after hearing her talk of her parents the other day, I realized how soft and vulnerable that heart truly was.

Whoever sent the package would pay for putting that look on Silver's face.

The knot in my gut only tightened.

She was a problem.

I barely knew her, but she was a problem. The woman

filled my mind more often than she should. If I didn't find a way to banish her from my thoughts, she'd become a weakness.

When I came to Glenvulin, I had none.

Then Akiva became one. Then Quinn, Cammie, the lads in the band, the villagers.

I didn't need the kind of weakness Tierney Silver could become.

The kind of weakness that would wreck me.

Maybe Silver's grandmother had been right about knowing yourself.

Because before her ... I didn't think there was anything left of me to be wrecked.

11. Tierney

The next morning, I climbed the hill to the B and B, my limbs heavy, like they were filled with rocks.

I'd slept poorly to say the least.

My phone call to Perri had consisted of her reassuring me I didn't need to put my name in the article if I was afraid for my life. I'd replied that I was only informing her because she needed to know about the threat. That I was scared, but it didn't mean I would back down.

"Halston Cole can go fuck himself," I'd whispered hoarsely into my phone.

I'd heard the pride in Perri's voice when she told me to take care of myself and to stay vigilant.

Still, I hadn't slept. I was worried that whoever had jumped on a ferry to deliver a dead bird to me was still in Leth Sholas.

———

Ramsay was working on internal cupboards in the bedrooms so my guests would have places to hang their clothes. I didn't want bulky furniture in the guest rooms but rather clever storage solutions that would give the rooms a sense of spaciousness and allow us to create larger adjoining bathrooms for each. Previously, guests had to share two bathrooms in the guesthouse and that wouldn't work for modern hospitality.

I'd caught sight of Ramsay as I wandered through the house, but he'd seemed preoccupied.

An hour later, I felt superfluous to the activity. "What can I do to help?" I asked Quinn.

My contractor's smile was kind. "Honestly ... a lunch run. It would save the guys going down to Main Street."

"Lunch." I jumped on the idea. "I can do lunch. I'll go get everyone's orders."

It took me twenty minutes to get around to everyone and I left Ramsay until last. Akiva wasn't with him today and was probably with Annie at the voluntary Leth Sholas Lifeboat Service station which I now knew locals abbreviated to the LS.

I might have worried about Ramsay's reliance on Annie, but I'd finally met her at the Fisherman's Lantern and she was a seventy-two-year-old widow who volunteered full time with the LS as their station manager.

Finally, I approached Ramsay in one of the back downstairs bedrooms. "Hey!" I called out before I walked in to give him a heads-up.

The banging from inside halted. Ramsay stepped away from his work. He swiped a strong forearm over his forehead, wiping the sweat from it. His biceps flexed with the movement, and I experienced an answering tug deep in my belly.

Over the last few months, his beard and hair had grown again, but he'd trimmed both before they reached the yeti stage.

"Aye?" he asked, studying the sliding closet door he'd fitted.

He did not give me the courtesy of looking at me.

Apparently, my interrupting him was an annoyance.

"I'm on lunch duty. Do you want anything from the bakery?"

Ramsay kept looking at that damn door like it was fascinating. "Anything. Whatever's left. Not fussy."

"That's extremely unhelpful."

"A sandwich," he bit out impatiently.

What the hell was his problem? I wanted to ask. To confront him and his suddenly shitty attitude toward me, but I was emotionally drained.

So damn tired.

Without another word, I walked out.

Quinn was outside conversing with one of the guys about the repair work happening on the roof. I nodded at him as I passed to get to my car. I'd taken to leaving it at the B and B since parking was tight behind my vacation apartment. Once per day, at least one of the workmen teased me about the bright paint job on my cute little Suzuki.

Mind on Ramsay's weird behavior, I opened the driver's door, and it took me a second to process what was happening.

Worms. A horror movie abundance of worms, poured out of the car.

They hit my feet before I could react.

I squealed, jumping back, shaking my legs, shrieking as I kicked off the live worms. My yells of abhorrence grew louder and louder.

"Fuck!" I heard Quinn's shout and then he was at my side. "Are you all right? Tierney, are you all right?"

I shuddered, pulling at my clothes. "Are they off?! Are there any more on me?"

He turned me efficiently, checking me over as I tugged at my tee, whimpering with revulsion.

"What the fuck?"

Both of our heads snapped toward Ramsay who'd obviously heard the commotion and come running.

He stared stonily at the worms slithering on the ground at my vehicle and wriggling over each other inside it. They'd filled the driver's seat and floor of my Suzuki. Ramsay's wolf-gray eyes snapped to me. "Worm bait." His eyes narrowed. I saw understanding dawn. "The bird was for you."

I shuddered, feeling nausea rise every time I looked at my vehicle. Leaning into Quinn, who'd put his arm around me, I shook my head.

"Deep breaths." Quinn rubbed my back in comfort. "Come on, let's get you some water while we wait for the police."

"No," I denied, pulling out of his embrace. "No police." I was afraid if the police were called, this would find its way into the media. And despite the continued threat, I was even more determined that Perri publish the article.

Worm bait.

Halston Cole was warning me what I'd become if I didn't stop.

Clearly he was getting desperate.

But this really did mean someone on Glenvulin was doing his dirty work.

Who?

Ramsay strode over to me and Quinn as Quinn tried to talk me into calling the police. He cut his friend off, reaching out to grab me gently by the chin, forcing my gaze to his. "Who is threatening you, Silver?" he demanded gruffly.

Ignoring the shiver of awareness that tingled across the bottom of my breasts at his touch, I yanked my chin from his calloused fingers. I lied. "I don't know what you're talking about."

Ramsay stared stonily into my eyes. "Bullshit."

"Ramsay, mate ..." Quinn placed a palm between us.

"She's had a shock. I don't think an interrogation is going to help matters."

"She doesn't want to call the police, even though she's had two threats made against her. You don't find that suspicious?"

"I think it could be anything, including some miserable fucker who's unhappy Tierney—an outsider, no offense—could afford to buy the guesthouse and they couldn't. The CCTV equipment is on order and it should be here by the end of the week. That should deter any more of this nonsense."

Although his expression remained calm, Ramsay shook his head at his friend. "You're a fool if you can't see she's lying."

I flinched and Ramsay caught it.

"What trouble have you brought to our island, Silver?"

Hurt, stupid hurt I shouldn't feel because I, ultimately, barely knew this man, echoed through my chest. I'd thought his persistence was somehow him being protective of me.

Of course not.

He was merely worried about the village and its people.

Which meant he didn't see me as one of them.

Maybe that's how they all felt.

Maybe trying to start over in Scotland was the worst idea ever because I might have Scottish blood running through my veins, but I hadn't been raised here, I didn't sound like them … I was an American.

I wasn't one of them.

The truth was if I thought I was endangering anyone here I'd leave, but I knew Cole was desperate. These sick threats were the actions of a frenzied, cornered criminal.

Deciding to ignore Ramsay entirely, I turned to Quinn. "Who can I hire to clean out my car?"

My contractor shot his partner a quick look before turning to me with a sigh. "I can get Forde here. He and his lads will clean it out and give it a thorough valet, as well as a safety check."

"I don't—"

Quinn cut me off with a wave of his hand. "It's happening. I'm also going to check in with Murray to see if he can find out if someone he's not familiar with bought a ton of bait down at the harbor. And I'll talk to Jack, the harbor master. See if he's noticed any unfamiliar faces hanging around. They have CCTV at the main ferry terminal. He could check that too."

"I don't want you to do that," I insisted.

"Well—"

"I said no." My voice rose with aggravation. "If someone is messing with me, then I am not going to give them the satisfaction of being bothered by it. Call Forde, tell him to send me the bill, and let me know when I can collect my car. Otherwise, do nothing." I handed over my note for the lunch order. "Sorry, but someone else will need to get lunch." With that I marched away from both men, hurrying downhill, grateful when they didn't follow.

I made it back to my apartment in record time and as soon as I locked the door behind me, I divested myself of all my clothes and got into the shower. As soon as the warm spray hit my skin, the sobs I'd been holding in escaped. I cried out all my fear and frustrations—my loneliness—as I scrubbed my skin and hair until it hurt, making sure there was not a single worm anywhere to be found.

My eyes were puffy and red by the time I got out of the shower, and I could barely breathe through my nose from all the snot. I missed my mom and dad with a longing that almost took me out at the knees. I missed that feeling of knowing I had a safe place to land when life got shitty.

Blowing my nose, I took a calming breath as I dried off

and changed into joggers and a tee. A check of the time told me it was a civilized hour in New York so I called Perri.

She picked up on the fourth ring.

Quietly, as calmly as possible, though I couldn't quite stop the slight tremor in my words, I told her what happened.

"Are you okay?" Perri asked.

"A little shaken. But fine."

"He's scared and he's making mistakes. Last night I got a phone call from someone using a voice distortion app. The fucker threatened to cut me up into little pieces if I didn't stop writing the article."

I blanched, sagging onto the couch. "Perri ..."

"I'm not stopping. It's not the first time someone has threatened to kill me over an investigation. The question is, do you need to back out? I'd understand if you want to."

I remembered sitting across from Halston Cole at a gala for a charity he advocated for. I saw him in my mind, the memory of him making polite conversation with my mom and dad, so smooth and seemingly benevolent. He'd socialized with my parents. He'd won my dad's trust and landed the position of CEO when my dad decided to step down.

His power, his legacy, was bestowed upon him by the same people he'd betrayed in the evilest of ways. Determination gritted my teeth. "I told you yesterday, nothing will stop me from bringing Cole down."

12. Ramsay

My alarm went off on my watch, alerting me to the fact that I only had twenty minutes to get across to Leth Sholas before the tide washed over the causeway. I stepped back from the dresser I was working on, analyzing my work so far.

I'd studied the images I'd asked Cammie for. Silver had a very specific design in mind for the Welsh dresser–inspired piece to pay homage to her grandmother. Since it was one of the few problems in Silver's life I could solve, I'd spent a few hours on it this morning.

Last night I returned to Stòr, and Akiva and I grabbed a quick bite to eat before I lost myself in my research. Hours later, I hadn't found a single thing that would account for the threats against Tierney Silver. It occurred to me it might be her ex, so I looked into Hugh, the man she'd blocked on her phone.

Hugh Inchcolm. Heir to a car manufacturing fortune. He and Silver had dated for around two years before rumors circulated about their breakup before she left for Scotland.

He didn't fit the MO. Threats from ex-lovers and stalkers fit a certain pattern and this wasn't it. Still, he was worth looking into, so I had a contact doing a deep dive on his background.

Quinn and everyone else (because, of course, one of the lads on-site told someone so the dove and worm stories had spread through Leth Sholas like wildfire) thought someone was pranking Silver. People were looking to anyone who had shown a dislike toward the American or been vocal in their opposition to her buying the guesthouse. There were only a few people on that list, and what Silver didn't realize was that the community here wouldn't put up with that kind of behavior.

Neighbor would turn on neighbor to get to the bottom of it.

She and I both knew this had nothing to do with our community.

Someone believed Silver was threatening the peace and that if she didn't stop, they'd kill her. That was the message in those threats.

And she was afraid. She was alone and afraid.

My gut knotted.

I'd spoken to Aodhan who owned the flat Silver rented and asked him to beef up the locks on the outer and inner doors. He was dismayed I felt it necessary, but he'd agreed.

For now, I'd gotten permission to leave my boat in the harbor, pointing directly at Silver's building. I'd mounted an onboard camera, so all I had to do was click onto the app on my phone to make sure all was okay outside her flat.

The app had remained open all night, and I kept shooting glances to make sure there was no movement on Main Street outside her door.

I didn't know why I was suddenly so obsessed with Silver's

safety. I only knew that if something happened to her when I was around to prevent it, it would fuck with my head.

There were no answers online to my questions. She didn't trust me to confide her secrets. Until she did, there was nothing any of us could do but be vigilant.

Tired from lack of sleep, I quickly returned to the house to pour more coffee into my flask. I grabbed everything I needed for myself and Akiva. "You're going to help out today," I told my dog as we jumped into my Defender. "You're going to stay with Silver."

My dog's ears twitched and her tongue suddenly folded out in an excited pant, like she recognized Silver's name. I chuckled as I drove out of the clearing in the woods. "Miss Plays It Cool doesn't know how to with Tierney Silver, eh?"

Akiva cocked her head at me, ears twitching again at Silver's name.

"Silver."

She panted happily.

I groaned. "You keep acting like that, she's going to know you like her."

―――

"Silver!" I called her name as soon as I jumped out of the Defender with Akiva. She was standing outside the B and B with Quinn. I was relieved to see an electrician installing security cameras on the outside of the building. The equipment arrived earlier than expected.

Silver turned at my call as Akiva bounded over to her. I watched as she crouched to greet my dog with just as much enthusiasm.

"Can you watch her today?" I asked without preamble.

Surprise rounded her eyes. "Akiva?"

"Aye. Annie can't today."

A quick glance at Quinn and the knowing smirk on his face told me my friend understood my motive. Akiva had never harmed a human being in her life, but that was mostly because she was trained. I knew without a doubt if someone attacked me, Akiva would jump into protect me.

She'd bonded to Silver and she'd protect this woman too.

"Oh. Well, of course." Silver looked at Akiva. "Are we hanging out today, beautiful girl?"

Akiva swiped her tongue up Silver's cheek and she laughed, tilting her head back out of the way. The sound was so fucking pure, I felt as ensnared by it as I did any time I looked into those big, hazel eyes.

Quinn cleared his throat, and I dragged my gaze off Silver and my dog.

My mate grinned at me in a way I knew I was in for it.

I glowered, silently threatening to maim him if he verbally suggested what his grin already hinted at.

"Thanks," I told Silver gruffly as I handed over some dog poo bags and treats. "Just in case."

She took them without meeting my gaze, keeping all her attention on Akiva.

Irritation zinged in my blood, but I told myself Silver putting an emotional wall between us was a good thing. Without another word, I strode into the building to get on with my work.

Quinn found me a few minutes later.

"Want to talk about it?" If he attempted to keep the smirking tone out of the question, he failed.

"Any suspicious packages arrive or anything strange, I want to know first."

At my gravity, he nodded. "You're worried?"

"These aren't pranks. I don't know what they are, but it's serious. I feel it in my gut."

Concern wrinkled his brow. "Okay. I'll make sure the lads know."

Quinn trusted my instincts. "Thanks."

About an hour later, I was up on a platform fitting moldings to the dining room ceiling to give the edges the swan neck cornicing that was reminiscent of the building's original Victorian grandeur.

Someone whistled, and I turned to look down.

Quinn.

He wore a grim expression. "Andy brought this to me." He held up an envelope. "Again, no name or address on it."

I muttered a curse under my breath and climbed down. Since the package didn't have a name or address on it, I didn't feel bad about opening it. Peering inside, I saw what looked like a single photograph.

"We got any gloves lying around?" I muttered to Quinn.

"Just work ones and they won't do."

I moved over to my tools and pulled out a pair of slim pliers. As delicately as possible, I clipped the very edge of the photograph and slipped it out.

Quinn hovered at my side as we peered at the image.

It was of an unfamiliar but attractive redhead. A candid shot of her on a busy city street. A swoosh of red paint or lipstick circled her head.

Flipping the photo over, I froze.

Across the back were the words:

THEN MAYBE THIS WILL STOP YOU.

"Well, fuck," Quinn bit out. "Who do you think that is, then?"

"My bet is she's someone our Ms. Silver loves very dearly." With that I brushed past him. "Where is she?"

"Last I saw her, she was out in the garden playing with Akiva ... Ramsay, don't bully her!"

I whirled back around. "What the fuck does that mean?"

He grimaced. "You come across like you're pissed off at *her* about this. That'll just make her clam up more. You saw her this morning. That is a woman who is mad at you. Trust me" —his eyes darkened—"I recognize the signs."

Considering his words and Silver's reaction this morning, I nodded grimly. "I'll be ... nice."

Quinn's lips twitched. "I doubt it but at least try to be kind."

TIERNEY

The air was a little damp, but the sun was trying to peek through the clouds above, and since a bit of drizzle didn't seem to bother Akiva, I kept her outside in the garden close to the house so Quinn could find me if he needed me. Quinn hadn't said anything about not taking photos of Akiva for social media, so I'd snapped a few beautiful shots of her against the backdrop of the water to upload later.

Now we were playing with a thick twig, Akiva proving she had jaws of steel as she clamped down and tugged *me* around the garden. I'd just tripped over a divot in the grass and Akiva had come bounding over trying to swipe my face with that pink tongue. Laughing as I tried to avoid the doggy kiss, gratitude swelled inside me and I found myself burying my face in her furry neck.

Ramsay had some balls treating me like *I* was a threat to Leth Sholas and then expecting me to look after his damn dog!

But for Akiva, I would do it because she was the only thing right now that could bring a smile to my face.

That was how he found us.

My jeans dirty and grass stained because I was kneeling in the garden, hugging his dog like she was my life raft.

"You all right?"

I jerked back from Akiva to find Ramsay blocking out the sun, a towering shadow of masculinity above us.

Akiva gave a happy bark and lunged onto her hind legs, pressing her forelegs to Ramsay's torso as she greeted him.

He rubbed her down with one hand. "Hiya, sweetheart," he murmured gruffly. "Down, Akiva. Down. Good girl."

I stood, moving to the side so I could see Ramsay better. He petted the top of Akiva's head as his stare pierced mine. Awareness scored through me like always. "What?"

Ramsay slowly raised his free hand, and something flickered between the clamp of a pair of pliers. "Take it by the handle," he commanded but in a much softer tone than usual.

Curious, I did as he asked and brought what I realized was a photograph to my face.

I froze at the candid shot of London about to get into a cab in New York. There was a bright red circle around her head.

"Turn it over."

Almost afraid to, I slowly flipped it.

Nausea rose and I swallowed back the sensation, not knowing what to feel more. Terror or fury.

"It arrived in an envelope with no name or address. Do you know what it means?"

Ramsay's tone was so gentle. Coaxing. Not demanding.

Yet I could barely take in his words.

"Cell." I thrust the pliers back at him. "Do you have a cell I can borrow?"

He frowned. "Have you forgotten yours?"

I shook my head. No, it was in the back pocket of my jeans. An unwitting traitor.

Ramsay pulled his phone out of his shirt pocket.

"I need to make an international call. I'll pay you back."

He impatiently waved off my offer, and I took the phone, fumbling for my own so I could find an email from Perri. At the bottom of the email was the number for the newspaper office. I dialed it on Ramsay's phone and walked to the end of the garden for privacy.

Thankfully, Ramsay stayed put. I kept my back to him as I called the newspaper and asked to speak to Perri. They took my name and I waited until eventually I connected to Perri's work phone.

"Tierney? What's going on?"

"Our phones are tapped. They tapped our cell phones. Or at least they tapped mine. How?"

Perri let out a curse. "Are you sure?"

"Yesterday I said the words *Nothing will stop me* to you on the phone. Today I got another unaddressed envelope and inside is a pap shot of my best friend London, the only family I have left, and she has a big fucking target drawn around her head. On the back of that photo are the words *Then maybe this will stop you*."

"Oh fuck," Perri hissed. "Fucking, fuck, fuck."

My heart was pounding so hard I could barely hear over it. "What do we do?"

"Dump your phone and get a new one. New number, everything. I'll send you a burner phone so we can safely stay in contact. That's if you still want to do this?"

The thought of anyone hurting London caused panic to constrict my lungs. "I think it's only fair she knows she's been threatened and ask her if she wants me to back off."

Perri sighed. "Tierney, we are so close to publishing this thing. If you tell her and she tells the wrong person ..."

"I trust her."

She sighed again. "Okay. Then let me know what you decide as soon as possible."

"I'll call her now. I'm using someone else's phone."

"Right. Talk soon."

London and I hadn't spoken on the phone in a few weeks. We had a video call about a month ago, but we'd been trading texts because every time I tried to video chat, she didn't pick up. But I knew her job kept her crazy busy.

I dialed her number and prayed she'd pick up. A quick look over my shoulder revealed Ramsay watching me patiently, Akiva at his side. I turned away, wondering at his change in attitude. Unable to resist, I glanced back and suddenly the favor he'd asked of me appeared different.

Now I wondered if Annie really couldn't watch Akiva today.

I wondered if Ramsay had only said that so he could leave his very large, very protective Alaskan Malamute with me.

Huh.

Turning around, I frowned out at the beautiful view ahead. Even on a cloudy day, it was stunning here, especially with rays of champagne-gold sunlight piercing through the mauve clouds and hitting the water in bursts of sparkling light. Sometimes remembering I lived here now was surreal. Glenvulin's tranquility was almost jarring against the current chaos of my life.

It was a shock when the line suddenly connected.

"Hello?"

"London, it's me."

"Nee?" London's voice and use of my nickname was a balm to my soul. "Are you okay? It's early." She was home and she was alive. And she was probably exhausted from working late and long hours.

"I woke you."

"It's okay. What's wrong?" she asked as I heard a male voice in the background asking something I couldn't quite make out. "It's Tierney," London replied. He said something else. "It's fine," my friend said in return and then I heard what sounded like a door closing. "Okay, we're alone. What's happening?"

Taking a shuddering breath, I explained. "Spoon ..." I used the nickname I'd called her since we were kids. "I can't go into details, but I'm working with an investigative reporter because ..." Tears threatened. London had been at my side through everything, including my parents' deaths. She was the only person I'd let see how broken I was by the loss. "My parents ... it wasn't an accident."

"Oh my God," London said in a jagged breath. "What do you mean? What is going on?"

"It has to do with the company. That's all I can say. But the person responsible knows that I'm working with a reporter and I've been threatened to stay quiet. But it's my mom and dad." I swiped at my freely falling tears.

"I know. Oh, babe, I know." I heard London sniffle, crying with me because that's the way it was. When I was in pain, she was in pain and vice versa.

"So I haven't backed down." I sucked in a breath, getting control of myself. "Until now. I got a threat against you."

London's voice was instantly hard and demanding. "What kind of threat?"

I told her about the photograph and the warning on the back.

"Well, fuck that," she hissed. "Do not let that stop you. I will be fine, Nee. Everyone knows I'm dating Nick and Nick has more power in this city—fuck, in this country—than most. They won't touch me and risk Nick's wrath."

For once, I might actually be grateful she was dating the prick. "So you're okay? You're okay for me to keep going?"

"Yes. If someone *killed* your parents, you have to bring them to justice. I know you. I know you better than I know anyone. And you won't be able to live with yourself unless you do this."

"I love you," I whispered, sucking back more tears. "I miss you like crazy."

Her voice turned husky. "You have no idea how much I miss you."

Something in her voice sent a shiver of warning up my neck. "Spoon ... are *you* okay?"

"You don't worry about me," was her reply. "I'm all good. Now go teach this asshole a lesson and tell me when it's done."

I still wasn't convinced there wasn't something going on with her, but just as she knew me, I knew London and she'd only feel cornered if I pushed. But I would fly out to New York as soon as it was possible to check in with my friend.

We hung up with another exchange of love and I turned to find Ramsay waiting. I strode across the garden as the drizzle began to turn to rain and handed him his phone. "Thanks."

He nodded and opened his mouth to say something, but I walked past him to hop up onto the concrete patio. Removing my phone from my pocket, I removed the SIM card first, then dropped both it and the phone onto the slab. I picked up a nearby bit of rubble and got down on my knees to start smashing the fuck out of them.

"Silver?" Ramsay caught me by the elbow and pulled me to my feet. I realized he'd been calling my name for a while. He bent his head to peer into my face, his grip on my arm gentle but firm. "Tell me what's going on."

I tugged out of his hold. "Bill me for the phone calls."

"Silver," he pushed. "I can help."

No, he couldn't. No one could help. I wasn't dragging more people into this only for them to become targets too. We were so close to the finish line. Ramsay, everyone, would understand soon enough.

"I need to run some errands. Do you still want me to watch Akiva?"

Ramsay's expression was tight with dissatisfaction, but he nodded. "Aye, I do."

And that's when I knew for certain Ramsay McRae had assigned me a very beautiful, very furry bodyguard and had no intention of letting me out of Akiva's sight.

13. Ramsay

The first call Silver made was to the *New York Chronicle*, one of the largest newspapers in the world. The second to a London Wetherspoon, a sous chef in New York. A quick search on the internet brought up a number of photos of London and Tierney together as teenagers. London was Tierney Silver's best friend and most definitely the redhead in the photo.

Someone had threatened the only family Silver seemed to have left.

Because she was working with a reporter at a newspaper?

I disliked the unknown.

I'd moved to Leth Sholas for anonymity.

To live out the rest of my life in peace.

If our newest resident brought trouble to the Isle of Glenvulin and that trouble ended up in the news, it might bring my own trouble to my doorstep.

Aye.

That was the only reason I found myself obsessing over the situation with Silver.

Of course it was.
I wouldn't *allow* it to be for any other reason.

14. TIERNEY

A few weeks ago, Cammie told me about the Isle of Kiln off the west coast of Glenvulin. It wasn't quite as small as Stòr and had a tiny population of only six families. It was twelve miles long and four miles wide, and the community of the island ran a privately operated ferry to and from Glenvulin. I'd been intrigued and wanted to visit, but that urge almost turned into desperation over the subsequent few days.

Word about "the incidents" had made its way around the island, and I'd been treated to concern, accusation, and lectures from the community. I'd even been interviewed by the island police, but I refused to report it as a crime so there wasn't much they could do. Quinn was as good as his word and Forde had taken care of my SUV and checked every inch of it over. I could deal more with people's wary glances and passive-aggressive comments than the McQuarries' genuine concern. Cammie was like a dog with a bone and was determined to find out what was going on with me.

As for Ramsay, I was avoiding him like the plague.

He was much too perceptive, and I was pissed that he only

seemed to care whether my troubles had the potential to hurt Leth Sholas. He didn't seem at all concerned that *I* was the actual target! I avoided him when I could, but I couldn't avoid everyone.

And I couldn't take much more of the constant attention on top of everything else.

London had been texting me regularly to check in.

Hugh used a new number to start blowing up my phone with "We need to talk, baby" texts and multiple calls. I was now starting to freak out about his persistence, but I didn't know how to handle it with all this other carnage going on, so once again, I blocked him.

And realized, as selfish as it might be, I wanted to block everyone.

So the Isle of Kiln called to me.

Instead of heading to the B and B that morning, I told Cammie I was catching the ferry to Kiln to hike around the island all day. I packed supplies and carefully checked the ferry timetable. Because the ferry to Kiln was privately owned, it didn't run as regularly as those to the mainland. There was one in the morning and one in the late afternoon, and that was it.

"I don't think this is a good idea." Cammie glowered, taking a sip of her coffee.

We'd grabbed to-go cups at Macbeth's Pages & Perks after I'd bought my lunch at the bakery to take with me on my island adventure.

"It's a splendid idea," I disagreed.

"Let me switch out my hair appointment today so I can come with you."

"Nope. I don't need an escort."

Cammie huffed. "Someone has threatened you three times, so I vehemently disagree."

"I am the only one waiting for the ferry," I reminded her.

"I'm pretty sure I'll be okay on Kiln with its population of twenty people."

"Fine." Cammie threw back the rest of her coffee. "But I'll be here on the Leth Sholas dock waiting for you at five o'clock."

"I'll be here," I promised as I reached out to squeeze my friend's hand. We'd only known each other a few short months, but it felt like we had a bond that transcended time. "It's not that I don't trust you with the truth. I'm ... bound by circumstances right now. As soon as I'm not, you are the first person I will explain everything to. All right?"

Her expression softened. "Okay. I'm just worried about you."

Emotion brightened my eyes. "You have no idea how nice it is to have people in my life again who worry about me. I don't take it for granted. I ... I hate having to keep this stuff to myself and I just need a day of not thinking about it."

"Aye, I understand." Cammie sighed and nodded beyond me. "Here's the boat."

The small boat, as it turned out, was operated by Donal Macintosh, a gruff man in his fifties. A few people disembarked before I boarded, and I was his lone passenger. We waited for ten minutes until Donal announced, "Just one today."

He pulled away from the harbor and I waved goodbye to Cammie who stood watching until we cruised out of sight.

"I've not seen you around. Tourist?" Donal asked loudly over the engine.

"No, I moved to Leth Sholas a few months ago."

"Oh, are you the lass who bought the B and B?"

It would seem the occupants of the smaller islands around Glenvulin knew of my arrival too. Talk about a close-knit community. "That's me."

"What brings you to Kiln?"

"I wanted to hike and explore."

"Not much to see."

"Merely natural beauty," I replied with a smile.

Donal liked that and nodded. "Aye, we have that in abundance. It's moorland, woodland, and grassland on Kiln. There's some boggy ground, so be careful where you put your feet."

"Is the main town close to the ferry dock?"

"There's not really a main town. Just homes dotted around the island. There's a restaurant and pub up from the ferry dock, though. It's mine. I close at four today, though, to run the ferry, so there's no point coming knocking anytime after that because nobody will be there."

"Good to know. Thanks."

Donal was quiet after that. As we approached Kiln, I could see a home with a thatched roof not far from where we'd dock.

"The museum." He pointed to it. "The bothy—do you know what a bothy is?"

"A small house, right?"

"Aye. Well, shelter, really. It's not what we'd consider a house nowadays. That one there is hundreds of years old. The museum welcomes donations."

I grinned. "I'll pay a visit and donate."

The dock on Kiln was literally a small wooden strip that would only accept a small boat in its waters.

"I head back to Glenvulin at precisely four thirty to pick up islanders who work there. I'll leave without you if you're not here because there's a storm coming in this evening, and we need to get back before it's unsafe to cross."

"I'll be here."

Donal helped me off his boat once he'd tied it to the dock. I headed to the museum first to donate and look around. There was no one there to attend to it, so I guessed it was an honor system. I stuck twenty pounds into the donation cup and crouched in through the small door. Goodness, people used to be so short.

Inside was dark and musty and I shivered as I felt its history wrap around me. I imagined the people who lived here hundreds of years ago, how hard their lives were in comparison to ours today. And yet I wondered if the simplicity of their existence made for happier human beings.

One end of the room was roped off, the floor there packed dirt. A large cabinet stood against the wall, and a closer inspection revealed it wasn't a cabinet but a bed. Crossing to read the sign next to it, I marveled at the ingenuity. It was so cold at night here in Kiln that back in the day, the residents slept inside the large cabinet and closed the doors to shield them from the chill.

I read all the information signs about life on Kiln centuries ago. Apparently, Kiln was a victim of the Highland Clearances (evictions of a significant number of tenants from the Scottish Highlands and Islands from 1750 to1860) and potato famine. There had once been over six hundred residents on this island, but the latter had led to a massive population reduction.

Snapping a few pics for my Instagram, I stepped outside to take photos of the exterior of the bothy with its thatched roof. Turning around, staring out at the water and views back to Glenvulin, I took a few more photos, including a selfie.

Donal had warned of a coming storm, but it had to be far off because all was calm and sunny.

I closed my eyes, drinking in the sound of the gulls overhead and the water crashing gently at the rocky coastline of this tranquil island.

Peace. Finally, a little drop of peace.

It took me three hours to walk from one end of the island to the other. Donal had been right about boggy ground, and I'd had to watch where I walked. I'd tried to stick to the single rough track that wove around the coastline, but I'd seen a sign for standing stones and had ventured off the path and into woodlands to find them. I did find them, but I also found mud and marshy ground.

Disappointed that placing my hands on the standing stone didn't send me careening back in time to find a handsome Highlander, I decided to find my way back to the main path.

I'd seen signs for a "free bothy," a house hikers could make use of if needed, a church, and two houses in the distance, but other than that, there was no one and nothing. The island was connected to a tiny piece of land by an old bridge and I'd stopped to take photographs of the turquoise water beneath it. Off the bridge was an even narrower, rougher track suitable for foot traffic and no more. It wound around the coastline of the tiny portion of land and I passed a cemetery. It was small as expected with stones congregated together and then spread out farther apart. Many of the names had been worn away by the coastal weather, but it was peaceful.

There was a house nearby, but no one appeared to be home, so I carried on a little farther until I came almost to the end of Kiln. It had a rocky beach where water the color of jade lapped at its shore. Climbing down onto it, I pulled off the blanket I'd rolled and attached to my backpack and laid it over the grass before it met the rocks.

Breathing in the crisp, sea air, I let the tranquility that clung to every inch of this place wrap around me. In the distance I saw the shoreline of a small island and one to my left. There was a dot of land farther out and to my right a cluster of islands. I'd stared at the map of the Inner Hebrides so many times, I was pretty sure that cluster was the Treshnish

Isles, but I'd have to double-check when I got back to Leth Sholas.

There was no signal on my new phone.

Utter bliss.

Perhaps an hour or so passed as I ate the gourmet sandwich from Leth Sholas Bakery. With the last bite, I was hit with a wave of exhaustion. I knew it was mental more than physical. Emotional more than mental. And with no one around but me and nature, I decided to take a nap before heading along the coastline on the other side of Kiln.

———

Splashes of cold hit my skin, pulling me back to consciousness. I blinked blearily, my vision clearing until all I saw was water. Confused, I sat up rapidly, a little dizzy from the abrupt transition.

The picnic blanket was scratchy beneath my palms, and I remembered where I was.

I'd fallen asleep by the water. Water that was now farther up the rocky beach and a moody blue beneath a darkening sky.

Shit.

I scrambled for my phone and gasped at the time.

It was four o'clock. I'd fallen asleep for three hours!

There was no way I'd make it back to the ferry in thirty minutes.

Shit, shit, shit.

Feeling my panic rise, I shook my head.

No.

There was no point in panicking.

With no phone signal, I was stuck on Kiln.

I sighed heavily at the thought of knocking on the door of one of the very few homes on the island and asking for shelter for the night. It freaked me out too. I mean, I was pretty sure they were all very nice, but this felt like the beginning of a bad horror movie.

The bothy.

I suddenly remembered.

There was the free bothy for hikers.

Hearing the water hit the rocks harder than before, I glanced up at the sky. It was growing broodier by the second. I needed to get to that building before those heavy purple clouds poured down.

I stuffed everything into my backpack, rolled and reattached my blanket, and hurried away from my picnic spot and onto the track that would lead me over the bridge to the main road on Kiln.

By the time I found the sign for the bothy, it was ninety minutes later and the rain that had hit my skin in spits of water was a sheet on the sea in the distance, headed straight for shore. I needed to reach the bothy before the downpour landed and I had to spend the night in wet clothes.

The sign for the free bothy explained the building had only cold water and no electricity, but I didn't care. I needed shelter. And I at once realized the people who lived here hundreds of years ago must have felt the same. I followed the directions down toward the water, winding around a narrow footpath carved into the grass until I saw the white building looking out toward Glenvulin.

Just as I reached the door, the rain started hammering down. There were two solar lamps sitting outside, and I had the presence of mind to grab them before I darted into the building and slammed the door behind me. I took a deep breath of relief as the solar lights flared to life.

Then I wrinkled my nose.

The bothy smelled musty and damp. There was a two-seater couch facing a disused fireplace and two armchairs on either side of that. Along the back wall was a sink and some counter space.

A look through the door on my left revealed a bedroom with bunk beds against one wall and a double bed in the center of the room. The blankets and pillows appeared clean and fresh, so someone was obviously looking after the place.

A spider scurried across my foot and I hurried further into the room. I shuddered as the lamps barely lit my way, but I caught the trickle of water flowing down the brick wall opposite the sofa.

The roof was leaking.

Chilled air blew over my skin and I shivered.

I was in for a freezing, miserable night.

15. Ramsay

I was finishing up for the day when I heard Cammie's familiar voice frantically shouting my name.

Hearing her distress, I jumped off the platform I'd been working on in one of the bedrooms as Cammie burst into the room. "What's wrong?" I demanded.

Her brows drew together, concern glimmering in her blue eyes. "It's Tierney. She wasn't on the ferry back from Kiln. Donal said she never showed, and he'd warned her to get back in time. It's lashing down out there now."

An image of Silver on the island by herself in this weather caused me discomfort, but I merely answered, "She'll find shelter."

Anger flared in Cammie's eyes. "There's someone threatening her, Ramsay. I tried to tell her not to go alone, but she was convinced since no one else got on the ferry, she'd be fine. But who is to say someone else didn't follow her out there? Maybe she missed the ferry because whoever is threatening her found her."

"Fuck." The word hissed between my lips as I considered

Cammie's concern. If there was even a remote possibility ... "I'll take the boat over."

"The water is rough."

"I'll go now before it gets worse. I'll let you know if I find her."

"I'll come."

"No. Quinn would have my head if anything happened to you. Anyway, I need you to watch Akiva."

Twenty minutes later, I left Akiva behind on shore with Cammie and headed out toward Kiln. The rain battered down, so I'd pulled on waterproof trousers and a hooded jacket to make the crossing. As the waves rocked my small boat, I cursed Tierney Silver and whatever this fucking hold was she had on me.

Beneath my irritation was something I didn't want to consider.

Because what if someone had gotten to her on Kiln?

"Fuck," I growled, steering the boat through the choppy waters. I could barely see a thing and knew too late I'd taken a big risk. Still, I'd been in worse situations in my life. Far worse.

By the time I reached the dock at Kiln, my boat had almost capsized twice and I knew I'd have to find shelter for the night too. There was no way I could chance traveling back in this weather. With sheer strength and physical will, I managed to get the boat tied to the dock next to Donal's and hiked up onto the main footpath. I had a backpack with supplies, including a portable VHF radio so I could update Cammie and Leth Sholas on our situation.

The SUV took me by surprise, because I hadn't heard the rumble of its engine over the crash of the water against shore. Its headlights blinded me before it suddenly swung to the side. I lowered my hand from my eyes and made out Donal Macintosh's bearded face in the driver's side.

"Donal?"

"Who is that?"

I approached the vehicle so he could see me better. "It's me! Ramsay!"

"McRae?"

"Aye!"

"Are you crazy coming over in this weather, man!"

"I'm looking for someone! You brought her over this morning!"

"The blond lass? Aye, I'm out looking for her meself! Bloody tourists!"

"Do you know which way she went?"

"She took the coastal trail!" He pointed ahead of us. "If she's smart, she made her way to the bothy!"

I knew which one he spoke of. The islanders here maintained the shelter for hikers who wanted to spend a night on the island. "I'll head that way. You head home. I've got this!"

He scowled. "Let me drive you a ways. It's ninety minutes by foot!"

Grateful, I nodded and rounded the SUV, jumping inside.

The sound of the weather dulled only somewhat as Donal righted the SUV and started down the coastal road.

"This lass something to you, then?" Donal asked quietly. "Considering you risked your very life in that water to get to her."

"Honestly, I didn't realize how bad the crossing would be. But she's a friend of Cammie's and Cammie was worried."

Donal nodded. "Well, she seemed like a smart enough lass. I wouldnae fash yourself too much."

"Is that why *you're* out looking for her?"

"I dinnae like to think of anyone out here by themselves in this weather. And once my wife heard there was a young woman out here alone, she radioed everyone on the island to see if they had her. No one has seen the lass. The wife wouldnae stop nipping my ear until I went out to look for her."

Because that was what a small community did for one another.

We fell into silence as he cautiously followed the road.

However, fifteen minutes later, as we came over the brow of a hill, we saw the light.

"That's the bothy," Donal told me. "Looks like she found it and the solar lamps."

Something in me eased. "Good."

"We've got another five minutes of track and then I'll need to drop you off at the path. From there you're probably another ten minutes by foot."

"Thanks."

A few minutes later, Donal stopped the SUV and I got out. He stayed there, lighting my way with the headlights until the footpath took me downhill out of sight. I couldn't hear him drive off over the crash of water against the coastline and I could barely see through the rain battering down around me.

At the sight of the bothy and that light shining in the small side window, I felt the sudden urge to throttle Tierney Silver.

Not so much for dragging me out here in this fucking weather ...

But for making me worry that I might not find her.

Or worse, I'd find her and be too late.

16. Tierney

Living the kind of privileged life I'd led, I'd seen more than most people in my twenty-seven years. I'd traveled the world and considered myself an adventurous person. London and I had once joined a camping tour in the Amazon Rainforest where the guide taught us survival skills.

Despite the deadly plants and insects there, I'd felt empowered by the experience.

Now I realized it was because I wasn't alone. I'd had my best friend and two badass guides leading our small group.

Moreover, I was free of any threats six years ago when we did that tour.

Sitting on the double bed in the bothy, my arms wrapped around my legs, listening to the weather crash around me, I was afraid. I was alone and afraid and I hated it. There were moments when the loss of my parents' hit me harder than others. Like when I bought the B and B and I forgot for a second and I picked up my phone to call my mom and then remembered I couldn't. The grief had hit me then like a crushing weight. Losing two people who were that intrinsically tied to my happiness had made me feel so unanchored, I felt like I was losing my mind. Now and then, I'd get hit with flashes of that intense grief and have to meditate my way through it.

Right then, I missed my mom and dad so much I could cry like a baby.

I wanted to call my dad and ask him to come get me, knowing he'd send the freaking coast guard and Royal Navy to do it.

"I miss you so much," I whispered hoarsely, tears stinging my nose.

I wasn't going to sleep a wink tonight.

And crying wouldn't help my situation, so I sucked back the tears. Blood rushed in my ears as I strained to hear anything over the sound of the storm.

My mind kept conjuring sounds. Like a door creaking open. A tap on the window.

Maybe the bothy was haunted.

"Oh, fuck a duck," I muttered, pulling my legs tighter against me. "Survived a week in the rainforest. Can't even survive a night in a haunted bothy."

A loud creak sounded, and I held my breath, my eyes trying to detect movement in the darkened front room. Shadows moved and my heart raced at the definite sight of the bothy's door opening.

I froze in terror as a huge figure stepped inside and the door slammed shut.

The scream rushed up my throat as the figure turned and then stepped into the doorway. The dim light of my solar lamp cast shadows over his face.

I sagged in utter relief. "Ramsay."

He strode into the room, the light now illuminating his expression.

And he was pissed.

He yanked his hood down and sprays of rain water hit my face. "How the bloody hell did you miss that boat?"

At his belligerent tone, my fear gave way to indignant anger. "Well, hello to you too!"

Ramsay yanked off the waterproof jacket, and I gaped as he pushed down the yellow waterproof trousers, only slightly relieved he had jeans on underneath. He disappeared out of the room and I heard him curse loudly as I imagined he found somewhere to dry them. Then he was back with the other solar lamp in hand.

"What are you doing here?" I asked more calmly, trying not to show him how freaking relieved I was to see him.

"Cammie was in a panic when you didn't show up, so I brought my boat over to find you."

"In this weather? Are you insane?"

"Apparently." He cut me a dark look. "So you're safe? You're all right?"

"I hiked to the other end of the island and I fell asleep by the water. By the time I woke up, I didn't have enough time to make it back to the ferry, so I remembered this place and reached it before the storm got really bad."

Ramsay let out a long, heavy sigh before he started rummaging in the backpack he'd brought with him.

"What are you doing?"

Instead of answering, he pulled out what looked like a walkie-talkie.

A VHF radio.

He held it to his mouth. "Half-Light, this is McRae. Over."

The radio crackled and then a distorted voice replied, "Meh-Rae—is Ha—ligh—you—kay?—er."

"All good. I found Silver. We're safe for the night. Over."

His eyes held mine and awareness sparked through me as I processed the situation.

I was alone in the bothy with Ramsay McRae and we had to spend the night together.

Wonderful.

"Will—Cam—ow. Stay—afe.—er."

"Thanks. Over."

Ramsay dropped his hand to the side and kept looking at me in that way that made me feel like he was peeling back all my layers. I shivered. His eyes narrowed. "Cold?"

I let out a huff of laughter. "Just a little bit."

"Hungry?"

I nodded. "I only brought lunch with me."

Ramsay promptly sat down on the bed and dumped his backpack between us. "I brought supplies. It's not much." He began unloading protein bars, packets of peanuts and chips, a couple bottles of water.

"Why did you come here?" I dared to ask.

Those wolf eyes met mine. "Cammie was worried someone might have gotten to you."

Just Cammie?

"I'm sorry I worried her. I haven't been sleeping well and didn't mean to nap so long."

He searched my face, expression grim. "You know ... it might help if you tell us what's going on."

I looked down at the food supplies. "Is that a chocolate chip peanut bar? Can I have it?"

There was no mistaking his frustration. It practically vibrated off him. But eventually, he replied gruffly, "Aye, knock yourself out."

Unwrapping the bar, I studied my companion as he took a swig of water. With his beard closely trimmed, I could see the bob of his throat as he swallowed, and I didn't know why the sight was so erotic. My eyes roamed over his broad shoulders.

The Henley he wore hugged his muscular biceps, the sleeves rolled up to reveal strong forearms. He had great hands. Long fingered, but big knuckled. I'd bet my life his fingertips were covered in callouses that would rasp across my skin like sandpaper.

I shivered again and looked away, reminding myself I was mad at the Scot.

And yet ...

He'd risked his life crossing the channel between here and Glenvulin.

For me.

He might say it was for Cammie ... but it was for me.

"Thank you for coming," I murmured. My eyes returned to him, and I realized it was against my will. I couldn't not look at him.

The handsome bastard that he was.

His silver-gray eyes gleamed in the low light. "You're welcome."

It wasn't the response I'd expected. I'd anticipated something sarcastic and disapproving.

If he was still frustrated at my inability to confide my troubles, he didn't show it.

Instead, he held my stare as if he too found he couldn't look away.

I could feel my breathing grow shallow with awareness. Afraid of the intensity of my attraction, I sought to break the silence. "You know, I once camped in the Amazon Rainforest for a week when I was twenty-one ... and yet, I think I was more scared to be alone in this little bothy tonight."

He quirked an eyebrow. "I wouldn't have taken you for the camping sort."

I grimaced. "Then you'd be wrong. But I'd be lying if I told you I did that tour alone. I had the best guides money could buy. My parents insisted."

"I'd have insisted too." Again his response surprised me.

Wondering if this time, forced to be with each other, he might actually open up a little, I tried once more to get to know Ramsay McRae. "Would your parents have insisted?"

He searched my gaze thoroughly. I didn't know what he was looking for ... but to my surprise, he replied, "Probably. I think. They died when I was eight so ..." He shrugged. "I'm an orphan."

The word clanged through me.

It conjured images of sad-faced little children, not tall, broad-shouldered capable Scots whose hands were almost twice as big as my own.

"I'm sorry," I whispered, shocked.

Ramsay shrugged. "It's my reality. I don't think my life has been worse or better than most because of it."

"So ... were you adopted?"

"No. It's difficult at that age. I spent the rest of my childhood in the foster system and stayed with foster parents across the north. Inverness, Aberdeen ..."

He was talking.

Ramsay was talking.

A surge of triumph moved through me even as his truth caused dismay. I hated that reality for him. As heartbroken as I was without my parents, I wouldn't trade those years together just so I didn't feel the pain of their loss. Ramsay had such little time with his. How lucky was I to have had the time I did?

"And you ended up in the Royal Marines?"

"I joined at sixteen." He reached for one of the protein bars and ripped it open.

I tried not to stare at his mouth as he chewed. "Did they become like a family? Your unit?"

"For a while. Do you pity me?"

There was something sharp in his tone I didn't like.

"Never. If I pitied you for losing your parents, then I'd have to pity myself and I don't. Plus, you're one of the most capable people I've ever met. I could never pity you."

Tension eased in his shoulders. "You're pretty capable yourself for a rich girl."

I heard his teasing, so I didn't take offense. Instead, I chuckled and took the bottle of water he held out to me. "My parents made sure of it. Yes, I grew up privileged. We had luxury vacations and I've seen more of the world than most people ever will. I've never wanted for anything. I don't know what it's like to be hungry or to be afraid I don't have the money to feed myself, to pay my bills. And I'm grateful for that. But, like I told you before, my parents wanted to make sure that's as far as my privilege went."

"What does that mean?"

Trying to think of the perfect example, I took a sip of water, searching my memory. I swallowed and wiped my lips with the back of my hand. "Okay, for instance, I'm fourteen years old and my classmate Carissa Yiu just had a slumber party that made Blair Waldorf's look like child's play."

"Who's Blair Waldorf?"

My lips twitched. "A fictional New York socialite known for her lavish slumber parties."

"Ah."

"You were probably somewhere on a covert operation when she made her splash into popular media," I joked.

Ramsay nodded as if that were probably true.

Hmm.

I wondered just what he did while he was in the Royal Marines. "Anyway, I begged my parents for a slumber party that would knock Carissa Yiu's slumber party out of the park. They adamantly refused. And when I threw a hissy fit, my mom made me volunteer with her at a homeless shelter. That shut me right up." I smiled fondly at the memory.

Ramsay swallowed a bite of his protein bar and murmured, "I think I'd get on well with your mum."

"Oh, she was a Scot through and through. She grew up with money, but my grandfather hadn't, so she was raised to appreciate everything she had. And she wanted me to be the same. My mom and dad kept me in check. I don't take any of the experiences they provided for granted."

Ramsay considered this. "Perhaps some of us had preconceived notions about you."

"Some of us being you?"

"I rarely judge a book by its cover. People are excellent at keeping secrets and are never really who you think they are. But ... I have to admit, you've surprised me a time or two and that's not easy to do."

Despite the cold, my cheeks flushed beneath his intense regard.

God, I wanted him.

I didn't think I'd ever wanted a man as much as I wanted this one.

Feeling breathless again, I racked my brain for a subject change. Pinned to the wall of the bedroom was a photograph of a Highland piper. "So, the pipes ... where did you learn to play them?"

Ramsay went with the new topic and to my continued shock, replied, "In the marines. They have a pipe band and as punishment for a prank I pulled on a member of my unit when I was seventeen, my corporal stuck me in the pipe band, and I was forced to learn the pipes."

"But you enjoyed playing?"

"I did. It had been years since I picked up the pipes, but when I settled in Leth Sholas, Quinn was looking for another piper. Some madness led me to saying yes." He shrugged, a far-off look in his eyes. "But being part of the band reminds me of my time in the marines. Of being part of a team, of a community. I'd lost that over the years, reverting to the orphan who grew up needing nothing and no one."

Grateful he'd shared so much, I responded softly, "I guess we all need someone. Even a man who bought an island just to be alone."

"Not alone. I have a dog." He flashed me a grin, and I felt a swoop of attraction in my stomach.

I chuckled, suddenly not afraid to let my feelings show in the heat of my stare. "You have more than a dog."

Blunt as ever, Ramsay replied gruffly, "I'm not a relationship type of man, Silver. I like sex and when I need it, I find someone uncomplicated to have sex with."

Perhaps it was because he couldn't run from me here, but I found myself answering boldly, "And I'm complicated?"

Ramsay gave a little huff. "Where do I start?"

"Somewhere," I insisted.

"Fine. One: You live in Leth Sholas. I don't sleep with women from Glenvulin. Two: You're a good thirteen years younger than me. I like women who know the score. Three: You're hiding something that potentially puts the people I care about in danger. Is that complicated enough for you?"

I raised my chin defiantly. "The only person potentially in danger is me, and we both know you couldn't care less about me."

"You believe that and yet you want to fuck me?" He quirked an eyebrow.

My skin flushed at his words. Not at the bluntness. But at the imagery they conjured. The thought of his big body moving over mine. *In* mine.

"I'm not looking for complicated either," I whispered, my voice hoarse with need.

Ramsay turned his head from me, and I saw the muscle in his jaw flexing beneath his beard. "Who is threatening you?" he asked the wall.

"Why do you care?"

"Silver." He flashed me a warning look.

I sighed and shimmied back up the bed and onto one side. "I'm tired. I think I'll try to sleep through this storm."

Without another word, I curled up on my side.

17. TIERNEY

"The blankets are clean." Ramsay stood and began removing his supplies from the bed. "You can get under it. I'll take one of the bunks."

A few minutes later, I'd kicked off my boots and gotten under the blanket. It might have been clean, but it smelled a little damp, like it had been changed a good few weeks before. I curled into a ball on my side and squeezed my eyes closed, trying not to think about how freaking cold it was now that the storm was raging around us.

"It's blowin' a hooley out there," Ramsay muttered, moving around the room.

"What does that mean?"

"Windy," he replied succinctly. "Will I turn off the lamp?"

My eyes flew open. "No! I mean ... please don't."

He didn't respond to that, but he also didn't turn off the lamp. I closed my eyes and heard creaking as Ramsay got into the lower bunk bed.

I tried to sleep, but my feet were like ice, and I couldn't rid myself of the chill. Shivering, I curled tighter into a ball, pulling the blanket up around my ears. My teeth chittered.

"You all right over there, Silver?"

I jolted at Ramsay's question; I thought he'd be long asleep. "I ... I c-can't g-get warm."

"Fuck," he muttered. "Do you want me to sleep in there with you? For body heat?"

The funny thing is, if any other guy had offered to do that, I would have known they were using the situation as an excuse to get in bed with me. Not Ramsay McRae.

I knew he genuinely was only offering his body heat.

"Yes," I bit out. Pride be damned. I was freezing.

Turning around, I watched him as he unfolded his large body from the small bunk bed and got up. He didn't hesitate or overthink things. Ramsay pulled back the blanket and slid into the bed.

"I'm going to hug you," I warned him as he settled down next to me.

His chuckle was almost enough to warm me as he raised his arm in invitation and I moved into him. He hissed. "Your nose is like ice, woman," he complained as I nuzzled my cold face into his throat.

My arms wrapped around his strong torso and I sank fully into his hard body as his arms pulled me tight.

Safe.

That was the word that clanged through my mind.

For the first time since my parents died, I felt safe.

Emotion clogged my throat and I swallowed hard, trying to focus on Ramsay's heat and not on my emotional reaction to him.

"You're so warm," I whispered, lifting my head from his throat to look at him.

He peered down at me in the dim light of the solar lamp.

"I've always run a wee bit hotter than normal," he murmured.

I grinned. "You are very hot."

Ramsay's lips twitched. "Are you going to use this situation as an excuse to flirt with me, Silver?"

"Are you really opposed to it?" I teased.

"Go to sleep," he ordered instead.

"I will ..." I held my breath, my heart suddenly pounding in my ears as bravery took over me. "If you tell me you're not attracted to me too."

Considering I was totally opening myself up to painful rejection, I stiffened with anticipation in his arms.

Ramsay searched my face, his hold on me tightening ever so slightly. "I can't tell you that."

I sucked in a breath, shivering with aroused triumph.

My gaze dropped to his mouth, surrounded by that trim beard. Slowly, slowly enough to give him time to object, I moved my head toward his. My breathing shallowed as the storm raging outside fell away and it was only me and Ramsay McRae.

A man I'd wanted to kiss from almost the moment we'd met.

The space between us disappeared and finally, eventually, my lips touched his. Just a tingling, tentative brush of mouth against mouth. His beard tickled my chin. I shivered again but not with the cold as I pulled back ever so slightly to look into his eyes.

He stared back.

Not objecting.

Waiting.

I held his gaze as I brushed my lips over his again.

His hands flattened against my lower back, fingertips putting a little pressure on me.

Not pushing me away.

He watched me with that intense stare as I whispered my lips over his again and arousal flushed through me, tingles of need exploding between my thighs.

From a barely there kiss.

My breathing turned jagged, and he pressed me closer.

This time when I brushed my mouth over his, I let my tongue touch his lips.

Suddenly I was on my back, his weight over me as he slammed his mouth over mine.

His tongue pushed into my mouth, licking mine in a kiss that had gone from barely there to full-on erotic. Ramsay McRae kissed me like he wanted to fuck me.

I groaned, my fingers sliding into his hair to pull him deeper, to kiss him back as thoroughly as he kissed me. My thighs parted, inviting him between them.

The hard heat of his arousal pushed against me, and I moaned as a flood of wet dampened my underwear. I'd never been this turned on in my life.

Ramsay ripped his mouth from mine, his breathing ragged as he gaped at me, shocked.

"Don't stop."

"Too complicated," he muttered, even as he glowered at my swollen mouth like he wanted to taste me again.

"I don't want complicated either," I said. "I ... I want ... an escape."

"You promise?" He searched my eyes. "You promise you understand what this is? And what it isn't?"

"I do." My chest heaved with excitement. "Please."

Ramsay bowed his head, taking a deep, ragged breath. "Not here."

No!

"Ramsay ..."

He lifted his head. "I'm not fucking you in this bed."

Frustration ripped through me. "Then you're going to have to bear witness to me getting myself off because I'm about to explode over here."

I was just as surprised as he was by my forthright words.

His lips curled at the corners. "I think I can help you out with that."

Shivering with want, I let out a sigh of relief as he tugged at the button on my jeans. My hips undulated into him as he pulled down the zipper and my belly rippled with anticipation at the feel of those calloused fingertips on my skin.

My hands curled into his shirt, tightening around the fabric as he dove beneath my underwear and hit wet.

Ramsay grunted, tensing against me. "You're fucking soaked, woman."

"Mmm." I arched my hips eagerly.

"From a kiss?" He pressed his lips to the corner of my mouth as his fingers found my swollen clit.

"I want you," I had no shame in admitting.

His groan filled my ears a second before it rumbled down my throat as he crushed his mouth over mine. He kissed me like it would be the last time. Thoroughly, hungrily. Fucking me with his mouth as his thumb rubbed over the slickened bundle of nerves between my legs.

The scent, feel, and sound of him overwhelmed my senses, and it didn't take long for the tension coiling inside me to build toward its breaking point.

I broke our kiss to pant, "I'm going to come."

"I want to feel it," he purred as he traveled downward to push inside me. His fingers were so thick, I could only imagine what his cock would feel like.

The very thought sent me over the edge and my orgasm ripped through me, my inner muscles clenching and unclenching around him as he finger-fucked me.

"Silver," Ramsay growled against my lips, murmuring my nickname over and over as he thrust in and out while I continued to shudder around them.

Eventually when my body stopped shaking from my climax, he gently removed his hand from my underwear. I reached for him through his jeans, his arousal straining his zipper. But he covered my hands.

"Not here." He pulled me into his arms, settling my leg over his hip so we were as close as two people could get without him being inside me. His hard-on pushed between my legs, renewing those tingles of lust. At my confusion, he tipped my chin to hold my gaze. "I can wait. When we get back to Glenvulin, I *will* feel that tight pussy of yours come around my cock. But for now, sleep."

I flushed at his blunt dirty talk, my body deciding for me that I liked it. "You're hard," I whispered the obvious.

"It'll settle eventually. Sleep." He pressed my head to his chest, and I snuggled against him, arching closer.

He grunted but said no more.

Within seconds, I was asleep in his arms.

18. Ramsay

"It's looking good."

I turned from taking a swig of water to find Quinn studying the built-in wardrobe in the smaller of the guest rooms. Akiva got up from her spot in the corner to get a rubdown from my partner.

Silver wanted hanging room and a place to put folded items, so I was creating both within the same tiny space. It allowed us to put in interior walls to provide the rooms with small adjoining bathrooms. All the plumbing and plasterwork for those were done. Our team worked fast and efficiently, which allowed me to get in and do what I was good at.

The bathroom fixtures were ordered and would arrive in two weeks, so I wanted to get as much of the woodwork done as I could before work really started in the en suites.

"Aye. Only two more rooms to go."

"You're not tired after last night?" Quinn gave Akiva one last pat before he straightened and my dog wandered out into the hall.

Hearing the smirk in Quinn's tone, I shrugged, pretending indifference. "Nah."

Silver and I had woken early in the bothy. She'd slept after I'd made her come, but I'd only gotten a few hours of shut-eye. It didn't matter. I didn't sleep long hours on a normal day. The storm petered off toward sunrise and I'd woken the warm woman in my arms and reluctantly dragged her out of bed. We hadn't spoken about what occurred, but the tension crackled in the air between us.

It took us almost ninety minutes to make it to the ferry dock, just in time to meet the islanders leaving for Glenvulin.

Donal stopped us before we got on my boat and asked Silver if she was all right. He explained he'd driven me to the bothy, something I'd forgotten to tell her, so caught up in this fucking inescapable attraction between us.

Touched by his concern, Silver had apologized for missing the ferry and kissed Donal's cheek in thanks. The man's ruddy face turned even ruddier, and he gruffly told her to "Get on with yourself," but I could see he was pleased by her attention.

She had that way about her.

A warmth that drew people.

Made them care.

Made me care.

Fuck.

Silver was quiet, contemplative, on our way back to Glenvulin, and I wondered if she regretted what had happened in the bothy.

After we'd disembarked at Leth Sholas harbor, I'd walked her down Main Street, nodding to locals as we passed, and stopped outside of the building I'd had under surveillance.

For perhaps the first time in a very long time, I wanted to let my sensible, logical side go piss in the wind when it came to Tierney Silver.

I wanted her.

And I knew if she still wanted me back, I was going to have her.

I refused to acknowledge the relief that had poured through me when Silver turned to meet my eyes and boldly asked me to come to her place that night.

"I'll pick you up instead," I'd replied gruffly. "Take you over to mine." My gaze had crawled up the building, assessing it. "We can't be loud here."

Her breath hitched and when I'd returned my attention to her, her eyes were filled with desire. "Tonight." She'd nodded with a small smile filled with the knowledge of her feminine power. Then she disappeared inside, and it had taken everything within me not to follow her up those stairs.

"Did something happen between you and Tierney on Kiln last night?" Quinn asked now.

I studied my friend, thinking not for the first time that he would have made a good spy. He was more perceptive than most if he could read me.

"Aye." I didn't want to lie to him. "Not sex. But something. It isn't serious."

He raised an eyebrow. "So you're going to sleep with her?"

I nodded because Quinn was about the only bloody person on the planet I didn't have to lie to and wouldn't.

"I won't tell you what you already know." Quinn considered me. "But the fact that you're letting your dick rule you should tell you something here."

Hiding my irritation, I asked blandly, "Like what?"

"That maybe it isn't your dick that's ruling you after all ... but something else entirely."

I sneered at the insinuation. "Believe me, it's only sex."

"If it was only sex, you'd find someone else."

"She's young, she's beautiful, and she wants to fuck me. Could you resist that?"

Quinn narrowed his eyes like he knew I was deliberately being an arsehole. "I hate to bloat your ego, McRae, but there are plenty of young pretty things who'd like to fuck you. You could have your pick and you know it."

I scowled, turning away. "Look ... if you think this will interfere with our business ..." I could barely spit the words out, "I'll finish it before it starts."

Honestly, I think Quinn stayed silent so long just to torture me. "Nah," he finally said with a sigh. "This is probably going to blow up in your face, but Tierney isn't the type of woman to take it out on me. She won't fire us because of you. But be careful. She's been through a lot and doesn't deserve to be used."

I whirled on him. "Is that what you think? That I'm using her?"

"You won't mean to."

"Tierney Silver is a grown woman. She's the one who doesn't want complicated."

Quinn shook his head. "Ramsay ... I know you know better than that." He walked out before I could reply.

Staring at the work I'd done, my mind roiled with Quinn's veiled remark. Frustration built with every second because he was right, wasn't he? Was Silver really a casual fuck kind of woman?

Maybe I did need to call this thing off before it got started.

I contemplated it as I moved through the house in search of my dog.

Then I spotted her as I crossed what would become the dining room out onto the garden. Akiva was outside with Silver. My dog was tugging her around the garden with the stick in her mouth while Silver laughed. It was a warm day after the storm and she wore only a tank top with her jeans. Her breasts strained against the material, bouncing with her laughter in a way that sent blood rushing to my dick.

As if she felt me, Silver suddenly turned, squinting against the sun.

Recognition lit her face and she gave me a sultry smile.
A visceral need tightened in my gut.
How long had it been since I wanted someone this much?
Ever?
Fuck it, I thought gruffly.
Tonight Tierney Silver would be mine.

19. TIERNEY

I was wearing a summer dress.

With my sneakers.

There hadn't been a day since I'd moved to Scotland when I hadn't worn jeans, and I found the dress in the back of my closet. Most of my stuff was in storage, but I'd packed a couple of nice dresses in case.

Tonight was my first "in case."

Still, I couldn't quite bring myself to don a pair of matching heels, considering we were taking Ramsay's boat over to Stòr. But I wanted to wear a dress. My legs were my best feature. At least I thought so, and people had told me over the years that I had great legs.

Ramsay hadn't gotten a chance to see my best feature and although he would have eventually, I wanted to look and feel good tonight.

The dress paid off.

As Ramsay helped me down into his boat that evening, his gaze was practically glued to my legs.

Ramsay waved away my offer of assistance, so I sat in the

boat and Akiva rested her head on my lap. Ramsay untied the small vessel from the dock and then started the engine. He drove us over to Stòr without saying a word. I noted his wet hair and the fresh scent wafting toward me. He'd showered somewhere. Probably at Quinn's.

Instead of being nervous about his renewed taciturnity, I enjoyed the cool breeze off the water and the way the sunset sparkled across the sound in deep pinks and mauves. I wanted to talk about how this was my first pink sunset in Scotland, but nerves clamped my mouth shut.

Last night I hadn't been nervous. Some bold woman overtook my body, and I was more forthright with Ramsay than I'd ever been with any man. That's how much I wanted him.

Now, however, I had butterflies.

And I didn't know why.

We were heading over to his island to have sex. There would be no rejection.

He wanted this too.

Right?

Looking back, it was ridiculous of me to worry that a grown-ass man with such decided opinions as Ramsay McRae would ever do anything he didn't want to do, but in that moment, my insecurities got the better of me. Because the man had not said a single word since he'd picked me up from my apartment. His damn dog showed me more affection!

Hadn't Ramsay told me before I was too young?

Too sweet.

Maybe he was remembering that I wasn't his type after all.

To my surprise, we didn't pull in to the small dock at the white cottage. Ramsay had a second dock closer to his house. Once we were safely anchored, he wordlessly helped me onto shore and Akiva ran ahead.

I tried to catch Ramsay's eye, but he avoided it.

Shit.

Then ...

He wrapped his big hand around mine, his callouses scraping deliciously against my skin, and he led me upward through the thicket of grass and onto a trail through the woodlands. With his free hand, he switched on his phone's flashlight and led us through the woods.

Biting my lip against a cheesy, girlish grin, I followed, my gaze veering between the path in front of us and his hold on my hand.

It felt like forever since someone had held my hand.

An ache scored across my chest.

Akiva barked in the distance and I understood why when the trees opened up to the clearing and Ramsay's home. His beautiful dog stood on the porch, impatiently waiting to be let in.

Ramsay's fingers tightened around mine and I hurried to keep up with him as he marched up to the house.

He cut me a look as he dropped his hold on me to open the door. "I need to feed Akiva first and then I'll cook us something."

That was the plan, after all.

He would be gentlemanly enough to feed me first.

But as we walked into his home and I drew in his scent, a need tightened in my belly and tingles awakened between my legs.

Ramsay moved around his kitchen, grabbing Akiva's dinner dish to feed her the organic dog food I knew he spent a fortune on. That was partially why her coat was so shiny and perfect. Affection warmed me. I loved how much he loved his dog.

He lowered to put the dish before her, his shirt stretching across his broad, muscled back as he reached out to pet her. "That's it, sweetheart. Good girl," he murmured as she ate.

Then he stood and turned to face me. His eyes dropped to my bare legs and traveled slowly upward until I felt like my knees were blushing from his intense perusal. When his gaze caught on my breasts, they seemed to tighten against the fabric of the dress, my nipples peaking into needy little buds.

"I know I promised dinner first ..." His voice was hoarse with sexual want. "But if I don't get inside you soon, I might lose my fucking mind."

Triumph—exultant, smug triumph—flooded me along with wet arousal. "I've wanted you inside me since the first time I walked through this door. Dinner can wait."

His eyes narrowed. "You should know I like to be in charge. If you don't like something we're doing, we stop, but otherwise when we're in there"—he indicated toward the bedroom with a jerk of his chin—"I'm the boss."

I shivered with excitement and knew I could probably come with his rumbling those three words in my ear. "Okay."

"To clarify, anytime we're having sex, whether it's in that room or bent over a table, I'm the boss."

An erotic image filled my mind, and I sucked in a breath. "Have you been thinking about bending me over a table?"

Ramsay took a step toward me. "Every time you lie and evade about the threats against you, I've wanted to bend you over the nearest surface and smack your arse until you tell me the truth."

"Oh." I wheezed out as my arousal deepened.

Funny. If Hugh or any ex had said such a thing to me, I probably would have sneered at them and told them to go fuck themselves.

Ramsay threatening to spank me ... okay, wow.

New kink activated.

What was happening to me?

His lip curled at the corner. "Then I'd fuck you until you screamed for me."

"Let's just ..." My skin felt like fire. "Let's just skip dinner."

He considered me, drawing his thumb over his bottom lip as his gaze swept over my body again. I shivered as his pale wolf eyes turned smoky.

Finally, he crossed the room to stand inches from me. He was so close I could feel the heat of him, smell that earthy sandalwood that made me want to bury my nose in his throat. Ramsay reached out and slipped his fingers beneath the right strap of my dress, his rough fingertips stroking my collarbone. "Did you wear this for me?"

I tilted my chin, something about his tone sparking my defiance. "What if I did?"

"Dress, jeans, bin bag ... Whatever you wore tonight was coming off as soon as we walked in this door." And true to his word, he grabbed the hem of the dress and I had the presence of mind to raise my arms as he yanked the material up and over my head.

He threw the dress behind him and it hit the sofa. Ramsay was too busy eating me up with his eyes to care he'd casually discarded a dress that cost more than most people's car payments.

I stood in a lacy matching bra and panties that I'd never wear on any normal occasion. Truthfully, I was Miss Comfort when it came to underwear. Cotton briefs all the way. But I'd dug out a peachy-pink sexy number that suited my coloring. Considering his domineering attitude, it occurred to me Ramsay was probably used to women who wore overtly sexual lingerie. Perhaps Ava wore red or black lace or didn't wear underwear at all.

Maybe my peachy-pink number was more girlish than sexy.

My jaw clenched in self-irritation as Ramsay drank in every inch of me.

I'd never been insecure about sex.

The reality was I'd slept with four men in my twenty-seven years and all of them had been disappointing. The closest I'd come to orgasming with a partner was with Hugh. My first three boyfriends were all very similar. Nice, good guys. But they'd also been very considerate during sex. Very gentle. And it wasn't until I confessed my frustration to London that she told me that because I was kind of an alpha in life, I probably needed someone more dominant than me in bed.

So I'd gone on a date with Hugh, despite my misgivings about him.

He wasn't particularly kind or gentle. But he was confident, self-assured. And he took what he wanted in bed. While I'd definitely been more aroused by him ... he was ultimately a selfish lover. He wanted blow jobs ... but he didn't like going down on a woman.

That was fine.

Just don't expect blow jobs in return, right?

And now here I was finally about to have sex with a *man* and his mere warning that he took control in the bedroom had soaked my lace panties through.

Yet, for the first time, I wondered if *I* wasn't going to be what *he* needed.

I didn't like that.

Suddenly, Ramsay took me by the chin and tilted my head back, his eyes searching mine. "Where did you go?"

Surprised by his perceptiveness, I moved to retreat and his grip on my chin tightened.

"Don't lie. Not in this."

Oh God. I didn't want to ruin the moment between us by being honest.

"Silver ... we don't do this unless you're absolutely certain you want to."

I knew that without a doubt. That with Ramsay, even if

he was "in control," I'd always be the one really in control. If I said no or stop at any point, we'd stop.

I trusted him and at once realized I hadn't trusted anyone like that since London and my parents. Not even Cammie or Quinn.

Why him? What was it about him that made me feel so goddamn safe?

"Silver."

I could feel Ramsay withdrawing, and I wrapped my hand around his thick wrist to stop him. "I've never worried about not being good in bed before ... because ... well, quite frankly, I haven't had the ..." I sucked in a breath and bravely spat out, "I haven't been with the right men before. I've maybe orgasmed once with a guy and the rest have been self-induced. Other than last night with you, I mean. Maybe it's a *me* problem."

His expression tightened.

I smirked unhappily. "I'm standing here in my underwear realizing you're probably very experienced and ..."

"And what?" Ramsay took hold of my hand that was wrapped around his other arm and gently lowered it until I cupped his arousal straining against his zipper. "I want you. You want me. Experience has nothing to do with it. Get out of your head and get in there." He jerked his chin toward his bedroom. "Wait for me at the foot of the bed."

The instinct to balk at his command was strong, even as arousal blossomed within me with immediate intensity. It was a confusing dichotomy and his lip curled as if he read that flash of defiance in my eyes and liked it.

"Go."

I pulled my hand free and reminded him through clenched teeth, "You get to boss me around, but only with sex."

His answering cocky grin almost melted me. "Aye, I can't imagine otherwise. Now go."

Despite his gruff delivery, his words had soothed my insecurities, and I found my hips swaying in invitation as I strode across his home and into his bedroom. I'd snooped in here the last time, thinking it very utilitarian. Bed, bedside tables, integral closets, and an en suite.

His bed, unsurprisingly, was made of solid oak. There were no throws or throw pillows.

Nothing feminine.

Except me in my peachy-pink lacy number as I turned to face the door and wait for him. I heard him mutter to Akiva and realized he was making sure she had everything she needed before he stepped into the bedroom and shut the door behind him. He'd kicked off his boots already.

Our eyes met and held, and there was that electric spark that had existed between us from the very first moment we'd met.

Holding my gaze, Ramsay pulled off his Henley and threw it to the floor.

I sucked in a breath, breaking his stare to take in his strong, broad chest. His biceps were bulky and sculpted, as were his pecs. But he didn't have some superhero eight-pack or even a six-pack. He was rock hard and defined, but in a manly, natural way. His chest was lightly furred and a happy trail led downward to what I knew was going to be a generous surprise waiting for me in his boxers.

He was sexy as fuck.

He was a *man*.

And when he unbuckled his belt slowly, pinning me in place with those wolf eyes, my inner muscles clenched with anticipation. My underwear was a goner.

Ramsay's lips curled as if he could read what undressing in front of me was doing to my body. Cocky Scotsman.

The sound of his zipper seemed overtly loud and sexual,

and I licked my lips, devouring him as he shoved down his jeans and boxer briefs and stepped out of them.

His cock ...

I didn't even know if I'd fit my hand around it.

It strained toward his abdomen, swollen and big.

Big man, big cock.

I clenched my hands into fists at my sides. "What now?"

20. Tierney

"Undress."

One word. A command.

Guttural. Needful.

Oh yeah, my Scotsman was as turned on as I was.

Feeling playful, I hesitated. "You don't want to do it?"

His eyes flashed. "Not tonight. Undress. Now."

"And then what?"

"And then I'm going to prove to you that you don't have a 'me problem.'" He referred to my words earlier. "We all have different ... tastes and needs. I like to be the one in control while we fuck. I like a woman to give up her control to me. It's what gets me off." He cocked his head in consideration. "But some people prefer to be the one giving up the control. Most people spend their days shouldering their world by themselves. Not having to think or lead when it comes to sex is a relief. To have their partner make the decisions for them. It's what gets them off. And there are different levels of that."

"Like ... BDSM?"

"Aye."

"Is that what you're into?"

"I wouldn't label myself as a dominant. I don't live that lifestyle. But I have a wee bit of kink in me." He flashed me that cocky grin. "Most folks do. *You* do. Take off your knickers. Now."

Shivering at his command, I slowly rolled the lacy fabric down over my hips and legs.

"Give them to me."

Biting my lip and squeezing my thighs together, I handed over the underwear.

As soon as his fingers touched them, Ramsay's eyes heated. "Soaked. Do you know why?"

I waited.

"Because you're one of those women who spends her days making all the decisions, carrying the weight of the world on her shoulders ... and you don't want to think when it comes to sex. You need someone to tell you where to stand, when to bend over, and how loud to scream."

My breathing grew ragged as my arousal intensified.

He was right.

He was so goddamn right.

"You don't have a 'me problem.' You just want a domineering bastard in your bed." He took a step toward me. "Domineering bastard at your service and happy to oblige. Now take off the bra."

I unclipped it and let it drop to the floor.

My nipples puckered in the cool air and Ramsay's tongue touched his lower lip like he was imagining taking them into his mouth. *Yes*, I almost begged.

Instead I waited for his next order.

He bridged the distance between us, his cock a heated prod against my stomach. Gripping the back of my neck, he tilted my head with a slight jerk that made me whimper, a wanton sound he muffled as he crushed his mouth over mine to kiss me. Hungrily. His beard abraded my skin, and I pressed my hands to his chest, curling my fingernails into his pecs as I held on, trying to meet his voracious kiss with my own.

God, he was even dominant in that.

It turned into a battle until I nipped his lip in aroused frustration and he released me, only to grip my face between his fingers and thumb. He studied me, breathing harshly against my lips.

"Are you going to play nice?"

Feeling wetness against my stomach where his cock pushed into me, I smirked. "I think you like me a little rebellious."

He grunted and released me. "Lie on the bed and spread your legs."

Skin flushed hot, I didn't even bother to countermand him. I was beyond ready.

I lowered my ass to the bed and slowly pushed backward until I was in the middle of it. My breath caught as Ramsay stroked himself in languid, loose-fisted pulls, watching me as I lay back on his bed, my arms bent, hands at either side of my head. Then I opened my thighs.

"Wider."

As another flood of wet surged, I stared at the ceiling in disbelief. Never in my life had I been this turned on.

"Look at me."

I lowered my gaze to his.

"Keep your eyes on me as I eat your pussy."

A little hiss of need escaped.

"No touching or I stop."

I nodded in agreement, though my brow wrinkled in confusion.

Did he not like to be touched?

"You'll touch me when I want you to touch me," he said as if he'd read my mind. "Just not right now."

I nodded again, too breathless to speak.

Then he was on the bed, his big hands pushing my thighs even wider. He reached beyond me for a pillow, and I huffed with impatience as he propped my hips on it to give him better access.

Then his lips were soft, gentle even, on my inner thigh, his beard tickling the sensitive skin there.

"Oh."

It was unexpected and seductive.

And lulled me into a false sense of what was about to happen.

Suddenly, he gripped my thighs, pushing my legs up and open wider as he dragged his tongue through my wetness.

A cry of surprise slipped between my lips as I held his gaze.

His eyes had turned to smoke. "You are fucking soaked. This is what you need, isn't it?"

"Yes."

"Are you going to come for me, Silver? Are you going to explode around my tongue as I fuck you with it?"

I nodded, frantically. "Please."

His answer was to push his tongue inside me.

"Oh my God!" I threw my head back at the sensation.

Then suddenly his tongue was gone. "I said look at me."

My eyes flew back to his.

He scowled. "You keep your eyes on me as I eat you out or I stop."

Remembering his earlier command, I nodded again.

He covered me with his mouth, his tongue searching until it found my incredibly swollen clit. He drew it between his teeth and tongue and sucked. Sensation ripped through me, and it took everything in me to hold his gaze as I cried out with the building tension.

I saw his satisfaction blaze in his eyes as he sucked harder.

"Ramsay!" My fingers clenched into the duvet beneath me.

He released my clit to push his tongue in me, his grip on my thighs bruising as he toyed with me. This wasn't how it had been with my boyfriends who had gone down on me because I'd been kind enough to give them a blow job. This wasn't a half-assed "returning the favor" moment.

Ramsay got off on this.

Got off on me squirming with building desire.

Got off on how wet and aroused I was for him.

His eyes flashed with triumph as his mouth and tongue moved over me.

The orgasm exploded.

Shocked by the intensity of it, I screamed.

Because I knew what that meant now.

Exploded.

Until that moment, I hadn't.

But right then, it felt like every part of my body was splitting apart from the center, the pleasure zinging through every nerve as I unwittingly broke eye contact, my lower body shuddering against Ramsay's face, my stomach muscles flexing uncontrollably.

When the aftershocks finally settled (and not fully—my inner muscles still fluttered like they knew they still needed to be satisfied by his cock), I melted into the bed.

I gasped as the pillow was ripped out from under my hips and Ramsay moved over me, reaching past me to his bedside drawer.

He pulled out a string of condoms and ripped one off, throwing the rest on the pillow above my head. My thighs spread without command as he moved between them, ripping the condom packet open.

With ease of practice, Ramsay smoothed the protection over his cock and then slid his hands under my ass to shift me up the bed. "Grab the headboard."

I reached above me and wrapped my hands around the

slatted frame, tugging my body up a little until I was more comfortable. "Did you build this headboard specifically with this in mind?" I teased.

Ramsay smoothed his roughened palms up my torso to cup my breasts. I arched into his touch as he brushed his thumbs over my nipples in teasing strokes. "I've never fucked anyone in this bed."

Oh.

I didn't know what to make of that.

His eyes gleamed. "But I can't say I didn't imagine tying a woman's wrists to the headboard when I built it."

"Do you ... do you want to tie me to it?"

"Aye." He squeezed my breasts. "Aye, one day. For now, you hold on to the headboard and you don't let go. Or I stop."

"I'm sensing a pattern," I hissed as his cock brushed my sex.

"Aye ..." He leaned down to brush his lips over mine. "And by how hard you came, suffice it to say, you fucking love it."

My grip on the headboard tightened. "You know I do, you arrogant bastard."

Ramsay grinned and sat up but only to take my thighs in his hands and lift my hips to meet his cock. Suddenly remembering how big he was, I tensed.

"Relax. I'll fit." He nudged into me slowly, his voice deepening to a growl. "You'll take all of me, Silver, and love it."

Yes, yes, yes!

"Tell me what you need."

"Ramsay!"

"Say the words." He stopped working into me. "Say the words."

God, the man had an annoying amount of willpower. "I need your cock," I huffed out.

"Where do you need it?"

"Inside me."

"Inside where?" he teased mercilessly.

Oh God. My cheeks flushed. "You say it!"

Thankfully, he didn't push me on it. "You need my cock in this tight wee pussy, is that right?"

My inner muscles squeezed, desperate to feel him. "Yes!"

With a grunt, Ramsay thrust into me, my swollen inner muscles clamping down on him like a pleasure-pain vise. My back arched, my hips rocking forward to pull him in as I cried out at the thick intrusion.

My grip on the bedframe bordered on superhuman.

"Easy," Ramsay said gruffly as I tensed around him.

He was overwhelmingly thick.

"Just relax. Relax around me, Silver. That's it." His big hand smoothed down my thigh and gently urged my ass up.

"Oh!" The shift in position drew him deeper in. "Ramsay!"

"I know." He bowed his head, not moving any farther. "Fuck, you're tight."

That was good, though, right?

"You feel amazing." He pulled out ever so slightly, the muscle in his jaw clenching as his hot eyes met mine. "Your pussy's heaven, Silver. God, I want to fuck you until I can't see straight."

"Then do it."

"In a minute." He rocked slowly in and out and my toes curled as pleasure zipped down my spine.

"Please," I begged. I needed more.

"I will, but you need to get used to me first." He kept up that steady, gentle rocking that tightened the coil of tension inside me.

Finally, I couldn't take it.

"More!"

"Aye." His eyes blazed. "You're ready now. Hold on tight."

He tugged my thighs around his hips, his grip unyielding, and then he began to fuck me. His teeth gritted, his cheeks flushing, his stomach muscles rippling as he drove in and out of me in powerful thrusts.

It was too much.

The sight of him, the feel of him, the scent of him. The way my breasts bounced vigorously with his rough fucking. The way his eyes roamed over my breasts and face, his hunger visceral and pouring into me. The thick drag of him in and out …

My climax ripped through me and Ramsay grunted as my pussy throbbed around him.

But he kept going.

He kept thrusting with a determination and stamina that floored me.

"You'll come again," he commanded through gritted teeth. "You'll suck the come out of me with this tight wee pussy."

My inner muscles clenched around him in response. "Ramsay!"

"Is this what you need?" He panted, his chest gleaming with a sheen of sweat. "You need my cock to fuck you into oblivion, Silver?"

"Yes!"

"My cock." He lowered over me suddenly, one hand wrapping around the bedframe, while the other cupped my left breast and squeezed. His biceps strained against his hold on the frame as he snapped his hips harder, faster. "It's my cock you need." His breath puffed over my lips. "Say it."

"Yours," I gasped in agreement, drawing my thighs up around his waist as the tension tightened inside of me.

"My cum." He pounded harder, his teeth flashing. "Fuck, I'd give anything to come in you bare, woman. Watch my cum spill out of your pussy." His gaze dropped to between us, watching himself thrust in and out as his filthy words pushed me closer to climax. "Look at you take me." His gaze moved back to my face. "The sweet wee princess likes to be fucked dirty and hard."

Just like that, I shattered around him, my inner muscles throbbing with such force he grunted as I inadvertently pushed his cock out.

"Fuck!" His eyes widened and his hips snapped, thrusting back into me with a forceful push. "Fuck!" His hands fell to either side of my head as he came, pumping inside me as I felt him release with a deep shudder into the condom. "Fuck," he muttered again, breathless. Then he ground his hips into me and met my gaze, his chest heaving. "Fuuuuuuck."

I laughed breathlessly as I finally let go of the headboard. "I'm going to take that to mean you enjoyed yourself."

Ramsay buried his head into the pillow by my neck, his chest still heaving against mine as I fluttered around his cock. Eventually, he lifted his head, and I turned to meet his eyes.

He seemed ... a little stunned, actually.

I tried not to be too smug. "You, sir, have a very dirty mouth."

His eyes roamed my face. "You liked it."

"I did." I blushed inwardly. "To my surprise."

"I liked how much you liked it."

"I got that impression." I grinned. "Came hard, huh?"

Ramsay's eyes gleamed with something that I might have called tender amusement on anyone else. "Look who's the cocky one now."

"Is this why you're so taciturn in real life ... you're merely saving it all for sex?"

At that, Ramsay threw his head back in laughter and it was the most beautiful sound I'd ever heard.

I clenched around him and his laughter faded out into a groan. "You're going to kill me, woman."

Staring up at his handsome face, my body replete in a way I'd never experienced, I saw him laughing in my mind again. Felt the way the sight caused an ache across my chest.

Oh boy.

If I was going to kill him ... Ramsay McRae was going to ruin me.

21. Ramsay

Not since my twenties had I been this raring to go again so soon after coming.

Only the reminder that Silver hadn't eaten before we traveled to Stòr got me out of bed. I pulled on some joggers and handed Silver one of my T-shirts to wear. Together, we stepped out of the bedroom. Akiva jumped off the couch with a bark and scrambled over to us for affectionate pets and reassurance. She would've heard the noise we were making and been confused by it most likely. More than anything, she was nonplussed that I'd kept her from the bedroom when usually she had free rein of the house.

I gave her one last pet and left Silver to shower my dog with affection while I made us French toast. Quick, easy. We could eat and then I could fuck her again.

I was already semi-hard just thinking about it.

Aye, there was no denying she and I had chemistry.

We settled at my small dining table. I enjoyed the way Silver kept shooting me pleased, hot looks in between each bite of her food.

The manipulative bastard I could be, I saw her soft, her

guard down, and I went in for the kill. I swallowed a bite of the eggy toast. "Who is threatening you?"

Silver's hazel eyes narrowed as she chewed. A few seconds later, she replied, "Did you think multiple orgasms unlocked your rights to know my business?"

Frustration irritated me. "Silver, this isn't a joke."

"I know it's not." She finished her toast and pushed the plate away. "We had sex, Ramsay. It doesn't mean I trust you with my big, dark secrets."

"You trust me," I uttered quietly with conviction.

Once upon a time, it had been my job to forge trust merely to break it. It meant I was almost always sure when someone was certain of me. And it meant nowadays I would rather cut off my own arm than break someone's trust.

Silver's certainty in me should have sent me running for the hills.

If I were a better man, I'd end it now.

Yet my blood burned hot for this woman. Insatiable. After so long of an almost numb contentment, feeling this level of *anything* was fucking addictive.

She sighed, lowering her gaze, hiding her expression. "Maybe I do. Trust you, that is. To a certain extent. But this secret isn't for me to tell." Silver looked up, eyes blazing. "The truth is going to come out. Everything will make sense soon. But I can't jeopardize the situation by telling anyone the truth just yet. Not even you."

Something strange ached in my chest.

It made me want to lash out at her.

I controlled the urge, recognizing I couldn't punish her for her honesty. "You think I'd spill your secrets, Silver?"

"No." I heard the sincerity in her answer and relaxed a little. "But like I said, this isn't only my secret to share, and I've made promises." She leaned toward me. "If I thought anyone would get hurt, I'd tell you. I'd tell the police everything. But it's not going to go that far. I promise."

"What about you? This person is only threatening you. Do you really believe *you* won't get hurt?"

She tilted her head to the side, contemplating me. Her hair slid over her shoulder, and I wanted to wrap the silky strands in my fist while I moved inside her again. "Do you care?"

Dangerous fucking question.

And she knew it.

In answer, I got up abruptly and grabbed our empty plates. As I dumped them in the sink, I ordered, "Get up and bend over the table."

"Are you serious? I've just eaten."

Considering the toast had merely been a light repast, I turned to face her and crossed my arms over my chest. "Do you want to come again or not?"

Silver's cheeks flushed and she slowly stood, muttering, "Arrogant, cocky bastard."

My lips twitched. "Bend over."

Arousal darkened her eyes. "I'm not wearing any underwear."

"I'm perfectly aware of that."

Her gaze dropped to my crotch where my cock proudly tented my joggers. "Well, you certainly have a lot of stamina for a man of your advanced years."

Little brat. I curbed my smile, covering it with a glower. "In ten seconds, I'm going to take care of my situation myself and leave you to deal with your own. Unless you bend the fuck over."

"You know you should really psychoanalyze why you are able to string together so many fully formed sentences when it comes to sex but not when it comes to normal, everyday conversation."

"I don't need to. It's called a calculated choice. Five, four, three—"

"Fine, God!" She adorably and somewhat hilariously sprawled herself across the table.

My amusement ended, however, when my T-shirt rode up over her perfect arse. The woman really did have the most astonishing pair of legs and arse.

"Are you happy?" Silver asked a little breathlessly, the right side of her face to the tabletop, her hands by her face. "I'm feeling very vulnerable right now, you asshole."

My lips twitched at the dirty comeback that immediately came to mind, but I let it slide as I crossed the room to her. My gaze flicked briefly to Akiva who was asleep on the couch and hopefully wouldn't interfere with what was about to happen.

Anticipation tightened in my gut as I cupped Silver's smooth, lush wee arse. Her breath stuttered as I caressed her gently, slowly, sliding my palms up her spine beneath the T-shirt and around to cup her tits.

"Ramsay," she murmured huskily, pushing her arse back into me, naturally spreading so I could stand between her legs.

I thumbed her hard nipples, looking forward to sucking on them until Silver writhed in my lap with unspent need. *Another time.*

Instead, I gave them one last caress and straightened.

Her gaze cut to me, her head lifting.

"Stay there."

She watched me take a condom out of my pocket. "You brought those with you from the bedroom?"

I did.

"You planned this?" Silver gaped. "To take me here?"

The corner of my mouth quirked and I deliberately didn't answer.

"This isn't the most comfortable, you know."

"In a minute, you'll feel differently."

Her eyes remained on my hands, watching me shove down my joggers to roll on the condom. "You're such an arrogant prick."

"You're full of compliments tonight, brat." I smacked her arse lightly, my cock throbbing not only at the flush it left behind but the shocked moan Silver emitted as she arched instinctively at the contact.

My heart raced a bit harder.

She was perfect.

I prodded my cock against her pussy and her fingernails curled into the tabletop. "Did you like that, Silver?"

"I ... I don't know ..."

Not wanting to push her too hard too fast, I eased back, squeezed her arse again, and drew my hand. It cracked against her skin, and she cried out. Her wide eyes flew to mine and she pushed up, putting her weight on her hands.

I thought for a second I'd misread her, dismay pushing through my arousal.

But she rocked her arse and whispered, "Again."

My hands shook with desire as I demanded, "Take off the T-shirt first."

Silver straightened to do just that, her tits bouncing as she jerked it off and threw it on the floor. Then she braced her hands on the table and stuck her arse out at me in invitation.

I took a mental snapshot of the erotic sight.

And then cracked a hand across her bottom once more.

"Oh!" She bowed against the table, moaning. "What the ..."

Gripping her hips, I guided my cock between her pretty thighs. "My wee heiress likes a spanking."

She looked over her shoulder at me, panting with arousal. "I guess so."

"But only naughty girls get spanked." I grinned wolfishly as I began to push inside her tight, perfect, wet heat.

Her breathing stuttered, arousal hooding her gaze. "Well ... I won't tell you my secrets. Isn't that a little naughty?"

Blood rushed in my ears as I groaned and pulled out. Unable to resist what she offered.

I spanked her harder this time and Silver moaned, thighs trembling, arms shaking to hold herself up. Gripping her nape, I used just enough force to press her down to the table. "Is that what you want?" I growled in her ear as I guided my cock with my other hand. "To be spanked and fucked until you can't remember your own name?"

"Yes!"

I thrust inside her, and she tried to move her hips but couldn't because I had her pinned.

She throbbed around me at the realization.

I squeezed her nape and rocked in and out of her. Her snug pussy dragged across every fucking nerve ending, but I controlled my drives. Slow, easy, but hard. Dominating. Like she wanted. Like she needed. Like I needed. Her body, however, instinctually tried to buck into my thrusts.

"Relax," I commanded. "Relax and take your fucking."

Silver groaned and did as she was told.

"Oh God, oh God," she whimpered. "I'm coming. I'm coming ..." Her pleasured cries filled the room as her inner muscles throbbed around me in tight-fisted tugs.

I released her nape to straighten, grabbing her hips to power harder, deeper. The sight of her sprawled across my table, her lower body shuddering with her climax, her lips parted on moans, and her gorgeous hair a tangled mess down her sleek spine ...

My orgasm hit me hard and I exploded, ropes of cum filling the condom.

Once we were both checked out, we were getting rid of the condoms.

I wasn't lying when I told her I wanted to watch my cum spill from her pussy.

I wanted her to see what she did to me.

That I might be the one in control ... but, fuck, she was the one with all the power.

Pulling out with a pleasured grunt, I shot a look across the room to see Akiva eyeballing us with distaste. I sent my dog a silent apology, disposed of the condom, and turned, pulling my joggers back up. Silver pushed off the table, her arse cheeks still pink.

"You all right?"

She chuckled, smoothing a hand down her breasts and torso. "Tabletops aren't the comfiest."

Remorse hit me. "Did I hurt you?"

Silver shook her head. "No, you were right, I forgot about the discomfort in favor of the stupendous orgasm."

"Still, bed next time." I gently reached out to caress a hand over her breasts.

She shivered into my touch, holding on to my arms. Her cheeks were still flushed with her climax. "I'm a little sore."

I pressed my hand to her pussy. "I didn't mean now. Where does it hurt?" I rubbed my thumb over her swollen clit, and she bowed into me, eyes fluttering.

"Ramsay!"

"Not there, then." I teased her, rolling her clit between my thumb and forefinger.

Her nails bit into my arms. "Oh my ... Ramsay ... Ramsay ..."

"That's right," I murmured against her lips as I rubbed harder at that bundle of nerves between her legs. "Say my name."

She shook her head. "I can't ... Again ... oh my ... Oh ... OH!" She arched into me, her expression tight with her coming orgasm. "Ramsay!" She shattered in my arms, and I caught her, wrapping her in my embrace.

Silver held on to me as her lower body shuddered.

I nuzzled against her ear, feeling her come. "Just a wee apology for the hard table."

She laughed hoarsely into my chest, melting into me.

Feeling her go limp, I quickly eased her into my arms, cradling her against my chest.

"Oh!" Her eyes widened ever so slightly and then she relaxed into me as I carried her into the bedroom and lay her gently down on the bed.

It would be the first time a woman had slept in this bed with me.

But I couldn't bear the idea of asking Silver to get dressed so I could take her back to Leth Sholas.

I told myself it was because I'd want her again in the morning.

That it was purely selfish, and I didn't care enough about her feelings to take care of them.

I'd always been good at lying to others.

As I got in bed beside her, pulling the duvet around us, letting Silver roll into my arms to rest her head on my chest … I remembered too late that I'd always been shit at lying to myself.

22. TIERNEY

The muscles in the back of my thighs made themselves known with a pulling ache as I climbed the hill to my B and B with coffee in hand. Two black Americanos — one for me, one for Ramsay. Last night, Ramsay had pushed my thighs to my chest as he fucked me. It looked like I'd need to restart Pilates if he was going to be bending me into different positions like that.

It was three days after we'd started our affair.

The day after our first night, I was sore enough from taking him that I needed a twenty-four-hour reprieve. Ramsay had looked so cocky about this, I wanted to smack the smirk right off his face and then ride him, despite the ache between my legs. Instead, I'd kissed him like I wanted to fuck him but wouldn't and he'd glowered at me afterward, knowing exactly my game.

The last two nights, however, we were back in business. I'd spent my evenings on Stòr being thoroughly distracted from the shitstorm of my life by the dirtiest, most thrilling sex I'd ever had.

In fact, I didn't know how I'd ever return to normal sex after this.

Would I have to have that awkward conversation with potential future partners—that I liked to give up control when it came to sex? That I liked to be ordered around and have filthy words whispered in my ear? That I liked to be *spanked*?

How did you even bring something like that up?

And surely it defeated the purpose to have to train my future partner to give me what I wanted in bed.

The very thought of being with anyone after Ramsay nauseated me.

Wasn't that a blaring alarm bell I shouldn't ignore?

Yet I did, in favor of enjoying my current favorite method of escapism.

Ramsay had dropped me off at my apartment this morning so I could change my clothes (I'd already showered with him, and let's just say things got a whole lotta dirty before they got clean) and check my emails while he continued onto the B and B. I had a bunch of texts from Cammie to whom I'd confessed. I'd quickly responded, planning to meet her this afternoon for a catch-up.

It had only been two hours since I'd seen Ramsay, and yet butterflies fluttered to life in my belly at the thought of seeing him again.

Those butterflies dropped dead as soon as I cleared the brow of the hill and saw Quinn talking to a guy in a suit in my large driveway.

That guy was Hugh.

What the hell was he doing here?

Blood whooshed in my ears. Not from fear. Not from mere annoyance.

From actual *fury* that this unwanted blast from my past was intruding on my new life. The very idea of his slimy ass anywhere near my island made me want to rip off his nuts. I marched toward him and Quinn. "What are you doing here?" I yelled accusingly.

The two men turned to face me.

Hugh looked immaculate in his three-piece suit, his hair quaffed to perfection. Skin smooth from weekly facials. Nails clipped and buffed and filed by the same aesthetician. He looked expensive. I knew without moving closer he smelled expensive too.

Yet Quinn towered over him by a couple of inches and a lot of bulk, his stubble screaming he needed a shave, wrinkles in the corners of his eyes from laughter and life, and his clothes and hands dusty and dirty from construction.

To me, my contractor looked like a million bucks and Hugh a snivelly little eel who needed to slither back from where he came from in his three-thousand-dollar suit.

My ex's expression hardened. "Me? Where the hell were you last night? The hotel owner said you lived on Main Street, but I got no answer and there were no lights on in your apartment."

My tone was filled with contempt. "You're stalking me now? Did the not answering your calls and blocking your number *three* times not send a clear enough message?"

Quinn's expression darkened. "See, I knew when he told me he was your boyfriend, there had to be a mistake."

Horror suffused me. "What? What reality are you living in?" I seethed at Hugh in disbelief. "No, Quinn, he's the slime who cheated on me back in New York. I dumped his ass almost a year ago, and he's been harassing me for the last few months. I have no idea what he's doing here now."

Hugh let out an exasperated huff. "I'm here to bring you back where you belong. I gave you time. What I didn't give you was permission to fuck off to Scotland and buy a piece of shit building on a fucking forgotten island!"

Was he insane?

I took a step toward Quinn, my hands clenched so tightly around the coffee cups, they leaked over the lid, dripping hot liquid down my hands. "Permission? I broke up with you and even before that, I didn't belong to you. I'm a free person who doesn't need permission from a spoiled brat who has never heard the word *no* in his life."

"We were only on a break, and *you* took off for Scotland. Despite that, I still came all the way here for you." He stepped toward me. "I've been patient. And this is how you treat me?"

"You're a narcissist," I whispered hoarsely, realizing there was no arguing with him. It was unbelievable to me that he'd made up this rhetoric about us in his mind. "You should probably see someone about that."

"You little—"

Quinn stepped in front of me, his tone threatening. "Take one more step toward her and I'll bury you in concrete."

A flush of gratitude moved through me.

"Look, you don't understand the situation here." Hugh spoke calmly now. "Tierney has been mentally unwell since her parents' death. *I'm* looking out for her."

"You bastard!" I dumped the coffee on the ground and then tried to shove past Quinn to punch this prick, but he held me back. "Breaking up with you does not constitute a mental health issue, Hugh. I didn't want to be with you anymore!"

He smirked. "No. But giving up millions of your inheritance constitutes it. So, unless you want me to petition the courts to place you under a conservatorship—which you know I'm perfectly capable of making happen—you're coming back with me. But first, you're going to tell me where you were last night."

"She was with me."

We all turned as Ramsay crossed the driveway and didn't stop his slow, menacing stride until mere inches separated him and Hugh. My ex had to take a step back and had the good sense to look nervous.

"Hugh Inchcolm. Heir to Pioneer Motors." Ramsay shocked me with his knowledge of who Hugh was. "Did I just hear you threaten Silver?"

"This?" Hugh spat at me. "You traded me for this?"

Ramsay's hand flashed out so fast, none of us saw it coming. He gripped Hugh by the throat and his feet scrabbled like a cartoon character's as Ramsay carried him across the drive to slam him against his Defender. Quinn held me back as Ramsay shoved his face in Hugh's. My ex looked terrified, his perfect hair mussed and falling over his forehead. "I know who you are, boy. I know what secrets are in your closet. And unless you want the police reopening the investigation into Michelle Schull's overdose ... you'll forget you know Silver."

Michelle Schull?

The tech heiress who overdosed six years ago?

Hugh turned a sickly green. "I ... I don't know what you mean."

"Oh, aye, you do. I've met many boys like you. You think you have power because of Daddy's money?" Ramsay sneered. "But you don't know anything about real power. With one phone call, I could make you disappear. Unlike you, I won't leave behind evidence. And dear old daddy isn't powerful enough to do jack squat about it." Then he leaned in and whispered something in Hugh's ear that made him literally tremble with fear.

What the hell was this about?

"Who are you?" Hugh asked hoarsely as Ramsay finally released him and stepped back.

"I'm the man who will hold you personally responsible if *any* harm comes to Silver. Do you understand?"

My ex shrugged his shirt and jacket into place and smoothed his hair. He shot me a look of arrogant fury. "When you realize you've fucked up your life and you come running back to New York, don't dare come running back to me too."

I was still vibrating with rage at his threat to put me under a conservatorship. "You're lucky I gave up those millions, Hugh. Otherwise, *I'd* make you fucking disappear for what you threatened me with."

He scoffed. "I can't believe I thought you were worth dragging myself to this godforsaken place. I hope you burn in hell here."

I felt Quinn's reassuring hand on my shoulder as Hugh began to march downhill.

"Oh, and, Inchcolm," Ramsay's voice carried toward him and Hugh stiffened.

He reluctantly turned and snapped, "What?"

Ramsay crossed his arms over his chest, casual, calm. Intimidating. His tone bland despite the words as he warned, "I've got eyes everywhere. You make any kind of move toward her and my face is the last one you'll ever fucking see."

Hugh's lips pinched together, and I knew him well enough to know he wouldn't take Ramsay's threat seriously until he looked into him. The question is, what would he find?

As my ex disappeared down the hill, Quinn pulled out his phone. My eyes were on Ramsay, but I reluctantly tore my gaze and thoughts (and a thousand questions) from him as Quinn spoke to the person on the other end of his call.

"Jack, it's Quinn. I need you to keep a look out for someone getting on the next ferry to the mainland. Male, thirties, American, dressed in an expensive suit—aye, that's the one. He came in yesterday, did he? Well, I need you to let me know as soon as he's dropped off on the mainland ... Aye ... okay ... thanks, Jack." He hung up, looking from me to Ramsay. "We'll know as soon as he's gone."

Ramsay nodded grimly, turning to me.

"What happened to Michelle?" I asked immediately.

She and I weren't close, but we'd partied a few times together. I knew she and Hugh had a thing before she overdosed. I'd always liked Michelle. People thought she was a vapid party girl. But I was one of the few people who knew her IQ was off the charts, courtesy of her genius father who owned one of the biggest tech companies in the world. I'd never heard Michelle say a bad word about anyone. Yet, I'd also thought she was broken somehow. She held a pain within, and I figured that's why she partied so much. It was her escape from whatever demons chased her, but we hadn't been close enough for me to find out more.

I remembered being at work the day the news broke. I'd only just returned from my South American jungle experience with London, and I'd started as GM at the hotel. The staff were gossiping about Michelle. I'd hid myself in a janitor's closet so I could cry without any of them seeing me. I'd been unsurprised by the news of Michelle's overdose, but I'd wished I'd tried harder to be her friend.

Now Ramsay had alluded that there was more to her death than meets the eye and that Hugh had something to do with it.

"I can't tell you that." He took a step toward me and even annoyed, I found myself wanting to lean into him. "Is Hugh the threat or is it something else?"

"I can't tell you that. You'll know the truth soon enough." Perri called yesterday afternoon. As per the legal process, they'd contacted the Silver Group to explain what story they'd be printing and ask for comment, and the company was scrambling their lawyers. It might delay the story going to print until all the legal stuff was signed off. "How did you know about Hugh and Michelle? Does it have something to do with your military background?"

Ramsay turned to Quinn. Whatever passed between them,

I was aware of Quinn departing, but I kept my gaze fixed firmly on the man I'd recently shared a bed with.

"Well?"

"Will you tell me if Hugh is the threat?"

"He's not the threat."

"Who is the threat?"

I clenched my jaw. "So you're saying if I don't tell you, you won't tell me how you got Hugh the narcissist to back off?"

"Is that your answer?"

"Ramsay ..."

He shook his head with an exasperated sigh. "You keep your secrets, Silver, and I'll keep mine." With that he gestured toward the house. "I want you inside where we can keep an eye on you until that bastard is off the island."

"Seriously? That's it?"

"It's your decision. You trust me to fuck you but not to protect you, that's entirely your prerogative. As it is mine to keep information to myself."

I huffed and strode past him toward the house. "Bullshit. You wouldn't tell me even if I told you who was behind the threats."

"Wrong. I would tell you."

I spun back around to face him as we reached the front entrance. "Would you tell me how you came by the information?"

He studied me carefully and then answered flatly, "No."

Hurt I wasn't sure I was allowed to feel rippled through me unpleasantly. I shrugged, hiding the emotion from him. "Then I guess I don't feel bad about keeping secrets." I turned and marched into the noisy house, intent on finding the farthest place in there to be from Ramsay right now.

Yet, that damned sense of gratitude my parents had instilled in me stopped me. I whirled around to find Ramsay in the messy large entrance that would become my reception, staring after me.

I shivered at the unguarded look on his face.

A worried expression he quickly blanked.

"Thank you," I gritted out. "For getting rid of him."

His mouth curled ever so slightly. "You can thank me later on your hands and knees."

The words echoed around the space and anyone who was close enough to hear over the noise would've heard him.

And they did.

A choked laugh from the dining room made me flush from the tip of my toes to my hairline.

I glowered at him. "You can forget it now!"

Ramsay laughed low and unbothered. "Aye, we'll see." Then he casually walked away.

"Cocky bastard," I muttered under my breath.

23. Ramsay

That was the problem with living on a small island.

Everybody eventually found out everyone's business.

It had been two weeks since Silver and I started having sex.

Now everybody fucking knew.

To be fair, it might have been my fault. I didn't know what I was thinking when I loudly made it clear what was between us at the B and B after Silver's ex showed up. I was self-aware enough to know I was thinking with my dick after that arsehole had triggered my territorialism. It was backward, it wasn't pretty, and I knew Silver wasn't mine.

But at that moment, she'd felt like mine to protect.

It still clung to me as she walked off without giving me her trust.

And now, because my pride was stung, I'd inadvertently let everyone know we were fucking.

They were smart enough not to ask me about us, but Silver told me she was treated to innuendo and outright interrogation from her neighbors about what was going on.

She had a charming way of telling folks to mind their own business without upsetting them.

I watched her now as I played the pipes. Silver watched me too, a heat in her eyes I recognized.

Aye, I was going to get very lucky tonight.

I didn't know why she found my pipe playing such a turn-on, but I wasn't going to question it.

We were in the middle of Johnny Harris's farm, about a five-minute drive from Leth Sholas. Every year during the summer, Glenvulin hosted a small wares festival for tourists, and Johnny rented one of his fields out to the council to use. Me and the lads were hired to play. Tents were put up around the large field and local craftspeople from all the islands came over to Glenvulin to sell their wares.

Silver had been excited about an antiques dealer from the mainland who was presenting a stall. She and Cammie had raced there first to look for stuff for the B and B. They must have finished up because they'd returned, Akiva at their side, to our stage to sit, drink ale, and listen to us play.

I noted locals glancing at her and grinning conspiratorially.

They could think what they wanted, I supposed.

What was between us was between us.

Whatever it was, I was nowhere near done having my fill yet.

In fact, this need for the bloody American had only gotten stronger every day.

The sex was ... it was fucking phenomenal.

That was saying a lot for a man who had sometimes used mind-blowing sex to unearth secrets.

I was pretty sure Silver was in agreement that she and I ... well ... best sex ever.

And yet, I still could not unearth *her* secrets.

At least there had been no more threats. She spent most nights on Stòr with me and on the nights the weather was too bad to chance even the short crossing, I'd stayed with her in her tiny flat.

My attention moved to Akiva who rested her head on Silver's lap, her eyes closed in a nap. My dog could sleep through anything, apparently. And she followed Silver everywhere.

My gut clenched with something like unease, and I looked away to focus on the music. There had been a couple of years the festival was delayed a day or two due to the weather. Another year it was cancelled completely. But the weather this summer had been some of the mildest I'd ever witnessed on Glenvulin, and today the sun was out, shining bright.

Everyone was in a great fucking mood because of it.

Even Quinn whose general mood had improved these last few weeks as he finally let go of the idea of making amends with Taran.

We finished the song and I announced, "Need a break. A drink. Back here in thirty?"

Quinn and the lads nodded, and we placed our instruments behind the stage for safekeeping. Murray and Laird headed off toward the beer stall. Quinn and Forde moved around the stage and walked toward Silver and Cammie before I could. Silver nodded at them in greeting but got up to wind her way through the chairs toward me with Akiva at her side.

"You sounded great," she said with a smile.

It had taken her a few days to get over being pissed about the secrets I was keeping from her. Silver knew it was hypocritical of her to stay mad at me and she compartmentalized things. She'd also told me she didn't believe in holding grudges. "You never know when the last time you'll see someone is. I don't ever want to have the regret of harsh words between me and the people I care about."

I didn't ask if that meant she cared about me.

But I liked her words.

I just ... I liked her.

That unease shifted through me again, but Akiva barked for attention, drawing me out of my darkening thoughts.

"Hey, sweetheart." I lowered to my haunches to give her a proper rubdown.

"I saw a piece at the antiques store I want your opinion on." Silver absentmindedly raked her nails through my hair, and I fought off a visceral, needful reaction to her touch.

I nodded and stood. "Show me."

A normal man would reach for her hand and guide her through the crowds of the festival. My fingers twitched as I watched Silver avoid bumping into a laughing couple. She tucked a strand of her hair behind her ear. Usually, Silver kept her hair up in a ponytail. It was only ever down when we were in bed. Today she wore it loose in a cascade of blond waves that glinted wheaten gold in the sun.

Heat tightened in my groin as I followed her hand when it dropped back to her side.

She'd never taken my advice to cut her nails, and I was glad for it. I loved the feel of them scratching down my back or digging into my arse as I took her hard.

When we met, I'd never imagined how perfect she'd be for me in that respect.

That she'd get off taking it how I loved to give it.

Fuck, she was making me insatiable. Like a teenager who couldn't get fucking off his mind.

I blew out a beleaguered breath and Silver heard it, even over the noise of the crowd.

Her head whipped to me. "You okay?"

"Aye," I bit out gruffly.

She frowned but let it lie.

Another thing I liked about her. She knew when and when not to push.

Suddenly, we were outside the antiques tent.

I raised an eyebrow. It must have been a small feat bringing all this stuff over from the mainland.

"That." Silver tugged on my arm and led me over to the back of the tent where a large Welsh dresser stood.

"How did she get this over?" I murmured.

"A large boat." A small, middle-aged woman appeared at my side.

"Is it worth it?"

"If your woman here buys it, it will be." She grinned cheekily.

I smirked. "I'm afraid that's not happening."

Silver smacked me gently on the stomach "Hey, why not?"

"It's not what you want." I frowned at the piece. "It's nothing like what you want."

"I can't find what I want."

Aye, which was why I'd finished crafting it for her. It was supposed to be a surprise. "Trust me. You'll find what you want."

She narrowed her eyes. "Oh really?"

"Aye, really."

"What are you up to?" She stepped into me, pressing her body to my side, her breasts pushing against my arm. "Have you done something that might be considered sweet and thoughtful, Ramsay McRae?"

My gaze dropped to her lush mouth. "Me. Never."

Her breath hitched at the low rumble in my words. A rumble she recognized.

"Are you buying the dresser or not?" the antiques owner asked from my other side.

I almost bared my teeth at the interruption. "Not."

Silver bit her lip to hide her amusement and leaned past me to answer politely, "That would be no, thank you."

"Fine." The woman made a huffing noise before she left us to engage with another customer.

Resting her hand on my chest, leaning deeper into me, Silver asked, "Did you build me a dresser?"

I sighed. "It was supposed to be a surprise."

Her eyes lit up. "Can I see it?"

"It's in my workshop."

"Maybe we should leave early." She ran her hand down my chest. "So I can see it and then thank you properly."

My words were hoarse as I fought to control my body responding to her invitation. "Sounds like a plan."

"How do you want your thanks?"

I narrowed my eyes and dropped my head to murmur the words against her lips. "My cock in your mouth."

She shuddered, eyes dilating.

"Silver." I squeezed my eyes closed and stepped back. "Not here, woman."

Her answering smile was smug. If I stayed in her vicinity right now, I was going to find a quiet spot behind a tent somewhere to fuck her.

"I'll see you in a few hours." I walked away abruptly, clicking my tongue for Akiva to follow me.

"Where are you going?" Silver called after me, laughter in her voice.

Vixen.

"Music to play!" I called back. "Places to fucking be that are not near you," I muttered. "Bloody death of me. Fucking forty years old, for fuck's sake."

"All right there, Ramsay?" Annie called out to me from a cheese stand. Amusement twinkled in her eyes.

"Fine."

"An awful lot of angry muttering going on there," she

insisted, her eyes darting toward the antiques seller's tent. "Someone got you in a bit of a tizz, has she?"

I bared my teeth at her in more of a grimace than a grin and strode off toward the stage.

Her laughter trailed behind me.

Bloody small-town living.

Why did I think moving here was a good idea?

24. Tierney

Our mingled panting filled Ramsay's bedroom as we came down from our energetic sex and subsequent mind-blowing orgasms.

I'd felt his sexual tension all day, to the point where he'd avoided me the rest of the festival, and then practically dragged me back to his boat like a caveman. As soon as we stepped inside his house on Stòr, he was on me. I didn't even get a chance to ask to see the dresser he'd apparently built for me.

Now, my inner muscles wouldn't stop quivering from the strength of my climax.

"Oh God," I moaned, pushing my hair back from my damp hairline.

The bastard Scot had brought me to the brink of orgasm so many times before pulling back until I was begging the asshole to make me come.

When he eventually did ... holy fucking fuck fuck.

Yeah, I was ruined.

He'd ruined sex with other men for me for the rest of my goddamn life, and I didn't even care. The experience with him was worth it.

Turning my head on the pillow to look at him, an aching pang lit across my chest. His eyes were closed, one arm flexed above his head on the pillow. He'd trimmed his beard so I could see all his rugged angles.

Ramsay McRae was the most beautiful man I'd ever met.

He'd scoff at that descriptor. Other people might even raise an eyebrow.

But to me he was beautiful.

And safe.

I thought of that Welsh dresser in his barn.

Maybe he wasn't as detached from me emotionally as he'd like to make out. I threw myself out of bed and chuckled at the way I swayed a little. There was a familiar throb between my legs, and I thought of that Ariana Grande song "Side to Side" as I crossed the room to pull on Ramsay's T-shirt.

"Where are you going?" His voice rumbled from the bedroom. He sounded relaxed. Content.

I loved that I could give him that.

"To check out my Welsh dresser."

Ramsay groaned. "Can it not wait?"

"Nope." I wandered out the door and stopped by the couch to pet Akiva who was now very used to our shenanigans. She kept out of the way but always looked at us when we reappeared as if to say *Again?* in what I imagined was beleaguered disgust.

She did, however, buss into my petting and when I crossed to the door, she hopped off the couch to follow me.

"Wait." Ramsay strode out of the bedroom, pulling up a pair of joggers.

My cheeks flushed at the sight of his gorgeous half-nakedness, his hair mussed from my fingers. Seriously, I was insatiable for him.

"Shoes." He pointed to my feet.

"I'll be fine."

"Shoes. There are wood shavings and pieces of metal in there. Shoes. Or I carry you." He pulled on his own boots with a warning, bossy glare that really should have pissed me off.

Instead, I felt warmed by his concern. I didn't show him that, though. I huffed, muttering about him bossing me around as I pulled on my boots.

"You love it," he grumbled, stalking out the door.

"Only when you're inside me!" I called back.

He flicked me a heated, amused look over his shoulder before marching to the barn to open the door.

Suddenly nervous, hoping for both our sakes I loved the dresser, I hurried with Akiva to follow him.

Ramsay hit the lights and gestured toward the back of the workshop. "Here." He guided me across the barn.

"It needs either a stain or paint, but I wanted you to choose that."

We stopped in front of it, and I gasped.

"No. No paint," I opined immediately. "Can I touch it?"

"O' course."

I smoothed my hand along the top of the sideboard. Like a traditional dresser it had a countertop and mounted to that was open cabinetry. Except Ramsay had added drawers between the top and the bottom to match the cupboards in the sideboard. There was space to display belongings on the countertop, maybe even put out breakfast items. And shelving on top to display the more elegant pieces I'd inherited from my grandmother's crockery collection.

What made it modern were the clean lines, sharp edges, no fancy frills. And the legs, which were slanted at an angle with a midcentury modern vibe.

What made it beautiful was Ramsay had created it using small planks of wood to give the effect of herringbone.

It was cool and contemporary while still being beautiful. Exactly what I wanted.

"It's stunning." I opened the cabinets, inhaling the rich scent of the wood.

"I'm glad you like it."

Turning to him, I slid my hands up his strong pecs and entwined my fingers behind his neck. It forced our bodies flush since I was quite a bit shorter than him. "It's perfect. Thank you."

Seemingly uncomfortable with my gratitude, he gave my ass a little pat. "You're welcome. Now, what color of stain to seal it?"

My lips twitched at his gruff subject change, and I studied the dresser. I couldn't wait to see it in the dining room. "It matches the dining table we chose as it is." He'd clearly paid attention to my overall design. There went my heart beating a little faster.

"So, a clear stain?"

"Yes. Please." I bit my lip against a giddy grin as I stared at the piece of furniture.

Maybe ... maybe he did care about me. Just a little.

———

Of course, I had to thank him properly.

A little while later, after I'd ridden him hard, we collapsed onto the bed again. I knew we were done for the night because Ramsay whistled for Akiva. We heard her pads hit the wooden floors before she appeared in the bedroom door. Ramsay's bed was huge, so it accommodated the large Malamute. She jumped onto the foot of the bed and spread out to go to sleep.

Before Ramsay could roll over to switch off his light, I asked, "What was your life like before you came here?"

There were a million questions I wanted to ask him. About his past. His life. If he'd ever been in love. We'd steered clear of how he knew about Hugh, what he knew about

Michelle, but that didn't mean I didn't want to know more. To give him the chance to confide whatever information about himself he was happy to share.

Ramsay was silent for a few seconds, and I shifted onto my side, tucking my hands beneath my cheek as I stared at him. Waiting.

He flicked me a look before staring at the bedroom ceiling. "I was in the marines. I moved around a lot."

"Why did you retire?"

"It's a young man's job."

"You were only thirty-four when you retired, though, right?"

"I was done."

At his flat, almost snippy response, I sighed internally. "Where did they deploy you?"

"All over."

My God! Frustration roared through me. It was like we were back at day one when he'd barely string three words together. I kept my frustration to myself. "Did you ... did you inherit your books from your birth parents? You mentioned before they were an inheritance."

His head whipped toward me, cutting me a narrowed-eyed look. "Silver."

The word held a gentle warning.

Ramsay's eyes spoke for him too.

The hope that had been building since he'd shown me the dresser turned cold and brittle and crumbled into dust. I clamped my lips shut.

He turned onto his side, giving me his back, and reached out to switch off the light.

As the room descended into darkness, I turned from him, not wanting to see his back in the shadows.

We're not that, his eyes had said.

Tears burned in mine, and I cursed myself for letting my emotions go there in the first place.

Ramsay was merely escapism.

Yes, the sex was phenomenal.

But it was only sex.

He wasn't a safe place to land after a couple of years of hell.

He was just ... a distraction.

The bed suddenly moved and I tensed, thinking he was going to get up and disappear into his barn like he always did when I tried too hard to get close to him.

It was such a shock, then, when I felt his grip on my hips. He pulled me into the middle of the bed, curling his body around mine. Spooning me. His strong arms held me close, and he leaned in to confess in my ear, "I don't like to talk about them. My parents. If ... I'll talk about them when I'm ready."

This time the tears that burned my eyes were from relief. I nodded and whispered, "Okay."

"You ever want to talk about yours, though ... I'm here."

"Ramsay ..." I was confused. So confused. One second we weren't that and now ...

"I ... it's not just sex," he murmured gruffly.

I squeezed my eyes closed, emotion thickening my throat. "No, it's not."

And for now, that was enough. I wiggled closer to him, covering his arm with mine and relaxing into sleep.

He seemed to understand.

Ramsay pressed a kiss to my bare shoulder and settled his head on the pillow behind me.

Just like that, I was safe again.

Problem was, I wanted to feel safe with him all the time. Not sporadically. Not only when we were having sex.

I wasn't sure Ramsay McRae could give me that kind of certainty.

25. Tierney

The sound of the coffee machine gurgling, bubbling, and hissing had become a familiar background noise to my biweekly coffee date with Cammie and Taran. The coffee dates had started at the same time as my affair with Ramsay, over three weeks ago.

My time with the dominating, talented Scot seemed short (which, it technically was) but also not short. Not short because there was a familiarity between us that time couldn't account for. Even though ... well, I barely knew anything real about him. I only knew the Ramsay McRae who had lived on Glenvulin for six years. Who he was before that ... I had no real clue. Although he'd promised he'd talk when he was ready, it clearly wasn't going to happen in a week.

So, all I knew was that he had connections that made Hugh almost pee his pants and I hadn't heard a word from that slimeball since our confrontation.

"Okay, I've tried to be polite and respectful about this, but my curiosity is killing me," Cammie announced abruptly.

I blinked at her changed tone because a few seconds ago,

she and Taran had been discussing helping at the Halloween fair (organization for which had already commenced despite it being at the end of next month). "Me? You're looking at me? What?"

My friend chuckled, shooting Taran a conspiratorial look.

Taran still wore the shell-shocked expression of someone who'd recently lost a loved one. I knew it well. Two weeks ago, I'd found her walking along the harbor by herself, and I'd joined her. I'd told her about my parents and that I was here for her.

The truth was, I hadn't needed to say anything else. She'd gravitated toward me ever since because I think I was the human equivalent of noise-reduction headphones. My empathy cut off the overstimulation of everyone else trying too hard to be there for her. They didn't mean it. They were simply being kind. But their kindness was suffocating her.

There was no pressure from me to talk.

No awkward weirdness.

I chatted with Taran like normal, knowing that if she wanted to talk about her mom, she knew she could.

Cammie had followed my lead.

Thus, our biweekly coffee dates in Pages & Perks.

Pushing through Taran's grief now was an amused smile.

It soothed me to see it.

"What are you talking about?" I grinned, naively unaware.

Cammie leaned in. She'd dyed her blond hair violet last week, and the light purple strands fell across her shoulders as she moved close enough to whisper, "Sex with McRae."

I gave a small bark of surprised laughter. "What?"

Taran covered a husky laugh with her hand. "She's incorrigible. Sorry. I told her not to ask."

The laugh had brought Cammie's head swinging around, her eyes wide on Taran.

Not wanting our friend to feel strange about the show of emotion, I cleared my throat. "Okay, what do you want to know?"

"For real?" Scooting her chair closer to mine, Cammie looked like an eager teenager, leaning in to hear the school tea at the back of the classroom. "Spill."

"This stays between us," I warned.

"Well, of course. We've lived here longer than you, you know."

I chuckled. "Yeah, and there's enough gossip flying around about me and Ramsay."

"Look, all I want to know is ... is he as good at it as he looks?"

Taran groan-laughed. "You're such a nosy cow."

Cammie, unsurprisingly, didn't flinch at the comment. Instead, she seemed delighted by Taran's amusement. "You've known that about me our entire lives." She turned to me again. "So ...?"

How good Ramsay was never failed to make my skin flush hot. God, my body literally readied itself for him at a mere thought. "He's ... the best sex I've ever had."

"Woo!" Cammie squealed, raising a palm up high.

Customers turned to look at us, but I laughed and gave her a high-five.

"Get it, girl." She lowered her voice. "One of us should."

"Things aren't going well with the postman from Oban?" Taran queried as if she already knew the answer.

"When you practically have to draw a roadmap to your clit, then no, things are not going well."

"Cameron McQuarrie, wash your mouth out!" an older woman called angrily from the line at the coffee counter.

Unfazed, Cammie gaped in mock innocence. "Why? Can you smell my coffee breath from there, Mrs. Wallace?"

I covered a laugh as Mrs. Wallace sniffed and turned away.

"Maybe if her husband knew where her clit was, she wouldn't be such a grumpy witch," Cammie muttered.

Taran leaned forward, lips twitching. "Maybe you could lower your tone when you're talking about clits and cocks in my store."

"No one mentioned cock." Our purple-haired friend turned back to me. "But speaking of ... Ramsay's?"

She really was incorrigible. "I'm not describing it."

"At least describe what it can do."

I laughed so hard at her petulant tone, I had to wipe tears from the corners of my eyes.

"I think if she does, you're going to feel very jealous," Taran mused perceptively.

Cammie raised an eyebrow. "Just because he's the best sex she's ever had doesn't mean he's amazing. It could mean our Tierney's had a poor showing in the past."

At her questioning tone, I shrugged. "It's both. Four boyfriends. The one who was at least decent at sex also turned out to be a narcissistic douche canoe."

"Hugh?"

"Hugh." I contemplated my past lovers. "My first real boyfriend was in high school—Blake. He was privileged but sweet. Too sweet, maybe. The sex wasn't good, but he was kind, and I think that's important for a first boyfriend. I broke up with him when we graduated. He went off to Harvard while I stayed in New York, studied hospitality management, and interned with the Silver Group. That's where I met boyfriend number two. Eddie was a young marketing intern. He was funny, sharp, nice but not too nice. Sex was okay. But he couldn't get over the differences in our background and he always felt not good enough and nothing I said could change it, so we broke up. Third boyfriend, Mikael, a couple of years older than me. Son of my parents' friends. Another so-called privileged brat, except he had all this guilt about it. We dated for eighteen months and probably saw each other six out of those. He traveled all over, volunteering with a water aid charity. I admired him more than I was attracted to him. But he was a good guy. Last I heard, he'd fallen in love with a young woman he met in Rwanda, and he married her, much to his parents' displeasure." I grinned, thinking about Mikael and how he always did what his heart told him to do. "He was my favorite of all my boyfriends. And I still didn't love him."

"Or have good sex, apparently. Until now." Cammie grinned and turned to Taran without thought. "What about you?"

I stiffened.

It was common knowledge now that Taran's fiancé had broken their engagement. He couldn't handle her grief. I felt such a kinship with her, knowing now that Hugh couldn't handle mine.

"I've the libido of a starfish," Taran replied flatly. "So, I don't care."

"In the future, you'll care again," I whispered.

"Surely there are celebrities you'd jump if you had the chance." Cammie tried to lighten the mood.

Taran gave her a half-hearted smirk. "If Brodan Adair weren't married, I'm sure he could unstarfish my libido."

Cammie chuckled. "He's getting on a bit, is he not?"

"Uh, no. That man will still be sexy as hell at seventy," Taran argued.

"Nah, give me some North Hunter over Brodan Adair any day."

"He's actually very nice," I offered.

Cammie gaped. "You've met North Hunter?"

"Yeah. He was at a gala in New York about five years ago.

He had his wife with him. She's stunning. And funny. I liked them."

Cammie made a face at Taran. "She's casually name-dropping. Sometimes I forget you used to socialize with the one percenters. I suddenly feel very uninteresting and unglamorous."

I chuckled, shaking my head at her teasing. "You could never be uninteresting or unglamorous."

"Aww, thanks." Cammie fluttered her eyelashes comically. She eyed Taran again. "What about non-celebrities? You have to admit, our wee island has a disproportionate number of hotties. There's nothing wrong if you contemplated potential *future* partners." Cammie's expression softened with something I'd call hope.

Realizing where her thoughts had gone, I tensed.

Taran's expression shut down, a hardness creeping into her eyes.

"What about Murray Shaw?" I blurted out, diverting any thoughts from Quinn.

She blinked, the hardness softening. "Murray? Isn't he married?"

"How can you have been back this long and not know he's divorced?" Cammie asked quietly.

She shrugged. "I haven't been paying much attention." She frowned. "Murray and I were never close. So ... he's divorced?"

To my surprise, Cammie's features tightened. "Aye ... he and his wife split and she took their daughter Kelly to the mainland."

Taran winced. "I didn't know."

"It was fairly recent and a fairly ugly divorce." Cammie frowned. "It was so ugly, anyone caught gossiping about it was swiftly shut down. Kelly visits for a few weeks during the summer and the odd weekend here and there."

"That sounds shit for Murray." Taran scowled.

"Aye, just the way Jill wants it to be. She and Murray finalized their divorce last year and Jill has turned into the ex-wife from hell. Such a cliché. It gives ex-wives a bad name when some of them are so decent they deserve a medal." She bit her lip, probably because she was thinking of Quinn's ex-wife whom I knew Cammie liked and respected.

Awkward silence fell over the table, and I could see Taran disappearing inside herself.

Desperate to keep her with us, I blurted out in a hushed whisper, "Ramsay ties me to his bed."

Their heads whipped toward me in unison.

My cheeks flushed. "A few years back, London told me I might need a bit of an alpha in the bedroom to get ... you know ... Well, nothing else was working for me."

Cammie's grin was slow and delighted. "But Ramsay knows how to dominate, huh?"

I covered my face with an embarrassed groan/laugh combo. My reply was muffled.

Fingers wrapped around my wrists, yanking my hands off my face.

Cammie snorted. "Repeat that, please."

"I like it." I wrinkled my nose. "I like giving him the control during those times."

She relaxed back in her chair with a sigh. "I shouldn't have asked. Now I'm jealous."

"Really?" Having not had anyone to talk about these new discoveries, I asked, "Are you ... do you like that too?"

"I'll try anything." Cammie nodded, taking a sip of her now cold cappuccino. "Him in control. Me in control. I have yet to date a man, though, who was authentically dominant."

"So, you like them dominant *and* submissive?" My curiosity peeled away any prudishness.

"Not submissive. I mean, I've tied a guy to the bed and it

was fun." Cammie shrugged as if we were talking about the latest floor tiles she'd chosen. "But I don't like a truly submissive guy. I had this one boyfriend who kept asking me if he was doing it right, and it was so off-putting, I had to fake it."

"Really?" Taran frowned. "I think that's kind of respectful and nice."

"Oh, it was. He was a lovely guy. And there are women and men out there who need that in bed and good for them. I'm not one of them. It's an ick for me. Isn't it an ick for you?"

"I don't know."

"Think about it ... he's asking you constantly if he's putting his fingers and cock in the right place. Fella, if you don't know by now, get out of there."

Unfortunately, I'd just taken a sip of my Americano and nearly spat it everywhere.

Taran chuckled. "We should not be having this conversation in here."

Cammie nodded. "That's a no. It's an ick for you too. I can tell."

Taran rolled her eyes but didn't deny it.

"So ..." Cammie turned to me. "Ramsay's definitely not asking if he's doing it right, is he?"

I raised an eyebrow. "I think me screaming through multiple orgasms is all the validation he needs."

With that they both threw their heads back in laughter and I joined them, feeling smug.

Not just about Ramsay.

But about this.

The three of us.

This friendship we'd forged.

My new friends in my new home.

Things were finally falling into place.

The B and B was on track to be finished by Christmas, and I already had weeks booked out for next summer. The threats against me had stopped, and Perri called yesterday to tell me the Silver Group were threatening to sue if they published. They knew they had enough evidence to print, but the newspaper's legal department were prevaricating over a statement Perri had obtained from the hotel resort manager because she hadn't fully explained all of her reasons for her investigation to him. Perri was sure legal would come around and they'd go to print next Monday.

It would be tough. I was bracing myself for the media frenzy. For the long legal battle. But my parents would get justice and so would the people they were trying to fight for. That's all that mattered.

The only things missing from my life were London and something real with Ramsay.

Because I knew I wanted that now.

I wanted to be with him.

After the night he'd admitted to me it was more than sex for him too, he hadn't pulled away. He hadn't put up a wall. In fact, every day I felt him grow more affectionate, tender with me. A little unguarded. I was hopeful he would really start opening up to me soon.

And maybe ... if I opened up first, he would.

I was going to tell him the truth about the threats instead of waiting for it to go to print. It would say to him that I trusted him, and I think our relationship needed that.

Sometimes, you had to be the one to give up your damn pride and make the first move.

Ten minutes later, Taran had to return to work and so did Cammie and me. We hugged our friend goodbye, waved to Ewan and Martha, and stepped out onto Main Street.

Cammie's ringtone suddenly blasted in her purse. While my ringtone was boring and traditional, Cammie's was a song by some Scottish band with a weird name. Biffy Clyro. It was loud, it was rock, and it was so Cammie.

"Oh, this is a client," she said, pulling her phone from her purse. "I'll catch you later?"

"Sure. Talk soon." I left her, heading toward my apartment. I had the urge to try to catch London on a video call so I could tell her more about Ramsay, that I was going to tell him the truth. She'd always been my best and favorite sounding board and it was weird not having her around all the time to talk to. Especially about the big stuff.

And Ramsay ... I knew he was the big stuff for me.

Maybe even the biggest. At least ... I knew I'd never felt this way about any man before.

It was raining, not a heavy downpour, only a drizzle. I was kind of getting used to it, so I didn't even bother to pull up my hood.

Then I saw the rainbow over Stòr. I bit my lip against the massive grin that wanted to spread over my cheeks as I strode toward the harbor barrier, pulling my phone from my purse to take a photo of it to send to Ramsay.

It looked so beautiful and vivid against the stormy clouds around it.

I was tempted to send it to him with a text that read: "Grumpy vs. Sunshine."

As a non-romance reader, he totally wouldn't get it.

I chuckled at the thought, taking a few more snaps before I turned back toward the road to cross it. My view was abruptly blocked by a broad chest in a dark hoodie and my heart jumped as I looked up into a masked face, fear ricocheting through me too late. A male voice that sounded distorted said, "Maybe this will shut you up."

He made a blunt movement toward me, and a sharp, burning pain radiated through my midsection. It was so brutal my knees gave out as he grabbed my purse and fled.

I pressed a hand to my stomach, using my free one to catch

my fall as I watched in disoriented horror as he took off down Main Street.

My hand came away from my belly covered in blood.

He'd stabbed me.

Surreal terror shot through me as I cried hoarsely for help.

Nearby cries of shock filled my ears as I fell onto my back, the sky a dark blur above me.

26. Ramsay

Because I'd been so focused on Silver's B and B, I had requests for freelance work piling up. Today, I wasn't needed on-site, so I headed over to the cheese farm this morning to fit a couple of bookshelves I'd built for them. Now they were custom milled into place in their café that abutted the farm.

My plan was to head back to Stòr to lose myself in my workshop. But first a stop at the bakery. Between my workouts in my home gym, the physicality of my job, and the sexual workouts I was getting regularly with Silver, I was hungry all the time lately.

Akiva waited outside for me and as I stepped out, she gave a sudden bark and took off down Main Street.

A hooded, masked figure, too tall and broad to be a woman, shot past me clutching a woman's handbag and threw his body over the harbor wall. Instinct had me racing across the street as the cries hit my ears. The man scrambled to his feet and unwound the rope anchoring a small speedboat. My eyes flew down Main Street to where Akiva had run to, where the cries for help sounded.

People crowded around someone.

A gap in them revealed what I'd dreaded from the moment Akiva tore away from me.

A familiar blond head on the concrete.

The engine roared, drawing my attention back as the hooded figure zoomed across the water in the speedboat.

Blood rushing in my ears, I searched the harbor until I spotted Jack, the harbor master. His face stretched with worry as he walked toward the noise. "Jack, call the police!"

His face leached of color. "What's going on?"

"That boat!" I pointed at its quickly disappearing silhouette. "That's our perpetrator! Call the police, now!" There was no time to wait. My boat wouldn't catch the fucker.

And she was the priority.

I ran down Main Street. "Move!" I bellowed and the crowd around her parted.

Silver's wide, shocked gaze met mine as she lay there panting hard, her hands covering her blood-soaked stomach. Rage and another feeling I couldn't acknowledge filled me. Memories of another woman staring up at me, eyes begging for help tried to intrude. Tried to fuck me up. I held the memory back. Forced myself to calm. For her sake. Akiva licked at Silver's face, whimpering.

"Akiva, back off," I commanded, and she did. But she sat on her rump like a guard dog at Silver's side as I lowered to my knees. "Ambulance?" I asked the crowd.

"On its way, Ramsay," a shaking, female voice said behind me. "They're going to get her to the helipad to airlift her to Inverness."

"Ramsay," Silver gasped out.

I pulled off my shirt and bundled it into a wad. "I'm going to put pressure on the wound, Silver. Okay?"

Her panting grew faster.

She was hyperventilating.

"Breathe with me, Silver." I took a deep breath in and out as I gently moved her bloody hands so I could quickly cover the wound.

Her breathing increased as I pressed down on it.

"Breathe." I breathed in and out. "Like me. Look at me, angel."

The pleading in her eyes almost undid me.

"Angel, breathe," I begged.

She took in a slow breath and released it.

"That's it. That's it. Good girl."

"They're here, Ramsay."

I glanced over my shoulder to see the island's only ambulance stop at the scene. Inside were our two paramedics—Forde, who was driving, and Laurie, the second medic. Forde managed the ambulance and volunteered to drive it when he could.

His face slackened when he saw me and Silver. Then he covered his shock and dismay as Laurie pushed forward. "What do we have?"

"Possible knife wound. I've kept pressure on it."

Laurie nodded grimly. "Keep the pressure on while we get Tierney onto the stretcher."

It was quick, efficient, though I nearly lost my shit when Silver cried out in pain as she was rocked a little too hard going up into the ambulance. Akiva barked from outside it and I frantically scanned the crowd.

Cammie was there.

I hadn't seen her arrive.

Her face was chalk white.

"Cam, can you watch Akiva?"

She blinked rapidly, tears falling down her cheeks. "Aye. Call me as soon as you can."

I gave her a jerk of my chin. "Thanks."

Then the ambulance doors closed.

"Ramsay."

I looked to Silver. There was so much blood drenching my hands. So much fucking blood, I was terrified a major artery had been punctured. "I'm here."

"Sorry," she mumbled. "So ... sorry." Her eyes closed and her hands went limp at her side.

27. RAMSAY

I'd lied.

Knowing there was no way the doctors would tell me what was going on with Silver. Knowing she had no immediate family left.

I'd informed the hospital in Inverness that I was Silver's husband.

Lucky for me, I was a paranoid bastard with a photographic memory. When I'd looked into Silver, I'd memorized small details, like her date of birth, without even trying. A quick glance at it and that information was stored in my brain.

I couldn't sit around. I'd been in contact with Jack. The police didn't catch the bastard who robbed and stabbed Silver, but a tourist had come forward to say he'd snapped a photo of the perpetrator and the boat. He'd handed over the information to the island police who, in turn, shared it with mainland investigators.

After that phone call, I'd called Jay and asked her to hack the island police to get the photographs.

Quinn, Cammie, they'd all called for an update, but I

didn't have anything yet. I told them there was no point in them traveling the five hours it would take to get here without more information.

I tried to detach myself from the situation.

Think on it as if Silver were a stranger.

Reevaluate her situation with my emotions removed.

Was there as much blood as I'd thought?

Surely, if there had been, wouldn't she have bled out in the helicopter?

But she was still alive, if unconscious, when the paramedics wheeled her into the hospital.

As much as I attempted to rewind the last few hours ... my mind kept conjuring horrifying images of Silver drenched in blood.

I couldn't ... I couldn't rationalize. I couldn't think logically.

Fear had clouded my perception. Truth be told, I had no fucking clue how bad her injury was.

All my training ... out the fucking window.

Maybe I'd been too long out of the game. Maybe the people of Glenvulin had made me soft. Fundamentally changed me.

Or maybe *she* had.

When I'd returned to the waiting room, I was aware of the looks from the other patients. Because of my height and size, it wasn't unusual to feel eyes on me. My size, in fact, had often been a hindrance in my job, and I'd found ways to try to diminish it through a careful use of body language while wearing clothing that made me blend in.

But the patients here weren't looking at me because of my size. A nurse had given me a shirt from lost and found that just about fit because I was bare chested after giving Silver my own. The same nurse had led me to a bathroom to wash Silver's blood off my hands.

Yet my jeans were splattered in her blood.

Now, a quick glance in the mirror on the wall revealed I'd streaked my cheek with her blood and hadn't noticed. Fuck. I got up to head to the bathroom again but was stopped when a doctor in scrubs appeared in the waiting room.

"Tierney Silver's family?"

"Me." I stepped forward and perpetuated my lie. "Husband."

The doctor nodded. "I'm Dr. Vincent, your wife's surgeon." He gestured for me to follow him outside the waiting room for privacy.

My heart rate increased.

"How is she?" I demanded as soon as we were in the corridor.

"Your wife has been very lucky, Mr. Silver. The knife didn't go deep enough to hit any organs or major arteries. We've repaired the wound, though it may leave scarring—it appears as if her attacker twisted the knife once he pushed it in."

Rage thrummed through me, but I kept my expression perfectly blank.

"She lost a fair bit of blood, so we've given her some. All her vitals look remarkably good considering."

Relief cut through my wrath. "Can I see her?"

"Of course. She's in the recovery ward. It might take her a while to wake up from the anesthesia." He started walking, and I fell into stride beside him. "We'd like to keep Tierney for a few days to monitor her recovery before we discharge her."

"Aye, okay."

"We have some forms for you to fill out. A nurse will be in with those. For now, I'll let you sit with your wife." He opened the door to a private room on the ward and I strode in. Only to stop abruptly.

In my worst nightmares, I'd imagined finding Silver with an oxygen mask over her face, breathing for her.

But she lay peacefully on the bed, unconscious, yet breathing on her own. She was hooked up to machines that kept an eye on her vitals, the sound of her heartbeat a steady rhythm in the room.

"Fuck." I ran a shaking hand over my beard.

"She's going to be fine, Mr. Silver," the surgeon repeated as he patted my shoulder. He left the room, closing the door behind him.

Slowly I made my way over to Silver.

Christ, she looked even younger than her age lying there. Such a baby face.

Too young.

Too sweet.

What the hell had she gotten herself mixed up in?

What the hell had I gotten myself mixed up in?

I reached out to stroke her cheek, knowing that I was on a dangerous path to ruin. After everything I'd fought my way through … all I'd wanted was peace. Peace on my fucking island. What had I been thinking getting mixed up with a woman who so clearly had a million secrets? Who so clearly had lost everything and wasn't only looking for a safe place to land … she was looking for a person who made her feel safe.

I huffed bitterly.

Aye, well, she chose wrong.

I couldn't keep her safe.

She hadn't trusted me enough to keep her safe.

Because I wouldn't let her in.

I couldn't.

Slumping down onto the chair next to the bed, I watched over her. I'd watch over her until I knew who was behind this. Because I knew this wasn't a straightforward pickpocket. No one came to a fucking island just to rob someone. Too many variables. Too many chances to get caught.

Then there were the threats we thought had disappeared.

I'd find who did this to her.

And then *I'd* deal with them.

Permanently.

28. Tierney

The beeping sound was annoying.

I kept waiting for it to go away, but it seemed to grow louder and more insistent. I groaned, fighting against the urge to open my eyes.

But I couldn't.

Even though my eyelids felt so heavy, it was almost like they'd been glued shut.

Finally, I got them open and immediately slammed them closed against the brightness.

"Silver?" a deep, male voice rumbled pleasantly in my ear. "Silver, I'm here."

Ramsay.

I tried again, pushing my eyes open and blinking rapidly against the lights that stung. Eventually my vision unblurred, and I stared into Ramsay McRae's rugged face.

Those wolf eyes were alight with concern.

"You feeling all right, Silver? Just give yourself a second. I'll go get the nurse." He stood up.

"Nurse?" Confusion had me turning my head on the

pillow. My body felt heavy, my brain sluggish. Where was I? "Ramsay ..." But he was already half in and out of the door and calling for a nurse.

A nurse.

The beeping.

I turned my head, my hair crinkling overly loud in my ears as I saw the machines next to the bed.

The bed.

I was in a hospital?

And like a rush of memories, it all came flooding back.

The masked figure.

The burning pain in my stomach.

The blood.

The fear.

Ramsay holding pressure on my wound.

Keeping me calm.

Then there was nothing.

"Am I okay?" I asked fearfully. "Ramsay ..."

He returned to my side, taking my hand between his. "You're all right, Silver. You're all right."

A few minutes later, a doctor introduced himself. He told me about my injury, the surgery, and my recovery time. That I had to stay in the hospital for a few days so they could monitor my situation.

And he kept referring to Ramsay as my husband.

It sounded nice.

Really, really nice.

"Water," I'd said in response. I needed water and to wake up properly. I still felt sluggish.

They let me angle the bed up but warned me I had to be very careful with my stomach and sutures.

Then the nurse told me and Ramsay the police would want to talk to us as soon as I was able.

Eventually, thankfully, they left us alone.

My gaze moved over my ... Ramsay. He was wearing someone else's shirt. It fit too tightly. I remembered him taking off his own to put pressure on my wound.

"I told them I was your husband so they'd keep me updated."

I huffed. "Isn't that illegal?"

"They should've checked my ID." He shrugged. "Tomorrow, when you've had some rest, I need to know if you know who did this."

I didn't want to wait until tomorrow.

I took another sip of water, my hand shaking so much, Ramsay reached out to steady it for me. Smiling in thanks, I nodded when I was done, and he put the cup at my bedside. "I was ... I was going to tell you. Everything. Today." I frowned. "Is it still today?"

"It's still today."

"I was going to tell you," I repeated, my throat a little hoarse. "I didn't want to keep it from you anymore."

"You can tell me tomorrow after you've rested."

"No. Now."

"It wasn't a robbery, was it?" At my furrowed brow, he explained, "The perpetrator stole your handbag to make it look like a robbery."

Shit. My wallet and car keys were in that purse.

I met his fierce stare with my own. My brain still felt fuzzy, but I needed to get the words out. "Last year, an investigative reporter from the *New York Chronicle* approached me. Perri Wilcox was investigating the death of her colleague. He was in the middle of several investigations, so she was trying to narrow down if one of them was connected to his death."

Ramsay frowned but nodded at me to continue.

"He was working with my mom and dad." Tears burned

my nose. The trauma of what I'd gone through hit me and the tears spilled over before I could stop them.

"Silver." Ramsay's voice was gruff as he reached out to stroke my cheek. "We can talk about this later. You've been through a lot today."

I cried a little longer, trying to get a handle on my emotions. "I'm sorry. Must be ... the anesthesia."

Ramsay held out some tissues. "Silver. This can wait."

"No, it can't. I th-thought I could handle it. That the threats were desperation ... I underestimated him."

His expression hardened. "Underestimated who?"

I wiped away my tears and snot, balling the tissue up in my fist. "My parents were on the board of the Silver Group. Over the years, my dad's family sold off more and more of their shares in the hotel empire. Dad gave up being CEO and sold even more. But they still owned a twenty percent share, which doesn't sound a lot but that's a big stake in a publicly traded company. It's worth hundreds of millions of dollars. And he still had great influence with the board. He voted to appoint Halston Cole as the new CEO."

Ramsay waited patiently for me to continue.

"Unbeknownst to me, around three months before their deaths, my parents were approached by a woman called Adila Binti Aziz. The Silver Group has resorts all over the world. After my father stepped down as CEO, he was like any board member. He had to trust Halston Cole was informing the board of all important company decisions. But he wasn't. They bought land on an island off the coast of East Malaysia to open a luxury resort. But it turned out the local government had allowed the Silver Group to displace some of the Indigenous people of the island from their village on the coastline. Their village was mowed down to make way for the hotel. If that wasn't bad enough, once construction began, it became clear that the new construction involved rerouting the islanders' water supply to fill the fucking pools in the resort." I jerked with my anger and hissed as pain ricocheted across my stomach.

Ramsay leaned forward. "If you can't tell this without getting worked up, we're stopping right now."

I bared my teeth at him in frustration. "I'm fine."

His lips twitched. "A wee warrior, I know. But you've only come out of surgery, and I don't need you ripping open your wound."

I softened my tone. "I'm fine. I promise."

He settled back in his seat. "So, what happened?"

"The islanders quite rightly had enough. They started protesting the construction. One day they were assaulted by private security Halston hired to protect the contractors building the resort." Guilt roughened my voice. My father had made it a point to avoid doing all the shitty things so many of the bigger hotel chains did in the name of their luxury properties. Halston had betrayed his legacy. But we'd let him by trusting him. "Adila was the assistant to the main contractor. She spoke Malay, which half of the construction workers spoke because it's the main language in that part of Malaysia. She also spoke with the islanders. It wasn't her job, but the main contractor put her in the middle of it.

"She tried to tell them that the islanders weren't violent and wouldn't become violent. But Halston insisted on the security team. One of the guards shot and killed an islander called Rahman Bin Raffi. He was a local leader. A husband. A father. Peaceful. Nonviolent. One day some of the protestors were getting a little out of hand. Rahman was trying to calm things down, but a guy on the security team got jumpy and trigger-happy and he shot Rahman." I blinked back tears. "Halston covered up the death. Paid settlements to the islanders and threatened them to keep quiet. He paid off the local authorities too.

"But Adila couldn't stay quiet. She believed from what she knew of my father that he wouldn't stand for it. So, she reached out to him to tell him what had happened, taking a huge risk in doing so. My parents being who they were, they flew out to meet with her. To get the full story. It was enough for them to look into it. Quietly. Not wanting to raise suspicions. At least they thought they were circumspect. Once they realized it was true, they decided the best way to deal with it was to make the truth public by bringing in an investigative reporter. Even if it meant ruining everything my father's family had worked for. My parents were *good* people."

The tears fell fast and free now. "They stood up for what was right, no matter the cost to themselves. I'm proud of them. I'm proud to be their daughter."

Ramsay nodded, squeezing my hand in comfort.

"Anyway, they got in contact with Ben Rierson at the *Chronicle*. And then they had a bit of luck drop in their lap. Henry Copeland, an intern in Halston's office, had accidentally been on the line when Halston took the call about Rahman's murder. His conscience forced him to take action. He stole copies of all the transaction documents for the settlements made to the Indigenous people of the island and the 'donations' to all the local authorities who helped cover it up. They thought they had him.

"But Halston must have found out. They all flew out to Bintulu to meet with Adila again. My parents got on a helicopter to fly to the resort under the pretense that they wanted to check out the new hotel. Their helicopter exploded off the coast."

He squeezed my hand harder.

I wiped at the tears that kept falling beyond my control.

"I didn't find out until last year when Perri came to me that it wasn't an accident. That same day, Ben was killed in Bintulu. They made it look like a violent street robbery. There was no reason for the local police to look into it beyond that. But they never found out who did it."

"You all believe it was Halston Cole quietening everyone who knew the truth?"

"Yeah. Henry Copeland and Adila disappeared off the radar. Perri and I tried to keep things quiet as we looked for him and attempted to find Adila again. Ben had copies of the documents, but we needed Henry's and Adila's statements. We found Adila in Australia. I don't know if she was being watched, but they tapped our phones."

"You realized it that day the picture of London showed up—you smashed your phone."

I nodded, mopping up my tears again.

"Halston was behind all the threats to you?"

"Yes. The *Chronicle* informed the Silver Group several weeks ago that they were running with the story and asked for their statement. Halston and the board tried to stop it, but the *Chronicle* will print it next week. The man ... the man who stabbed me"—my lips trembled with remembrance—"he said 'Maybe this will shut you up.'"

Ramsay's features hardened, his eyes flashing with wrath. "That fucker thought killing you would stop the story? Is he insane?"

"Desperate." I slumped, exhausted, into the pillow. "He's desperate and not thinking clearly. Making everything worse. Perri told me that the Malaysian officials Halston bribed aren't concerned for themselves. All the transactions for the money they received were put through as legitimate donations. Legally, this won't touch them. *They* didn't kill my parents." I sucked in a shaky breath. "Or an innocent reporter. Halston paid off the investigator who examined the crash. We found a money trail that's proof Halston paid money to the investigator who signed it off as engine failure. But we have no evidence of what actually happened to the helicopter. It was destroyed and with it any evidence to support our claims that he killed my parents. And there's none for Ben. No evidence. Just one hell of a coincidence. We knew we could only get him on covering up manslaughter. Until now." I scoffed bitterly. "If we can prove he did this to me ... it'll be worth the knife in the gut to nail that evil bastard to the wall."

29. RAMSAY

Silver was asleep by the time I left. Cammie had driven five hours north to be at the hospital, leaving Akiva with Quinn.

I didn't arrange travel back to Glenvulin.

Instead, a few hours later, I found myself in London.

I'd slept on the flight and showered and changed in my hotel room before making contact with an old colleague.

We met a few hours later in a gentlemen's club in Mayfair. James was a member and called ahead so they'd permit my entrance. It was the best place to meet because it was the one place in a city known as the City of Spies where the walls didn't have eyes or ears.

"It's been an age, my friend."

At the familiar, clipped Etonian accent, I stood from the table where I awaited him. James grabbed my hand to shake it with both of his. "It's good to see you, McRae, but you're taking a bloody chance showing your face here."

"It's good to see you too," I replied sincerely. And then grimly, "It's worth the risk."

"I'm intrigued."

A few minutes later, coffees ordered, James unbuttoned his suit jacket to sit comfortably. "So, why am I at the club at this ungodly hour?"

I swallowed my pride. For her. "I need your help."

———

Thirty-six hours later

The good news, our sources were sure there was no imminent threat against Silver while she was in hospital. That didn't stop me from calling in a few favors. Now she had twenty-four-hour protection with bodyguards at her hospital room door. James's authority meant the hospital had to comply with the security measures.

Knowing Silver would be all right in my absence was the only reason I got on the private flight to New York using an old alias. When you were lucky enough to have the option to retire, like I had, you weren't supposed to have access to powerful resources. Yet "supposed to" was a phrase that often hadn't sat well with me. Lucky for the higher-ups, I'd been fucking good at my job, and I was allowed a certain leeway others weren't.

And they owed me.

They knew it.

James knew it.

So when I called, he came through.

We'd spent the last day piecing together the puzzle. Jay had sent me the photographs the tourist had taken of Silver's attacker fleeing the scene. The registration number on the boat was visible. It was registered to a rental company in Oban. We hacked the rental company's computer system, but the boat had clearly been rented under a false name. James pulled the

CCTV footage from traffic cameras and any businesses who had a view of Oban Harbor.

We found the fucker with a traffic camera.

James started running facial recognition.

As we waited for it to ID our suspect, we uncovered everything we could about Halston Cole's schedule. From there we looked at the best place to corner him alone and the security measures I'd have to breach to do it without being caught.

Which was why, thirty-six hours after meeting James in London, I found myself in the men's restroom of a members-only club in Manhattan.

I'd flown via private jet. James had arranged the delivery of the club's staff uniform to my hotel room upon my arrival. We'd planted one of my aliases in the club's staff database because each staff member had to sign in and out digitally with a key card.

From there I'd entered the "highly secure" club with embarrassing ease. Despite my unfamiliar face, they believed so much in their own security no one even questioned my presence.

Before I'd arrived, James contacted me with pivotal information. Silver's attacker was a criminal from Glasgow. A bit of a local gun-for-hire called Shawn Prescott. He'd been paid by local thugs and crime families to "deal" with undesirables. Scotland's Specialist Crime Division had been working on nailing the slippery bastard for years, but it turned out his previous clients were smarter than Halston Cole. They'd always dealt in cash. Cole couldn't.

Not only did James's team find a digital money trail from his bank account to Halston Cole's personal fucking bank account, but they also found email communications between them that revealed he was the one behind all the threats to Silver. Most importantly there was a recent communication that detailed a new job: to *silence* Tierney Silver. He thought making it look like a robbery would avert suspicion. The absolute moron. Cole's defense might argue he didn't mean for Prescott to kill her, but with all the other evidence the news article would reveal next week, Cole's lawyers would have a hard time defending him. Shawn was arrested, and the police found the weapon with blood on it. A simple DNA test would prove it was Silver's.

We had them.

All because the fucking bastard thought Silver was a young woman on her own whom he could easily target. He probably also assumed a small country like Scotland wouldn't have the resources to put the pieces together. We did. The police would have gotten there. It just would have taken them longer than it took my sources.

Halston's ignorance and arrogance was his undoing.

He didn't see me standing at Silver's back.

Now he was about to endure a lesson on exactly what that meant.

When I spotted Halston in the dining room, I wanted to break his neck. Instead, I made sure I was the one delivering his coffee and I dosed it with a liquid laxative. My palms were unusually sweaty at the familiar situation but I pushed away bad memories. I focused on what needed to be done. Large reading glasses obscured most of my face and I changed the way I walked and held myself to diminish my size.

Thankfully, the bastard was the kind who didn't acknowledge servers. He didn't so much as glance at me when I brought the coffees to the table he shared with another Silver Group board member, Darren Polson. It wouldn't surprise me if they were there to discuss the upcoming article in the *Chronicle*.

I'd put a Cleaning in Progress sign on the nearest restroom, knowing it would deter others but not a man who was about to shit himself.

Now I waited in the restroom for Halston to make his inevitable appearance.

He came barreling into the room, almost slamming the door in my face before rushing into a stall.

Completely unaware of my presence.

Calmly, I locked the restroom door with the key I'd stolen from the cleaning supply pantry.

I'd only dosed Cole enough to send him running to the toilet to relieve himself.

It wasn't enough to keep him there in crisis. I didn't have time for that, though it would have been satisfying to put him through it.

Even though I knew how to move without sound, he was making such a fucking fuss in there, I slipped into the next stall and closed the door, leaving a gap so I could see out into the main room. I took savage pleasure in his muttered cursing and bitching.

Thankfully, it was over as quickly as it started.

I listened to him clean up, flush, and leave the stall to wash his hands.

I waited.

There were no mirrors near the hand towels.

The fucker was oblivious.

As soon as he crossed the room to dry his hands, I was on him before he knew what hit him.

I slammed his face off the tiled wall, the crack of his nose a satisfying echo as his knees gave out, his head bobbing. Grabbing him in a chokehold from behind, I flashed a large knife in front of his face. Halston made a gurgling noise, frantically trying to shake me off.

"If you make a move or even a squeak, I'll gut you like a pig."

"Who are you?" he gritted out, his voice nasally from the nose break.

I squeezed his neck harder until he smacked my arms, struggling to breathe. Finally, I released him just enough so he wouldn't suffocate.

Bringing the knife closer to his face, I felt him tremble against me.

"This club is supposed to be the most secure club in Manhattan, yet here I am. I hacked their visual security and right now, their security team's system is on a forty-minute time delay. They have no idea they're not watching live footage. No one saw me serve you. No one saw me come in here. No one saw *you* come in here." Courtesy of James. Again. I owed my friend. "What is my point, you ask?"

He panted between gritted teeth, and it wouldn't have surprised me if the arsehole had pissed himself.

"My point is"—I pressed my lips to his ear—"there is nowhere you can run from me. I could slice your throat right now and no one will stop me. You'd die and it would be a fucking unsolved mystery for the rest of eternity."

He whimpered.

"Shawn Prescott has been arrested for the *attempted* murder of Tierney Silver."

Halston stiffened. I wanted to open his throat there and then.

Unfortunately, that wasn't the plan.

"That's right, arsehole. You failed. She lived. And the knife was in Prescott's possession and has Tierney Silver's blood on it. The authorities have already found a digital money trail leading from Prescott to you. It's all in motion and there's nothing you can do to stop it. In about five minutes, the FBI will be here to arrest you."

He whimpered again.

"It's over for you. But I'm here for one thing only. To warn you that if you come for Tierney Silver again while justice awaits you, I won't just cut your throat. I'll cut a little bit of you off, piece by piece, over a prolonged period. I'll make your death the most painful, horrifying fucking thing you can imagine. And *I'll* get away with it. You think you know power ... but you've never seen real power until now." I leaned in, hissing between my teeth with my rage. "I have *governments* at my back. There's nowhere in the world you can go that I can't find you and no one will care when I make you disappear. Do you fucking understand me, you feculent fuck?"

Halston sobbed and gave a jerk of his head.

I wanted to kill him.

This man had taken everything from Silver.

I wanted to kill him.

But I knew that would do her more harm than good.

Need for vengeance controlled, I tightened my arms around his neck until I felt him grow limp. Releasing him, I lay Halston down on the tiled restroom floor and checked his pulse.

It took a lot of training to be able to choke someone into unconsciousness without killing them.

He was still alive.

Glasses back on, knife concealed, I unlocked the door and strode out unhurriedly.

I'd left the building before anyone even noticed I was there.

A few minutes later, I watched from across the street as the FBI arrived. Another ten minutes passed before I witnessed them march Halston Cole, face bloodied, nose broken, out of the club in handcuffs.

30. Tierney

When I woke up again, Cammie was by my side. I don't remember if we spoke because I fell into unconsciousness soon after. The beeping from the machines roused me the next morning.

I turned my head on the pillow, instinctively searching for Ramsay, but there was no one there.

He wasn't there.

Fear crawled over me as I lay in the hospital bed, remembering how easily that masked stranger had gotten to me. Had hurt me.

I wanted my mom and dad.

The sob burst out of me before I could stop it.

My parents would have been the first people at my side. Would have parted oceans and chartered a goddamn F-15 fighter jet to get them here as fast as possible. I was twenty-seven years old, and I realized that I could have been fifty when they died, and I still would have felt like a lost little kid without them.

I sucked in a breath, pulling my tears back in because the ache in my gut was making itself known.

I was lucky, I reminded myself.

I was lucky to feel this kind of pain from their loss.

Not everyone had parents like mine.

It was a privilege to have been loved like that for so long.

So now I had to deal with it and face this world without them.

I could do it.

They'd made me strong enough to do it.

It didn't mean I didn't feel relief wash over me when the door opened and Cammie stood there.

She appeared rumpled and tired as she moved across the room with a coffee cup in hand. "I wanted to get back before you woke up." Cammie's expression fell. "Have you been crying?"

My lips trembled as I attempted to keep the emotion in check. "No."

Cammie slid into the chair next to me, placing her coffee aside so she could take my hand in hers. She tenderly brushed the hair off my face. "Liar," she whispered. "Are you in pain?"

"A little."

In response, she hit a button above my head that I assumed was for the nurse.

"I only went out to wash up and grab a coffee."

"Have you been here all night?"

She nodded, squeezing my hand. "Of course. Where else would I be?"

Just like that, I started to cry again. This time in gratitude.

―――

The nurse, Janet, arrived not long later, muttering under her breath at two shadowed figures outside my door. I shot Cammie a questioning look.

"I'll tell you in a minute," she whispered.

"Everything all right?" Janet said as she rounded the bed.

"I'm a little sore," I murmured, wincing as a sharp throb echoed across my torso.

"Aye, it's time for another dose of pain relief." Janet moved a switch on the IV that was hooked into my hand, and I realized the top of my hand where it pierced a vein hurt too. "That shouldn't take too long to work. Now, can I get you some breakfast? It's continental. A wee bit of toast, that sort of thing."

I nodded, not really hungry but knowing I needed to keep up my strength.

"You're on fluid restrictions. Only water today, all right? But we'll see if we can get you a wee tea or coffee tomorrow." Janet winked at me with a smile and disappeared out of the room.

"God, I'd give anything for a coffee." I eyed Cammie's cup with envy as she took a sip.

She winced. "Don't be jealous, babe. It's vile, but I need the caffeine."

I chuckled and then groaned as pain sliced through my gut. "Don't make me laugh."

"Shit, I'm sorry, I didn't mean to."

"Not your fault." We shared a small smile and then mine fell. "Where is he?"

Her brow furrowed. "Ramsay left yesterday. Put Quinn in charge of Akiva. Put private security outside your hospital door."

My eyebrows shot up my forehead. "What? How?"

"No idea. But they're the real deal."

"How can he afford private security?"

Cammie huffed. "Oh, I have my suspicions Ramsay McRae is absolutely rollin' in it. I have no idea how he made the money, but he's *rollin'* in it."

He'd chosen not to stay by my side but he made sure I was protected? "Did he talk to the police before he left?"

"No, but the police haven't shown up yet. I thought they'd be here by now for a statement. Maybe they'll turn up today."

"Where is he, then?"

Cammie's eyes narrowed. "I don't know. But Quinn is being cagey about it. To no one's surprise, I was vocally pissed off that Ramsay left and didn't come back. Quinn ... well, he alluded to the idea that Ramsay is going after whoever did this to you."

My mind raced. My first thought was fear for him. What if he was throwing himself into this mess with Halston Cole?

My second was ... *Who* was Ramsay McRae?

What exactly did he do in the Royal Marines?

"He didn't leave you alone." Cammie's tone was reassuring. "Quinn says he's never seen Ramsay so cold, so focused. He's ... Christ, I'm worried he'll kill the bastard who did it if he finds him."

I flinched thinking about Halston.

Maybe it wasn't Ramsay I needed to be worried about.

Cammie left midmorning to get something to eat in the cafeteria after I insisted. Once she was gone, I had nothing to do but stare at a blank wall and worry about what Ramsay was up to. They'd taken my belongings, so I didn't have my phone. Cammie had thoughtfully reached out to London because I'd given her London's number in case of an emergency. She said London's boyfriend, Nick, picked up, and she'd informed him about my attack. He'd promised to let London know.

"He was kind of a rude prick," Cammie huffed.

Yeah, that sounded like Nick.

I just hoped he didn't send London into a panicked tailspin.

Cammie had only been gone around ten minutes when Janet appeared to let me know two police officers had arrived to talk to me. I assured her I was up to it.

The detective inspector was an older man who looked to be in his midfifties. Tall, broad of shoulder, and a little soft around the middle. His partner, a detective constable, was a younger woman. Maybe late thirties, early forties.

They introduced themselves as DI Peter Bishop and DC Louise Branford. Everything seemed normal at first. They took a statement from me about what happened.

But then DI Bishop said, "We have the suspect in custody."

Shocked, I stared at them. The guy was masked and he got away by boat. I hadn't expected them to find him. At least not this soon.

"A tourist took a photo of the boat and through that we found a registration. It led us to the suspect and the weapon. It had your DNA on it."

I reeled with shock. "Th-that's amazing."

The officers shared a look, and the man offered a frown of his own. "It really is. It's astonishing how quickly he was found. You must have friends in very high places, Ms. Silver."

"What do you mean?"

"Well, we were provided with information that leads us to believe an American, Mr. Halston Cole, hired the suspect to attack you. Are you familiar with Mr. Cole?"

What the actual fuck?

I gaped at the officers. "Uh, yeah, he's, um, the CEO of my family's hotel business."

"We're working in coordination with the FBI and yesterday they arrested Mr. Cole. Do you know why Mr. Cole would attack you?"

Deciding it didn't matter now because the article went to press next week, I quietly explained the situation.

The officers exchanged looks as they noted everything down. "Well ..." DI Bishop seemed stumped on what to say. "Corporate manslaughter is a new one for us. But, uh, thank you for the statement. We'll be in touch once we have more information."

They departed bemused and left me wondering what the hell they'd meant by the statement "friends in very high places."

Somehow, I knew without really knowing that this was all Ramsay.

Somehow, he'd not only found the man who did this to me, but he'd found evidence that led back to Halston Cole.

That raised the question: Where was Ramsay now?

31. TIERNEY

The next two days seemed to drag on forever. I insisted Cammie leave to get some sleep, so she booked into a nearby hotel and returned the next day.

Ramsay hadn't shown again, but Cammie told me there were two new guys guarding my door. How Ramsay had gotten away with planting private security in a public hospital ward, I had no idea.

My surgeon told me I was healing nicely and my vitals were great, that they were happy to discharge me in the morning. I was surprised by how quickly I was allowed to leave until Cammie informed me that was standard with the National Health Service these days. They always needed beds and thus worked to unburden the system by discharging patients as expediently as possible. It didn't worry me. I'd rather be home.

About an hour later, because there was no cell signal inside the building, a nurse came in to let Cammie know someone had called the ward for her. When she returned, she told me the call was from Ramsay and he was on his way. He'd be there in the morning to take me home.

It irritated me to have my life managed without discussion,

but I didn't let Cammie see. She didn't deserve my frustration. Instead, I told her to go home, that I would be fine on my own. Reluctantly, she left, and I had a fitful night's sleep, stressed about who Ramsay was and what he'd been up to while I recovered in the hospital.

The next morning, I opened my eyes and found Ramsay sitting in the chair, watching me. His expression was soft, unguarded. I watched him close down as soon as he realized I was awake. His features hardened into a cool, detached facade.

Dread knotted my gut.

"Mornin'." Ramsay straightened in the chair. "Do you need anything?"

"Where were you?" My voice was still gritty with sleep.

"Taking care of some things." He stood. "I'll get the nurse."

"No, I'm fi—" My words faded to silence because he'd already left the room.

He returned with Janet who asked if I wanted breakfast before they discharged me. I wasn't hungry, so I shook my head. She glanced between me and Ramsay with a wrinkle between her eyebrows, as if she sensed our tension.

Before any more could be said, however, he left again to wait for me outside. There were no shadows at my door, so he must have dismissed the private security, people I never got to meet or thank.

Janet waited outside the shower for me in case I needed assistance. The hot water felt great, but I was exhausted and sore. The attack had taken its toll on my entire body, not just my gut. Being the sweetest person alive, Janet offered to braid my wet hair, which I gratefully allowed her to do. Cammie had brought clean clothes for my discharge per the hospital's recommendation: clean underwear, yoga pants with a low waistband, a long-sleeved loose tee, socks, and comfy sneakers. Stretching my arms up to put on the tee hurt like a bitch, so I learned quickly to keep my arms as low as possible while dressing.

Finally, I was ready to go. Hospital policy dictated I had to leave in a wheelchair, and Ramsay was waiting with it in the room. We shared a loaded look before Janet steadied me as I lowered into it.

My surgeon, Dr. Vincent, showed up to go over the meds I needed to take during my recovery and to discuss my suture aftercare. Once I signed my discharge papers, Dr. Vincent turned to me with a gentle smile. "We'll coordinate with your local doctor's surgery for the check-up appointment so you don't have to travel all the way up here. If your doctor thinks you need to see me, we'll arrange that then, but I'm optimistic your wound will heal nicely."

"Thank you, Dr. Vincent. For everything."

He gave me another kind smile, an expression that changed when he looked up at Ramsay. "Next time, please don't lie to medical professionals about your legal relationship to a patient. NHS Scotland has a confidentiality obligation that you put at risk. Thankfully, in this case, Ms. Silver has retroactively granted us permission to share her medical information with you, Mr. McRae."

If Dr. Vincent thought Ramsay would show some kind of remorse for lying, he was sure to be disappointed. Ramsay stared stonily at him. I had to give it to Dr. Vincent because he wasn't intimidated. His lips turned down in disapproval, but his expression softened when he looked to me. He pressed a hand to my shoulder and squeezed. "Take care of yourself, Tierney."

"Thank you, Doctor."

Ramsay was silent as he guided my wheelchair out of the hospital entrance toward the visitors' parking lot. Then he grumbled, "He has a thing for you."

"Who?" I scowled, confused and annoyed by the subject when we had many more important things to discuss.

"Your bloody surgeon."

"No, he doesn't." I shook my head. "You're just annoyed because he called you out for lying about being my husband."

"He fancied you. He kept touching you unnecessarily."

I shook my head. "Really? This is what we're going to talk about?"

"Nope." His lips smacked together over the word harshly and he didn't speak again until we reached an unfamiliar vehicle. "I rented a car that's easier for you to get into."

My eyes burned at his consideration. Goodness, the attack had triggered my emotions like nobody's business. I blinked back tears and murmured, "Thank you."

When Ramsay wrapped his strong hands around my biceps to help me stand, I looked into his face. His beard needed a trim, and he had dark circles under his eyes. But he wouldn't meet my gaze. It was like he was right there in front of me ... but he wasn't at the same time.

My belly fluttered with nervous butterflies as he helped me ease into the passenger seat of the car. I was never more grateful that he hadn't brought his Defender because trying to get up into it would have been a nightmare. Even trying to get into my little Suzuki was going to be a hassle for a few days. Not that I would be driving anywhere for a while yet.

I waited as Ramsay returned the wheelchair to the hospital.

I couldn't work out if he was being distant because he knew the inevitable slew of questions that were about to be fired his way ... or if he was being distant for a much more worrying reason.

Ramsay got into the driver's side, and I realized he'd had to push the seat way back to accommodate his long legs. He held out a plastic bag to me. "They forgot to give you your belongings. Since the bastard took your bag, it's only your phone in there."

"Oh." I took it and pulled out my cell phone. Disappointment flooded me. "The battery is dead."

"The car will charge it." He lifted a cover on the armrest to reveal a rubber pad for wireless charging.

"Great, thanks." I set the phone on it. I was sure London and Perri had tried to call me and was eager to switch my phone back on.

Ramsay didn't speak as we drove out of Inverness. He didn't even look at me. I knew he felt me staring, but he kept his focus on the road ahead.

I studied him. The way his big hands moved elegantly across the wheel as he turned the car. His rugged handsomeness. The weariness beneath his eyes. I wanted to reach over and caress his cheek. Inhale his masculine sandalwood scent that made me think of wicked nights in his bed.

Longing.

That's what I felt. I stared at him with longing because as much as I didn't want to think it was true, I already knew what was coming.

Hurt and anger caused me to turn from him to watch the world pass by out my window.

I wanted answers. However, I needed some time because once I had my answers ... I guess that would be it between us.

After about an hour of tense, awful silence, I reached over to switch on my phone. I had several missed calls from Perri, texts from Taran, Aodhan, Quinn, and a few other villagers wishing me well. Quinn also kept me up to date on the B and B.

There was nothing from London.

Not a thing.

It didn't make sense.

Had Nick told her?

I called her, but it went to voicemail. "Hey, Spoon, it's me. Did Nick give you Cammie's message? I've just gotten out of the hospital. I'm okay. Okay? Call me. I love you."

Worried now for London because it was not even in the realm of imaginable that my best friend wouldn't call me upon hearing I'd been attacked, I pondered if maybe she'd done something impulsive like jump on a plane to see me. Maybe her flight had been delayed and she was in the middle of travel hell?

"No answer, then," Ramsay said his first words.

"No."

"That isn't like her?"

Feeling petulant about him asking me a question when he hadn't offered up *anything* to me in the past few hours, I ignored him and called Perri.

"Remember it's early there."

Oh shit. Of course. I wasn't thinking. I hung up quickly.

But a few seconds later, Perri called me back.

"Tierney?" Her voice was high pitched with anxiety.

"It's me. I'm okay."

"Oh my God. Thank fuck. Halston's arrest is all over the news. We hit publish on our article at midnight because we were afraid someone from the police would leak the info before we could."

My pulse raced, realizing the UK had woken up to our story.

Ramsay sensed my tension. "What is it?"

"Perri says the *Chronicle* published the article last night."

"Who are you talking to?" Perri asked.

"A ... friend."

A 'friend' who was muttering curse words under his breath.

"I wanted to give you a heads-up because I think your little island will be invaded with the media once they track you down."

"I'm surprised they weren't already waiting outside the hospital."

"Yeah, lucky. But you're good?"

"I will be."

"Fuck, Tierney, I ... I am so sorry about this. I really didn't think he was stupid enough to do something like that."

"Well, thankfully, he was. This only helps our case."

She snorted. "You know, you would make an excellent investigative reporter with that attitude. You have balls of steel."

I laughed softly. "Nah. I think once this all blows over, I'll be happy with my remote little life."

I felt Ramsay's attention, but I turned to look out the window, my throat closing with emotion.

Because I had been stupid enough to believe my remote little life would include him.

Perri and I chatted more about what to expect next. As soon as we hung up, Ramsay connected his phone to the car and called Quinn. Quinn asked how I was and then Ramsay told him about the article.

"Aye, everyone's already talking about it. The whole island is abuzz now that they know who is behind the threats against Tierney. Some apologies have also been made to those who were accused," he said, a hint of amusement in his tone. "You can imagine how that went. But we're all proud of Tierney and what her parents were trying to uncover."

There went my throat constricting again. I couldn't speak. Ramsay took one glance at my face and replied for me, "Silver's a wee bit emotional right now, but she's grateful."

An ache panged across my chest and with it, hope.

Had I read him wrong?

Was he ... I was so confused.

"We're here for you, Tierney," Quinn replied softly. "And I'll warn everyone about the media frenzy, but I think most of us already knew to expect it after reading the article this morning."

After the call with Quinn, Cammie called to check in. She was with Taran.

I felt their love and kindness wash over me.

Even as I continued to worry about London.

About Ramsay.

About the media.

Around the halfway mark in the journey, I had to ask Ramsay to stop so I could relieve myself and because I was getting faint with hunger. He pulled into a large service station that had several fast-food options.

He insisted on rounding the car to help me out and he stayed glued to my side as *I* insisted on walking by myself. My wound radiated pain up my torso and down across my stomach. Frustration blazed through me as I realized I wasn't going to be up and on my feet quite as quickly as I'd thought.

Ramsay saw my struggle, took hold of my elbow, and led me directly to the restroom. I stopped him. "You're not coming in with me."

"You need help."

"I'm peeing on my own." I gritted my teeth and used what strength I had left to get myself into the restroom and to a toilet cubicle.

Self-pitying tears welled in my eyes as I took care of business, my stomach throbbing the entire time. This overly emotional crap was not helping anything!

Willing myself to keep it together, I got out and over to the sinks to wash my hands. I was out of breath and hot all over. I had to take a minute, resting against the counter. Maybe it was time for some pain relief too.

Ramsay waited outside the door and slid an arm around

my waist before I could say a word. "Lean on me now," he demanded.

So I did.

People were looking at us, but I no longer cared. I needed a seat, pain relief, and food. I told Ramsay as much.

"I should have brought the food to the damn car," he muttered.

"I still needed to pee," I whispered as I slid into a booth.

He grumpily took my order, and I didn't get mad at his mood because I knew he was annoyed I was in pain.

And there I went getting all hopeful and optimistic again.

Because surely if he cared this much about me ...

While Ramsay ordered the food, I googled the article. It was difficult not to start sobbing in the middle of the restaurant as I read Rahman's, my parents', and Ben's story in black and white. Perri had added my attack and Halston's arrest into the finished article. Now the whole world knew what had been done to my family for trying to tell the truth.

Pride, almost unbearable pride, burned through me.

My parents had been so strong in their convictions. They'd gone after the answers they needed, even if it hurt them.

With that in mind, when Ramsay returned with the food, I lunged. Verbally. "How did you find the guy who attacked me so quickly? How did you connect it to Halston? Where did you disappear to?"

"I called in a few favors." Ramsay shrugged before taking a bite of his burger.

"What kind of favors? With whom?"

"Old friends."

"Ramsay—"

"Eat your food before you pass out."

I took an aggressive bite of my burger, glaring at him the whole time.

Something hot but tender lit his expression as he stared back.

As if he realized it too, he looked down at his food.

I waited until I'd finished my burger. "Who are these friends you speak of?"

"Just old friends."

"Seriously." I hissed, leaning across the table and then wincing with pain. "Fuck."

"Stop exerting yourself."

"Stop lying to me."

He scowled. "I haven't lied to you."

"Then stop evading. Did you go after Halston?"

"I'm going to get your pain meds out of the car." He got up before I could say a word and disappeared out of the restaurant.

Emotionally wounded, I sank back against the booth and reached for my phone. I wanted to talk to London. I wanted to tell her everything and ask her what she thought about Ramsay.

There was still nothing from her.

Concerned and a little depressed, I didn't push Ramsay further. I took my pain relief. I ate and let him eat. Then he gently guided me back to the car.

For the next few hours, I stewed in my own emotions. By the time we reached the car ferry that would take us over to Glenvulin, I was close to tears again. "I trusted you with my story," I suddenly spoke into the silent vehicle. "I don't understand why you can't trust me to tell me the truth."

Ramsay sighed. "Be honest, Silver. You only told me the truth because there was no other option. That's not trust."

Anger flushed through me. "I told you I'd already decided to tell you that day that fucker stabbed me, but he got to me first!"

"Calm down." Ramsay glowered. "You can't get worked up right now."

Knowing he would be obnoxious and not respond if I didn't lower my tone, I continued quietly, "I trust you."

A muscle in his jaw flexed as his gaze shuttered.

I swallowed over and over again, fighting back my tears. I wouldn't give him my goddamn tears. Clenching my hands into tight fists, I concentrated on my indignation instead.

Quinn called as we made the crossing.

The media were already there and waiting.

Thankfully, we were able to drive past them off the ferry, though Ramsay almost mowed them down and they nearly blinded me with their cameras. The Leth Sholas police unit was very small, but they blocked the exit from the ferry terminal with two large Defenders so we could get out with a police escort while the Defenders blocked the paparazzi from following us.

My heart rate slowed as soon as I knew they couldn't follow.

To my surprise, Ramsay drove me into a residential area of Leth Sholas. "Where are we going?"

Instead of answering, he pulled up outside a bungalow. Taran stepped through the front door of the one-story home.

The police car parked behind us as a precaution.

Taran hurried around the car and opened my door. "You're staying with me while you recuperate," she offered without preamble.

I gaped up at her. "No. You've got enough going on."

"I want you here," she assured. "It'll help me too."

"The media." I gestured behind me to what we'd left in our wake at the harbor. "They'll camp outside the house."

"Then let them." Taran stepped aside and Ramsay was there, sliding his arms under my ass.

"What are you doing?"

"No more walking today," he said gruffly, easing me out of the car and into his arms as if I weighed nothing.

Even though my anger toward him still burned hotly, I held on tight and enjoyed the moment.

Mostly because I worried it might be my last time in his arms.

The thought made me sick to my stomach.

Inside the bungalow, Taran directed Ramsay to the back of the house and into a bedroom with a double bed. My suitcases were stacked in the corner. "What?"

Ramsay lowered me onto the bed. "You can't get up and down the stairs of the flat, so the flat is done with. Aodhan already knows."

I narrowed my eyes. "Well, that's a little high-handed, don't you think? Where am I supposed to go when I'm healed up?"

Taran appeared in the doorway. "You're staying here until the B and B is ready."

Gratitude mingled with dismay. "I can't impose like that."

She gave me a sad smile. "Honestly ... having you here ... it's kind of selfish of me. I ... being here without Mum is hard. And after reading your story today in the paper ... maybe it would be nice to have each other right now."

This time my tears fell before I could stop them. "Thank you," I whispered, wiping them away, though the salty taste of them lingered on my lips.

Feeling his stare, I looked up at Ramsay.

He seemed ... conflicted.

Until he washed away the expression with that cool disinterest he was so good at adopting. "I'll make sure the journos don't bother you."

With that, he brushed past Taran and was gone.

Taran frowned, turning back to me. "What ... is everything all right there?"

No.

Everything most certainly was not.

32. Ramsay

Akiva pressed her warm, furry body to my legs as we sat with Quinn at a corner table in the Lantern.

I rubbed a soothing hand down her back. My girl had missed me. More than that, she was smart, and she hadn't seen Silver since the traumatic moment on the harbor. She was anxious and in need of comfort.

"Bottom-feeding scum," Quinn muttered, glaring over my shoulder to the bar.

I knew there were a couple of journalists there having a drink.

"Not all." I shrugged. "The woman who helped Silver … that kind of reporting matters."

"Aye, but these guys are tabloid scum." Quinn threw back the last of his pint. "They're not welcome here. They shouldn't have served them. If Aodhan was here, they wouldn't have gotten served."

"Ignore them."

"You're lucky they don't know who you are."

"Who am I?" I asked dully.

"Tierney's … you know."

As if she'd heard her name, my mobile buzzed, and I turned it over. The screen said *Silver Calling*.

I switched off my phone.

When I looked up from it, Quinn's expression had turned ... withering. This time it was directed at me. "What?" I snapped.

"I know your moves, McRae." He gestured to my phone. "You're going to end it with her, aren't you?"

My chest felt like a fucking ton weight crushed down on it, but I didn't deny it.

Shaking his head, Quinn let out a huff of disappointment. "After everything you did for that woman ... everything you've risked. Make it make sense."

It didn't need to make sense.

All that mattered was Silver was safe.

But I couldn't be what she needed going forth. She was noble like her parents.

I wasn't noble.

I'd become the darkest part of myself to protect the world while they'd used the best of themselves to do the same.

If Silver knew the truth, she'd turn her back on me.

I'd known only loyalty to my country.

To people ... well ... I'd learned far too young that unless you wanted your spirit crushed beyond imagining, when it came to people, *you* had to leave *them* before *they* left *you* behind.

33. Tierney

Despite the lack of rain, the island still smelled like it. It had rained every day since my return for the past ten. Today was the first morning I'd woken up to dry skies, though the sun was trapped behind a cavalcade of pale gray clouds. I missed waking up to a view of the harbor, which made me realize how much I'd miss it once I moved into the B and B. The harbor-view rooms were, of course, for the guests.

Taran always left super early to open the coffee shop. She'd been reluctant to leave me at first, but to both of our surprise, Ramsay had shown up the first few days to make sure I was all right. He wasn't warm or tender about it. But he was there. He'd also brought private security to keep the tabloid journalists off the property.

For once, I didn't push him to explain how. Or what was going on between us.

I let it go for ten days and allowed myself time to heal instead.

Too afraid to look online at what the rest of the world had to say about the story, Cammie informed me the commentary was positive toward my family. The B and B's social media profiles had gained a ton of new followers from the notoriety and Cammie took over going through all the messages of support and sympathy that had flooded my DMs.

The Silver Group had fired Halston Cole, but they weren't innocent in this. When the *Chronicle* informed them of the story, they should have fired him then, but they wanted to protect the company name more than seek justice. As it was, apparently the resort in question had been inundated with cancellations, and human rights protesters from all over had descended upon it.

Halston had not only been charged with my attempted murder but with the murder of my parents and Ben. The charges of manslaughter were separate and being brought by Rahman's family against the security guard who killed him. Halston would be directly charged with subverting the course of justice once the case of manslaughter was proven. Rahman's family was also suing the Silver Group for covering up Rahman's death.

The *Chronicle* had started a crowdsourcing fund for their legal fees when I'd offered to pay them. Perri had reminded me I didn't have an unending well of wealth now, and I had my own legal fees to cover so she'd initiated the funding page for Rahman's family.

Yeah, it was a big legal mess.

And the truth was, it might never go to court.

A judge had to decide whether there was enough evidence against Halston to move forward.

It was a waiting game.

I'd been stuck in Taran's house for days waiting for the media leeches to fuck off. On day four, a UK celebrity was caught on film kissing someone who wasn't his wife, which took the UK paps off the island. On day seven, the US paps left because they hadn't seen a peep out of me, and they had other stories to cover.

I knew they'd come swarming again if the case went to court, but despite everything I'd been through, I wouldn't change it. All that mattered, all that had ever mattered since I discovered the truth, was bringing justice to Rahman, my parents, Ben, and all the islanders affected by the displacement.

Taking in a deep breath, I didn't mind that my pace was slower than usual as I walked to the B and B. I no longer had pain from only walking a little. Every day since the paps and the private security had departed, I'd gone for a walk, increasing my steps daily, not pushing too hard. But it was so good to get some air after feeling cooped up. I'd thought the villagers would be angry with me about the paps, about the threats and drama, but I was greeted with nothing but kindness and generosity. People brought around meals and gifts and offered to help me when they saw me walking slowly down the street. Everyone knew about my coffee addiction, so someone always brought me an Americano.

I felt loved and taken care of by the entire community.

Except Ramsay.

Sure, I felt taken care of ... but he didn't touch me. He hadn't touched me in a week. I wasn't talking about sex, of course. In general. No touching. No affection. No tenderness.

He was all business.

And the last few days ... he'd disappeared entirely.

In truth, I was more in emotional knots over him and London than the looming legal battle or trying to complete the work on the B and B through it all. All that seemed manageable. But Ramsay ... he'd never been manageable. Or more, that my feelings for him had never seemed manageable. Too big, too fast, too everything.

Then, of course, there was my best friend and all my worries about her. London had called the day after I arrived home from the hospital, hostile and hurt, demanding to know why I hadn't told her I'd been attacked. Stunned, I'd relayed what Cammie told me about telling Nick and then I informed her I'd left a voicemail on her phone.

There had been silence and then London had whispered hoarsely, "What? No. I don't have any recorded calls or voicemails from you or Cammie."

I promised her I wasn't lying.

We'd talked for a little while and she said she'd fly over, but I told her not to. I wanted her to, but it was a long flight, and I knew it wasn't easy for her to get time off. When London texted me two days later from a new number without explaining why she had a new number, my mind started racing. Why *hadn't* Nick relayed Cammie's message? Why didn't London see the voicemail or calls? Why did that mean she needed a new number?

I thought about my concerns regarding Nick in general. After the blinders had been lifted about Hugh, it worried me that he and Nick were such good friends. I'd grown to think of them as two peas in a pod. Were they two peas in a narcissistic, controlling pod?

Now I was anxious about London on top of everything else.

London wasn't a problem I could solve right now while I was still recovering.

But Ramsay ... Ramsay was a problem I knew I needed to face, or I'd drive myself crazy.

By the time I reached the hilly driveway that led up to the B and B, I felt a little twinge in my gut and my limbs were shaky. What shocked me more than anything was how much my whole body needed time to recover from the attack. I grew exhausted easily and couldn't wait for my energy levels to return to normal.

"Ms. Silver."

I turned from where I'd stopped to take a moment's rest.

The young man walking toward me was familiar. Dressed

in paint-splattered coveralls, I recognized him as a member of Quinn's crew. He had a coffee cup in hand as he hurried toward me, his brow furrowed.

"Fit like?" he asked.

I stared at him in confusion and then down at my feet because I knew the Scots sometimes pronounced *foot* as *fit*.

He chuckled. "Jus' askin' how ye are? Should ye be oot and aboot like this?" he asked in his thick Scots accent.

I gave him a tired smile. "I've been walking a little farther each day. And I miss the B and B. Sorry, I didn't catch your name."

"Greig," he offered, pronouncing it like *Greeg*. "Ah dae all the plasterwork an' painting fer Quinn."

"Greig. Hi. You're not from Glenvulin, though, right?"

"Originally Banff. Noo Oban. I stay wae a friend here in Leth Sholas an' then heid back tae Oban at the weekends." He gave me a cheeky smile as he offered me his arm. "Want tae lean on me?"

Greig was good-looking with close-cropped auburn hair and a strawberry blond beard. He had freckles and light blue eyes. He was also probably only a year or so younger than me and yet he seemed too young for me to find attractive.

Ramsay had ruined me for men my own age.

He'd just ruined me, period.

Asshole.

Gratefully, I took Greig's arm, and we began our ascent. "I thought I could make it. I've been getting better every day."

"I think ye'are amazing. Most folk might hole up in their hoose after what ye've bin through."

I wanted to. But I knew that was a path to nowhere good. When I first left the house, I'd been constantly looking over my shoulder, feeling vulnerable in a way I'd never experienced. Over the last few times, that feeling of needing to be hypervigilant had eased somewhat.

It helped to know my attacker, Shawn Prescott, hadn't been granted bail.

"Thanks. You ... gotta get on with it, right?"

"Ye were born tae be an islander, Ms. Silver," Greig replied with a grin. "Even if ye are fair trauchled by this here hill."

I chuckled because clearly, I hadn't hidden how out of breath I was by the climb. "Trauchled. I've never heard that one. Exhausted, though, right?"

"Aye."

"Your accent is so different."

"It's the Doric dialect. Even Lowlanders huv a hard go understandin' it. Yer doin' weel. Even if yer pechin."

I merely smiled in response because I didn't understand the last part.

After a second, Greig cleared his throat. "Ye're, um ... ye're pals wae Cameron McQuarrie, right?"

My lips twitched with knowing. "I am."

"I dinnae s'pose ye'd think she'd be interested in a bloke like me?"

"What age are you?"

"Is that a factor?"

"You definitely seem younger than Cammie."

"Och, age is merely a number."

"And yours is?"

He grinned. "Twenty-four."

I grimaced.

Greig scoffed. "Och, it's no' that bad, is it?"

"She's nine years older than you, and I think she likes her men a little older than her."

"*I* think she can be persuaded."

I laughed. "Then why did you ask?"

"So ye can tell her the gid-lookin' painter-decorator fancies her and it'll move things a long a wee bit fer me." Greig winked.

My amusement made my breathing even worse as we finally made it to the top.

Greig frowned. "Ye need tae tak a wee rest noo, all right? I'll get Quinn."

"I'm not here to see Quinn."

"McRae?" Greig guessed and then nodded. "I'll go find him fer ye."

"Thank you."

He raised his coffee cup to me. "Remember tae tell Ms. McQuarrie whit a fine man I am."

"It would help if you didn't refer to her by her surname like she's your teacher!"

He stopped at the doorway and flashed me a wicked grin. "Maybe I'm intae that kind o' thing."

I let out a bark of laughter and then winced as slight pain flared across my gut.

With a groan, I forced myself across the driveway and round the front to the garden.

Akiva lay in the grass, face between her paws, eyes closed.

This time the ache I felt was in my chest.

I'd missed her.

Her eyes flew open as if she sensed me and she lunged to her feet, barking. Anyone else would back off, intimidated, but I recognized her happiness. She launched at me, her paws on my chest, and I ignored the impact on my body. Instead, I pulled her into me, petting her and covering her head in kisses.

She whimpered in response, her cries telling me she'd missed me too.

Tears burned in my eyes, and I buried my face in her furry neck as she swiped at me with her tongue.

"Akiva, down!" Ramsay's authoritative voice rang out across the garden.

Akiva whined but obeyed, sitting on her rump to stare up at me, tail sweeping across the grass, back and forth, back and forth. She trembled against the urge to launch herself at me again.

I frowned at Ramsay as he walked out of the new bifold doors I hadn't even noticed until now.

"Did she hurt you?" he asked gruffly as he came over to pat a reassuring hand over Akiva's head.

"No. She was fine."

Ramsay's gaze washed over me, like he didn't believe me.

Probably because I was grimacing and exhausted.

"Did you walk all the way here?"

Not in the mood to argue about my well-being, I waved off his question. "Look, we need to talk."

His scowl deepened. "So you walk all the way here with a fucking knife wound?"

"I'm fine."

"You're pasty and sweating and look ready to pass out. C'mon." He swept me off my feet before I could protest.

I grappled for his neck, grunting as my wound throbbed. "That didn't help! What are you doing?"

"Taking you home. Akiva." Ramsay whistled for her, and she raced after us as he bridal-style carried me to his Defender.

"This is ridiculous. Put me down."

He did.

In his Defender.

Frustration boiled toward fury as he and Akiva rounded the vehicle and got in on the driver's side. Akiva stopped mid jump into the back to swipe my cheek with her tongue, and her sneaky affection softened me somewhat.

But only somewhat.

"What did I tell you about bossing me around?" I gritted my teeth as Ramsay started the engine. "Only okay in the bedroom."

"*And* when you do stupid things like walking across the village when you're supposed to be resting."

"I have been resting. For days. Dr. Vincent also told me to exercise in increments. Which I have been doing."

"Fourteen days. You were stabbed fourteen days ago." Ramsay drove down the hill away from the B and B. "Stop trying to push your recovery."

Seething, I waited until we were parked outside Taran's, which was literally a two-minute drive away. Walking "across the village" was nothing. He made it seem like I'd walked miles and miles.

"We need to talk."

"Akiva, wait here." Ramsay jumped out of the Defender, and I threw open the passenger side. "Wait!" he practically barked.

If I could set someone on fire with my eyes, Ramsay McRae would have been ash. "Don't even think about carrying me again!"

He ignored my wrath but gently eased me down out of the four-by-four, "letting" me walk on my own.

"You're not going anywhere." I pointed a finger at him. "After everything I've been through, I deserve two minutes of your time. And I swear if you drive off right now, I will just walk back to the B and B."

Ramsay slammed the driver's-side door shut, his belligerence clear, and gestured for me to lead the way into the bungalow.

Despite my need to be in control of the conversation, as soon as I saw the sofa, I lowered myself into it and released the breath I'd been holding.

Ramsay stood in the middle of the living room, arms crossed over his chest. He swept his gaze over the room, taking in the photos and artwork and clutter of ornaments that had belonged to Taran's mom. She hadn't had the heart to go through any of it yet, but I was hoping once I was better, I could help her with that.

Finally, his attention returned to me. "Do you need anything?"

"Answers."

At his instant closed expression, I huffed bitterly, "I don't expect answers regarding Shawn Prescott or Halston. I know I'm not going to get them. But I want answers about us."

He remained expressionless, not even shifting his feet. "It was a casual thing between us."

Even though I'd suspected it was coming since the moment we'd left the hospital, it still hurt like a motherfucker. Yet I wouldn't give him the satisfaction of crying. Even if I needed more than that. I needed to know *why*. "So ... when you said it was more than just sex between us ... what did that mean for you?"

That muscle in his jaw ticked and he made an exasperated sound. "Can we not do this?"

"You want to end it without an explanation?"

"I just did." His gaze returned to mine. Cold. Glacial, even. "I told you when we started sleeping together that it was all you'd get from me. It ran its course. We're done."

"You must think I'm an idiot." My expression clearly advertised my disgust because his features hardened and he looked out the window to avoid me. "Suddenly after I get stabbed and you go off doing God knows what on my behalf, it's over? You don't do what you've done for someone who is only a *fuck*." Tears threatened now, but I held on tight to them, forcing them down.

"And what have I done?" His question was gruff.

He still wouldn't look at me.

"I don't know the details. But it couldn't have been easy. You had to use some major resources to find Prescott that fast."

"What do you want from me?" Ramsay's head whipped

toward me. "I'm trying to bow out of this without fucking hurting you!"

"You don't think this is hurting me?"

His shoulders slumped. "I'm sorry, Silver. I am. But I told you. I warned you. I do life alone." With that, he exhaled a shaky sigh. "I don't want things to be strange between us. I'd rather we part as ... friends."

Friends?

He wanted to part as friends?

I let out a slightly hysterical huff of laughter. "Okay," I said, sharp sarcasm stinging my words. "Let's be friends. Maybe we can get coffee sometime and you can tell me about your latest casual fuck and how she compares to me. Sound fun?"

Ramsay had the audacity to give me a wounded look before turning toward the door and saying over his shoulder, "I'm not doing this."

"You're a coward!" I called after him. "When it matters the most, you're a coward!"

Taran's front door slammed shut so hard behind him, the walls shook.

34. TIERNEY

The beautiful thing about small-town living was that everyone rallied around each other during difficult times. The entire community had my back and were looking out for me as another week passed in my recovery.

That didn't mean they weren't gossiping among themselves now that it was public knowledge my affair with Ramsay was over.

The not-so-beautiful thing about small-town living was that everyone was in everyone else's business.

It was interesting to me from a human perspective that no one gave me pitying looks when I returned wounded from being stabbed on Main Street by an "assassin for hire." No, they'd looked at me like I'd survived a war.

But getting dumped by a guy ... that got me pitying looks.

And wasn't that fucked up?

I was pissed.

I was pissed at Halston Cole and Shawn Prescott.

At Leth Sholas for not treating me like the walking wounded over my actual physical wound but over a guy breaking up with me.

At Ramsay for lying. For his mixed signals.

At myself for getting involved with him when I knew it was going to hurt in the end.

I hadn't realized how bad it was going to feel. It was worse than the knife wound—that I could take a million times over this bullshit.

Mostly I was angry that I could feel this way about someone I didn't know very well. He hadn't really shown himself to me, so how could I ... how could it feel like he'd broken my heart?

I'd have to be in love with him for that to be true.

How could you love someone who only showed half of himself to you?

In desperate need to feel anything but this low, simmering seething, I'd jumped on the chance at a girls' night. I could now walk without getting exhausted and my wound only hurt if I jerked my body a certain way. Cammie invited Taran and me to the Lantern, promising Quinn and Ramsay wouldn't be there because a folk band was playing and it wasn't their thing.

It was the first time being out in the village that I didn't feel like everyone treated me to pitying, sympathetic looks. Our neighbors raised their pints when we walked in, and a group of fishermen very kindly gave up their table so I could sit.

We bought them a round as a thank-you and ordered a round of ale for ourselves.

It was a nice night. I'd told Cammie about Greig and had teased her about the attractive young decorator ever since, which was fun. Moreover, since I'd moved in, we'd both noticed a change in Taran. Having me there really did seem to help pull her out of the black hole of grief. Now she joked more with us and even opened up a little about her mom and her failed engagement.

The folk band was made up of three women and a man—a

female vocalist, two fiddle players, and a bass violinist. They played a few songs, then took a break so the pubgoers could enjoy socializing among themselves. Then the band would play another few songs and break and so on and so forth.

It *was* a nice night.

For about an hour.

Then Ramsay and Quinn walked in.

"Oh shit," Cammie muttered under her breath. "Ladies, I'm so sorry."

Taran glanced over first, her expression tightening as she and Quinn locked eyes for a moment before she turned away.

I was afraid to look at Ramsay.

But I ... I couldn't help myself.

He didn't even look my way. He found a space with Quinn to squeeze in at the bar.

They didn't come over, if only to say hello to Cammie.

"Arseholes," Cammie huffed. "Big man babies."

"I might go." Taran shifted, reaching for her purse.

Cammie covered her hand to stop her. "Please don't. You ... I say this with the utmost kindness and understanding ... eventually, you have to coexist with him."

They shared a long, loaded look.

Finally, Taran nodded, and the tension drained from Cammie.

Not from me.

"I'm not leaving," I said at their questioning stares. "I was here first."

Cammie smirked, but the band began playing again before we could speak.

Still, I felt everyone watching us. Waiting to see if any drama would unfold. I tried to focus on the band, but I could see Ramsay out of the corner of my eye turning to watch them too.

Unfortunately, I noticed the lead singer, an attractive, very tall, very voluptuous redhead closer to Ramsay in age, staring in his direction as she sang. When her lips turned into an inviting smile, I stiffened, following her line of sight.

Sure enough, she and Ramsay were locked in a staring contest.

Was he fucking kidding me?

Cammie shifted beside me, and I didn't even need to look at her to know she'd noticed.

The whole pub probably noticed.

When the song ended, the vocalist thanked us, and the band began packing up their stuff.

Taran shot me a worried glance because I was glued to what was happening, waiting on edge for it to play out.

Sure enough, the redhead strolled over to the bar, introducing herself to Quinn and Ramsay. Quinn quickly turned to talk to the person at his other side and Ramsay bent his head as the redhead spoke in his ear.

Jealousy was like a knife wound across my chest—and I could say that with authority now.

"This is unbelievable," Cammie hissed.

"Don't look." Taran angled her body toward me. "How's the B and B coming along?"

I couldn't.

I couldn't engage in banal discourse.

Instead, I watched as the redhead and Ramsay barely made any conversation before they moved from the bar.

To walk out together.

It felt like my heart was cracking in two.

"Watch yourself with that one, sweetheart!" Cammie suddenly called over the noise of the pub, hushing everyone into silence.

I couldn't even be embarrassed.

I could only process the pain.

Ramsay and the redhead halted.

"He'll cut out your fucking heart," Cammie spat at them.

I didn't know how the redhead reacted because I was staring at Ramsay.

He met my gaze, and I couldn't hide my feelings. I wanted to so badly because he didn't deserve them.

And I hated him for it.

I *hated* him.

There was nothing on his face. No hint that he even cared.

The redhead nudged Ramsay, and he jerked his head round, following her out the door.

"What an absolute prick." Cammie slammed her pint down on the table.

"Would you calm down," Taran snapped at her. "You making a scene only made it worse for Tierney."

It was true.

But I couldn't speak.

And I knew Cammie's intentions came from a good place.

Cammie flinched. "Shit. Tierney, I'm so sorry. I ... I can't believe him ... I'm sorry."

Slowly, the room returned to normal, but I could sense everyone watching me. Quinn's sympathy was clear even from across the room, and I fought the urge to bolt. Rather, I stood, reaching calmly for my purse. It was new since Shawn Prescott had stolen mine after he stabbed me.

I'd been stabbed three weeks ago and my lover not only dumped me, but he'd walked out of the pub with another woman.

I hated him.

"I'm going home."

"I'm coming with you." Taran snatched up her purse too.

Cammie grabbed my hand. "I'm sorry."

I squeezed hers in reassurance. "In the morning, I'm going to love you for what you did. But right now ..." My lips trembled dangerously. "I need to leave."

My friend nodded, pale with guilt, as she stood too. "Let's all go."

With my head held high, I got out of there without bursting into tears.

It was only once we were off Main Street and there was no one else around that the tears flooded out of me before I could stop them.

Taran and Cammie hugged me, protecting me inside an emotional and physical cocoon of friendship, as I sobbed for the first time since Ramsay ended things between us.

I promised myself it would be the last time I cried for him.

35. Ramsay

Lying in bed, I stared at the ceiling, trying to sleep and failing.

Akiva, sensing my turmoil, had her head on my chest, comforting me. I stroked her head and tried to close my eyes again.

As soon as I did, I saw Silver in the pub. Looking at me with such pain and betrayal and hatred.

My eyes flew open, and I cursed under my breath.

Despite having left the disappointed folk singer outside the rental she was staying at with the band, I couldn't shift my guilt. I hadn't slept with the redhead. After seeing Silver's face in the pub, I couldn't do it.

There was this pressure, this unpleasant sensation, crushing down on my chest.

I'd thought I could fuck a random woman and send a message to Silver. So that she wouldn't feel bad about things ending between us. She'd feel like she'd made an escape. That somehow, we'd all move on.

But seeing her face and realizing I'd done that to her in front of everyone …

What a cruel fucking thing to do.
And more proof I didn't deserve her.

36. TIERNEY

Six weeks later

"Don't you think this could have waited?" I asked for the millionth time.

Cammie answered with patience, even though she'd be well within her rights now to snap at me. "No. We need the dresser so we can arrange the dining room. Having one space completely finished will be amazing for your social media. And I know you're off on your travels tomorrow, so I'll take all the photos and load them to the B and B socials."

My friend and interior designer had already explained her reason for getting me and Greig in a pickup truck borrowed from Forde to collect the Welsh dresser Ramsay had built for me. Three times she'd explained it.

I saw Greig and Cammie exchange a look of sympathy and I blanched.

It had been six weeks. I didn't want people looking at me

with those pitying looks anymore, but it was hard after Ramsay's colossal assholian move at the Lantern. Sure, it was common knowledge he hadn't slept with the folk singer, because said folk singer had complained to Taran and Ewan the next morning at the coffee shop about it. Ewan had proceeded to tell everyone. Now people were creating narratives in their heads about why Ramsay didn't sleep with her, and I didn't need their narratives when I was trying not to overanalyze the ones my own heart produced.

In the end, it didn't matter. He'd still humiliated me in front of everyone and that was enough for me. I was done. We were done. I'd avoided Ramsay as much as possible and we hadn't spoken since. I could have spent days in my bed, crying and bemoaning the end of something truly special, but I'd spent too much of life lately grieving. I didn't want to grieve someone who wouldn't grieve me back.

Instead, I got on with life and with healing. We'd celebrated Halloween and the only island festivities I avoided was the Halloween ceilidh because the pipe band played at it. Thankfully, Ramsay avoided the haunted trail that Cammie and Quinn's parents allowed to happen on their land. It kind of reminded me of an American haunted hayride. I helped out. It kept me busy, distracted.

Now it was a cold and wet November. Ramsay and the pipe band were on Skye this weekend to do a couple of gigs, and Cammie had decided it was the perfect weekend to put all the finishing touches on the guesthouse dining room. The first completed room in the B and B.

Because Greig was smitten with her, she'd roped him into helping us collect the Welsh dresser from Ramsay's barn.

I was shocked Ramsay had given Cammie the keys.

Pulling up outside his home, however, I hadn't expected to get slammed by so much emotion.

What I'd had with Ramsay took place over a month, a

short span of time in the grand scheme of things, but it had been the kind of passionate affair I didn't really believe existed between two human beings until it happened to us.

And that hurt so fucking much because it was like any loss. You mourned the loss of possibility too.

"You okay?" Cammie asked as Greig jumped out of the vehicle.

I avoided her question. "I hope you're not leading him on."

Cammie nudged my shoulder. "Stop changing the subject."

I gave her a serious look. "Are you leading him on?"

"He's young, he's sexy, and he wants me." She shrugged. "I'm tired of searching for 'the one.' We're having fun."

"Oh." I hadn't realized they were ... "So, you're already ...?"

"Last night." She waggled her eyebrows. "For a young 'un, he knows what he's doing."

A banging on the hood of the truck brought our gazes out to the windshield to where Greig waited with a cocky smirk. "If ye twa are done gossipin' aboot ma talents, can we get a move on?"

I mentally promised to grill Cammie on this situation afterward as I chuckled and got out of the truck. The clearing, protected by the trees, offered a reprieve from the harsh coastal winds. Amusement fled as I stared at the house, tucking my chin into my scarf as I contemplated it. Since I'd been avoiding Ramsay, I hadn't approached him to ask for the things I'd left at his house. I kept hoping he'd leave them with Taran at Pages & Perks or give them to Quinn. But they never appeared. Now was my chance to get them back.

Before I could overthink it, I walked up the front porch.

"Uh, where are you going?" Cammie called.

Ramsay had a Beware of the Alaskan Malamute sign next

to the front door. I lifted it up and saw the spare key taped to the wall of the house. He didn't know I'd noticed it when I'd been out on the porch one morning.

I untaped the key and tried it in the front door. It opened, and I paused.

No alarm.

Glancing down at an open-mouthed, round-eyed Cammie, I explained, "I left some stuff that he never returned. I'm getting it back. I'll be out to help you as soon as possible."

"Is this your way of avoiding looking at the dresser and feeling soft emotions toward McRae?" Cammie deduced with eerie perceptiveness.

"Partly. But mostly I want my shit back." I strode into the house and shut the door behind me.

I squeezed my eyes closed, leaning against the front door.

The house smelled like him.

It took me a second to gather the courage to open my eyes.

Memories cascaded over me.

While he'd never confessed much to me, I'd told him a lot about my past, about my parents, sharing little anecdotes about my childhood and travels. He'd listened with patience, like he was truly interested. I'd never had that before.

And then, of course, there was the stupendously amazing sex.

Bent over the dining table.

On the sofa.

Against the wall.

Even on the rug in front of the fire one particularly chilly summer evening.

Shrugging off the images that flooded my brain and erogenous zones, I moved through his space, searching for the books and tablet. My heart leapt into my throat because they were in the exact same place I'd left them. I was sure of it.

There was one of my paperbacks on the coffee table.

One on the edge of the kitchen counter, next to my tablet.

I picked them up as I passed, frowning as I stared warily into the bedroom suite. The rest of my stuff—toiletries—should be in there.

Most of the memories were in that room.

Tears of frustration burned my eyes, but I blinked them back. When I'd promised that night Ramsay left the Lantern with the redhead that I wouldn't give him anymore tears, I'd kept my vow. It hadn't been easy. There had been some close calls over the weeks.

But I was determined to be strong. Not just because I'd recovered better than anyone could have expected from my attack, not just because I was determined not to grieve him, but because I had to live on this tiny island and see this man all the time. There was no other option for me but to compartmentalize the month I'd spent with him.

And get over it.

I had to move on.

Throwing my shoulders back, I strode into the bedroom and veered off into the bathroom first.

Staring at his vanity ... I paused.

All my things were still here in the exact same place I'd left them.

The spare electric toothbrush I'd bought to keep here. My extra makeup bag. Deodorant. A hairbrush. It was all where I'd left it. It was like ... he'd cleaned and then put all my stuff back in the same place.

I absentmindedly rubbed at the ache in my chest as I looked at my reflection.

If I closed my eyes, I could see Ramsay behind me at this sink. Hands on my hips. Lips trailing across the nape of my neck, which he knew was a sensitive spot for me. His bathroom was a wet room, so there was a massive walk-in shower where we'd explored each other's bodies with an abandon I'd never experienced before.

Anytime I'd caught glimpses of Ramsay since he ended it, my immediate thought was one of vulnerability—this guy knew my body better than I did. He'd seen a side of me no one else had. He knew what I sounded like when I came. What my expressions were. How much I liked to be dominated. That I loved when he talked dirty while we were having sex. That I could come while he spanked my ass and told me the things he wanted to do to me.

This was knowledge only the man who shared my bed should know.

Except he no longer shared my bed. And he still knew.

One day, when I met someone else, Ramsay would always be walking around knowing these things about me, even as I gave them to another man.

It was disconcerting and one of the reasons it was harder to "just get over it."

My hands curled around the vanity, and I sucked in a big breath, letting it out in a shaky exhale. "You can do this," I whispered.

Striding out, I walked into the kitchen and found the cupboard where Ramsay kept shopping bags. I took one and began putting all my stuff into it. In the bathroom, I searched for my perfume, the one thing I'd really wanted back. It was expensive and I didn't have another bottle at Taran's.

It wasn't there. I could have sworn I'd left it there.

Forcing myself to, I walked out into the bedroom, avoiding the bed itself.

There.

On Ramsay's bedside table was my perfume, sitting on the paperback I'd been in the middle of reading. I hadn't left either of them there.

Confused, I slowly made my way over, staring down at them.

Why was my perfume and book on *his* bedside table?

Emotion clogged my throat.

Did that big asshole miss me?

No.

He ... if Ramsay wanted me back, he'd have said something by now.

Or would he?

I didn't know what the man was hiding from me, but was it enough to make him push me away?

He hadn't slept with the folk singer ... Was it guilt ... or was it that he didn't really want her?

Why did it matter?

In my frustrated anger, I reached for the perfume too fast and knocked it over the back of the bedside table. I winced as it clattered to the floor but thankfully didn't smash. Grumbling, I dumped the shopping bag on the bed and leaned a hand on the wall behind the table to reach down the crack between it and the furniture. Not quite able to reach it, my hand slid down the wall for balance and landed on the wall light. The weight caused the wall light to flex downward and I let out a little cry of dismay, thinking I'd broken it.

But then ...

A creaking sound brought my head up as a draft of cool air hit me. I gaped in shock.

The wall beside the light had opened.

Opened like a freaking door.

I straightened, a million questions and thoughts running through my head.

Of course, curiosity got the better of me, and I found myself pushing the wall open farther. The movement hit sensors and light spilled into the secret room.

Ramsay had a secret ... *war* room?

I stepped into it, my breathing heavy as my heart raced.

There was a bank of three computers that suddenly lit up with images of forestry, coastline, and the clearing outside. Sucking in a breath, I moved toward them, my gaze bouncing between the screens that had split views.

Of Stòr.

There were cameras all over the island.

There were even cameras at the little white house with the dock. Ramsay had told me it was the home the previous owner built, but Ramsay only used it as storage and it had a bed, in case anyone needed to use it. There was a camera inside that building and outside it facing the water.

A terrible thought crossed my mind, and I scanned the cameras for the inside of this house.

There were none.

Only cameras on the outside. I could see Cammie and Greig at the pickup truck.

Relieved to discover he hadn't been filming me inside his home without permission, I stepped back to take in the walls.

They were covered. With weapons.

Different kinds of handguns and rifles. Knives.

More weapons than any one man needed.

This was ... this was the kind of room a man who was running from serious shit kept.

Is this ... is this what he'd been hiding from me? Literally.

The sound of the front door slamming had me skittering out of the secret room. I instinctively pushed the light back into position and the wall closed.

I studied the mastery of the woodwork, the way the wall paneling masked the line of the door, and I knew Ramsay built this himself.

Footsteps had me quickly reaching for my perfume bottle. I'd just dumped it into the shopping bag when Cammie appeared in the bedroom doorway. "Are you done?"

"Yeah."

Her gaze swept the room, and I knew something cheeky flirted on her tongue by the quirk of her lips. Then she saw my expression and whatever she was going to say died. Instead, she asked, "Are you okay?"

Still reeling from the shock of the secret room, I covered whatever was on my expression with a half-truth. "Just ... memories. Let's go. Okay?"

"Sure. Greig and I got the dresser in the truck."

"Already? By yourselves?"

"We're strong." She shrugged and I could see her looking around the house as we walked out. "McRae has a shit ton of books."

"He inherited them from his parents."

"He told you that?" she asked, surprised.

"Yeah. He had his moments, you know." I stepped outside and waited for her to clear the doorway. Locking it, I then put the key back where I'd found it. "Let's go before the tide changes."

Cammie slid her arm around my shoulders, hugging me into her side. "You're amazing, Tierney Silver. A total badass. And he doesn't deserve you."

Her words rang in my head as we reached the truck and I saw the Welsh dresser in the bed. Ramsay had stained it with a clear finish like I'd wanted. It was beautiful. I placed the bag of my stuff in the bed too since there wasn't much room in the cab.

And he doesn't deserve you.

I turned back to look at the house, thinking of where I'd found my stuff.

Thinking of the hidden room that spoke of a man who led a secret life that was frankly a little scary.

And he doesn't deserve you.

Is that what Ramsay thought too?

Was that why he'd broken us?

If that was true, it hurt worse than anything.

Because I knew it was impossible to love someone who didn't really love themselves.

Any kernel of hope I'd been clinging to, a hope of some miraculous reconciliation ... it withered and died with that realization.

37. RAMSAY

The urge to get on the ferry to Glenvulin was strong. Somehow, however, I forced myself to get on the stage for our midday gig in Portree on the Isle of Skye.

We were booked again to perform that night in Broadford before traveling back home the next day.

I had to get through an entire twenty-four hours without giving in to the need to race back to Leth Sholas to make sure Silver didn't give me away.

Only instinct kept me on Skye.

The instinctual belief that Silver wouldn't betray my secret.

When the truck had approached my house, the app on my phone went off to alert me. I knew, of course, it was Cammie because I'd reluctantly given her the keys to my workshop to collect the dresser she couldn't bloody wait another day for.

Then my app alerted me because my front door had been breached.

Checking the camera feed, I saw Silver take my spare key I had hidden.

Nosy bloody woman knew where it was.

I hadn't set the alarm on the house and probably should have.

Hoping she was there to pick up the stuff she'd left and not to violate my privacy, I'd decided not to call the VHF radio in the house to tell her to get the fuck out.

But then a second alert came over the app, and this one was worse.

While I had no cameras inside the main house, I had one in the hidden room off the bedroom.

I saw on the feed as Silver stood inside the small room, staring around in abject shock.

She jolted as if she'd heard something and then quickly stepped outside, and the wall closed.

She'd found the wall light that opened the door.

In all the time she'd spent in my bedroom, I'd been very careful to keep her on the other side of the bed so she never found it.

I had to hope like hell she didn't tell Cammie. Or anyone.

Quinn, Forde, Murray, and Laird knew there was something up with me. I was taciturn. More than usual. But I couldn't tell them why. Instead, I got through our performance on autopilot. We ate. They exchanged looks they thought I couldn't see. I knew Quinn suspected I was pining for Silver because he'd fucking told me. After I nearly took his head off in response, he hadn't said it again. Yet I knew he was thinking it.

We drove to Broadford, and I let the lads talk among themselves while I checked my outdoor camera. Sure enough, the recording showed Silver stepping out of the house with Cammie seconds after she'd closed the hidden wall. They left quickly.

Gut churning, I left the lads at the guesthouse bar, promising to meet them before the gig, and disappeared into my room.

I brooded for a bit. Checked in with Annie to see how Akiva was doing. Resisted the urge to call Silver. Finally, it was time for the gig.

After we finished, I switched on my phone and found I had a voicemail.

From Silver.

Miraculously, I got through a late dinner with the lads before excusing myself to head back to my room to listen to her message.

The sound of her voice reawakened that crushing weight on my chest.

"Hey, it's me. I know we haven't talked in a while." I heard the shakiness in her voice as she took a breath before continuing. "I did something. When we were collecting the dresser, I remembered where you kept the spare key, and I went into the house to get my stuff. My books and tablet and toiletries. And, uh, I broke the wall light by your bed. You know the one. I ... I didn't mean to invade your *private space*. I'm sorry. I'm really sorry, Ramsay. And I'm sad." She let out a huff of hurt laughter and I hung my head, hearing the pain in her voice. "I'm sad you didn't feel like you could show me who you are. Or who you were. I ... Anyway, I'm not going to tell anyone about the wall light. I wanted you to know that." She let out another shaky breath. "Goodbye, Ramsay."

Silence echoed around the small room.

I scrubbed a hand over my face.

Silver was smart. She'd kept the message vague because she perceived the truth even if she didn't realize it herself. And she knew from her own experience, it was possible someone was listening who shouldn't be.

Smart.

Kind.

Sweet.

Fierce.

Passionate.

Capable.

Strong.

Independent.

My perfect match when it came to sex.

Resilient.

Honorable.

Good.

I missed Silver like I missed a fucking limb.

Gritting my teeth in frustration, I glared at my reflection as I caught it in the mirror on the wall.

In my life, I'd known brutal moments of unhappiness.

I'd known pride.

Satisfaction.

Contentment, even.

But happiness ...

I might have known it as a child, before my parents died. I think I did, considering how traumatic losing them was.

But I hadn't known it since. Not until her.

Realization scored through me along with something else I'd rarely felt until Silver entered my life.

Panic.

"You self-sabotaging bastard," I muttered angrily at my reflection.

38. TIERNEY

Ramsay never responded to my voicemail. If he'd chosen to speak to me in person or merely ignore what I'd discovered, I wouldn't know because fortuitously for me, I had a flight to catch the next day.

In the six weeks I'd spent recuperating, dealing with the slow, stressful, legal stuff for Shawn Prescott and Halston Cole, and seeing the B and B come together, I'd also been worrying constantly about London.

Her texts were infrequent, her calls even more so, and that didn't make sense. Considering what I'd been through and was dealing with, London would have been the first person calling me every day to check in. Now she was cagey and uncommunicative, and I couldn't sit by and let it go on.

Two weeks ago, I'd asked my doctor if I could fly. She'd suggested another two weeks and so I'd booked my flight for the Sunday. The day after we'd collected the Welsh dresser and I'd discovered Ramsay's secret room.

I'd barely slept, and Taran knew there was something up with me, but I'd hoped she'd put it down to my upcoming travels and concerns about London. She and Cammie had offered to accompany me, but I'd only bought a one-way ticket because I didn't know how long it would take to figure out what was going on with my best friend. And I wasn't leaving New York until I was satisfied she was safe and happy.

We'd had a friend in high school, Shay. We weren't best friends like London and I were best friends, but the three of us used to hang out a lot. When we were seventeen, Shay started seeing this older guy. Trevor. It was noticeable to me and London that Trevor quickly grew controlling. One of the things he used to do was constantly check Shay's phone and talk shit about her parents and us, trying to separate Shay from all of us. Shay broke up with him after a few months and he'd hassled her for a little while until her new boyfriend put the fear of God in him. The memory of Trevor's behavior, along with the ick Nick had always given me, had my alarm bells ringing.

I'd left in the middle of the night for my flight from Glasgow to New York. It was one of only a handful of airports in the UK that offered direct flights to my home city. I arrived at four o'clock in the afternoon my time, but it was only eleven in the morning in New York. Despite my exhaustion, I wanted to get onto eastern time as quickly as possible, so I forced myself to stay awake, checked into my hotel, ordered room service, and had a shower. By the time I was ready, I knew London would be at work.

The restaurant in Manhattan was fancy, but I needed to be discreet with my return to the city. Therefore, I wore a ball cap and sunglasses as I left the hotel. I'd chosen a hotel in Soho near Nick's apartment building to be close to London. However, she was the sous chef of a French restaurant in Midtown. According to live maps, it was as quick to grab a cab as it was to get the subway, so I chose a cab.

London was fifteen the first and only time she really got her heart broken by a boy. She'd been in love with a guy we'd met while on vacation at the Cape. One day he'd kissed me, and I'd immediately told London. But telling her that the boy she loved had tried to cheat on her with me, her best friend, was the first time I ever had butterflies facing London. I was so afraid she'd blame me. My mom warned me she might at first but also claimed London would come around.

In the end, London hadn't blamed me. She was devastated, but she also felt bad for me that he'd put me in that position. Because that's the kind of friend she was.

That day as I got in the cab, it was the first time since the summer we were fifteen that I had butterflies going to visit the woman I considered a sister.

The city passed me by, and now that I'd eaten and showered and was no longer in a plane daze, I drank in the place that had been home for most of my life. The buzz of vehicles and people, the tall buildings, vendors, stores, and chaos of life —there was a familiarity to it, a nostalgia. It was like a childhood house filled with memories … but it no longer felt like home.

It stunned me into silence in the back of the cab.

Because … Leth Sholas felt like home.

I'd hoped for it as soon as I walked off the ferry in Half-Light Harbor and experienced that feeling of rightness.

And my dream came true.

It was home.

New York might not be that for me now, but London still was. She was still my home too.

After paying the driver, I slipped out of the vehicle and stood in front of the French restaurant that wasn't open for another hour. The scent of food and traffic fumes hit me as soon as I got out of the car.

It was funny, but I hadn't realized how crisp and fresh the air was back on Glenvulin until I stood in New York again. It felt like a smog across my chest. It wasn't the first time I'd noticed the air quality difference. I'd been lucky to travel all over. Most cities were like that. Smog. Fumy. A chaotic potpourri of opposing scents.

Pushing my longing for my Scottish island aside, I stepped up to the restaurant. I could see staff inside. I took off my ball cap and knocked on the glass front door.

Laurent was still the maître d'. A tall, handsome Frenchman in his forties, Laurent was fun-loving with a wicked sense of humor. But he could turn on the cliché pompous Frenchman schtick for the clientele in an instant. Right now, he was shooting me an imperious look as he took his time approaching the front door. As always, he was impeccably dressed in an exquisitely fitted three-piece suit.

As he neared, I took off my sunglasses. "Laurent, it's me!" I called out, not wanting to say my name aloud.

Recognition crossed his expression and he unlocked the door, letting me in. "Tierney, what are you doing here?" He bent down to brush barely there kisses to both my cheeks.

"Hey, how are you?" It was lovely to see him, but I was impatient for my best friend. "I'm here to see London, of course."

Laurent's brows drew together. "London? But ... surely you know London does not work here anymore?"

With that, it was as if the rug had been ripped out from under me. I reached for Laurent instinctively and he placed a steadying hand around my biceps.

"Tierney, are you all right? Do you need to sit down?"

Call it jet lag on top of shock. I blew out a breath, trying to remain calm so I could get some answers. "What happened? Why doesn't London work here?"

He scowled, releasing me. "I have my suspicions. London quit two months ago. Said she was reevaluating her life."

"What?" *Two months!* "She didn't tell me. Is she ... is she still living with Nick?"

"Who knows."

What did he mean? Laurent and the staff here were London's friends. They didn't only work together, they socialized together because they were the only people who shared the same crappy schedule. "You haven't spoken to her lately?"

He tsked and shook his head. "London pushed us"—he gestured to the restaurant—"all away these last few months. I tried to talk to her. So did Cynthia." Cynthia was his girlfriend and the restaurant's sommelier. She and London were good friends. At least, I thought they were. "But she stopped answering our calls and texts. When she quit, that was the last we heard of her."

"That doesn't make sense." My unease grew by the minute. "Did you notice anything off about her behavior?"

"Oui." Laurent nodded, anger flashing in his dark eyes. "Little bumps and bruises she tried to hide. Cynthia tried to get her to open up ... but she was completely shut down. Sorry." He shrugged unhappily. "We did try, but she didn't want to talk."

I felt sick to my stomach. "Are you saying Nick is abusing her?"

"I don't want to say anything without facts."

And they'd left her to it? I glowered at him. "You suspect it and you let her leave? You didn't do anything?"

"Do what? You cannot help someone who does not want to be helped."

Like hell!

Throwing him a look of disgust, I stormed out of the restaurant, shoving my hat and sunglasses back on.

It took me fifteen minutes to find a cab, and I cursed myself for not jumping on the subway. By the time we reached Nick's apartment building in Soho, I'd had to talk myself down several times from a ledge that might lead me to murdering Nick!

Nick's building, unsurprisingly, had every amenity possible beneath the apartments. It also had twenty-four-seven doorman service, a receptionist, and key card security. Nick had a private elevator to the penthouse on this side of the building, which meant I couldn't go up. The doorman let me in, and I asked the guy at reception to call Nick's apartment, hoping the asshole was at work and London would be home.

My wish came true, and London agreed to let me up. I was vibrating with anxiety when the receptionist swiped a key card over the pad on the wall beside the private elevator.

As the elevator rose, I did a little meditative breathing to slow my pulse. It helped. A little. The doors opened, revealing Nick's large, stylish home. It was an open-plan concept with floor-to-ceiling windows along two walls overlooking the city.

I'd seen his home before. Therefore, my attention wasn't on the expensive furnishings and one-of-a-kind artwork I'd always thought were pretentious.

I was looking at my best friend who stood before me.

Her pretty face was gaunt, her cropped T-shirt and cardigan drooping on her small shoulders, her baggy jeans barely clinging to her slim hips. It wasn't only the weight loss that shocked me.

It was the way she stood almost hunched into herself, a hand wrapped around her opposite wrist, knuckles white with nervousness. It was the hollowness in her stunning turquoise eyes.

She forced a wide smile and reached for me. "What are you doing here?"

I walked out of the elevator and into her arms, feeling how delicate and fragile she was, and I had to fight back tears. Burying my face in her neck, I trembled, trying to hold back the emotion and failing.

"Hey, hey, hey ..." London tightened her embrace. "I've got you. I've got you."

It was so typical for London to be in the midst of something awful and still offer me comfort.

Pulling back, I ignored the tears drying on my cheeks and took her in.

Her lush red hair was in a messy topknot, so it only accentuated the hollowness of her cheekbones. Her freckles were covered with a thick layer of foundation, which wasn't her usual style. When she wasn't at work, London wore multiple piercings in her ears and a small hoop in her nose. She didn't wear any jewelry now. "Oh, Spoon, you don't look like yourself at all."

Her expression tightened and she dropped her hold on me.

The sleeves of her cardigan had pushed up when she embraced me. I caught sight of the dark smudges around her forearms, and fury flushed through me.

"Are those bruises?" I reached for her, but London quickly shoved her sleeves down and crossed her arms. A huge diamond glinted on her ring finger, momentarily stunning me. Not just because London tended not to wear rings because she had to take them off for her job but because my friend was engaged.

And she hadn't told me.

"You're engaged?" I whispered.

London glanced unhappily down at her finger. "He proposed last night."

Shouldn't she be the happiest woman in the world then? "You look *miserable*."

She flinched. "What are you doing here without warning?"

I gaped in shock at her sharp tone. "What am I doing here? Do you mean what am I doing here after being stabbed?"

She flinched again. "Silver ..."

"Where have you been?" My anger made me push even as a voice in the back of my head told me to stop. "I got stabbed. I got dumped by a man I'm pretty sure I'm in love with, even though I also kind of hate him. I'm juggling two legal battles against the man who stabbed me and the man who ordered my murder after murdering my parents. What am I doing here? Where the fuck have you been? Why didn't you tell me you got engaged?"

Tears filled London's eyes as she stumbled back from me.

And I cursed myself.

Whatever Nick was doing to her ... the last thing she needed was one more person emotionally wailing on her.

"I'm sorry." I hurried to apologize. "I'm so worried about you, Spoon. Laurent said you quit two months ago! He said that you've been cagey, that you dropped all your friends, that you came into work a few times covering up bruises and injuries. Now you're standing before me not looking like you at all and there are definite bruises on your arms." I took a step toward her. "Did he do this to you?"

Fear seemed to swallow London's entire face. "I ... you should probably go. I'll come to you. Just let me know where you're staying, and I'll come see you." She gently shoved me toward the elevator.

"Spoon." I took her hand. "Please."

"I wanted to quit my job." London was breathless now. "I'm taking time to figure out what I want to do, okay? And I d-don't l-look like myself because you took off for Scotland and left me behind." She none too gently shoved me onto the elevator. "You don't get to come here and judge me when *you* left *me* behind. Nick didn't leave. He's the only person who hasn't left me and he won't."

Oh God. "Spoon"—I reached out to stop the doors from closing—"that's not true. I know you better than anyone. Remember that. No matter how much physical distance is between us, I will never truly leave you. I got on a fucking plane as soon as I could after the attack to make sure you're okay."

Her lips trembled as she tried to fight back tears and I saw her. I saw her buried behind the fear in her eyes.

"I won't leave you alone in whatever this is," I vowed. "I'm not leaving New York until I know you're okay. I'll be back. And if you need me, I'm staying at the Winton. Room 201." I let go of the door. "I love you, Spoon."

The doors closed between us, but I caught London's sob before I was shut out from her.

I swiped angrily at my own tears, vowing to get her out of whatever mess this was with Nick.

Whatever it cost me.

39. Ramsay

I stepped back from the built-in closets in one of the guest bedrooms. Greig, Andrew, and Mikey, our decorators, were making their way through all the rooms, painting walls and paneling and hanging the wallpaper Silver and Cammie had chosen. As they finished up, I went in at the back of them to add the final staining to the built-ins and custom shelving.

Turning, I took in the space. It didn't have any furniture in it yet and the curtains needed to be hung, but it was coming together nicely. Silver would have a business to be proud of once it was finished.

I moved out of the room, past crew who were buzzing around the place doing all the finishing work. The wide, Victorian staircase had been given a new lease on life, the rails sanded down and repainted, the carpet ripped up, the stairs themselves painted, and a new carpet runner fitted down the center. Quinn had floor protectors everywhere. I watched my step as I took the stairs down into the large reception hall and turned, heading toward the back of the house and the dining room that had been opened into the morning room by removing that wall Silver had busted out.

It was the first completed room and Quinn was trying to keep everyone out of it. He had floor coverings down, though. I strolled in, thinking about how Silver hadn't seen it in real life yet.

Because she'd taken off for fucking New York.

A flare of panic cut through me. Gritting my teeth, I walked through the dining and morning room to push open the large bifold doors that led out into the back garden. Sure enough, Akiva was enjoying the winter sun, a rarity on the island. She lifted her head in greeting as I crossed the grass to pet her.

It was too late in the year to do much with the gardens, so the landscaping was on pause until spring. Lowering to my haunches, I scratched behind Akiva's ear and stared out at the view.

All I saw was the coastline to the mainland.

Where Silver had gone, traveling to Glasgow to jump on a plane to New York.

A week ago.

Cammie said she'd left to see her friend London. I knew Silver was worried about her.

But Cammie also said Silver had planned to only go for a few days.

Yet she still hadn't returned.

Quinn had been communicating with her via email.

What if ... what if she didn't come back?

What if she sold the B and B once it was renovated and decided to stay in New York? To be near London.

To get away from me.

There was that crawling, tight feeling traveling up my chest again.

Fucking panic.

Not like me at all.

"Nice day. Cold, but nice."

I glanced over my shoulder to find Quinn behind me. I grunted and looked back out at the water. I was warm from working inside. The brittle air over the sound was a welcome reprieve.

"Out here brooding? Again?"

"I don't fucking brood."

"Mate, you've been brooding since Silver got attacked." Quinn crouched to pet Akiva, and my dog basked in the attention, her eyelids lowering comically. At this angle, she almost looked like she was smiling.

"Since when did Akiva like you this much?" I changed the subject.

"Akiva's always loved me. I have a way with the ladies," Quinn joked. "Stop avoiding the question."

"You didn't ask a question."

"All right, stop avoiding the subject."

I didn't answer. Just gave Akiva one more scratch and a kiss on the nose before I stood. "I better get back to work."

"You're worried she's not coming back." Quinn stood too.

At my stony silence, my friend sighed.

"Ramsay ... *I'm* worried she's not coming back."

There was that fucking panic again.

"I'm not worried for me, though I like her and we'll all miss her." My friend took a step toward me. "I'm worried for you."

"Quinn—"

"I know it's not easy to admit when you care about someone. Especially for someone like you. But take it from me, mate ... it's not worth the lifetime of regret."

My gaze sharpened on my friend and business partner. On the pain I saw in his expression.

His sincerity was uncomfortable, but I gave him my attention as he continued. "A long time ago, I let pride and fear get in my fucking way. I didn't fight for what I wanted. For who I wanted. And while I wouldn't change having Heather and Angus, there is this regret that hangs over everything now. Knowing that I fucked up so badly with Taran. It was there long before she ever came back. What I felt for her fucked up my marriage. Because I married the wrong woman. And now I can't have the right one ever again. She's gone for me." Quinn swallowed hard and looked out at the water, visibly fighting back emotion. "Wouldn't wish that on my worst enemy. So, I certainly don't want that for you, McRae."

Fuck.

I scrubbed a hand down my face.

Then I looked at Quinn.

Really looked at him.

And I saw what I'd always seen but told myself my friend could deal with.

That beneath his easy-going facade there was a lack of contentment.

Definitely a lack of happiness.

I hated that for him.

Quinn was a good man.

Better man than me.

And without Silver … I was staring at a window into my future.

I glanced down at Main Street. "It's never too late. Taran's here. You sure you want to give up yet?"

"Am I to take advice from a bloke who let his woman go?"

"Will you watch Akiva while I go to New York?"

Quinn grinned. "I can watch Akiva."

"If I go to New York to bring Silver back, you have to try again with Taran." I pointed a warning finger at him.

He scowled. "I think I've laid my pride at her door enough times."

I raised an eyebrow. "You tried to find an opening with her just after her mum died. After her fiancé left her. It was never going to happen then. She needed time. She might even need a wee bit more time. But you *will* try again."

Quinn's brow wrinkled as he considered my words. "I'll think about it. Not saying I will. Just that I'll think about it. But you need to go to New York."

I held out a hand to him. "Shake on it."

He shook his head but took my hand in a firm grip. "Deal."

"Deal."

40. Tierney

This had to be one of the longest weeks of my life.

I hadn't seen London since that first day.

While trying to remain incognito, I'd visited the apartment building in Soho every single day and been turned away. London wasn't picking up the phone or answering my texts.

I left her a daily voicemail too.

I'd been trying to consider what hold Nick had over London. My best friend had always been so fiercely independent because of how shitty her parents were. She'd always been the one in the driver's seat in a relationship because that's what made her feel safe. In the past, if a guy had tried to take control, she would dump him at the first sign.

Nick had somehow emotionally manipulated my friend. She feared him. I could feel it emanating from her.

How, then, did I convince her that she didn't need to be afraid of him?

Last night I'd left her another voicemail.

"It's me again, Spoon. I wanted to say … no one is too big or too powerful that they can't be fought. Haven't I proven that with Halston? The sad reality is that there are people out there who don't have any power, who bad people target because they can. But you aren't one of those people, Spoon. We grew up with a privilege that means we have a certain amount of cache too. We can find something on Nick. Is it playing dirty? Yes, but I don't care if it means getting you out of there. You can come back to Scotland with me. Be the chef at the B and B. You'll be safe there. No fear. No guilt. No shame. Not anything but safe. Please. Please, London. Talk to me." I was careful not to remind her she was the only family I had left. Or make it about me. I didn't want to be another person in her life emotionally manipulating her.

Because I was sure that's what Nick was doing.

I was certain of it.

Striding into the coffee place around the corner from my hotel, my worries weighed down my steps. I could see Perri already at a table, tapping away on her phone while she waited for me.

The *New York Chronicle*'s building was in Midtown, and I'd arranged to meet Perri around the corner from it to catch up in person.

My friend, because I thought of her as a friend now, stood as soon as she saw me and enveloped me in a warm hug. I squeezed her, holding tight to the tears of gratitude that wanted to spill out all over her. We pulled away, and I gave her a watery smile instead.

She chuckled and gestured for me to sit. "Don't look at me like that or my ego will get out of control."

I laughed and sat across from her. "How are you?"

"Things have been a little crazy since the article. But more to the point, how are you? What brings you back to the city?"

I didn't tell her my worries about London or that I missed my friend.

We chatted for a while. I told her my lawyer had called yesterday to tell me the case against Shawn Prescott was going to court and the court date would likely be set for some time next summer. We still didn't have word on the case against Halston Cole because it was more complicated, but we'd hear from the presiding judge in the next few weeks whether it would go to court.

My lawyer had no doubt that it would.

"It's a tough time ahead."

"But worth it?" Perri asked.

"It's worth it for me."

"And for Ben's family," she reminded me. Ben's family didn't have the evidence to prove Ben's death had been ordered by Cole, so their only hope was that he'd pay for what he'd done to my family and to the islanders he'd regarded as a nuisance he could plow through.

Perri asked about my B and B and promised to book a vacation to come and see me. We chatted for a bit longer before she had to get back to work. I stayed at the coffee shop after she left, checking my messages from back home. Trying not to think about the fact that Ramsay had never responded to my voicemail.

Concentrating on London had made it easier to not think about the man I'd left behind.

I answered texts from Taran, Cammie, and Quinn, and then left the coffee shop to do a little shopping. If there was one thing New York had over Glenvulin, it was the stores and the restaurants. I'd noticed Taran loved a purse of mine, so I wanted to spoil her with something pretty as a thank-you for letting me stay with her. Cammie always wore unusual necklaces, so I was on the hunt for something special to bring back for her too.

As I turned the corner, distracted by a million things, I wasn't looking where I was going and pain ricocheted up my shoulder as I collided with someone walking in the opposite direction. I stumbled as a male voice snapped "Watch it," and I opened my mouth to apologize.

And stopped when our gazes locked.

Hugh.

Of all people.

Hugh's expression slackened with surprise. "Tierney. You're back?"

"No, I'm not back." I skirted around him, not wanting to engage with him at all after his visit to Scotland.

"Wait." He grabbed my biceps, and I shrugged him off with enough force he dropped his hold and raised his hands in surrender. "I'm not … Sorry. Look … I wanted to say, I read the article in the *Chronicle*. I'm sorry about what happened to you. Are you doing okay?"

He actually thought we could have a normal conversation. I guffawed. "Seriously? We're not doing this. Ever. The world knows why I gave up the shares in my company and that it was for a pretty good reason. Good luck trying to put me under a conservatorship now, asshole."

Hugh had the audacity to blanch.

"Yeah, did you think I'd forget that horrendous threat?"

"I shouldn't have said that." He nodded, fake remorse etched carefully into his features. "I said it in the heat of anger."

I scoffed. "The fact that the thought even entered your mind tells me all I need to know about you, Hugh."

The fake remorse fell as easily as it appeared. "Is that right?"

I took a step toward him. "What happened to Michelle?"

Rage flashed in his eyes and he bent his face toward mine, hissing in warning, "Nothing. And you and your boyfriend better leave well enough alone." How easily he switched from remorseful to aggressive was slightly terrifying. "I'd have thought a knife in the gut would've smartened you up, sweetheart." He moved to leave me behind with a sinister smile thrown over his shoulder, but my rage at powerful men like him getting away with actual murder overtook my sense.

I grabbed his arm, my fingernails biting into him. "If that was a threat, I'd think again. If you haven't noticed, assholes who do very bad things tend to find Karma once I dig up their shit."

Hugh almost bared his teeth at me but seemed to think better of retaliating. Instead, he shrugged off my grip and marched around the corner out of sight.

I trembled with anger.

At him.

At Nick.

At Halston.

With Halston, I'd only half dealt with it. We still had the trial. The verdict.

Hugh had gotten away with whatever he'd done to Michelle and God knows what other controlling crap he'd tried to pull with women.

And Nick ... he was abusing one of the people I loved most in the world.

If I could help London get away from Nick, then at least one of them would be dealt with for good.

It was difficult, though, when my best friend didn't seem to want help.

Thoughts of shopping abandoned me and I found myself walking back to the hotel instead. If I were a painting, I was sure I'd be shrouded in wintry dark clouds of grim thoughts. As I moved through the lobby heading toward the elevator, however, a familiar voice called my name.

A shot of adrenaline spiked through me as my head jerked left.

Walking slowly toward me was London, wearing big

sunglasses and a ball cap. Her fingers threaded nervously together in front of her as she approached.

Not wanting to draw attention to her, I reached out, took her hand, and hit the call button for the elevator.

We didn't say a word as we waited and then stepped inside. I swiped the key card over the panel and we rose to my floor. The whole time I kept her hand tightly wrapped in mine.

I could feel how violently she was shaking, but I held it together as I led her into my hotel room.

The door closed behind us and I waited for London to make the first move.

She dropped my hand, her arm trembling as she raised it to take off the cap and sunglasses.

Fury exploded through me, and I had to suck in a breath to contain it.

Her right eyelid was swollen and there was dark bruising all around the socket and top of her cheekbone. A sob burst out of London, and I grabbed her to me, wanting to shelter her from Nick with my entire being.

I tried not to cry, but I couldn't stop the tears.

When one of us was in pain, we were both in pain.

She clung to me so hard, her fingernails bit into my back, but I didn't care. I held her as she rattled both our bodies with the force of her sobs.

41. Tierney

I called for chamomile tea and snacks as London cleaned herself up as much as she could in the bathroom.

She stayed in there when the room service arrived and didn't come out until the server was gone. If he'd noticed my eyes were red and swollen from crying, he didn't comment.

"Sorry for breaking down like that," London apologized quietly as she approached the sitting area.

I pushed a cup of chamomile toward her. "Don't be. *I'm* sorry I couldn't keep it together for you."

The corner of her mouth quirked up. "You cry, I cry. I cry, you cry."

That was true.

It always had been.

London slipped into the chair opposite me, her shaky hands reaching for the hot cup. "I don't know how I got here," she whispered.

I knew she didn't mean to my hotel.

"You can tell me anything, you know. Nothing you say will ever make me love or admire you any less."

Tears flooded her eyes again. "But I let him do this to me."

I controlled my anger. "You didn't *let* anyone do anything to you."

"He wasn't like this at first." She smirked bitterly. "He was charming. I thought his confidence was sexy. The sex was great." Self-flagellation glowed in her eyes as she looked at me. "You knew, though, didn't you? These last few months that's all I kept thinking was that you knew something was off about him and you tried to tell me, and I didn't listen."

"London—"

"Why couldn't I see it?" she hissed. "I saw it in Hugh. I saw what a creep he was. Why couldn't I see it in his friend? Why did I let this happen?"

"You didn't let anything happen. This happened *to* you."

"It was ... it wasn't like this at first," she repeated. "It was gradual. Little negative comments about my job and my friends. Things I let get in my head over time because they were, like, my deep buried insecurities. How did he see them? How did he pluck them out and use them against me?" She swiped at a tear in frustration. "Stuff like ... how I worried I wasn't good enough at my job. That maybe I couldn't handle the stress or the hours. That my friends there weren't really my friends but liked that my name could get them into places." Shame paled her features. "That you left me behind because you didn't love me like I loved you."

I covered my mouth to cover a sob.

"I'm sorry," she cried. "I know that's not true."

"I'm sorry I left you," I apologized through my tears. "I'm sorry you've been going through this alone."

London huffed, wiping at her cheeks. "I was the one who told you to go. And you had big-world shit going on, Silver. I let you down, not the other way around."

"I don't believe that. I will never believe that."

"He said I did." She turned to stare out at the city. "Nick

said I was a shit friend and that I didn't deserve you. Of course, that was weeks after he told me you were a shit friend and I deserved better." She chuckled unhappily. "By that point, I knew he was a fucking asshole. I just ..." London tentatively touched her cheek. "I tried to leave after the first time he hit me. He was being a pretentious asshole, and I was starting to really not like him. I said so. He punched me. I was so stunned I barely heard him threaten to kill me if I left. Every time I tried to leave, he would remind me he had the kind of power that meant he could kill me and get away with it. And I believed him."

"London ..." I didn't know what to say. What to do that would make it all better.

"It was easier to give him what he wanted." She shrugged, vacillating it seemed between high emotion and numbness. "I quit my job. Became his little arm ornament. My parents love him." London scoffed. "They met him at this stupid fucking art gala thing last month and told me that they were so proud of me."

I shook my head in disgust. They'd seen her last month, seen how much weight she'd lost, that she'd quit a job she loved, and they didn't think anything was off about that?

"When Nick didn't tell me that you got attacked ... I tried to leave again. And when he hit me, I fought back. He had to go into work with scratches down his face." London curled her lip. "It felt good. I felt like me again for a second. And I thought, I can do it. I could leave him. Even if I had to really hurt him to leave, it would be better than this hell I was currently living. He wanted me to hang around the apartment, meet up with his colleagues and clients' wives and girlfriends for shopping and lunch. Our parents didn't even force cotillion on us, Nee, but *he* wanted me to be the perfect New York socialite. I didn't know if I was more terrified or more bored out of my fucking mind."

The fire in her voice gave me hope because it belonged to the London I knew and loved.

"I was going to leave." She nodded. Then desolation crushed her features. "But then he told me that he was the reason Halston had you stabbed."

I gaped. "What?"

Guilt tightened her features. "He tapped my phone. Every conversation you and I had got back to him. And he threatened Halston to back off me but also told him that you weren't going to stop because of the threats. So *I'm* the reason you got attacked."

"No!" I shot out of my chair to pull her into my arms. "You are not the reason."

"I'm sorry."

"Please." I smoothed her hair back. "Please don't apologize." Cupping her face gently between my palms, I took in her black eye and vowed, "We're getting you away from him."

"When I got your voicemail last night ... something in me snapped. We got into a huge fight"—she gestured to her eye—"he warned me not to leave the apartment today. But I can't stay. I'm afraid if I stay, I'm going to kill him or he's going to kill me."

"That's not going to happen. We are going back to Scotland. And if you want to, you can work at the B and B with me."

For the first time, I saw hope in London's eyes. "I want to get away, to come with you, but ... I don't have my passport. He locked it in his safe along with all my credit cards, my driver's license, and my old phone. He doesn't know about the new one. I asked Cynthia to get it for me. I still owe her money for it."

It made my stomach churn that she'd been forced to ask her friend to buy her another phone. I wondered if Cynthia had kept that from Laurent, considering Laurent's blasé attitude. Maybe not all of London's friends had abandoned her after all.

The fact that the asshole had locked her passport and driver's license in a safe ... How much I wanted to hurt Nick was on par with how much I wanted Halston Cole to suffer for eternity.

The passport issue was certainly a problem, but one I was determined wouldn't stop us. "Let me figure out a plan. Tonight, you stay with me. Does he know I'm here?"

"No."

Something occurred to me. "Hugh might tell him. I bumped into that prick today." I worried my lip. "Okay, we're safe at the hotel for at least a night, but if we haven't figured things out by tomorrow, we'll move hotels."

"I'm sorry I'm putting you through this when you've been through so much already."

"You're not putting me through anything. I love you. We protect each other. We always have."

Her lips trembled. "I love you too."

A few minutes later, at London's request, I called down to see if the adjoining room was available. I understood she needed some alone time to decompress, but I worried about her, even with only a wall between us. However, for the past six months, everything she wanted had been taken from her through threats and violence, and I wouldn't take even the slightest thing from her merely because *I* needed her close.

Thankfully, the room was available, and I hurried down to the lobby to collect the key card and the key for the adjoining door.

After London disappeared inside her room to shower, I sat on the edge of the bed and tried to figure out how the hell we could get into Nick's safe.

When the knock sounded on my hotel room door, my pulse instantly raced. Fear made my knees shake as I crossed the room on tiptoes to peer into the peephole. All I saw was darkness, and I realized a body was covering it.

The darkness disappeared as the person stepped away from the door, frowning at it.

Confusion and relief burst through me with recognition.

I fumbled for the door, throwing it open. I stared up into Ramsay's rugged face, those piercing eyes looking right into my soul. For a moment, I wished I could throw my arms around him and hold on tight.

Because he'd made me safe.

Even now, after everything, he made me feel safe.

I kinda hated him for that too.

Crossing my arms over my chest, I covered my wealth of emotions with what I hoped was calm blandness. "What are you doing here?"

42. Ramsay

I could see right through Silver.
 Knew every nuance and flicker of emotion in her eyes and across her gorgeous face.

She was as relieved to see me as she was belligerent and confused.

That gave me hope.

I'd gotten a red-eye from Glasgow to New York and arrived in the early hours of the morning New York time. My hotel had twenty-four-hour check-in and was a block from Silver's. I might have asked Jay to track her down.

After sleeping for a few hours, I'd showered, eaten, and immediately made my way over to the Winton in the hopes of catching Silver in her room.

Here she was.

Standing in front of me like the best fucking thing I'd ever seen.

And her eyes were bloodshot and swollen.

I stepped toward her without thinking. "Have you been crying?"

Silver retreated warily. That hurt like a motherfucker. "What are you doing here, Ramsay?"

At the sound of a door opening down the corridor, I glanced along it to see a guest leaving their room and a housekeeper coming off the lift with a cleaning cart. "Can I come in?"

Her brow wrinkled in confusion, Silver stepped back with a nod and held the door open. As I moved past her, I studied her slightly swollen eyes and saw the tear tracks through her makeup.

She *had* been crying.

At my close perusal, Silver turned away and shut the hotel room door.

The room smelled of her perfume.

Memories of burying my nose in her throat just to inhale her pushed in and I shook them off. Now was not the time for that. "Christ, hotel rooms in this city are a fucking rip-off, aren't they?" London and New York were two of the worst cities for charging an absolute fortune for rooms you could barely swing a cat in.

"Is that why you came all the way to New York? To complain about square footage?"

Smirking at her sarcasm, I lowered myself onto the edge of the bed.

She raised an eyebrow. "If this is about the wall, I told you I won't tell anyone."

I suppose she had every reason to think my coming here was for something selfish. In truth, it was. Only it wasn't for the reason she assumed. My gaze washed over her. Despite the tear stains, Silver was beautiful, sexy. As always. However, she'd abandoned her usual Henley and jeans for a long-sleeved jersey dress that clung to her figure. My gut clenched at the way it followed the exaggerated curve of her narrow waist into her generous tits and gently sloped hips. "You're stunning."

Silver leaned her shoulder against the wall. "Somehow I doubt you came all the way to New York for a booty call."

I flicked her an annoyed look. "You know me better than that."

"Do I?" She pushed off the wall, dropping her defensive posture. "Because last I checked, I don't know who you are."

"That's not true. Look ... you've probably guessed by now, but I didn't keep my past from you because I didn't trust you."

She narrowed her eyes. "Does Quinn know about your past?"

Fuck.

I held her fiery stare. "Aye, he knows. He's the only one from Glenvulin who does."

"If you told Quinn but not me, then you trusted Quinn but not me."

Frustrated, I growled, "I don't care if Quinn judges me for my past. I care if *you* do."

Silver sucked in a breath, her shoulders slumping. "Do you think I would?"

I shook my head. "No. I just used it as an excuse. To push you away."

"To protect me?"

"Maybe. Maybe it's more that I didn't think I deserved you."

She let out a huff and strode slowly over to a seat at the small table. I noted the two cups of tea. "I think maybe deep down I knew that."

"Is there someone else here?" I tensed, alert.

Her gaze darted to the cups, and she shot me an unhappy look. "London is in the next room."

"She okay?"

"Why are you here, Ramsay?" she repeated instead.

Leaning forward, I held her gaze, needing her to see the

truth in mine. "I don't have a pretty past. I did things in the name of king and country that were necessary but not pretty. Not good."

Her stunning eyes grew wet. "Can you tell me?"

"Some of it. I came all the way here to tell you what I can."

"Okay. I'm listening."

I took her in, her calmness, her openness, her ability to be vulnerable but strong. Her bravery. Tierney Silver was fucking remarkable.

And I knew then she was it for me.

She was the one.

And it was going to hurt like hell if I had to walk away from her.

But I started talking, anyway. "You know my parents died when I was young."

Silver nodded, unconsciously leaning closer.

"I went off the rails. Got into bad shit. When I hit sixteen and another foster home, I knew I was on a path to jail or death. Ultimately, I didn't want that to be my mum and dad's legacy. They were both educated and intelligent, and they would have wanted better. My dad was a professor of English literature. I inherited all those books from him. Mum was a neuroscientist. Her mother had a very rare type of Alzheimer's. She died at only forty-one with the disease. It set my mum on a path for researching a cure. Both of my parents dedicated their lives to education before they were killed in a car accident. It would have destroyed them to see me throw my future away."

"So, you joined the Royal Marines?"

"I did. It was during my first big operation, where my commanding officer was killed, that things changed. I led the men. Got us out of a situation that we probably shouldn't have gotten out of. The higher-ups realized I was a particularly strong strategist and that I had a photographic memory. They ran a few tests."

"What kind of tests?"

"Different kinds of personality tests, IQ tests. I scored high on those." I shrugged.

"How high? Genius high?"

I nodded. "I was twenty-one years old when MI6 recruited me as an agent. They recruit people from all walks of life to be agents, codebreakers, analysts."

"MI6, as in James Bond?" Silver stared wide-eyed.

Tender affection thrummed through me. "Not quite. I mean, it's inextricable now with the Bond mythology. But espionage is neither loud nor high profile. Aye, there have been times the details of an operation have made it into public consumption. However, discretion and secrecy are key. I wouldn't walk into a bar and announce who I was while I was on an operation." I huffed at the absurdity.

Silver gaped, pretty lips parted wide. "You're serious. You're an ex-secret agent?"

"Retired."

"I, uh, yeah, uh ... I'm going to need more information."

I could give her more but not detailed. "Historically, MI6 recruited from the upper classes. My few remaining friends at the agency are such people, but the Soviet Union used that strategy against us, infiltrating Cambridge University to find people they could turn into British traitors. Convince them to join the British Secret Service and then pass those secrets along to the Russians. So, MI6 diversified. But even today, members of the intelligence community use private spaces in London, elite clubs like Whites and Boodles to meet." Only a few weeks ago, I'd met James in one.

"You were a spy." Silver slumped back in her seat. "An actual spy?"

"MI6 has around thirty-two hundred officers running

covert operations across the world. They use fake companies as a cover for clandestine operations. I worked in many of them over my fourteen-year career as an agent. One of my longest jobs was where I earned my engineering and construction qualifications. It was a cover, of course. My real job was to infiltrate, undermine, covertly acquire intelligence, or use blackmail, bribery, sometimes physical violence, to persuade foreign agents to betray their country and hand over top secret information. I had fifteen aliases in my time with the Secret Service. I infiltrated terrorist organizations and aided in the dismantling of international plots, not just against the United Kingdom but her allies." Here came the dirty truth. "I betrayed people I befriended, romanced, and worked with. Sometimes people who didn't deserve my loyalty, and sometimes people who were pawns in a bigger game. I was loyal only to my country, and I never looked back at the people who got hurt because I was so fucking good at my job."

Silver studied me silently. Her eyes roamed my face. I wondered if she could hear my heart slamming against my ribs.

Finally, she tilted her head in consideration. A familiar mannerism I'd missed. "What do you want me to say? Do you want me to judge you for doing a job very few people in this world can do? A job that ultimately protected your country?"

I sighed. Heavily. "I need you to know … I've been a ruthless bastard. I've hurt people. Your parents died trying to do what was right. I lived doing what I thought was right, not caring who died as a consequence."

"I think you do care. I think it lives with you every day. The choices you made."

Lowering my gaze, I didn't argue. Because she was right.

"Is that why you retired early?"

No. That was another story. One I hadn't spoken of since that night with Quinn. It wasn't a tale I enjoyed telling.

But for her …

"All agents have an officer. Your officer runs the operation, details what they want and how they want it, and the agent acquires and passes along the intelligence to them. Usually, we met in London. London is called the City of Spies for a reason. Not only because of James Bond. It's because beneath everyone's noses, London is a crossroads. It's full of exiles and dissidents. Spies from all over the world move through the streets of London trying to collect intelligence."

"You were one of them."

"London was my home base. And aye, it's where I met my officer more often than not." Grief tightened sharply in my chest. "Her name was Natalya. She was my officer from the beginning and had been a foreign spy, recruited by MI6 when she was a university student to betray Russia. After she acquired the intelligence they needed, she was recruited into the agency permanently. She was twelve years older than me." I took a deep breath, not wanting to hurt Silver but wanting her to understand. "I fancied myself in love with her."

"Oh." She lowered her lashes, covering her expression. "Were you two ...?"

"No. Natalya fell in love with another British agent about a year after moving to London. By the time she and I met, she was very happily married to Ian. There was never anything on her side. She loved her husband. Deeply. And he loved her."

Silver met my gaze again, concern in her hazel eyes. "What happened to her?"

"When ... when we plan to meet to pass intelligence on, an officer will walk what we call an antisurveillance route. They'll establish a theme. For instance, shoe shopping. Natalya would take detours into stores pretending to look for a pair of shoes so that if anyone was following her, they'd think she was just shoe shopping. If she spotted the same person on her route, we called it a double sighting and we'd abort the meeting.

"That day, she met me, and she told me she'd wasn't sure if

she'd had a double sighting. I was angry because even a sliver of doubt meant she should have aborted. But we were in the middle of a highly urgent operation, and she wanted the information I'd acquired. The next thing I knew she started seizing in the restaurant. I tried CPR, but she was dead within seconds. A sniff of her drink revealed a hint of almond. Toxicology reports proved she'd been poisoned with a liquid form of cyanide." I dragged a hand down my face at the memory of her sightless eyes staring up at me.

"I'm so sorry," Silver whispered, sincere emotion in her words.

"It wasn't even for the intelligence I'd given her. It was a state-ordered assassination. After twenty years, they killed her for betraying Russia."

"Oh God." She covered her mouth, shaking her head.

"Ian, her husband, blamed me. And I didn't blame him for blaming me. The meeting should never have happened, and I have no idea how I missed that someone had the opportunity to poison her drink. I should have protected her, and I didn't."

"So you retired early?"

"I couldn't attend Natalya's funeral because Ian didn't want me there. But only agents and officers attended. No outside friends or family.

"And I knew that would be me if I died on the job. Except there would be no grieving wife. I was a fucking ghost. That's what I was. A ghost."

"And you didn't want to be that anymore."

"I didn't realize that was why I quit. I thought it was guilt. Failure. I thought I wanted to be alone. Of course, quitting meant starting over as someone new. Especially after what happened to Natalya. Ramsay McRae is my sixteenth and last alias."

Her lips parted in surprise. "It's not your birth name?"

"No. No one but me and the agency know my birth name. I became Ramsay six years ago, and that's who I am. The agency paid well, but I dabbled in high stakes gambling during my career and accumulated what I called my safety net in case I needed to disappear. I bought Stòr. But then I got Akiva. And Quinn." I smiled at Silver's small chuckle. "And everyone on Glenvulin." I held her soft gaze. "Then you showed up."

"The nosy American," she teased, though her eyes were still dark with all the secrets I'd revealed.

"I have traveled the world and met many people, Tierney Silver ... but I've never felt what I felt the moment we met."

"What did you feel?"

"Like I already knew you," I confessed gruffly. "Like you knew me."

She blinked and her tears slipped free. "That's how I felt too."

"You scared the shit out of me."

Silver laughed, wiping at her wet cheeks. "I bet I did."

I grinned, that hope building in my chest. "There's nothing I wouldn't do for you, woman."

"What have you done for me?" she whispered. "What happened with Halston? What do you know about Hugh and Michelle ...?"

If I was disappointed Silver needed more answers, I didn't show it. Because I'd told her there wasn't a thing I wouldn't do for her. And I meant it.

43. TIERNEY

My heart raced so fast, I could barely hear over the blood rushing in my ears. Ramsay's story was unbelievable and yet I believed every word. A part of me wanted to throw my arms around him so he'd know that I didn't judge him for his past.

If anything, I admired him more than ever for what he'd done for his country. Even if he wasn't proud of the details—details I didn't need to know—I would never understand the choices he'd had to make. So, I was in no place to judge.

However, I needed to know everything he'd kept hidden that had to do with me.

I had to.

Ramsay seemed to understand that. "I pay a hacker called Jay to check things for me. She also has a program running to remove any photographs of me that end up online. To keep people from the past who might recognize me from uncovering my whereabouts."

"Is that why you have the secret wall room?"

"Aye. There's a satellite dish hidden at the back of the house that connects to the internet as well."

I gaped, momentarily forgetting big-picture stuff. "We could have been streaming Netflix? I could have checked my emails?"

His lips twitched. "Aye."

"Seriously?"

He shrugged. "I was under the impression you rather enjoyed the way I kept you entertained."

Heat flushed through me as the Scotsman smoldered. "None of that just yet."

"Just yet?" He raised a hopeful eyebrow.

Getting back on track, I huffed. "You were saying about Jay..."

"Jay." Ramsay nodded, serious again. "She helps me find things."

"You mean hack people?"

"Sometimes. After you told me about Halston, I got some help from Jay but also from an ex-colleague. James and I came up in the agency together. From totally different backgrounds, but we were good friends. If I trust anyone from that life, it's him. He's now a senior officer and will probably one day take over as chief. Anyway, he used all the resources at his disposal to track down Shawn Prescott and connect the dots to Halston."

"And he got away with that?" I asked because I didn't want Ramsay or his friend getting into trouble with their *government* for me.

"Aye. There's no way to say this without it sounding arrogant as fuck, but my government, and other governments, owe me. I've protected them economically and I've prevented cyber and biological weapon attacks against several countries. They owe me, and they know it."

"Like James Bond," I teased, trying to break the heavy tension.

Ramsay flashed me a quick grin that made my belly swoop with attraction. "Aye, I guess in that way like James Bond."

"That's where you disappeared to when I was in the hospital?"

He shifted, pushing up to stand, pacing back and forth for a second.

This sudden need to burn energy made me uneasy.

"Ramsay, what did you do?"

"He never saw my face."

"Who never saw your face?"

"I flew here. To New York. James helped me infiltrate Cole's club. I dosed him with a laxative and while he was alone in the bathroom, I broke his nose, almost choked him to death, threatened him that if he didn't stay away from you, I'd make him disappear for good."

My lips parted and a little sound, half gasp, half strangled laugh, escaped me.

I would have paid to be a fly on that bathroom wall.

"Are you … are you telling me that you … you threatened to kill Halston Cole *and* you made him shit his pants?"

Ramsay's lips twitched. "Unfortunately, he made it to the loo in time, but he was quite distressed by the sudden, violent bowel movement, if that helps."

Perhaps it was the strain of this entire day or weeks or months, but I laughed until I could barely breathe and was wiping tears from my eyes.

When I eventually calmed, Ramsay was on his knees before me, studying me with a warmth and tenderness he usually tried to hide. I reached out instinctively and smoothed a hand down his unshaven cheeks. His stubble prickled my palm and I shivered, remembering the feel of it as he kissed me … and as his face brushed my inner thigh.

"Thank you," I whispered.

"You don't need to thank me." He covered my hand. "I told you. I'd do anything for you."

"And Michelle?"

Ramsay's expression tightened with sympathy. "Hugh overdosed her. He slipped too much GHB into her drink, trying to loosen her up. Her respiratory system failed."

Horror suffused me. I felt sick. I'd lived with a man who had dosed a woman he was dating. I shuddered.

Poor Michelle.

"That son of a bitch," I wheezed out.

"James looked into it for me. Hugh's father has friends in high places. It was a team effort from all those bastards to make it look like Michelle was at fault. They considered it easy enough since she was a well-known party girl."

Those bastards. The level of corruption was devastating. "What did you threaten Hugh with doing?"

"The men who helped Hugh out of the scrape, they're holding on to evidence that they use every now and then to force Hugh's father to do their bidding. James could easily acquire that evidence. I threatened to use it if Hugh didn't leave you alone."

Before I could respond, there was a knock on the adjoining door, and it suddenly opened. Ramsay turned to look over his shoulder as London stepped into the room in the hotel bathrobe. Her hair was wet and slicked back from her face.

And her black eye was more prominent than ever.

"Oh." She halted, her good eye widening. "I didn't ... who is ..."

"London." I stood, my tone reassuring. "This is Ramsay."

Ramsay slowly rose at my side and London's eyebrows lifted as she took in the size of him.

Feeling his tension, I looked up at him and saw the muscle

flexing dangerously in his jaw. "Who the fuck did that to your face?"

44. Ramsay

My purpose in coming to New York was to show Silver who I was and hopefully win her back.

Now, I put my selfish wants to the side.

I'd seen the worst of humanity as my time as an intelligence agent. Abuse I'd sometimes had to ignore because it interfered with the bigger picture.

This, I didn't have to nor could I ignore.

London was understandably brittle and was reluctant to explain her black eye when Silver asked her permission to confide in me.

"You can trust him," Silver had promised.

Because she trusted me.

After everything … she trusted me.

I felt about ten feet tall.

London gave her the go-ahead, so Silver told me about London's fiancé Nick. His abuse over the last few months. The control. Everything spoke to a very typical pattern in emotionally and physically abusive relationships. The abuser would systematically attempt to isolate their victim from the world. It made them easier to manipulate, control, and threaten by first creating the isolation and then insisting they were the only people who could be counted upon. That they were the only people who loved them.

I'd seen it many times, and it didn't matter who you were, how strong you were, how independent, how fierce … it could happen to anyone. Staring into London's eyes, I knew more than anything her struggle would be with herself and the irrational blame she laid at her own feet. Even once we got her free and clear, her path to freedom from her misplaced shame would not be an easy one.

As I took in the friends, it was only seeing them together in real life for the first time that I recognized how close they were. It was clear Silver hurt when London hurt. She'd taken on her friend's troubles even while dealing with her own. I worried about her. Yet it made me more determined to win her back.

To be the person she could lean on. To be the person to shoulder the weight.

And I had broad shoulders.

I'd shoulder the world for her.

They laid out their plan to bring London back to Scotland but explained London's passport was locked in Nick's safe. My brain was already at work, figuring out our next move.

"Do you know what kind of safe it is?"

"Digital." London shrugged wearily.

"Fingerprint, retinal, or code?"

London frowned. "Um, code. I think I know it. I've been waiting for him to open it again and watched him put some money in it the other night."

Well, that made things easier.

"Nick isn't … he's a powerful stockbroker. His family are the Hustons. Old money. They made their fortune in railroads back in the day and then became one of the biggest financial investment groups on the East Coast. Their company is publicly traded now, but they still have a lot of influence and power. Not to mention, Nick is best friends with Hugh Inchcolm. Tierney's ex. Heir to Pioneer Motors."

I sneered. "I know who Hugh is. He's not a problem. If your worry is Nick's connections, we can deal with that."

"How?"

I pulled out my phone. I didn't want to take advantage of James, but this was a wee bit above Jay's pay grade. It was Tuesday afternoon in London and James was probably at work where there were eyes and ears everywhere but, still, I called him.

A few rings later, my friend picked up. "Twice in as many months when I hadn't heard from you in a year."

"Sorry to call again."

"I'm not sorry. How can I help? Is this about your lady friend? Again?" James's tone was teasing.

"Actually ... kind of."

"I hope she's not in trouble. Or anymore trouble. I've been following the case. Cole will see justice one way or another."

"Thank you. I actually need a deep dive on someone. Nicholas Huston. A New York stockbroker."

"As in the New York Hustons? The finance family?"

"That's the one."

"Specifics?"

"Skeletons. Dangerous, rattling skeletons."

"Why?"

"He thinks he owns the women who date him. I'm trying to free someone from him."

"Doesn't he sound charming. I'll get you what you need. Give me a few hours. I have a meeting first."

"No problem. I owe you."

"You owe me several." James chuckled before hanging up.

I turned to the women.

Silver stared at me in a way I knew too well, and I wished we were alone so I could take advantage of it.

London narrowed her good eye. "Who the fuck are you?"

45. Tierney

Despite everything between us still up in the air, I wanted to jump Ramsay. Spy mode Ramsay was hot. Hot Ramsay distracted me from the utter avalanche of information I'd had to process between London's devastating revelations and Ramsay's intense ones.

The only thing that stopped me from getting into bed to let the last twenty-four hours wash over me was London. My determination to help my friend. I was profoundly moved by her trust in me—that she knew I wouldn't share her story with just anyone. That if I trusted Ramsay she knew she could too.

I could see his instinctive fury over the idea of any man hurting the woman they were supposed to protect. Yet he'd put that aside and gone straight into problem-solving mode.

He'd explained to London he'd been in the military. That seemed to assuage her questions. Better yet, his confidence that we'd get her back to Scotland with us, his air of capability, seemed to reignite the flame of determination in London's eyes too. I was worried with everything Nick had put her through she wouldn't want to return to the apartment.

Ramsay had even given her the option not to. It would be harder without her, but he'd get her damn passport back.

London had shaken her head, tilting her chin in that stubborn familiar way. "I'm doing this. I need to do this."

We understood. As much as we could understand.

She needed to feel like she'd taken back control of her destiny.

My gut knotted unpleasantly as we approached the apartment on foot. I resisted the urge to reach for London's hand because it would be to comfort me and not her. London had her game face on behind those huge dark sunglasses.

"You ready?" Ramsay asked her.

London nodded. "I want it over with."

The doormen eyed Ramsay as he ushered us in ahead of him, but London said, "They're with me."

Ramsay strode at our backs like a bodyguard as we walked through the marbled entrance toward the penthouse elevator.

"Uh, Ms. Wetherspoon!" the guy at reception called out but London ignored him, fumbling to get her key card out of her pocket. She swiped it over the keypad, but it bleeped red. She cursed and tried again.

"Ms. Wetherspoon." We all turned to stare stonily at the receptionist. He was a tall, broad-shouldered young man wearing a light gray suit and the shiniest shoes I'd ever seen.

"Andrew?" London gestured to the elevator. "Why isn't my key card working?"

She sounded impressively calm and "normal."

He glanced at me and Ramsay before giving London an apologetic grimace. "Mr. Huston asked us to deactivate your key card. The penthouse system has been updated with a different code, so you'd need the new key card to access it. I, uh ..." He lowered his voice. "I'm under strict orders not to give you a new key card."

That piece of shit!

He knew after she'd tried to leave last night that she'd try again. As soon as she left the apartment, he made it so she couldn't access it again without him. What an absolute psychotic bastard.

A flush stained London's cheeks and I could see the telltale signs of her fuse readying to blow, but Ramsay placed a calming hand on her shoulder. "That's no problem, Andrew. I'm sure it's a misunderstanding. London will give Nick a call." He nodded politely and guided us back toward the exit.

Trusting he had a plan, we followed.

As soon as we were outside, I cursed. "What now?"

Ramsay held up a finger, telling me to wait before he again pulled out his phone. I smirked. Him calling in resources was becoming almost comical. As if he saw the thought in my eyes, his gleamed with warm amusement. I almost melted right there on the sidewalk. This version of Ramsay, this not hiding how he felt about me Ramsay, was going to be my undoing.

"Key cards use either a magnetic strip, NFC, or RFID technology," he said, as if I knew what any of that meant. "Jay can find out what system this building uses, but it doesn't really matter if the code is transmitted via radio waves or not. We need access to the building's digital database. Jay can hack it, switch it back to the old code, and we can get into the penthouse with London's original key."

Grinning as he hit the call button on his phone, I mused, "I hope you pay this Jay very well."

"Oh, I do."

Then something occurred to me. "You two didn't ... you know?"

"Really?" London nudged me. "Can you be a jealous girlfriend later?"

"I'm not his girlfriend," I replied without thinking, my eyes darting to Ramsay.

He scowled. "Jay's just a friend. And no, you're nothing as

simple as my girlfriend. But when this is all over, I hope you'll consider being my woman again."

The way he said "my woman" in that growly, deep accented voice ... I was inappropriately turned on. "Why is that hot?" I asked London as Ramsay started to talk with Jay. "That shouldn't be hot, right?"

London gave me a sad shrug. "It was hot."

Oh God, what a serious idiot I was being. I reached for her hand and squeezed. "Sorry."

"Don't be." She tightened her fingers around mine. "After everything you've been through, I want nothing but the best for you."

"We all okay?" Ramsay asked as he snapped his phone shut, eyes darting between us. And I knew he saw everything. He always had.

"We're good. What's next?" London demanded.

"We walk out of sight of the building for the next fifteen minutes, giving Jay time to do what she needs to do." He gestured with a nod down the street and we followed.

Two young women in exercise gear walked toward us and one of them spotted Ramsay and nudged her friend. Their mouths parted as they stared at him like he was a big ol' water bottle after an intense workout. Eyeing his tight ass in his dark jeans, his broad shoulders in his navy T-shirt, I was equally thirsty for him. Ogling him continued to keep my mind off the shittiness of London's situation.

"Hey." One of the women nodded at Ramsay as she passed, her lips curling in invitation.

To my delight, he didn't acknowledge her, not even to be polite.

"I'd climb that man like a tree," her friend groaned as they passed me and London.

"He's not exactly inconspicuous, is he?" London whispered, threading her arm through mine.

"Nope." It made me wonder how he managed to be invisible as a spy. I guess, for him, that wasn't part of his skill set. Or maybe it was. I couldn't imagine ever not noticing him when he was in the room.

"Are the women on your island as thirsty for him?"

"No one who's been obvious about it," I murmured back. "It's more tourists and visitors who flirt with him. But we don't have to talk about me and him right now."

"I need to talk about something or I might scream. Nick blocked me from getting into an apartment I naively thought was ours, not his, and somehow, it's almost as bad as him punching me in the face. Anyway, distract me. Are you two back together?"

I wanted to press her about her feelings, but I granted her wish and didn't. "I don't know. We had a lot to talk about this morning and then this ... so ... I don't know."

"Does he want you back?"

Nervous excitement fizzed through me. "He does."

"Do you love him?" she whispered.

Emotion clogged my throat and I nodded. "So much it kind of terrifies me."

"I guess that's your answer." London leaned in closer. "I never loved Nick. He excited me at first and I guess I was caught up in the great sex ... but I never loved him, which somehow makes me feel worse that I got into this situation."

"You never loved him because some part of you knew he wasn't right for you. That shouldn't make you feel worse, Spoon."

"My point is ... I think, before I knew what he was really like, I was going to settle for him because I didn't really believe in love. Not the kind they talk about in books and movies. But this is love." She gestured to Ramsay, who was much farther ahead than us now on the sidewalk. "The way he looks at you. Him doing all of this. He's only kind of doing it for me. This is mostly for you. He looks at you like he'd do anything for you."

I gripped her tighter, forcing back my tears as a wave of confusing emotions flooded me.

Hope, happiness, surreal disbelief that I'd found the one and he felt the same way about me.

Guilt that I might have this while London was going through hell.

Rage at Nick for putting her through hell.

Ramsay suddenly glanced back at us and waited for us to catch up. "Let's wait around the corner here." His gaze sharpened on my face. "What is it?"

"Nothing." I shook my head.

His expression said he didn't believe me, but he let it go, though I felt him watching me as we waited for Jay to do her thing.

46. Ramsay

Silver was looking at me in a way that gave me hope. But I couldn't let my mind wander to that.

We had a job to do.

The receptionist, Andrew, stared open-mouthed as the elevator doors to the penthouse opened.

London, cool as a cucumber considering the circumstances, waved her fingers at him. "I got the key from Nick. Like we thought, just a misunderstanding."

The receptionist nodded, and we stepped into the elevator.

"You're good at this."

London glanced up at me. Her tone was brittle, bitter. "You get used to masking your true feelings when it might get you punched."

Silver muttered angry curses under her breath.

I ground my teeth together, promising Nick Huston a wee bit of retribution once London was free and clear.

The elevator doors opened to a swanky apartment with an impressive square footage that would make most New Yorkers weep with joy. There was no time for looking around. "Safe?"

London shoved her sunglasses up her face and I saw that beneath her outward calm, she had a deer-in-the-headlights look that spoke of oncoming panic. "This way."

We followed London left down a hallway off the main open-plan living area and into a large bedroom suite. Behind the wall the bed was set against was a walk-in closet. She shoved aside a row of suits and there was the built-in safe.

"I'll start packing for you." Silver caught sight of a duffel bag and pulled it down from a shelf.

London murmured her okay and selected a six-digit code. The safe bleeped red. "Fuck."

"It's all right." I attempted to keep her calm. "Maybe the last digit was wrong."

"Yeah." She nodded, her breathing increasing. "He moved slightly so maybe it was three instead of six." She pressed in six digits, but it wasn't the same as before. The safe bleeped red. "Fuck, fuck, fuck!" London slammed a palm against the side of the black metal box.

"It's all right," I repeated. "Last time you entered 498126. This time you entered 489123. Try 498123."

"I did?" She gaped up at me. "Oh. Okay." With trembling hands, she selected the code I'd suggested.

The light on the safe turned green, and the door swung open.

London let out a slight sob before she reached in to pull out her passport and wallet. "This is it." Turning to me, she blinked back tears. "Thank you."

I nodded, giving her shoulder a squeeze. "No problem."

Two minutes later, Silver looked up from shoving a top into the duffel bag. She was slightly sweaty and out of breath. "Done."

"Already?"

"I packed what you needed to get started. Underwear, a

few pairs of jeans, a couple of tops. It's stuff I recognized as yours before you met Nick."

"Is there anything here you need before we go?" I asked.

"No. Everything else is his. Let's go."

Unfortunately, we all heard the elevator ping as we departed the bedroom suite. London's steps faltered as a man in an expensive suit stepped out of the lift.

I waved a hand at London and Silver to stay behind me but to keep walking. Nick Huston was recognizable from the images that had popped up on my quick Google search. Good-looking and not in a smooth way like Silver's ex. He had a sharp-edged quality to him. No warmth in his cool blue gaze as he faced us.

Nick was smart enough not to dismiss me, giving me an assessing, wary look before he turned his focus on London. The bastard didn't even hide the avarice in his eyes. His expression told me he thought he fucking owned London.

"How did you get in?"

London pressed into Silver's side behind me. "Key card."

"I had the key card changed."

"I don't know what to say. It still worked." She shrugged. But her voice shook. The cool, collected calm from earlier was gone. "I came to get my stuff."

Nick laughed softly. "You really think you're leaving me?"

Some of her fire crackled to life again. "This is the third black eye you've given me, Nick. Of course I'm leaving you."

"So, you brought muscle with you." Nick sneered at me.

I wanted to wipe that fucking sneer off his face. Permanently.

"You can tell people you dumped me. I don't care."

"I won't be doing that." Nick took a step toward her, anger tightening his jaw. "Because you're not leaving me. What did I tell you would happen if you tried?"

"You piece of shit," Silver hissed. "Don't you threaten her."

"Like I'd listen to you, you cunt."

My hand was around his throat before he could blink. His eyes popped out of his head as I squeezed and thrust him back against the hallway wall. Nick clawed at my hand, pushing at my wrist. He thought because he could beat up a woman half his size, he was strong.

I enjoyed making him look and feel weak.

"You come near London again, you contact her, threaten her, or try to directly and/or indirectly harm her in any way, *I* will deal with you. And that is the last thing you want." I released him, stepping back.

Nick bowed over, coughing as he clutched at his now bruised throat. Wrath morphed his handsome features into something monstrous. But he was nothing compared to what I'd faced in this life. I'd sooner be afraid of Akiva.

"I don't even know who you are," he wheezed.

Silver pressed into my side, trembling with her anger. "This is the man who nailed Halston Cole to the wall."

Nick straightened, his surprise evident.

"Yeah." Silver nodded, eyeing him like he was a piece of shite on her shoe. "I know you're the one who told Cole I wasn't going to back down and you're pretty much the reason I got stabbed."

What the fuck?

I moved toward Nick on instinct, but Silver grabbed my arm, halting me. "This is me holding him back from fucking you up permanently."

I bared my teeth at the prick.

Silver continued. "You don't want to mess with him. And you really don't want to mess with me, Nick. Not again. Trust me when I say that you're just a big fish in a small pond. We will annihilate you if you ever try to contact London again."

Like a switch, Nick's eyes welled up as he turned his attention to London. "Baby, are you really going to stand there and let them treat me like this? I love you! I am the only one who really loves you."

"Bullshit," London and Silver said in unison.

Silver quieted, though, glancing at her friend.

London stared blankly at Nick. "You have taken the last you're ever going to take from me. I left the engagement ring I didn't even want in the safe."

His nostrils flared. "The safe?"

"Yeah. I have my passport and wallet again. So, I'm leaving. Everything in that bag"—she pointed to the duffel Silver still held—"is everything I brought with me. Nothing you bought me. I don't want anything from you. We're done."

His hands flexed at his sides as if he wanted to react physically, so I moved in front of her, raising a finger in his face. "Fucking try it."

"This isn't over."

Aggravation writhed through me, but I kept a leash on it. Nick wouldn't be a worry for very long. James had sent over information before we'd entered the building that promised as such. "Unless you want me to crush your throat, you'll step back and let us pass."

Reluctantly, the piece of shit did so.

I ushered London and Silver onto the elevator.

Then I looked back at Nick and grinned.

Like I knew something.

Because I did.

He had the good sense to look uneasy.

Silver and London were silent as the elevator descended. London lowered her sunglasses back down to cover her black eye. They didn't speak as we walked out. London handed over the key card to Andrew who gaped at her in shock. The doorman pulled open the door, and she gave him a nod as we followed her out.

It was only once we'd made our way down the street that Silver's best friend finally spoke. "This isn't over. He won't give up."

"You don't have to worry about Nick. He's going to be preoccupied with other things very, very soon."

Her head whipped toward me and though I couldn't see her expression behind the glasses, I could feel the sharpness in her words. "What does that mean?"

"A friend of mine with resources." I turned to Silver. "James."

She nodded.

"Who is James?" London demanded.

"Like I said, a friend in a high place. The FBI are gathering evidence against Nick for insider trading. Apparently, he's bribing tippers to provide him with information he uses for personal gain and for specific clients. By the end of next week, he'll be so tied up in a legal shit show, he'll not only not have time to follow you to Scotland, legally he won't be allowed to leave the country."

Silver let out a huff of disbelief and relief.

London staggered back against a storefront and Silver dropped the duffel to make sure her friend was okay.

She waved her off, sucking in deep, shaky breaths. "It's ... it's over. It's really over."

"It's really over," Silver promised.

London looked up at her. "I won't believe it until we're in Scotland."

"Then there's no time to lose. Let's go home."

"I don't know what home is."

"It's with me." Silver pulled her into her arms. "We're family, Spoon. I've got you." She looked up at me over London's head and mouthed "Thank you."

I gave her a nod. "Told you. I'd do anything for you, woman."

She smiled through wet eyes before squeezing them closed as she tightened her embrace around her friend.

47. Ramsay

I'd never liked the feeling of uncertainty.

Rarely did I feel deflation. Mostly because I always entered situations with managed expectations.

Yet as I let Akiva out of the truck, watching her hurry toward the porch, I experienced both sensations weighing me down.

The evening temps were dropping to low single digits now, though my house was protected from the coastal winds by the surrounding forest. Still, there was a distinct wintry chill in the air as I let us both into the house. And it wasn't merely my mood.

We'd returned to Scotland five days ago. I'd barely seen Silver, let alone discussed our relationship.

True, she'd been preoccupied moving London into the bungalow with her and Taran. The little I'd gleaned from our short interactions and texts, Taran was happy for the company. Silver hadn't visited the B and B much, once to show London quickly around, twice to agree on some final details. But from the former interaction, I saw London struggling, so I understood the woman needed Silver. They'd bunked down together in Taran's bungalow while she tried to process everything she'd been through.

It wasn't the most opportune time for me and Silver.

"Miss her, though," I told Akiva as I dished up her dinner. "Do you, sweetheart?"

Akiva stared up at me impatiently.

"Right. Don't ask you questions when there's food on the go, eh?" I lowered her plate and gave her head a scratch before striding into the bedroom. I wasn't particularly hungry. Quinn and I had eaten at the Lantern with his kids. Quinn only had them every second weekend starting on a Friday evening. Reading between the lines, it had taken a lot to get Heather out to the pub. Heather had turned from a bubbly wee kid full of questions into a taciturn teenager who could barely look up from her phone. Angus, on the other hand, hero-worshipped his dad and was full of constant chatter. It didn't stop Quinn from shooting his daughter equally concerned and agitated looks all evening.

Kids had never been something I'd allowed myself to want.

For so long, I thought I'd end up dead before I retired. My job wasn't exactly conducive to a normal family life. Once I retired, I'd shut myself off from the possibility of family.

Now ... Silver opened a future I hadn't expected. Her distance, however, rattled me. Was it really because she was taking care of London? Or had she changed her mind about me now that we were back?

"Fuck." I slumped down on the bed, dragging my hands over my face. This was why I'd tried to avoid the connection I'd instantly felt with her. That kind of connection messed with your fucking head.

Akiva started barking, alerting me.

I stood and marched out of the bedroom. "What do you hear, girl?"

She raced toward the front door, and I tensed at movement by the living room window.

"Ramsay, it's me!" Silver's voice turned her shadow into a familiar face behind the glass.

Anticipation thrummed through me as I strode to the door to unlock it.

Silver smiled up at me from the doorway, her ridiculously bright SUV visible in the clearing behind her. It was a welcome as sight.

"What are you doing here? Did you text?" I asked as she petted an excited Akiva.

"No." She bit her lip, uncertainty flickering in her gaze as she gave Akiva one more rubdown and straightened. "I wanted to surprise you, so I made the crossing before the tide came in. I'm, uh, kind of stuck on your island with you again. Is that okay?"

Relief shuddered through me along with emotions too big to articulate. I flashed her a wicked grin before I swept her up into my arms to swing her inside, shutting the door with a kick of my boot.

Silver laughed, wrapping her arms around my neck. "I guess it's okay."

48. Tierney

Goodness, I'd missed this man in more ways than one. It had taken a supreme amount of self-control and love for London to put her first. Truthfully, focusing on getting her settled on the island, letting her grieve, was selfishly helpful for me too. It gave me time to think about Ramsay and what I wanted.

We needed to talk about the future and what we both wanted out of it.

But I wanted to try.

And that night I couldn't wait anymore.

I left Taran and London watching a paranormal teen show on Netflix. I was relieved that my two friends had bonded quickly. It gave me some room to explore my feelings.

The plan was to talk to Ramsay.

But as soon as he swept me into his arms, I knew all of that could wait. I *needed* him.

Perhaps I expected his usual dominating, passionate, *throw me on the bed and fuck me until I saw stars* fare.

So, I was surprised when he gently lowered me to the foot

of his bed. He held my gaze, *his* intense and filled with desire and tenderness as he yanked off his shirt in one swoop of rippling biceps. Never looking away, making me breathless with his intensity, Ramsay kicked off his boots, then unzipped his jeans. He drew them and his boxer briefs down, tugging off his socks too.

My skin heated as I took in his masculine nakedness, my belly clenching deep and low. I'd seen him naked so many times, but I'd never get enough. And I wanted him to be the only man I ever saw naked again for the rest of my life.

Heart racing, I licked my suddenly dry lips as I looked at Ramsay's impressive cock.

He stroked it, his gaze turning low-lidded as he turned and sat down on the edge of the bed. He placed his hands behind him, spreading his muscular thighs, his cock bobbing between them.

"Come to me, angel."

I crossed to him, and he reached for me, gripping my waist in his strong hands. Ramsay coasted his palms down my back, over my ass, giving my cheeks a squeeze. "I've missed you," he admitted gruffly.

Caressing his cheeks, feeling his close-trimmed beard prickle my palms, emotion thickened my throat as I whispered, "You have no idea how much I've missed you."

"Good," he grunted, making me smile. "Boots off."

I kicked them off, my breaths growing shallow with mounting lust. Then he unzipped my jeans, the zipper loud in the silence of the room. My belly clenched again and my wetness intensified. Steadying myself on his shoulders as Ramsay tugged down my jeans, I lifted each leg to help him discard them. Holding my gaze again, he slipped his thumb beneath my underwear, pushing against my clit.

I moaned, arching into the pressure.

"Always so wet for me, angel."

"Yes."

"Is it just for me?" he asked.

I opened my eyes at the territorial question. "Yes," I promised. "Only you."

Satisfaction hardened his expression as he wrapped his free hand around his cock. "Good. Because this is only for you."

I swayed as he circled my clit and then he stopped but only to grip my hips and pull me to his face. Ramsay nudged his nose against the fabric of my panties, pushing close to breathe me in, mouthing me through the material. I gasped, threading my fingers through his hair as his palms smoothed down my ass and under the panty line to cup my bare cheeks. His tongue pushed the fabric against my clit, and I groaned as it triggered another wave of arousal.

Impatience rode me, but Ramsay seemed in the mood to take his time.

He leaned back to peel my underwear down my thighs but just enough. He left them mid-thigh and looked up at me as he slipped two fingers in me. I inhaled sharply at the pressure and his cool gray eyes turned hot.

"I forgot how good you taste. How good you feel. So fucking hot and wet and tight." He ran his tongue up my opening, tasting me even as he finger-fucked me. "So mine."

"Yes." My fingers tightened in his hair. "Yours."

"Take your top off. Bra too."

I followed his orders, shivering at the hungry way his eyes ravaged me as my nipples peaked in the cool air. Dropping the shirt and bra at our feet, I waited for his next move.

He pushed me back so he could lower himself to his knees and then pull me to his face again.

"My underwear," I gasped out, wanting to shove them down my legs.

"Keep them there." His eyes flashed. "Do you even know how sexy you look right now?"

Before I could answer, he buried his face between my legs and began to lick and suck and *devour* me. His beard scratched and tickled my inner thighs, adding a spectacular element of sensation.

My cries filled the bedroom as the tension coiled and tightened like a spring. Ramsay steadied me with strong hands on my hips until the tension tightened too far and I exploded.

Knees trembling, I grabbed his shoulders, shuddering against his mouth as he drank up every drop of my release. Ramsay settled back, holding me steady. My skin was so hot, I felt like I was feverish and my inner muscles still throbbed as if searching for the thicker sensation of his cock.

He stood and wiped a thumb over his lip. "On the bed."

I moved to push my underwear down, but he gently touched my chin with two fingers.

"Keep them where they are and lie down on the bed on your back. Arms up."

It was a little awkward to get onto the bed with my panties around my thighs, but I knew what arms up meant and I eagerly crawled onto the bed for it.

Sure enough, Ramsay moved around the room as I settled on my back, his cock a purple-red, pulsing and veiny, and clearly in desperate need to be inside me.

He opened the bottom drawer of his dresser and pulled out the soft leather rope. From his bedside table he pulled out the condoms. I raised an eyebrow at how he tore off the packet to put aside.

Ramsay smiled slightly, though his expression was too intense with need for real amusement. "I'm going to take you many times tonight."

Oh.

My stomach muscles clenched. "I want that too."

"Oh I already know that, angel," he said with a cocky arrogance that shouldn't have been hot but totally was.

Then he proceeded to loop the ties around my wrists, drawing them just tight enough before he tied them to the headboard, securing me to it.

I followed him with my eyes as he strolled to the bottom of the bed, tearing open the first condom packet. His gaze roamed hotly over me as he rolled it on.

"Are you planning on taking off my underwear at some point?"

Ramsay nodded as he stroked himself. "Merely looking my fill first."

"Ramsay, please." I tugged on the ties, loving the tension on my arms that told me I was trapped.

His for the taking.

I spread my thighs, the fabric of the panties stretching dangerously.

He groaned. "What do you need, angel?"

"You. I need you."

"Do you need my cock?"

"Yes!"

"Do you need my cock in that snug wee pussy?" The words were guttural with desire.

"So much. I need you so much." I arched my back, yanking harder on the ties. "Ramsay."

He moved onto the bed.

His gaze stopped on the still red scar of my knife wound.

Tears burned my eyes as he reverently pressed a trail of gentle kisses over it. Ramsay looked up at me. "Warrior woman."

I smiled, blinking back the tears. "Don't you forget it."

With a wicked grin, his response was to reach for the underwear. He tore them in two and I let out a huff of laughter because I wasn't even surprised. It wasn't the first time he'd ruined a pair. Smoothing his rough palms down my inner thighs, he pushed my legs apart to move between them. Lifting my hips off the bed, he gripped my thighs wide and nudged against my entrance.

"Too young. Too sweet." His eyes narrowed, his jaw flexing as he pushed slowly into me.

"What?" I gasped.

"That's what I used to think. That you were too young. Too sweet."

"And now?"

He smirked. "You're still too young. Too sweet for the likes of me." He gritted his teeth on another groan as I arched into the slow, overwhelming sensation of him filling me. "You're also too much mine for me to ever let go now."

"Never let go," I gasped as he bottomed out and my inner muscles throbbed around him. God, I'd missed him.

"Never," he promised gruffly.

I expected a rough, beautiful fucking.

Instead, Ramsay's drives were measured, building the tension inside me in excruciatingly wonderful slow thrusts. I tugged on the ties.

"Take it, angel," he demanded. "There's nothing for you to do but take my cock."

I relaxed my arms and gave myself over to him.

"That's it. Good girl." Ramsay bared his teeth as he increased his thrusts. "Your pussy drives me mad. If I died coming inside you, woman, I'd die a happy fucking man."

I laughed. "Literally."

His grin turned a bit feral as he increased his thrusts.

"Come on me, Silver. Come like a good girl on my cock."

Those were the words I'd needed.

Shaking and clenching and shuddering around him, my cries echoed off the walls as the restraints pulled my arms tense against the power of my climax.

Then to my surprise, Ramsay reached over me, tugging the ropes free. "I want your hands on me," he explained before his mouth took mine.

I smoothed my hands down his muscular back, feeling his heat, his need, kissing him back as voraciously as he kissed me. He rocked into me as I touched him wherever I could reach as he finally broke the kiss to breathe. Ramsay held my eyes as he moved over me and inside me.

Making love to me.

An orgasm began to chase my last, and I moaned against his lips. His expression was hard and soft all at the same time as my nipples dragged against his chest with his close thrusts.

My fingernails dug into his waist as my climax built.

"I love you," Ramsay suddenly murmured, holding my gaze. His next words were said with a groan of need and emotion. "Silver, I love you."

My body reacted first, clenching around him tightly before pulsing with release. "Ramsay!" I cried, clinging onto him as he grunted with the strength of my orgasm. "I love you too!"

He took my hands, pinning them above me as he rose on his knees to drive into me a few more times before his release overwhelmed him. His bellow ricocheted across the room as he tensed before shuddering between my legs. His cock throbbed inside me, and I moaned with the sensation. And it kept throbbing until Ramsay finally collapsed over me with a long groan of utter satisfaction.

As I fought to catch my breath, I caressed my hand up the contours of his back until I cupped the nape of his neck. "You ... you love me?"

Ramsay slowly lifted his head to study my face. He did it like I was the most precious thing he'd ever seen. It was the most unguarded expression I'd ever seen from him. "Of course I do. I have from the very beginning."

Joy I didn't think I'd ever feel again since losing my parents suffused me, and I laughed at myself and the sentimental tears that rushed to my eyes. "Me too," I promised as he buried his face against my throat. I wrapped my arms tight around him, holding him to me like I never wanted to let go. "From the very beginning."

49. Ramsay

Silver lay in my arms, her cheek to my chest, her fingers trailing up and down the ridge between my pecs. Akiva had finally ventured into the room and sprawled herself across the foot of the bed.

Utter repletion and contentment glued me to the mattress and to the woman in my arms.

"Ramsay's an alias?"

The question surprised me, but it also didn't. More than anything it surprised me it had taken her this long to ask. "Aye. But it *was* my middle name."

"Will you tell me your birth name? I promise I won't tell anyone."

Only the agency knew my birth name. Yet I found myself replying, "Logan. Logan Ramsay Ferguson."

"Oh."

"What?"

"You ... you're definitely more of a Ramsay McRae than a Logan Ferguson."

I chuckled. "Is that right?"

Silver nodded, her tone serious. "Yes. You will always be Ramsay McRae to me."

I smoothed a hand down over her hip, her skin like warm silk beneath my calloused palm. "Aye, me too. This is the first place I ever really felt like me. The real me. So, aye. You're stuck with me as Ramsay forever."

"I know we got a little carried away during and post-sex … but, uh, we should probably talk about the forever stuff," Silver whispered tentatively.

I tensed. "Meaning?"

"We haven't spoken about what we both want. I know there's an age gap so … I know it's too soon to be talking about it, but I think we should know if there's even a future for us before we get any deeper into this."

At her nervous words, I tilted her chin to look into her eyes.

She seemed wary. Uncertain.

"Spit it out, angel."

"I want kids," she blurted. And then winced. "Not right away. But I want … I want a family."

Ah.

Of course, my Silver wanted a family. After she'd lost so much of it.

I relaxed and her eyes widened as she felt my response.

"Do you?"

"Honestly?" I caressed her cheek with my knuckles. "I never thought a family was in my future. I never let myself dream about it. Until you."

"Really?"

"Before the marines, before MI6 … I used to think about meeting the right person and having kids with her. Creating a family for myself again after losing mine."

Silver pressed a slow kiss to my chest over my heart.

"I ... I don't talk about it a lot. Losing my parents. Because it's hard. Everything I've been through and the terrible things I've seen people do ... and losing them is still the worst thing I've ever experienced."

Emotion trembled on her lips, and I knew she understood better than anyone.

"I don't talk about them a lot and that's the way it is." I gave her a squeeze so she knew it wasn't because I didn't trust her.

Silver nodded in understanding.

"Giving up the idea of making a family for myself again was one of the hardest sacrifices I made for the job."

She pushed up, resting her chin on her hand on my shoulder. "And now?"

"It's hard for me to wrap my head around the thought." I gently pushed her onto her back, smoothing her hair away from her gorgeous face. "But I'd want that with you. I see that with you. You. Me. Kids."

"Akiva." Silver grinned, biting her lip in that fucking adorable way of hers.

So happy.

She looked so happy.

It was difficult to believe I was the reason.

"And Akiva."

"So, kids ... yes?"

I nodded, heat flooding through me as I slipped my hand between us to tease her pussy. "We'll have a lot of fun trying too."

She gasped, arching into my touch. "When we're ready. I want you all to myself for a while."

I kissed her in savage possessiveness I kept on a tight leash, pushing my fingers into her snug, wet heat. My want for this woman had never dulled, only grown exponentially, and I wondered if it would always be like this. Or if it would eventually ease into something that felt more manageable to bear.

As I settled between her legs, as she opened to me, I thought, *Fuck being able to bear it*. This uncontrollable want was the best fucking thing I'd ever—

An alarm blared from behind the wall, jerking us apart.

Disbelief coursed through me.

Silver's eyes were round with uncertainty. "What is that?"

"My perimeter sensor alarm." I rolled off her and hit the wall light. The door to the hidden room opened and the motion sensor lights blared to life along with my monitors.

"Ramsay, what is going on?" I could sense Silver in the doorway.

"I have perimeter sensors set all over the island. Except at the crossing, though I have a camera there. If someone gets on my island from a less conspicuous point, I'll know." I clicked through the camera images of nighttime on Stòr. There was nothing at the main crossing because the tide was in.

"There." Silver reached past me pointing to the third computer screen. In the top right-hand corner, the camera attached to the outside of the white cottage showed movement. Clicking on it, I dragged the timeline back a few minutes and saw the small boat pull up at my dock there. The infrared revealed three figures climbing off the dock and onto the island.

"One of the sensors is on the dock," I explained tightly, watching as the three drew up to the cottage.

Three men. In camouflaged fatigues. Armed to the teeth.

Silver's breathing was sharp and shallow at my back. "Who are they?"

"I don't—" I cut off as one of them spotted the camera and looked directly into it. "Fuck."

After all this time.

"What? Who is that?"

"Ian Kingston." I looked over my shoulder at Silver, panic thrumming beneath my calm facade. "Natalya's husband."

Her nostrils flared. "Has he been looking for you? Why?"

I straightened from the monitors, focused on them and Ian's movements. "He blamed me for Natalya's death. He thought I was the reason the Russians discovered where she was. That I blew her cover and our meeting that day was the confirmation they needed to assassinate her."

"How did you blow her cover?"

"Because my previous operation had been in Russia. I was working undercover in Moscow as an English language and literature professor at the university." Uncertainty that too much information about my past might drive her away caused me to hesitate. With Ian on my fucking island, maybe I should deliberately drive her away.

"Don't." Silver reached up, taking my face between her palms. "I see that look. Don't you dare push me away because of this."

Fuck. No one instinctively understood me like her. It scared the shit out of me. "If you hadn't noticed, you are currently in danger because of me."

"What happened in Moscow?" she insisted.

I took her hands in mine, lowering them between us but not letting go. "I was there to get close to a research professor. I can't share the details of the research but suffice it to say, the British government was interested in acquiring the professor's data. She ... she was interested in me romantically, so ..."

Silver squeezed my hands. I saw the flicker of discomfort on her expression. But she pushed it aside. "You had a relationship with her."

"It wasn't demanded of me, but I would do what I needed to do to succeed at an op. Unfortunately, she wasn't only a research professor. She was working for the FSB—Russia's counterintelligence agency."

Silver frowned. "They knew her work was appealing to foreign governments."

I nodded, unsurprised at how quickly she grasped the situation. "She was already on high alert and when I realized the professor suspected me, Natalya arranged my extraction. However, the Russians looked into me and through me—"

"They found Natalya." Silver's gaze turned back to the monitors. "Ian blames you."

"Aye."

"Why now? Why after all these years? Surely, he could have found you before this?"

Aye, he could have.

I suspected I knew why he'd come now, but I didn't want to scare Silver. "I'm going to lock you in this room."

Her eyes flared. "No, you are not. There are three of them out there and they're armed."

"And I won't be able to focus unless I know you're safe."

She jerked her chin in defiance. "Behind you on the wall is a .22 small bore rifle and I know this because my dad's idea of bonding was to take me to an outdoor rifle range every other weekend."

Shit. I remembered she'd told me that when we first met.

"Now I'm not saying this to be arrogant, it's just the truth—my dad harped at me for years to shoot competitively because I am a crack fucking shot." She gestured to the gun. "Does it extend to two hundred yards?"

A dichotomy of feelings hit me at once. Pride. Fear. And arousal. I reached for the gun, taking it off the wall. In the drawers beneath the computer, I found the bullets. "Load it."

Silver loaded it as if she were at the Olympics.

"This is not the time to be turning me on, woman," I murmured thickly.

She rolled her eyes. "Men."

I looked back at the monitors. Every time they tripped one of the cameras, it flared to life on the screen. My fear for Silver was pushing to the surface, but I couldn't and wouldn't force her to hide. It wasn't who she was. Even if that scared the shit out of me. "They know where the house is. They're coming."

Despite her bravery, her voice shook as she asked, "What's the plan?"

I would kill Ian for putting Silver through this.

"We're both still naked, so clothes first. I'll give you something dark to wear."

Akiva jumped off the bed to watch us dress. Feeling our tension, she gave a wee yip. "Ssh, sweetheart. Be quiet."

"What will we do with her?"

"She'll try to protect us, so I'm locking her in here."

Silver nodded in agreement, her cheeks pale, eyes dark with worry.

I marched back into the room with the monitors and cursed as I saw what they were doing. They had the house surrounded on three sides. They had to know I knew they were here after Ian saw the cameras, and yet they'd left the back of the house uncovered.

Because they didn't think I'd run.

As I armed myself, I laid out the plan to Silver.

"I'm not leaving you," she hissed.

"I know." Fuck, did I wish it weren't true. "But I need you at a distance." I took the rifle out of her hand and clipped the infrared scope to it. "If you get a clear shot of any of them, you take it."

Exhaling shakily, she nodded.

"Ian's on the east side of the property. I'm going to take out the guy on the west and north. By then, Ian will reveal himself. If you see him, you take the shot."

"Okay. Who ... who are the other guys?"

"No idea. Mercenaries more than likely."

"Oh my God."

I cupped her face, pulling her toward me. "You can still hide in this room. I'd prefer it."

"I can't. I'm sorry. I can't leave you."

Squeezing my eyes closed, I nodded, then pressed a hard kiss to her mouth. Then I pulled out my phone and connected it to the Wi-Fi for calling out.

"What are you doing?" she whispered.

"I have the internet, remember."

"So, I could have been calling people this whole time?" she grumbled under her breath.

I flashed her a weak smile as the call connected.

"I'm afraid to even ask why you're calling at this hour," James said in greeting.

"Ian Kingston has breached my island with two armed men."

"Fuck."

"My thoughts precisely. They have my house surrounded. I have Tierney with me."

"I'll send out a team."

"Be quick. If ... *you'll* protect her if I can't."

Silver's expression tightened with fear. And anger.

"I'll get someone there as quickly as possible. What information can you provide?"

I relayed what weapons I could see on them, that they had infrared goggles, wore camouflage, and the formation I suspected they were taking to surround the house.

"Use the code name *Silver* to identify yourself to the team. ETA twenty minutes," James said. "The helicopter will land on your island, so stay out of the northwest."

"Thank you."

"Don't die, my friend. Not now when you might actually start to live."

"Aye, all right, no need to get sentimental."

I heard his sharp, worried laugh before we disconnected. Silver held my gaze. "Ready?"

"As I'll ever be."

I tapped the camera app on my phone so I could keep an eye on Ian and his men who had drawn as close as possible to the house without being seen. We closed the hidden room and then shut Akiva in the bedroom, much to her dismay. But I couldn't handle it if anything happened to her, and she was too protective of me and Silver.

Silently, I opened the back door and as Ian stepped out into the clearing at the front of the property, I gestured for Silver to run into the trees.

My fucking heart went with her.

"I know you know we're here, Logan!" Ian's clipped, English-accented voice ricocheted around the entire clearing. Akiva began to bark from the bedroom.

I slipped out the door too, silently making my way along the rear of the house. At the gap between it and the barn, I checked the cameras on my phone. Seeing I was clear, I moved past the gap and along the back of the barn.

Ian's voice continued to echo across the property. "You're not a coward! So come out and face me!"

His men were starting to move. Towards us.

I prayed Silver stayed hidden as I moved straight into the path of one of the guys. We were close enough that I heard the crack of bracken under his foot. Slipping behind one of the thicker trunked oaks that sat among my birch trees, I controlled my breathing until it was barely perceptible. So the light from my phone didn't give me away, I shoved it in my pocket and chose one of the knives strapped to my hip.

Another crack over my shoulder to my left had me practically shaking my head. Whoever Ian had brought with him could do with some training. Senses alert, I waited until I felt him draw up beside the tree. I whipped around the back of it before he even had time to process my presence.

He tried to fight.

Even attempted to aim his handgun.

In a series of rapid moves, however, I disabled him with knife wounds to his upper chest, gut, and arms. When he dropped the gun and tried to reach for his own knife, disoriented and dazed by the speed of my attack, I wound my arms around his neck and squeezed until he lost consciousness.

The prick was lucky I didn't kill him.

I hid his weapons in case he woke up and then checked the cameras on my phone. As I noted the second man had moved and Ian was on my porch, the sound of a gun firing exploded through the trees.

It was so loud, I was sure it would be heard on Leth Sholas.

Fear crashed over me as I pulled up more feeds.

Finally, I found him on one of the cameras installed on a tree.

He was slumped on the ground, clutching at his stomach.

Silver had shot the other guy.

"Good girl," I murmured, proud and terrified. "Now stay put."

I could see Ian moving swiftly, constantly on alert, toward the gunshot. I had to get there first. Before he spotted Silver.

I hurried as quietly as possible around the barn and across the clearing toward the woods on the west side and saw Ian find his man. He lifted his gun, pointing it as he scanned the trees beyond.

Just stay hidden. Just stay hidden.

I slowed as I approached and unholstered my SIG Sauer P266. It was the same weapon Ian held. The same weapon we'd both trained on. Back when we were still on the same side.

My night vision was good, but nothing compared to what Ian's was with those goggles. I tried to watch where I put my feet as he came into sight. Gun trained on him, I approached. "Lower your weapon."

Ian spun, not lowering his weapon. He pointed it at me one-handed.

He surprised me by pushing the goggles up onto his forehead. Then he clasped both hands on his gun and held it as steady as I did, despite the wrath that emanated from him. All his training went up in smoke, overtaken by his emotions. By his monstrous grief.

"Why now?" I asked, hoping like hell James's team was already on the island. I merely had to keep Ian talking long enough for them to get to Silver.

"Why do you think?"

"I didn't kill her," I reminded him. "I cared about her."

"Do you think I didn't know you wanted to fuck my wife?" Ian scoffed. "Everyone knew. She knew. She felt sorry for you."

Maybe once upon a time his words would have hurt. But no longer. "I'm sorry I failed her."

"Not as sorry as me. Do you know what the past six years have been like for me while you hid away on this fucking island?"

I didn't answer.

"You don't know ..." His words released with a harsh grief that felt as fresh as the day Natalya died. For him it was. He hadn't moved on or even tried to. "There was no point in killing you. It wouldn't bring her back. It wouldn't give her the justice she deserved. A quick end is more than you deserve."

I was afraid to ask again.

Because I knew.

I knew why he was here.

"But it's different now. Now you can feel what I've felt." He laughed sharply. "To everyone's disbelief, the great Logan Ferguson has fallen in love."

"Don't." The word escaped me before I could stop it.

"Oh, make this sweeter for me, please. Beg a little more."

"You'll ruin your life. The agency. Everything. Gone."

"What life?" he shouted, the question careening through the trees. "I have no life without her. Because of your fucking ineptitude. And they still act as if you're this legendary agent and all the while you screwed up! You screwed up, and Natalya paid for it! Why can't they see that?"

"Ian ..." For Silver's sake, I had to pretend like I didn't agree with every single word. "You need help."

"I don't need help," he replied calmly, his gun hand never wavering. "They would have discharged me from the agency if I required help."

They should have.

Clearly, he'd been smart enough to hide how broken he was from the agency's psychotherapist.

"I was doing quite well, actually," he said almost conversationally. "Even met someone. She's not Natalya, but she was a lovely distraction for a while. Until someone in James's circle mentioned he'd helped you out. And for whom. And for why. A woman. Something just ... something just snapped, Logan. Do you understand? Do you understand at least why I can't let you have what you stole from me? Where is she? I know she's here. We watched her take the crossing earlier and that is her vehicle in the clearing, is it not? Is she hiding in the house or the barn?"

He didn't know she was the one who'd shot his companion.

Good.

"I won't let you hurt her."

"Whatever happens here, she *is* going to die, Logan. Either

I kill you first and then I kill her, or I kill her first and then kill you." I saw his weapon lower ever so slightly to my gut and his finger tense on the trigger.

The shot rang out a second before my trigger finger moved.

50. Ramsay

A strip of moonlight highlighted Ian's face in the dark. His expression was frozen with wrath as a dark dot appeared on his forehead milliseconds after the shot sounded.

Like a puppet cut from his strings, his knees collapsed beneath him and he fell face-first onto the packed dirt.

Dead.

Bracken snapped and leaves crunched as I lowered my weapon, surprise rooting me to the spot for a second.

Until Silver appeared, the rifle at her side, her face slack with pale shock. "Told you I was a crack shot," she whispered.

Relief and pride and adrenaline crashed through me as I bridged the distance between us. She released the rifle to fall into me, wrapping her arms around me as tightly as I embraced her.

"Thank fuck, thank fuck, thank fuck," I murmured, my hands moving over her, to feel her, to reassure myself she was alive and unhurt.

"I ... I killed him."

I pressed a hard kiss to the top of her head. "I know. But he would have killed us."

"I know. I heard everything he said."

"I'm sorry." I bent my head to murmur in her ear, "I'm so sorry."

"Don't." Silver pulled away to look up at me. "It's not my fault Halston Cole is a psychopath, and it's not your fault Ian Kingston lost his mind when he lost his wife. Okay? *We* didn't do this."

I kissed her, probably too hard, too bruising. But for once, I couldn't control my emotions as I pressed kisses to her mouth, her cheeks, her forehead.

"We're okay," she comforted me. "We're going to be okay."

They were on us before either of us realized.

Because real professionals were like fucking ninjas.

"Hands in the air," a deep, Scottish accented male voice called out.

I raised my hands, looking up and around to see they had us surrounded. "We're good." I called out the code word. "Silver!"

The sound of weapons being lowered had me reaching for Silver again. The team moved toward us. The man who'd spoken identified himself. "Captain Reynolds, Special Forces." He shook my hand and nodded at Silver. "I was going to say you were lucky our unit had stopped at the barracks off Skye on our way home from an operation ... but it seems you didn't need us after all."

I suspected Reynolds was E Squadron, a secret unit of the Special Forces, mostly because they were the unit who reported not only to the Ministry of Defense but to MI6.

"I appreciate you coming all the same."

Reynolds nodded. "Is everyone all right?"

"Two injuries." I gestured to Ian's body. "One fatality."

He took it in stride as someone who dealt with death on a daily basis. "Where are the others?"

I told him and his team moved out to secure the two men.

Silver began to shake violently against me. "I need to get my woman inside and warm. She's going into shock."

"I-I'm f-fine ..." Her teeth chittered together.

Reynolds and I shared a look. "I'll escort you inside while my team secures the property." He guarded us as we rounded the house. I could hear the buzz of voices reporting to him in his earpiece as his team searched. "I heard you retired six years ago. Seems you haven't lost your touch."

My grip on Silver tightened as I guided her onto the porch. "I only took out one man. Silver here took out Ian and the other."

The captain nodded. "Impressive."

I wasn't sure Silver would agree.

Guilt wracked me despite her earlier words, but the urge to push her away, to protect us both from feeling too much, didn't reemerge like I'd worried it might.

No. I was so deep in this with her now, it would take my death or the end of the fucking world to tear her away from me.

Maybe not even that.

I pressed another kiss to her temple as I led her inside.

It seemed we were in this strange thing called life together now.

Until the very end.

Epilogue
TIERNEY

L eth Sholas at Christmastime was spellbinding. Yes, it was cold and wet and windy, but that didn't stop all the Christmas lights on Main Street from creating magic across the harbor. The way the water reflected the lights was so beautiful, I could have walked along the harbor all night long.

For the first time in weeks, it felt like we'd made it out of the storm.

I watched London stroll around the finished kitchen in the B and B, touching everything, opening cupboards, pulling out the equipment she'd asked for and then neatly placing them back.

Cammie, Quinn, and Ramsay stood out of the way with me, Akiva at my side too.

London suddenly glanced over at us, her cheeks flushing ever so slightly. "Being watched like you guys are spectators isn't creepy or weird at all."

A soft laugh escaped me. "Sorry."

But I wasn't.

My best friend wasn't quite herself yet, but every day she

grew closer and closer to the London I used to know. I didn't think she'd ever be that person again. How could she after what she'd been through? Yet I felt her relax more and more as she began to feel safe here.

And at home.

The B and B was complete. We were ready to start welcoming our first guests in the new year. To my utter delighted surprise, Ramsay was moving into the B and B with me. He was, of course, keeping his place on Stòr, not just because it was his workshop but so we had privacy whenever we wanted. My eventual goal was to have someone else move in and manage the place so I could move onto Stòr permanently. So we could start a family.

Despite what had happened there, it hadn't made me afraid of the place. In fact, I felt like Ramsay's island had protected us. And I'd protected us.

It cost me more than any one person should have to pay, but I couldn't feel anything but right in what I'd done to protect Ramsay.

I couldn't lose him.

I'd lost too much already.

What happened on Stòr would remain a carefully guarded secret. Ramsay's old boss didn't want anyone finding out one of his agents went rogue. The rest of the world would believe Ian Kingston died in service to his country. That didn't seem fair, really, but life wasn't always fair.

And I guess I didn't care too much, as long as I had Ramsay.

The last few weeks hadn't been the easiest.

Yet I'd always gotten through my darker emotions by focusing on others. I focused on Ramsay and our relationship, and I focused on London.

Nick was facing federal charges, so we hadn't heard a peep from him.

His best buddy, Hugh, wasn't faring well either when evidence of his involvement in Michelle's death mysteriously ended up in the hands of the *New York Chronicle*. There was no covering it up now that it was public. New York society was currently in an uproar that their two golden boys were facing serious prison time.

My case against Shawn and Halston were both going to court, and I had that to look forward to in my future. With Ramsay at my side, though, and after everything we'd been through, I felt strong enough to bear it. To see my parents, Rahman, and Ben finally find justice. I had hope that they would get justice.

I had more hope now than ever.

"Do you like it?" I asked.

"You know I love it." London looked away, and I saw her lips tremble as she struggled to hold back her emotions.

"Why don't you show London the view?" Ramsay read the room, as always, and pressed a kissed to my temple.

I gave him a grateful smile and he gave me a sexy wink before I ushered my friend out of the room.

Taking her hand, I led her through our beautiful dining room and out the patio doors. It was a freezing cold day, but for once, the low winter sun hung in the sky, casting beautiful dapples of light across the water beyond Leth Sholas.

London sniffled at my side as she stared out at the view.

I moved to her, sliding my arm around her shoulders. "Hey, hey, are these good tears? Because you know you don't have to stay here if—"

"No, no." London relaxed against me. "I'm grateful. Three months ago, I honestly thought that bastard had me trapped. I let him make me believe it. I could never have imagined then that I'd be standing next to my best friend in this beautiful place that has brought me so much peace."

"Spoon," I whispered, my throat thick.

"Thank you." She turned to me. "Thank you for being the only person who ever really gave a shit. For bringing me here. For everything."

"You don't need to thank me for that. My life isn't complete without you in it. This"—I gestured between us and out to the harbor—"this is a totally selfish move on my part. Plus, I get an awesome chef out of it."

London laughed, wiping at her cheeks. "You're so full of shit."

We chuckled at that before I hugged her to me, holding her tight.

Her parents had once again cut her off when they found out she'd left Nick.

They didn't seem to care that he'd been abusing her.

Bastards.

My parents would've found a way to destroy Nick if they'd been alive.

Thankfully, he'd done that to himself, anyway.

"I'm going to head inside to start the dinner." London gave me one last squeeze and strolled back into the B and B. That was our purpose for coming this afternoon on Christmas Eve Eve. Not only to tour the completed space but to cook for Quinn, Cammie, and Ramsay as a thank-you. Or for London to cook and me to host.

Wanting one last look before the sun dipped behind the horizon, I wrapped my arms around myself, burying my chin in the much-needed woolly scarf tied around my neck.

A year ago, I'd stood right here and imagined a quiet life.

I hadn't gotten that yet.

But I'd gotten so much more than I could ever have wanted. I'd go through all the hard stuff again to end up right here.

As if hearing my thoughts, Akiva was the first to appear at my side. I reached down to scratch behind her ears.

Then I sensed him before I felt him. Ramsay's chest pressed to my back as he slid his arms around my waist, pulling me into him.

I covered his arms with mine and snuggled against this strong, resilient Scot who had given me everything I never knew I needed.

"Is London all right?" His voice rumbled in my ear, making me shiver.

"She will be. I think this place is slowly healing her. Like it did me."

"Good." He kissed my cheek, his beard tickling my skin.

"*You* healed me."

Ramsay's breath caught behind me.

"I know you feel guilty about Ian. About a lot of things. But you healed me. I wouldn't change a thing, as long as I ended up right here with you."

His hold on me tightened as he nestled his chin against my temple. "Then we did that for each other. I can't even ... I can't contemplate what my life would be like if you hadn't shown up. Fucking empty, that's what." He exhaled shakily.

"I think this place drew me here to find you."

"Aye." The word was a rasp of deep emotion.

"Let's stay here forever."

"I can live with that." He kissed the side of my head. "Though I'd follow you anywhere, woman."

I smiled, chest aching with love, and a little smugness. "No following required. We're not leaving. Ever."

We stood in peaceful silence for a few minutes, watching the sun set over Half-Light Harbor. As Ramsay murmured into my ear that he loved me, I told him I loved him too. And then I made a wish.

I wished for London to find what I'd found here.

I wished the same for Quinn and for Cammie and for Taran.

And I wished for them to find it without the carnage and drama I'd had to go through to find Ramsay.

Well, as long as the love part came true, I could leave it up to fate to figure out how the rest should play out.

Acknowledgments

A few years ago, while visiting the Isle of Skye, I had a kernel of an idea for a new series. However, at the time I was entrenched in the world of Ardnoch in the Highlands, so that idea had to wait on the sidelines for its moment. The day I sat down to write *Half-Light Harbor*, I was at once giddy with excitement and nervous about trying to create a place readers would find just as magical as Ardnoch. But I truly hope Leth Sholas is another beautiful Scottish escape for you all.

Series starters are always a mix of wonder and stress because I put extra pressure on myself to do a great job setting the stage for the series with book one so readers will want to keep coming back for more. In those moments, I immerse myself in my fictional worlds and, as always, I'm surrounded by very understanding loved ones. To my friends and family, thank you for always supporting me and my quirky writerly ways. I love you a lot!

To my amazing editor Jennifer Sommersby Young: I'm so grateful for you. You can never not be my editor. Okay? Yes? I appreciate you more than I can say!

Thank you to Julie Deaton for proofreading *Half-Light Harbor*, catching all the things, and for being one of Ramsay's first fans.

And thank you to my bestie and PA extraordinaire Ashleen Walker for helping to lighten the load and supporting me more than ever these past few years. I really couldn't do this without you.

The life of a writer doesn't stop with the book. Our job expands beyond the written word to marketing, advertising, graphic design, social media management, and more. Help from those in the know goes a long way. A huge thank-you to Nina Grinstead, Christine, Kim, Kelley, Sarah, Josette, Jaime, Ratula, Meagan and all the team at Valentine PR for your encouragement, support, insight, and advice. You all are amazing!

A huge thank you to Sydney and JR for doing all your techy ad magic to deliver my stories into the hands of new readers. You both make my life infinitely easier and I'm so grateful!

To Katie and Jenna at Lyric Audiobooks: Ladies, thank you, thank you! From stellar production, to beta listening (I live for your beta reactions, Jenna!!), to finding me the most amazing narrators to work with, to getting my audiobooks into the earholes of brand new listeners. I do not have enough ways to say how grateful I am to you both!

On that note, a huge thank you to Shane East and Stella Hunter for once again knocking the audio for *Half-Light Harbor* out of the park!!

Thank you to every single influencer and book lover who has helped spread the word about my books. You all are appreciated so much! On that note, a massive thank-you to Tierney Page at Tierney Reads for inspiring Tierney's name!

And as always, the biggest thank you to the fantastic readers in my private Facebook group, Samantha Young's Clan McBookish. You're truly special. You're a safe space of love and support on the internet and I couldn't be more grateful for you.

Thank you to the incredible Hang Le for creating stunning covers for this book. You brought *Half-Light Harbor* to life with these!

As always, thank you to my agent Lauren Abramo for making it possible for readers all over the world to find my words. You're phenomenal!

Finally, to you, my reader. Thank you for reading. I couldn't do this without you.

Here With Me
The Adair Family Series #1

If you loved Ramsay and Tierney's story, you'll devour the *USA Today* bestseller *Here With Me*, the first book in the *Adair Family Series*.

Settled in the tranquil remoteness of the Scottish Highlands, Ardnoch Estate caters to the rich and famous. It is as unattainable and as mysterious as its owner—ex-Hollywood leading man Lachlan Adair—and it's poised on the edge of a dark scandal.

After narrowly escaping death, police officer Robyn Penhaligon leaves behind her life in Boston in search of some answers. Starting with Mac Galbraith, the Scottish father who abandoned her to pursue his career in private security. To reconnect with Mac, Robyn will finally meet a man she's long resented. Lachlan Adair. Hostility instantly brews between Robyn and Lachlan. She thinks the head of the Adair family is high-handed and self-important. And finding closure with Mac is proving more difficult than she ever imagined. Robyn would sooner leave Ardnoch, but when she discovers Mac is embroiled in a threat against the Adairs and the exclusive members of the estate, she finds she's not yet ready to give up on her father.

Determined to ensure Mac's safety, Robyn investigates the disturbing crimes at Ardnoch, forcing her and Lachlan to spend time together. Soon it becomes clear a searing attraction exists beneath their animosity, and temptation leads them down a perilous path.

While they discover they are connected by something far more addictive than passion, Lachlan cannot let go of his grip on a painful past: a past that will destroy his future ... if the insidious presence of an enemy lurking in the shadows of Ardnoch doesn't do the job first.

GRAB YOUR COPY ANYWHERE BOOKS ARE SOLD

Made in the USA
Columbia, SC
24 October 2025